D1375083

the HOUSE
on
VESPER SANDS

Paraic O'Donnell is a writer of fiction, poetry and criticism. His essays and reviews have appeared in the *Guardian*, the *Spectator*, the *Irish Times* and elsewhere. His first novel, *The Maker of Swans*, was named the Amazon Rising Stars Debut of the Month for February 2016 and was shortlisted for the Bord Gáis Energy Irish Book Awards in the Newcomer of the Year category. He lives in Wicklow, Ireland with his wife and two children.

paraicodonnell.com

@paraicodonnell

Also by Paraic O'Donnell

The Maker of Swans

Leabharlanna Poiblí Chathair Baile Átha Cliath
Dublin City Public Libraries

the HOUSE on VESPER SANDS

Paraic O'Donnell

WEIDENFELD & NICOLSON

First published in Great Britain in 2018
by Weidenfeld & Nicolson
an imprint of The Orion Publishing Group Ltd
Carmelite House, 50 Victoria Embankment
London EC4Y ODZ

An Hachette UK Company

1 3 5 7 9 10 8 6 4 2

Copyright © Paraic O'Donnell 2018

The moral right of Paraic O'Donnell to be identified as
the author of this work has been asserted in accordance
with the Copyright, Designs and Patents Act of 1988.

All rights reserved. No part of this publication may be
reproduced, stored in a retrieval system, or transmitted
in any form or by any means, electronic, mechanical,
photocopying, recording, or otherwise, without the
prior permission of both the copyright owner and the
above publisher of this book.

All the characters in this book are fictitious, and any resemblance
to actual persons, living or dead, is purely coincidental.

A CIP catalogue record for this book is
available from the British Library.

ISBN (Hardback) 978 1 4746 0039 2
ISBN (Export Trade Paperback) 978 1 4746 0040 8
ISBN (eBook) 978 1 4746 0041 5

Typeset by Input Data Services Ltd, Somerset

Printed in Great Britain by Clays Ltd, Elcograf S.p.A.

MIX
Paper from
responsible sources
FSC
www.fsc.org   FSC® C104740

www.orionbooks.co.uk

'. . . what will become of my soul . . .'

Elizabeth Parker, linen sampler embroidered in
cross-stitch with red silk, *ca* 1830, Victoria and Albert Museum, London

'But the angels are spirits, and when they are spirits
they are not angels;
when they are sent, they become angels'

Augustine of Hippo, *Expositions on the Book of Psalms*

'Come back! Even as a shadow, even as a dream'

Euripides, *Herakles* (trans. Anne Carson)

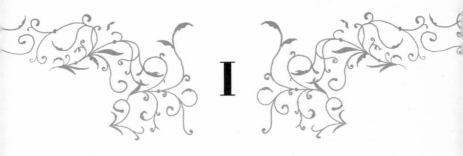

I

REQUIEM ÆTERNAM

February, 1893

I n Half Moon-street, just as she came near to the house, Esther Tull felt the first gentleness of the snow.

She paused at the front steps, setting down her case and extending a gloved hand to the railing. It was not that she felt weak, though she had feared she might. The pain was returning, but it was not yet more than she could bear. It was only that she wanted to look up. The longing was small and simple, and it came to her the moment the first flakes touched her cheek. How delicate they felt. Tender, almost, in the rawness of the air. As a child, Esther had felt a peculiar wonder when it snowed. It was like an enchantment, altering the world and making it quiet. She wanted to lift her face, as she had done then, to the soft tumble of smudges crowding the darkness.

She resisted the urge. She would not look up. There was no joy in such things now. Not in this place, on this of all nights. Instead, taking her left hand from the railing, Esther tugged her right free of its glove. She turned it cautiously, offering her cupped palm to the air, closing her eyes as she waited. A faintness that was almost nothing, then a tiny ache of cold.

At the front door, she collected herself before raising her hand to ring. She looked about her, considering. The servants' entrance would have been more usual, but for some time now she had been directed not to use it. Esther was given no explanation for this

3

practice and knew better than to inquire further. She twisted the brass turn to sound the bell. Some time would pass, as always, before Mr Carew saw fit to admit her. No doubt he could bestir himself when the occasion demanded it, but as she turned in from Piccadilly she had heard the striking of half past eight from St James's. At this hour no other callers would be expected. Not at this house.

When he appeared at last he greeted her in his usual fashion, lowering his chin in its swaddle of jowls and raising his hand before he spoke to conceal some imagined cough.

'Well, Miss Tull.' He glanced at the air above her. 'That is a bad dose of weather you have brought. We must hope it will not delay His Lordship's return.'

Esther said nothing in reply. She stood just as she was on the top step, waiting until he should bid her come in. Mr Carew gazed out into the street a moment longer, then returned his attention to her, as if remembering that she was present. Stooping towards her, he made a show of plucking something from her coat, examining his fingertips as he drew them away.

'Come along, Miss Tull.' He adjusted his bulk, making just enough room to let her pass. 'You will be no good to us perished upon the steps.'

Esther followed him through the grand entrance hall, where objects particularly prized by Lord Strythe were mounted on pedestals or loomed in dim recesses. She had never cared to examine these closely, or thought it her place to do so. She was usually conducted without ceremony to the servants' stairs at the rear of the house. But Mr Carew paused now before a vacant plinth.

'His Lordship waits upon Lady Ashenden this evening, who is giving a gala ball in his honour. It is to be a grand affair, by all accounts. You will recall the specimen that was mounted here?'

Esther looked in discomfort at the pedestal.

'I'm sure you would, if you saw it again,' Mr Carew said. 'It is a rare bird, Miss Tull, a most notable creature, His Lordship says, that was found in Manchuria or some such place. It has a proper name, but you would have no use for that. It is very like a phoenix, I am told. A great prize, even in such a collection as his. Do you think you could name the price of it?'

With both hands, Esther clasped the handle of her sewing case. Her discomfort had sharpened, though she hoped she gave no sign of it. She shook her head.

'Come now.' Mr Carew placed his feet a little apart and thrust his hands into the pockets of his trousers. It was an unseemly posture, but he felt quite at liberty in her presence. She averted her face.

'You are paler even than usual, Miss Tull. I trust you are not unwell?'

Esther drew in a careful breath. 'I am quite well, Mr Carew.'

'Well, then,' he said. 'You must give me your guess as to its price. You do not mean to tell me that you are a woman who does not know the price of things?'

He did not disguise his smirk. She had lived honestly for many years, but it had not always been so. It was useful to them – to Lord Strythe and his underlings – to keep her in mind of what they knew.

'I cannot imagine what the price of it might be, Mr Carew. I am no judge of such things.'

His features lapsed in dissatisfaction. 'Miss Tull,' he said. 'Permit yourself one guess, if you please.'

Esther drew her shoulders back and let out a long breath. 'Ten pounds,' she said.

Mr Carew arched away from her as if in horror, bringing the

back of his hand to his brow. 'Oh, Miss Tull,' he said. 'Ten? Ten pounds? Is that a great sum, do you think?'

He looked away, shaking with voiceless laughter.

'Ten pounds, she says, for a bird that is very nearly a cousin to the phoenix? For a bird that might have taken wing from the ashes of a fire? Why, it is very nearly priceless, but such is His Lordship's generosity that he intends to offer it for auction at the gala. The proceeds are to go to his new institution.' When Esther made no reply, he grew stern again and repeated himself. 'Such is his generosity, Miss Tull.'

She could not bring herself to respond, only lowering her head in a manner that might appear deferential. She sensed that he was not entirely satisfied by this, but he was distracted at that moment by the appearance of a serving boy. He was a slight youth of thirteen or fourteen – Esther had seen him on other occasions – and encumbered by a mass of white flowers very nearly half his own size.

'Begging your pardon, Mr Carew,' he said. 'I was to give you word, you said, when the arrangement come in.'

'Go and stand them in water, you mongrel, before the carpet is ruined. The dust from the lilies is a curse. Has the instrument-maker come?'

'No sign yet, sir.'

'Be sure to tell me when he does. There are instructions from His Lordship. Get along with you now.' Carew produced a plump pocket-watch and clucked at it in disapproval. 'Come, Miss Tull,' he said, as if the delay had been of her making. 'We haven't the whole night to stand around gawking.'

The workroom was on the fourth floor. Mr Carew was not sprightly, and he made slow going of the climb. At each landing he paused to fuss over some small task – to rub at an unseen smear or inspect the wick of a lamp – until he had recovered his breath. Esther had often chafed at having to keep to his pace. She knew the way well enough, and might have made the ascent alone in half the time, had the circumstances been otherwise. But she was glad tonight to remain unseen at his back, and to be spared any greater exertion. The climb had disturbed the wounds. She was conscious now of a rupturing, of a seeping heat. Some sound might escape her, if it worsened. Something might show.

Mr Carew lumbered onwards, giving no sign that he had taken notice, and she saw nothing else that seemed out of the ordinary. A footman stood aside as they approached, a cloak of freshly brushed velvet draped over one arm. Behind certain doors, when they passed, subdued conversations could be heard, or the muted clamour of servants at some obscure but pressing business. In this house, a great deal happened that went unseen.

It was furnished handsomely enough, but sparingly lit. Lord Strythe was known to dislike the gaslights that were now seen in many fine houses, and many rooms had no more than a scattering of oil lamps. They burned less brightly, he maintained, but with a purer light. The drapes and wallpapers were in sombre shades, or they had aged to give that appearance. They had been chosen in the time of the last Lord Strythe, and his son had given them no further attention. His Lordship had never married, and in the ordinary course the ordering of such things might have fallen to his sister. But Lady Ada did not live at Strythe House. Her opinion in these matters was not sought.

When they reached it at last, the uppermost floor was in darkness as always. The landing was no more than a narrow passage, unfurnished save for a table and chair by the door of the workroom. It was here that Mr Carew stationed himself while Esther was occupied within. As was her habit, she waited at the head of the stairs, following only when he had lit the modest lamp on the table and lowered himself to his seat.

'There now, Miss Tull,' he said, examining a handkerchief that he had put to his brow. 'Our penance is done for another day. Your present commission is to be completed tonight, I gather, and then we may hope for a few weeks of ease. Do you know what Lord Strythe says of us?'

Esther shook her head, though she knew very well. This exchange was repeated on each occasion, with hardly a word altered in its sequence.

'He says that we must be quite the pair of alpinists by now, and fit to scale any peak in Europe.' He set his hands on his midsection, as if to contain his merriment. 'Quite the pair of alpinists. Oh, dear me.'

He waited, and Esther made a small show of amusement, prompting a sudden blossoming of pain. She brought in her elbows, raising her case a little before her.

'Oh, he is a great wit,' Mr Carew continued. 'A great wit. Keep an eye on Miss Tull, he says, for she has the indomitable spirit of the mountaineer. At any moment, she might bound away to make an attempt upon the Matterhorn. And do you know, I think he may be right. But you will not bound away just yet, Miss Tull?'

She looked down at the handle of her sewing case, which she gripped so tightly now as to whiten her knuckles. 'I am very tired, Mr Carew, and I fear there is a long night ahead. I understand that there is – that there are new measurements. There is always a great deal to be done when the measurements are altered on the last night.'

He said nothing, but looked for some moments over her person, as if making a careful inventory.

'It is an elaborate garment,' she added. 'It calls for a good deal of fine work.'

He would hear the unease in her voice, surely, if she had not betrayed herself with some other sign. She had felt something again, a quick coursing against her skin. It would show somewhere. He would see.

'Quite right, Miss Tull,' he said at length. 'Lord Strythe is particular in his requirements, as you need not remind me. I will not keep you from your work any longer than can be helped. But before we go in, I will trouble you to open your sewing case and lay out what is in it.' He swept his forearm across the yellowish tablecloth as if to clear a space, though it was bare save for the lamp. Then he settled himself in his chair with a look of complacent expectation.

'What is in it.' She repeated the words as if she were a simpleton, and was conscious of a faint rasp of effort in her voice. To add to her other discomforts, she now felt a tightness take hold of her face and neck.

'You do not seem quite yourself this evening, Miss Tull. Yes, lay out what is in your sewing case, please. We will do the same again when you are leaving. It is no great novelty, surely? How am I to know you have taken nothing if I do not know what you had going in?'

'It has been some time, Mr Carew. I had thought that perhaps . . .'

'That perhaps we had come to trust you again. His Lordship is a reasonable man, Miss Tull, but he is not a fool. It has hardly been a month since we discovered those items among your belongings.'

'I meant only to finish that piece of work at home, Mr Carew. I knew it would be missed. What else could I have intended? What do you take me for?'

At this Carew's look darkened, and he rose with slow emphasis from his chair. Esther shrank from him, though she knew his outrage was feigned. She had not meant to say so much.

'You forget yourself, Miss Tull,' he said. 'You have been accused of nothing. Not lately, at least. His Lordship's instructions were plain, all the same. Nothing is to be brought beyond what is needed from your sewing box, and above all nothing is to be taken away. Lord Strythe believed he had made himself understood. But perhaps he had not.'

She felt herself sway a little on her feet. It was not only the pain. She had taken no supper, nor any sustenance at all since morning. 'He made himself understood, Mr Carew.'

'Very good, Miss Tull.' He lowered his face so that his brow was very near to her own. 'I am very glad to hear it. Then you remember the matter that most concerned him?'

'I remember.'

'You remember his words?'

'I remember – I remember, Mr Carew, but not the exact words.'

'His Lordship employs a good many servants, and engages any number of tradespeople. Between them they have many duties, but they have one in common. Do you recall what it is?'

'Yes, Mr Carew.'

'Well, then? Must I draw it from you like a tooth? What is the first duty of a person employed in His Lordship's household?'

'Discretion, Mr Carew.'

'Again, please.' Raising his hand, he gathered up the broad flesh of his ear.

'The duty of discretion, Mr Carew.'

He waited a moment longer before drawing his face away from hers. Even with her own eyes lowered, Esther felt the insistence of his gaze. 'Very well, then,' he said, resuming his seat. 'In your own time, Miss Tull.'

It was the work of some minutes to empty her case entirely. She had been ill at ease already, and grew clumsy under his scrutiny, piercing her cuff with a bodkin and letting a pair of scissors tumble from her grasp. When she had put out all she had, the little table was covered almost to its edges. The garment that had been commissioned was indeed an intricate piece of work, and the machine could be used only for the plainest of stitching. There was hardly an implement in her possession that she had not had call to use in these last weeks.

Mr Carew took hold of the table lamp and passed it slowly over the bobbins and thimbles, the needles and hooks, pausing now and then to turn something over or hold it up for inspection. She wondered if he knew the purpose of even half of these items. Taking up a stiletto, he held it to the light, so that a dull gleam passed along its length. It was used only to puncture eyelets, but its long point was keen, and it might easily do worse than that. Mr Carew set it down and returned the lamp to its place. He yawned as he turned to her, taking no great trouble to cover his mouth.

'The case itself, Miss Tull, if you please.'

There was considerable satisfaction in Mr Carew's face as he accepted it. He held it open beneath the lamp first, agitating it a good deal as he peered into each corner of its interior. Then he reached inside and began a thorough examination with his fingertips and the flat of his palm, so that she doubted there was a square inch of the lining he had left untouched. Finally – and by now the slackening of his expression revealed a measure of disappointment – he held the case upside down and shook it.

'Well, Miss Tull.' He reclined in his seat with a look of displeasure and gestured impatiently at her things. 'Clear all this away, will you, so that we may get on with our business. Such a production you made of it. Did I not say you had nothing to fear?'

Esther began packing away her sewing kit, not meeting his eyes. Would he attempt to search her clothing? He had not gone so far before, but might be moved to it by some new suspicion. She replied with as much evenness as she could manage. 'Those were not your words, Mr Carew, but perhaps that was your meaning.'

He gave her a keen look, but pursued the subject no further. When she had gathered up her things, he went to unlock the door. While his back was turned, she made the last of her preparations. With small and careful movements, she adjusted her clothing. It was to ease her discomfort, in part, but that was not her only concern. She had made certain alterations, in places that were hidden from view. She would depend upon them, when the time came.

'There now,' said Mr Carew, as they entered the workroom. 'All neat and tidy. Whatever else may be said about us, let no one give it out that we keep a slovenly shop. What do you say, Miss Tull?'

Again, he had made the same observation many times, and always in the same words. This time, at least, he did not wait for her response. The workroom was always cold, and he never stayed longer than he must. With a wheezy sigh, he slouched towards the great iron strongbox that stood in the corner opposite the door. Esther watched his movements carefully, taking note of the pocket to which he returned one key before drawing out another.

'You might oblige me by looking away, Miss Tull.'

Esther turned her back, since it humoured him to have her do so. She knew by now what was kept in the safe. Mr Carew had great notions of his own shrewdness. Perhaps his master did, too, since he was entrusted with so much, but in truth he was often inattentive. She had taken those opportunities that came. She had seen enough.

She stood in silence as he brought the pieces of the gown to the workbench, taking care to give no sign of unsteadiness in her posture. She heard him return to the strongbox, his tread ponderous and shuffling. It would take him three trips, or even four. It was not only the dress that was locked away, but the box of cards on which the measurements were marked. These were made from other items of clothing, procured in a manner she did not care to guess at.

She listened carefully when he returned to lock the safe. The hinges were apt to creak, but she had greased them with oil from the Singer sewing machine, applying only a little at a time. There was a dull clang as he shouldered the door closed, but that could be avoided with gentleness. The hinges themselves made no sound at all.

She turned, hearing him approach the bench again.

'There you are now, Miss Tull.' Mr Carew said this with a small flourish, as if to emphasise some act of benevolence. 'You have all you need, I believe.'

Esther waited. Nothing must be rushed. There must be no appearance of urgency.

'Thank you, Mr Carew.' Her tone was not curt, exactly, but neither was it courteous. She had repeated the words before her looking-glass, adjusting the set of her jaw by degrees, until she was sure of the effect they would have. Mr Carew was accustomed to her deference, and when he found it lacking he favoured only one form of correction.

He approached her, standing so close that his knees pressed faintly against her outer skirts. His breathing had slowed now, but it was laboured still. She felt it against her cheek. He smelled of plum cake, of must and snuff.

'Is everything to your satisfaction, Miss Tull?'

'Yes, Mr Carew.' She did not soften her voice. Not yet.

'Are you quite sure?' He leaned closer. 'Is there something you would like me to put right?'

'Nothing, Mr Carew.'

He raised his hand, and she felt his fingers curl about her nape. 'You know you may come to me, Miss Tull, if you want for anything. I will be glad to see to your needs.'

Esther raised her face to his, and as she did so she made a small show of distress and contrition. This was all that was required. As Mr Carew studied her with satisfaction, Esther made a movement he did not detect.

'Forgive me, Mr Carew,' she said. 'It is only that I am tired. My sister is unwell, as you know, and I sat with her for much of the night.'

'There now, Miss Tull.' He turned away, his attention already elsewhere. 'We have each our cross to bear. I will leave you to your work. The door must be locked, as always, but you need only knock. I will be at my little station outside the door. Now, that reminds me. Where did I put down my newspaper?'

He had left it on the workbench, almost at his elbow, where he could not have failed to notice it. He waited until Esther picked it up and handed it to him, a small act of reparation that completed her penance. He unfolded it as he crossed to the door, peering at the ghoulish illustration that took up the greater part of the front page.

'Heaven help us, Miss Tull. It seems a resident of Southwark was found devoured by his own cats. What has the world come to, that such things can happen not three miles from us?'

He continued tutting and clucking as he let himself out, and when at last he locked the door behind him Esther released a long quiet breath. She allowed herself to slump a little, now that

14

she was no longer observed, and to loosen her clothing where it pressed against the injured place. She had imagined this moment many times, fearing always that her courage would fail at the last. She had prayed, though she knew the wickedness of doing so. The Lord could not be called upon by those who had chosen her course.

Yet the strength had come. It held now even as her posture slackened, like a wire that had been drawn taut at her core. She had saved the drug until the last possible moment, being unused to its effects. She had done the stitching without it, fearing it would leave her insensible, only binding her jaw with a leather strap to keep herself from screaming. The relief, when it came, had made her weep. The opium had done its work, but she had endured the worst without it. Whatever strength she had found had some other source.

When it was done, she had swabbed the stitches with a solution of carbolic acid, then examined her work in the looking-glass. The words had appeared backwards, and she was not confident in her letters on the best of days. But she had taken her time over it, meaning to be sure. There was a small satisfaction in that, and in preserving the neatness of her work even at the height of her agony. She had taken a fleeting pride in her efforts, but had seen that in the next moment for the sin that it was. She had turned away from the glass to dress, lest she make herself late.

Esther roused herself. She had much to do still, and the danger had not passed. From a pocket sewn to the inner part of her petticoat – this was the first of the alterations she had made – she drew out a wad of ragged gauze that she had soaked in spirits. Reaching beneath her clothing, she dabbed at the skin around the stitches. She did so without looking, since she could not risk unclothing herself further, and kept one hand clamped to her mouth in case a sound should escape her. She withdrew the swab at intervals to examine it, refolding it and readying a clean patch once a portion was saturated. It was not that she feared for the cleanliness of the wounds – with that, at least, she need not trouble herself – but she was anxious that the stitches might be too much obscured by blood. They must be plainly visible, or nearly so, or her efforts would be wasted. It was a small part of her plan, and might have been done without if she had only one purpose, but it was not only a matter of saving those who could still be saved. She had made a promise and meant to keep it. For a little longer she must conceal her purpose, then the moment would come. She would bear witness, in the end, whatever might become of her soul.

She stooped to unlace her shoes, wincing as she worked them off. The pain had sharpened, but she refused to give it her attention. These were the moments that mattered most. She must be quick and exact in every movement, and above all she must be silent.

Esther kept to the edges of the room, where the boards under her stockinged feet had less give. Her father had taught her that, many years ago, and a good deal else. She remembered him fondly enough, for all his wickedness. Reaching the strongbox, she paused to listen, just as he would have done.

Stealing is half waiting, girl. His face was long gone, but she could still raise his voice. *Stealing is half waiting, and the other half is listening.*

A minute passed, maybe longer. Mr Carew coughed once, but no other sound came. From a narrow pocket sewn into her cuff, she drew out the key. He had felt nothing when she took it from him. She had learned her skills at her father's side, in the low places of Spitalfields that she had known as a child. She had renounced them years before, but they came to her again without effort. She had learned an honest trade when her father was gone, but one that had kept her fingers nimble. She had not forgotten.

The lock was stiff, but gave without a sound. She had greased it too, working the oil in with a crochet hook. Again she waited, closing her eyes this time to sharpen her hearing. Nothing. She eased the door open by a fraction. Silence still. Another inch.

She stopped dead. The noise had been slight – a momentary shudder of heavy iron before her hand stilled it – and Mr Carew's hearing was not keen. But in this silence even he might have been disturbed. Esther glanced at the workbench, where her sewing case lay open. She did not wish for it, in spite of all his petty cruelties, but she had given it thought. If he discovered her now, she would have nothing to lose by it. She was quicker by far, and would close the distance in three strides. He would find out then what use a stiletto might be put to. She would do what she must.

But no, he only coughed again, and presently she heard a low chuckling. He had found something else to amuse him in the *Illustrated London News*. Esther returned her attention to the strongbox door. In one movement, soft but swift, she opened it halfway. It was all she needed.

The crystal vessels were arranged on a tray that occupied the whole of the middle shelf. It was lined with velvet, and each bottle stood in its own recess. There were eleven in all – there had been twelve, but one recess was now empty – and until now she had only glimpsed them. They were beautifully made, fluted and intricately faceted, and gleamed mutely in the yellowish light. A man in Antwerp had fashioned them, that much she knew, and to His Lordship's particular design. Nothing like them could be had in all of England, Mr Carew maintained. It was more than he ought to have said, but he took a pitiful pride in such things and a braggart is a poor keeper of secrets. Esther did not know everything, perhaps, but she knew enough.

Of the eleven vessels, eight were empty and discoloured. They could be used only once, that much she had learned, too, and yet each was returned afterwards to its place. When they had put it to use – later tonight, perhaps, she did not know – they would bring back a ninth blackened bottle. They would see then what had been done, but that was a moment she would not witness. It was a pity.

The remaining three were intact. At first glance they too appeared empty, but their stoppers were in place still and cloaked in a rich wax. At the base of each lay a dark fraction of viscous oil. The resin, she had heard them call it. It became a vapour, when the air touched it, that was necessary somehow to their purpose. She knew no more than that, and did not wish to.

It was these vessels that mattered most. The Dutchman would make no more, for reasons she had not discovered. He had died, perhaps, or there had been a dispute. Another craftsman might be found, but it would be no easy matter. They were not priceless, these bottles, but they were something near to it.

From a hidden fold in her skirts, Esther worked free what she had made. It was a satchel of sorts, fashioned for strength from sailcloth. It was divided into chambers or pouches, and each of these was lined with quilting so that the vessels would make no noise when they were carried side by side. With the utmost care, she grasped the neck of an intact bottle and lifted it from its place. It was a heavy thing, though it held what could hardly be more than an ounce of fluid. Still, it was smaller than she had judged and disappeared entirely when she slipped it into its pouch. That was good. Better too much room than too little.

Again Esther waited, though each moment now was a struggle. *Wait, girl. Wait and listen.*

She tucked the second bottle into the satchel, where it nestled softly by its neighbour, then waited again. Ten seconds. Twenty. She took the third vessel.

When it was done at last Esther returned to the workbench. Taking a moment's ease on her stool, she allowed her gaze to wander. The gown itself had a sad, vacant splendour, even without its sleeves. The gloves and the veil had been laid out too, and those few pieces of lacework that remained unfinished.

She would be free of all this, as she had yearned to be for so long. It was not fondness that detained her in these last moments, but some necessity that she could not name. It had not come into her plans to spend time in prayer, but she felt now that it was called for. She knelt before the gown, since it was a way of being near to the one who was to have worn it. And to the others, who had gone before. It was a way to honour them.

Another thought came to her. From the box that had been set on the table, Esther drew out the newest card. However the measurements were taken, it was done with great exactness, down to the eighth of an inch. She scanned the columns, sounding them out in a whisper, and as she did so the girl's slight form came to her, as surely known as if it were cradled now in her arms. She touched the card, leaving a dim smirch of blood, and for a moment she closed her eyes.

When there was nothing else to keep her, Esther stood for a moment with no particular purpose. She smoothed down her skirts and put a hand to her hair, but did not otherwise concern herself with her appearance. She looked for the last time about the room, and wondered if some great surge of panic would flood her thoughts.

There was nothing, nothing more. It was time.

Esther stooped to retrieve a low wooden step from beneath the workbench, turning it over to inspect its feet. She had lined them with felt so as to soften the noise. She set it carefully beneath the window, waiting afterwards for ten or fifteen seconds, then stood on the step and worked at the catch above the sash. This too had been oiled in preparation, and came free with only a small effort. The sash itself gave easily in its frame, just as it had done when she tried it last.

She could not see the lights of the Walsingham House Hotel, when she had hauled herself out and stood upright. She had imagined she might, but the rooftops opposite obscured the better part of the view. At the end of the street a man stirred in a spill of lamplight. Beyond that, she could make out Piccadilly and the dark fringe of Green Park. Nothing more.

Esther drew the first vessel from its padded chamber and held it before her. She rocked it gently, watching the slow gleam of the resin, then leaned a little way outwards and let it fall. The sound it made was small. Delicate, almost. She did not look down. That was the one thing she knew she must not do.

She caught sight of the man again. He had crossed the street, moving quickly now. Esther paid no attention. They had set someone to watch, perhaps. He had seen her and knew that something was amiss. It would make no difference, not now. It was too late. She took the second bottle from the satchel and let it fall. Then the third.

She allowed herself a moment then. It was something she had promised to herself, that before the end there would be an unburdened instant, belonging to her alone. She took a long breath and released it. Her own living warmth, turned to mist in the cold. But it was not as fierce as she had imagined, that cold, and there was very little wind. She took her place on the ledge, spreading her arms a little way to steady herself, and it was only then – sensing its intimate scatter against her knuckles – that she remembered the snow.

It was everywhere, when she lifted her face, massing now with soft insistence. It felt tender almost, like a final kindness, and when the moment came it was not like falling at all. She offered herself, nothing more, and the waiting air was swift and sure. It knew her for its own, and it rushed now to gather her up, to take her, at last, and carry her weightlessly from the earth.

II

KYRIE

I

When his knocking brought no one to the door, Gideon Bliss retreated from it to make certain of his bearings. He knew that he was in Frith-street, having flagged down a hansom cab to confirm the point. The cabman had been put out of temper, finding that Gideon did not intend to engage him, and had made it known that of course it was fucking Frith-street, adding with some bitterness that he was not a fundament of fucking knowledge for them as wasn't even going nowhere.

Gideon drew out his uncle's letter to examine it once more, though he had spent much of the train journey poring over it and knew certain passages almost by heart. Neuilly had written a good deal that struck him as troubling or mysterious, but he had not been unduly perturbed, reasoning that he knew very little, after all, of his uncle's life and habits. He had the comfort, too, of having been taken at last into the reverend doctor's confidence, and decided that for now he must simply do as he was bid, trusting that all would come to light in due course.

In certain practical matters, moreover, his uncle had been admirably clear. A change in his circumstances, he explained, had obliged him to quit his former rooms near London Bridge, and to take new lodgings in Soho. He had given exemplary directions, knowing his nephew's acquaintance with London to be slight, and Gideon had not strayed from these in the smallest particular. He was in Frith-street, just as he ought to have been, having entered it by way of Shaftesbury-avenue. He had continued almost as far as Soho-square, following his uncle's instructions, and had counted off each doorway that he passed. It was the right house. He was almost sure of it.

He knocked again, as vigorously as politeness permitted, and as he waited he made a careful examination of the doorway. No number appeared on the door itself, and although it was difficult to tell – since the hallway within was in darkness – he could see none displayed in the fanlight above it. Indeed, when he drew back to peer again at the upper windows, not a single light could be seen in any part of the house, nor any other sign of human occupation.

Gideon drew his coat about him, beating his hands together as he deliberated on his best course. He had not minded the cold until now, having kept up a brisk pace all the way from Liverpool-street, but it was not a night for waiting out of doors. He was mindful, too, that it was growing late. Hearing a church bell strike half past eight as he made his way along High Holborn, he had anxiously quickened his step. Although he had visited his uncle in London once before, to be summoned in this way was a thing without precedent. Having been kept for so long at a remove, he saw a chance at last to find favour with his guardian and did not mean to let it pass. It would not help his cause to arrive at an uncivil hour.

He looked up, hearing raised voices, and saw two figures approaching along the footway. The gentleman's hat was askew on his head, and the lady's cape was loosely fastened. Their progress was unsteady, but they appeared to be in high spirits. Seeing them turn in at the next door but one, Gideon hurried towards them.

'Good evening to you, sir, madam.' He lifted his hat, skidding a little as he came to a halt. 'I do beg your pardon, but I wonder if you might tell me the number of your residence.'

They turned haltingly to face him. The gentleman's arm was slung about the lady's waist, and she supported herself in part by clinging to the lapel of his overcoat. He smoked a cigar, but paused now in the act of raising it to his mouth. 'You hear that, Bella? Like doves cooing, it was. *I do beg your pardon.*'

'It was lovely, Mr Townsend.' Bella shifted her grip on her companion's collar, the better to bring herself upright. 'I do like a nice speaking voice. Say something else, my love.'

Gideon tugged his cuffs to his palms and gave a small cough of embarrassment. 'I mustn't detain you, madam, since the evening is so cold. I meant to trouble you only for the number of your house.'

'The number of it?'

'Yes, madam.'

Mr Townsend wheeled into proximity. 'What for?'

'Sir?'

'The number. What do you want to know it for?'

'Ah,' said Gideon. 'Of course. I am visiting my uncle, you see, who resides, I believe—'

'Your uncle?'

'Yes, sir.'

'Your own uncle, and you don't know where he lives? Ain't much hope of us knowing if you don't.'

'Forgive me,' said Gideon. 'I'm afraid I have not explained the case well. My studies keep me in Cambridge for much of the time, and I have not yet had the opportunity to visit my uncle at his present address. I am almost certain that this is the house, but I find that there is no number on the door. If you would be kind enough to give me yours, I shall be able to deduce my position.'

Bella beamed at him. 'That was beautiful, that was. Just beautiful. Weren't it, Mr Townsend?'

'Like a lark,' Mr Townsend replied. 'What's he saying, though?'

'Mr Townsend!' Bella pivoted gaily towards him and prodded at his belly. 'Ain't you supposed to be a wark of clurks? Hark at me! A clerk of works, I mean to say, with a bit of schooling about you. What's the number of your uncle's place, my pet?'

'Number six, madam. It is a boarding house, I understand, where he has taken rooms.'

'Well, that explains it,' said Mr Townsend.

'Forgive me, sir. What does it explain?'

'Why there ain't a number on the door. No point, with sixes. The screw comes loose, it tips over – next thing you know, it's a nine. No good to anyone. You'd have been off by three.'

'Yes, sir.' Gideon tried to keep the impatience from his voice. 'I do see your point.'

'And what if there was a six *and* a nine?' Bella said, gurgling with amusement. 'You do know what a six and a nine make, darling?'

Gideon bowed his head by a fraction. 'Unless I am much mistaken, madam.'

Bella and Mr Townsend slumped for a moment in merriment. Gideon looked about him uneasily, taking advantage of their distraction to retreat by a pace.

'Oh, the wickedness we must answer for,' Bella said, composing herself a little. 'Don't pay no attention to us, my love. This is number four, so you ain't missed your mark. Your uncle one of Mrs Coombe's lodgers, then?'

'I am very much obliged to you, madam. My uncle did not mention his landlady's name, and I myself have yet to make her acquaintance. I had been knocking for some time when I saw you approach, but it appears she is not at home either.'

'Oh, she'll be at home, right enough, but you can knock till you turn blue for all the good it will do you. Deaf as a post, Mrs Coombe is, at least when it suits her. Here, he ain't that copper, is he? Your uncle, I mean?'

'Copper? No, madam. My uncle is a clergyman. Are you acquainted with the Reverend Doctor Herbert Neuilly?'

'Old Nelly?' She pressed the heel of her hand to one smeared eye, a fondness softening her expression. 'It never is.'

'What you talking about, old Nelly?' Mr Townsend said.

'It's what we call him. Never could say his name the proper way, but he don't mind. Nice old bird, your uncle is. Always about his good works. And soft in his ways, bless him. Not like some of them vicars.'

Gideon had never witnessed his uncle's softness for himself, and received this account with a small jolt of resentment. 'I am gratified to find that my guardian is so well thought of,' he said. 'I must confess, though, that I am rather at a loss. My uncle keeps irregular hours, I know, but he expects my visit. Indeed, he summoned me here on a matter of urgency. It did not occur to me that I might not find him at home.'

'That's the way with him, my pet. Has to make sure this one has a bed for the night and that one has tuppence for a bowl of soup. Even brings them home sometimes, if they're in a bad way, though Mrs Coombe don't thank him for it. What's this matter of urgency, then? He's all right, ain't he? He ain't poorly?'

'No, nothing of that kind,' Gideon replied. He was about to say more, but it occurred to him that he had no ready answer. All he could say with certainty was that his uncle had been uneasy in his mind. He feared for those in his care, and spoke in dark terms of others who wished him ill, but he had seemed reluctant, in his letter, to state the case plainly. He meant to unburden himself,

Gideon had assumed, only when he and his nephew could converse at their ease, and yet he was not at home to receive him on his arrival.

'It is kind of you to inquire,' he said. 'It is a small private matter, nothing more. All the same, it is peculiar that it should have slipped his mind.'

'Well, that's the way of it,' said Mr Townsend, whose interest had now dissipated. 'It'll all come out in the wash, as the good book says. You coming, Bella?'

'Look at that now,' said Bella, paying no attention. 'I said we'd have snow.'

Gideon turned up his collar, looking about him with quiet apprehension. 'Well, then,' he said. 'There is nothing to be done, I suppose. I shall have to come back in the morning.'

'Here.' Bella lurched towards him and squeezed his forearm. 'You all right, my pet? He's forgotten, that's all. He's full of high notions, bless him, but he's hardly fit to dress himself in the mornings. Ain't got the sense of a day-old chick. You'll see your old uncle in the morning, and all will be well with the world.'

'Yes.' Gideon said weakly. 'Yes, I'm sure you're right.'

'You'll be all right, won't you? A proper lost soul, you look like. You got somewhere else you can go? I'd take you in myself, only I ain't got but a bed and a bucket. You can hardly put your elbows out up there.'

'You can put your knees out all right,' said Mr Townsend, who had now grown surly. 'If you ain't forgotten how.'

Gideon straightened, collecting himself, and briefly lifted his hat. 'You have been most kind, madam. And you, sir. I will make other arrangements and return in the morning, just as you say. It is no great matter. Now, it is indeed coming on to snow, and I must keep you no longer. I bid you both goodnight.'

With that he took his leave, turning once more towards Shaftesbury-avenue. He strode away briskly at first, and for a time he kept up an easy and purposeful appearance. But before long his weariness began to tell, and a despondency settled on him as he contemplated his circumstances. To begin with, there was the question of where he was to spend the night. His uncle made only the most frugal provision for his living expenses, and this unexpected excursion to London had been scarcely within his means. The purchase of his third-class ticket from Cambridge had left him all but penniless, and he doubted that he could pay for his board in the poorest kind of dosshouse.

It was a difficulty that he might have alluded to, had he and his uncle been on more familiar terms, but he had made no mention of it when replying to his letter, confining himself instead to decorous expressions of duty. He was most concerned, he had written, to learn of the reverend doctor's difficulties, but delighted nonetheless to have his confidence in the matter. He would come by the earliest possible train, and it was his earnest hope that he might be of some small service.

That much had been truthful enough, but he had not been wholly candid. His eagerness to come had not sprung entirely from his sense of duty. He looked forward to seeing his uncle, naturally, but on reading the letter his thoughts had turned first to someone else. He was by no means certain that he would encounter her again – indeed, he knew almost nothing of her present circumstances – but that had not hindered his imagination. He had thought of her first, and in the days since then he had thought of little else.

He might, he now reflected, have turned his mind to more practical matters. For all his great hopes, he had considered his course of action only to the point of presenting himself at his uncle's door.

Beyond that, he had formed no plan, and as he trudged onwards in the cold, he berated himself for his foolishness. In Cambridge, when the nights were mild, a fellow could shin up a wall in one of the quieter lanes and make a bed for himself in a well-tended boat shed or the camellia house of a Dean of Studies. But this was London, whose shrouded vastness was almost entirely strange to him, and in these unfamiliar streets he had no notion of where he might find shelter.

It was not only the cold that he contended with. He was stiff and footsore, having spent the better part of the day travelling, and as he crossed what he believed to be Old Compton-street, he was reminded that he was also wretchedly hungry. His last meal – a tepid and gristly pie – had been taken in a railway station tea-room at eleven o'clock that morning, and it seemed that one could walk no more than twenty paces in Soho without passing a hostelry or eating-house of some description. Gideon kept clear of their windows and signboards when he could, but hawkers busied themselves among the crowds, competing with formidable energy for passing trade. One such fellow, wearing the costume of a circus ringmaster, propelled him forcibly to the doorway of his establishment, refusing to release him until he had recited the bill of fare in its entirety.

'And when you've ate your Dover sole, sir, you might find the entertainment to your liking. Look at them girls in there and tell me you ain't peckish. A nice mannerly specimen like yourself, sir, with a soapy look about him? Why, you may be sure of opening an oyster or two.'

Gideon freed himself and lurched away, turning blindly into Shaftesbury-avenue. He was resolved now to seek out whatever pitiful shelter was to be had in this place, even if he must find a carter's yard and conceal himself under a heap of sacking. He looked about him for some quiet side street, but was drawn instead to a narrow alley that he might have overlooked but for its curiously ornate archway. A plaque was set into the stonework, whose inscription he paused to read.

ST ANNE'S CHURCH
SOUTH ENTRANCE

The alley was unlit and indifferently cobbled, obliging him to pick his way with some caution, but he came at length to a narrow yard beneath the hulking flank of a church. The light was hardly better here, but after a moment Gideon made out a modest porch. It was covered, if nothing else, and enclosed on three sides. Venturing inside, and finding it passably dry in places, he concluded that he was likely to do no better.

He had paid no attention to the doorway itself, and only as he lowered himself to huddle against it did he discover that the door was unlocked – that in fact it stood very slightly ajar. Warily, he rose again and peered through the crack. A moth fluttered from it, and for a moment he felt the obscure thrum of its wings against his cheek, but there were no other signs of life. With the utmost gentleness, he pushed the door a little way inwards. It was heavy and stiff, and in spite of his efforts it yielded with a good deal of noise.

Gideon clamped a hand to his mouth, but stood otherwise motionless. He listened intently, prepared to flee at the slightest sound.

But the silence seemed restored, and at length he persuaded himself that he had disturbed no one. He slipped inside. For fear of the noise, he did not close the door behind him, keeping still once more as he took his bearings. The church lay in darkness, but a great arched window was set into its apse, admitting a feeble suffusion of gaslight from the street beyond. It was enough to orient himself by, and to make out the bulk of the altar and the orderly ranks of the pews.

He crept forward, keeping close to the wall as he sought out some quiet recess in which to settle. He meant to conceal himself without delay, not wishing to squander his good fortune. But St Anne's proved to be a parish church of the plainer kind, laid out to a simple plan. It offered no quiet side-chapels or colonnaded aisles. Indeed, there was hardly even a transept to speak of. Growing anxious, he shuffled towards a narrow door by the chancel, where the vestry might commonly be found.

A faint sound stilled him, just as he was about to try the handle. It was dry and ragged, like the scrape of a straw broom against stone. Gideon scurried at once behind a pew. He heard it again, when his breathing quietened, coming at unrushed intervals, like a slow measure followed by a rest. With that thought the recognition came to him, and he reproached himself for his dull wits. Breathing. It was the sound of someone breathing.

When he had mastered himself sufficiently, Gideon put his head out by a fraction. The sound seemed to be coming from somewhere near the altar, though it was hard to be certain. An empty church was apt to produce strange echoes. It was regular yet unsettled, as when a person is at rest yet not quite at ease. Gideon cleared his throat gently.

'Hello there,' he called out. 'I hope I did not alarm you. It is a bitter night, and I came in only to have some respite from the cold.'

No answer came. The breathing continued just as before, quiet and undisturbed.

Rising from behind his pew, Gideon ventured closer. 'Hello

there,' he called again. 'Have I the honour of addressing the rector of this parish? My name is Gideon Bliss, sir. I am the nephew of the Reverend Doctor Herbert Neuilly, with whom you are perhaps acquainted. I am a man of God myself, sir, at least in a small way. I will shortly return to Cambridge, preparatory to the taking of holy orders.'

Here Gideon departed from strict truthfulness, since he was by no means certain of his vocation, but he intended only to put the stranger's mind at rest. He crept on, straining to make him out in the gloom, and kept up his intermittent attempts at conversation.

'Could I trouble you, sir, to raise an arm or give some other sign, so that I can come forward and make myself known? You may not have caught my name, I fear. I am Gideon Bliss, a reader in divinity at Selwyn College, Cambridge, where I hope to take my degree before casting my little boat onto the great waters of the – oh, my.'

Gideon halted, his arms slack at his sides. Before the altar, silent and unmoving, lay the figure of a young woman. He stood for a moment in bewilderment. His first thought was that she had crept in from the cold, just as he had, but she had made no effort to conceal herself, to say nothing of keeping warm. She lay on the cold stone flags before the altar itself, with no covering but her thin white shift, and in plain sight from those foremost pews. Perhaps she wished to be discovered, having taken shelter here after falling ill. Her breathing was laboured, certainly, yet her posture betrayed no obvious discomfort. Indeed, Gideon was struck by her peculiar stillness.

'Miss?' He approached her cautiously. 'Forgive me, miss. I took you for a priest of the parish. We find each other in the same predicament, if I am not mistaken. I meant to pass the night here too, owing to a temporary difficulty in the arrangement of my

35

lodgings. You will not take it amiss, I hope? I will settle down in some other part of the church, and make no sound if I can help it.'

Still she did not speak, or give any sign at all that she was aware of his presence. He listened again for her breathing, and was re-assured by its faint persistence, but he was troubled nonetheless. How frail she was. How narrow her wrists appeared in the loose folds of her shift. He took another step towards her, raising his hands to show her that he meant no harm.

'Miss?'

He saw her face, since the shadow of the altar no longer hid it. He saw her face, and for a moment his reason faltered. He put a hand out, as if to steady himself, and all that surrounded him seemed to recede.

It could not be. It could not be.

He had seen her first at St Magnus-the-Martyr by London Bridge, where his uncle had been given rooms on taking up a lecturing post. In the summer months, to ward off any rupturing of his tranquillity, it was the reverend doctor's custom to find some oc-cupation for his nephew that would keep him away from London. Since June, therefore, Gideon had been consigned to a bleak par-sonage in the fens, where he was to undertake a course of private study. In his letters, however, his meek petitioning had grown more insistent, and at last his uncle had consented to receive him for a week.

Gideon's welcome was not especially warm. His living quarters were modest, Neuilly explained, and his work left him little time for entertaining. Gideon might make use of the library, which was ample, and was otherwise free to amuse himself within re-spectable bounds. In practice, it was Gideon's purse that limited his amusements, since it did not occur to his guardian to grant him any allowance beyond the ordinary. On one occasion, when it had stayed wet for the whole of the afternoon, he paid a penny to be admitted to a saloon near Victoria Station, where feats of daring were to be performed by a troop of Cossacks. Gideon saw very little, however, being much jostled by other spectators, and he fled when a horse kicked over a brazier, setting fire to a painted backcloth and giving rise to a stampede. In the three days that followed, he did little more than walk the streets, wandering eastwards along the wharves as far as the Tower or westwards to St Paul's Cathedral. By the fourth day of his visit, he had begun to think with fondness of Cambridge, and he resolved to lay out a pretext for returning that would give his uncle no offence.

At the supper table that evening, he waited an hour and a half for the reverend doctor to join him. His guardian's habits were irregular, and it was by no means certain that he would return home at all, but he appeared in the end a little after nine o'clock, at which hour the housekeeper was on the point of retiring and would serve them no more than plates of cold pork and cheese. After she had withdrawn, Neuilly occupied himself for a time with an item of correspondence, seeming so thoroughly absorbed that Gideon began to wonder if his presence had been overlooked.

'Well, nephew.' Neuilly looked up at last. 'You have found your lodgings satisfactory, I trust? You want for nothing?'

Gideon hesitated. 'Nothing, sir. I am very grateful indeed for your hospitality.'

'Indeed.' Neuilly looked away as if distracted, removing his spectacles to rid them of a smear. 'And you have found London tolerably diverting? You have been to see St Paul's, I gather. Wren had a hand in this church, you know, or put his name to the plans in any event. It is a handsome enough place, I suppose.'

'Oh, yes,' Gideon agreed, thumbing the edge of his plate. If he was to broach the subject of his return to Cambridge, he must do so soon. His uncle was apt to rise abruptly from the table after taking his meals. 'Notably so, sir. It struck me at once.'

The reverend doctor contemplated him for a moment, then pushed his chair back and took up his letter again. 'We have received a visitor of sorts,' he said. 'You will welcome the news, no doubt. I'm afraid I am poor company for a boy your age.'

Gideon looked up. 'A visitor, uncle?'

Neuilly toyed absently with his letter, smoothing out the corner of the topmost page. 'After a fashion,' he said. 'In my ministry, as you may recall, I tend to the needs of the poor. To young women, in particular, who are so much preyed upon when circumstances turn against them.'

'Yes, sir,' Gideon said, though in fact he knew nothing at all of his uncle's work beyond what little he had observed. 'You have spoken of it in general terms.'

'There is one young girl in particular,' Neuilly said, 'over whom I have taken particular care. An orphan, alas, whose prospects would be poor indeed if she were left without aid. I had found her lodgings and a position – she is a flower-maker, this girl – but a difficulty has arisen with her present engagement. She arrived last evening, and will stay with us for two days – three, perhaps, if my plans are hindered. Her name is Tatton, Miss Angela Tatton.'

'Ah,' said Gideon, lowering his eyes. 'Angie.'

Neuilly blinked slowly.

'Forgive me, uncle. It came to me just now that I have seen a young woman below stairs whom your housekeeper addresses by that name. It occurred to me that she must be the visitor you refer to.'

'I see,' said Neuilly. 'How observant you are. Yes, that is the girl I mean. Mrs Downey will find some occupation for her during the day and otherwise keep company with her, since we must ensure that there is no appearance of . . .'

He made a fastidious gesture, at which Gideon discreetly lowered his head.

'But in the evenings, perhaps, you might think of passing the time with her in some improving manner. Some little education will do her no harm, and I prefer to keep her from wandering abroad when she is at leisure. You might read to her from some suitable works, or instruct her in her letters. You would not find it tedious, I hope?'

Gideon was momentarily absorbed. The morning had been bright, and he had seen her first as he came in from the river, halting by the scullery door when a rift of sunlight caught the stillness of her face. She was intent on her work, forming a lattice of pastry with quick and delicate movements, but was troubled by a fly that settled at intervals on her skin. She looked up at last, as she brushed it away, and he hurried onwards. But he could see, even now, the place where she had touched her cheek, leaving a dusty figure of flour.

'Nephew,' Neuilly said, mildly vexed. 'You will not find it tedious?'

'Forgive me, sir,' he said, realising that he had fallen silent. 'No, indeed not. On the contrary, I should be delighted.'

'Miss Tatton?' He crouched over her, whispering her name in wonderment at first, but growing anxious when he could not rouse her. 'Won't you wake up, Miss Tatton? Do please wake up.'

She stirred at last and opened her eyes, but gave no sign that she had seen him. Indeed, he could not be sure that she recognised her surroundings at all.

'Miss Tatton, it is Gideon Bliss. What has happened to you? How did you come to be in this place?'

She turned towards him slowly, her gaze oddly vacant. She would not know him, he was sure. He feared for a moment that she could not see him. But she smiled faintly, as if at some small puzzle that she had solved. 'I knew you'd come,' she said. Her voice was thin, faded somehow. 'You had to go back to your books, you said, but your heart wasn't in it. I knew.'

'Angie.' Unthinkingly, he moved to grasp her arm, checking himself only at the last moment. 'Miss Tatton. You do know me, after all. How glad I am to see you. I did not want to go back, you are quite right about that. My uncle wished me to, but I – well, I had other hopes.'

'Other things,' Angie said. 'You were put here for other things.'

Gideon dropped his gaze. She had spoken those words on another occasion, and perhaps she had not meant them unkindly. Something had not quite been offered, and not quite refused. It was the gentlest reproach that might still be felt. He encircled her wrist, and with the faintest pressure allowed his thumb to graze her skin.

'Heaven help us,' he said, recalled to himself by how cold she was. He worked his coat from his shoulders and settled it about her. 'How long have you been lying in this place, Miss Tatton? You are half petrified. And what possessed you to come here on such a night? Could you not have gone to my uncle, if you had nowhere else?'

Angie closed her eyes, perhaps to gather her strength. Her breathing was shallow and frayed. 'My name,' she said after a time. 'The name you had for me. Do you remember?'

Gideon thought for a moment. 'Angie Tatton,' he said. 'Angie Tatton in ribbons of satin.'

She shook her head weakly. 'Not that. Everyone called me that. The other name.'

He looked away in discomfort. His name for her. He had whispered it to himself many times, late at night, but until now he had only once spoken it aloud. It was a moment before he could bring himself to say the words.

'Look at you,' she said, smiling again. 'Always too shy by half. That was it. Maybe that's what I'll be now, young master. Maybe that's how you'll remember me.'

'Angie?' Her eyes had fallen closed again. 'Speak to me, Miss Tatton, please. Tell me what you mean. Tell me what the matter is.'

'I can feel it, young master,' she said. 'They gave me something, and I can feel it happening.'

'Angie!' He shook her again. 'Stay with me, Angie. You must tell me what happened so that I know what is to be done. Who gave you something? What did they give you?'

Her head lolled, and Gideon feared that she had slipped entirely from her senses, but with a struggle she fixed her gaze on him again. 'He kept me safe as long as he could. Found new places, when they got too close. But it weren't just me they were looking for. They found him, young master, and brought him here first. Gone now. He's gone.'

'Who, Angie?' He cast a look about the darkened church, recalling with a lurch of dread that he had not closed the door behind him. 'Who took him? Is someone coming back for you? Someone who means you harm?'

'We must keep it hidden, your uncle said. Keep the brightness hidden. But we couldn't, in the end. I'll be all brightness soon, that's what they said, and ain't that a special thing? I should be happy. But it was black, the air. Like something made of nothing. I can taste it still. I can feel it.'

'Angie,' he said, clutching her shoulders. 'Miss Tatton, listen to me. Someone has poisoned you, I think, and you are delirious.

41

I will go for help. I will fetch a doctor here, even if I must pick someone's pocket to pay him. I will come back soon, do you hear? I will come back to you, I promise.'

He put a hand to her face, forgetting himself in the tumult of his feelings. Her skin was cold, but dewed faintly as if by a fever. He stroked her cheek, freeing a slip of hair that had clung to it, and with trembling effort Angie covered his fingers with her own. He brought his face very near to hers.

'Too shy, always,' she said. 'Too shy for your own good. You have to go now, young master. They'll be here soon, and they'll find you too. It's too late for me now, I can feel it. You have to go.'

'Angie, no. Never say that. I shall call the police. I shall fetch a doctor and he will – and you will be—'

He broke off, a sob rising in him, as Angie's fingers curled feebly about his neck, drawing him to her. They were frigid still, but her lips, as they parted under his, were warm and living.

'See?' she said, releasing him. 'Other things. You were put here for other things. Now go.'

He drew away, dazed from her, and so lost in her face that for a moment he suspected nothing. But she was staring past him, her scream a hoarse rasp as the rag was clamped to his mouth. He was slowing then, even as he began to struggle, clawing emptiness and breathing only the strange deep sweetness now, remembering nothing else. He saw her once more, as he was hauled up, the sense almost gone from things. He saw it, or thought he did. The brightness of her.

The brightness of her, and then the dark.

II

When her knocking brought no one to the door, Octavia Hillingdon was not unduly perturbed. No doubt she would have been refused admission in any event, and she had been quite prepared for this eventuality. Her plan was a simple one, but it required that she settle upon some distinguishing feature among the uppermost parts of the building. Descending the steps, she retrieved her bicycle and crossed the street, conducting it alongside her as she set off once more in the direction of St James's Palace.

She scanned the roof line opposite as she did so, and was so much absorbed in this that she very nearly collided with a newsvendor, a weathered and black-shawled woman of above sixty who berated her and her 'contraption' in the coarsest terms.

Octavia begged her pardon, though she did so with a certain briskness. The woman presented a formidable obstacle and had hardly been disturbed. '*News and Post* a ha'penny!' she bawled, holding that evening's edition stoutly aloft. 'Ha'penny the *News and Post*!'

'What have you on the front page?' Octavia inquired. Among those belonging to the better papers, the *Evening News and Post* was regarded with a degree of disdain, but she maintained a certain professional curiosity. 'May I look? Has another vagrant been found who resembles a long-lost duke?'

The woman backed away, folding the newspaper primly at her side. 'I only hump them out here and flog them, miss,' she said. 'I don't get them off by heart first. Pay your ha'penny, and you can look all you like.'

'I am on my way to an engagement and cannot carry a newspaper,' said Octavia. 'I will give you a farthing for a look at the front page. Come, the night is cold. It is coming on to snow, and you have half a dozen copies yet to sell at this hour.'

'Ha'penny,' said the woman, gathering herself resolutely beneath her dark rags. 'I should be asking for more, by rights, the fright you gave me. I still ain't over the shock of it.'

Octavia could not help but laugh. 'Very well, then, a ha'penny it is. And when I have looked over the front page you may have it back to sell again for your trouble. Does that seem fair?'

The woman regarded her grudgingly still, but handed over the paper, drawing a fresh copy from a broad satchel and resuming her cries. Octavia scanned the front page with a practised eye, passing over the death notices and the claims that were made for sauces and corn cures.

'"Spiriters feared abroad once more",' she read aloud, having settled on a headline. 'What is this now?'

'Them Spiriters,' the woman said. 'Been at it again, they're saying.'

For a moment Octavia's vision dimmed. She grasped the frame of her bicycle and pressed her eyes shut. *Not now.*

But there was nothing more. She blinked, and drew in a careful breath. 'Yes, but who *are* they?' she continued. 'What exactly have they been at? "A pall of fear has once again fallen over Whitechapel and surrounding districts, occasioned by the recent disappearance of another young girl. Talk has again turned to the shadowy malefactors known only as the Spiriters." "Shadowy malefactors", indeed. It is like something from a bad novel.'

'Name and address is up at the top, miss, for them as wants to write a letter in. I'll be sure to tell them to expect it.'

Octavia laughed again and took up her bicycle. 'Quite right,' she said, setting off again. 'You are a working woman, and I have detained you long enough. Goodnight to you, madam.'

She turned into Cleveland-row, quickening her pace against the cold, and came after a little way to a narrow back street that gave on to an irregular and gloomy court. To the rear of the grand establishments of St James's-street she would find their kitchens and coach-houses, and it was by this route, she supposed, that servants and tradesmen reached them. Crossing again to the far side of the lane, she searched the upper reaches of houses, fixing once more upon the high chimney stack of gaunt sandstone she had observed from St James's-street. She cast a last look about her, then unlatched a narrow gate and proceeded at a breezy pace towards the kitchen door.

Beyond it was a dingy passageway lined with milk cans and coal scuttles. A porter hoisted up his bucket of potato peelings to let her pass, but his expression was dimly perturbed.

'I shall be leaving my bicycle in the passageway,' she told him brightly. 'One hears of so many thefts nowadays. I do hope it won't be an inconvenience.'

She passed from the cellars and storerooms to the busier regions surrounding the kitchens themselves, drawing increasing scrutiny as she did so, and as she reached the foot of the servants' stairs, she was accosted at last by an agitated young man who wore a morning suit beneath his immaculate apron. She bid him a crisp good evening and moved to pass by him, but he raised his gleaming salver to block her way.

'Pardon me, miss,' he said. 'You are in the wrong place.'

'Indeed I am,' Octavia replied. 'I am at the bottom of this staircase, and I should like to be at the top. Would you be so good as to let me pass?'

'Miss.' He was hardly more than a youth, really. His complexion was poor and sallow, and he had rather too much oil in his hair. 'All Souls is a *gentlemen's* club, miss. You're in the wrong place.'

Octavia climbed to the next step, and her proximity forced him to adjust his outstretched arm. 'Tell me,' she said, 'is Mr Jermyn here this evening? He is the head of the domestic staff, is he not?'

Something of the young man's confidence leached from his face. 'It's his night off, miss.'

'My grandfather sends him a consideration with his Christmas card. Do you know my grandfather, Mr Felix Hillingdon? He is a sentimental creature, you see, but rather forgetful, so I keep a list for him. Perhaps I ought to add your name. I'm sure he'd be upset if you were overlooked.'

He winced in discomfort as she inched further upwards. 'My compliments to the gentleman, I'm sure,' he said. 'But he'd tell you the same thing if he was standing here now, same as any member. Ladies ain't admitted, miss.'

'Perhaps he would.' Octavia edged upwards again, obliging him to stretch his arm still further. 'My grandfather is a man of tradition, it's true. But rules are one thing. An assault on his granddaughter's person is quite another.'

'An assault on your—'

'Well, indeed.' Octavia rose by another step. Hardly half an inch now separated her uncovered collarbone from his hand, whose slight tremor she could now discern. 'I'm afraid I don't see how else the situation could be perceived.'

The young man swung awkwardly aside, contorting himself so as to keep his salver from tipping over. By the time he had righted himself, Octavia had reached the top of the staircase.

'Come now, miss, please,' he called after her. 'The constables will have to be sent for.'

'What a splendid idea,' she said, pausing at the top of the staircase. 'The members would applaud your vigilance, I am sure. But they may take a different view when the matter is reported in the papers. "Constables were called last evening to a scene of disorder at All Souls club in St James's-street, where they found that a young lady, having entered the premises only to seek directions, had been detained below stairs by domestic staff and subjected to improper advances." The form of words may vary a little, but you have the idea, I'm sure.'

She turned to look down at him.

'My own paper won't carry it, of course, since the proprietor and the editor are both members here, but others will be glad to, especially if I have saved them the trouble of drafting the fair copy. My name is Octavia Hillingdon, young man, of the Mayfair *Gazette*. Do feel free to give the constables my name.'

The dining room, when she located it, proved to be a grand but sepulchral chamber, with the brownish and looming appearance of places where the tastes of gentlemen have gone unchecked. Only two of its tables were occupied, one of them by a fantastically aged creature who sat hunched over a bowl of soup and that morning's *Times*, motionless and quite possibly asleep. At the other, just as she had expected, was Mr Healy.

He greeted her with a bland look when she had seated herself, finishing his mouthful with a show of indifference, then swigging from his claret glass before he spoke. 'Miss Hillingdon,' he said. 'You imagine this intrusion to be amusing, no doubt.'

'I imagine no such thing, Mr Healy. *I* certainly don't find it amusing. I find it tiresome. In fact, since I arrived at your office to submit my article, fully fifteen minutes before the appointed time, I've been having an exceedingly tiresome evening.'

Mr Healy sawed at his beef. 'I do employ a deputy, Miss Hillingdon.'

'Mr Benedict is of a very nervous disposition, as you know, and hardly trusts himself to check the railway timetables. I did ask him to accept my pages, but he would not hear of it. It would not do to interfere, he said, which is just the answer he gave me the last time you missed our appointment, and the time before that.'

'I shall be returning after my dinner, as always. You might easily have waited.'

'Oh, yes, I might easily have perched in that draughty corridor for three hours, watching Mr Benedict gnaw at his pencils and wondering how many toes I'd lost to frostbite. How very gallant you are, Mr Healy. In any case, I was in a hurry. I had just got back from the House of Lords, and I have a ball to attend at Ashenden House. One can't very well write about society if one never ventures into it.'

'What has the House of Lords to do with society? Debutantes have not begun coming out in the ladies' gallery, surely? Here is the porter, by the way, to bring this bit of foolishness to an end. Did you wish to pass me this article of yours before you are carried out?'

Octavia set her packet of pages on the table, propping it up with a salt cellar. 'For fear you should overlook it,' she explained. 'Lady Ashenden is giving the ball to honour Lord Strythe, the Earl of Maundley. He has established a benevolent foundation of some kind for injured work girls. I went to Westminster, where a bill on their working conditions was to come before the Lords. I felt I ought to begin by observing the man in his daily element, so that the reader may form her impression of him in the round. Or *his* impression, come to that. It isn't unimaginable, I hope, that a man might glance at my page.'

Mr Healy swelled his cheeks, prodding at the tablecloth with the handle of his fork. 'If you are so interested in these work girls, you might think of looking into this Spiriters business. Some of the weeklies have shown an interest, and it has done them no harm.'

'The *illustrated* weeklies, you mean?' Octavia waved away the porter, who was by now hovering at her shoulder. 'Well, quite. One expects no better of those. It is sensational nonsense, Mr Healy. What has it to do with the lives of working women?'

'What has it to do with working women, she asks, when there are scullery maids and match girls disappearing left and right. Why, it is just the sort of thing your Mrs Besant has always worked herself up about.'

Octavia straightened in her chair. 'Mrs Besant no longer concerns herself with such things. She has left for Paris, or so I understand, where she has taken up with an occultist of some kind. In any case, the Working Conditions Bill—'

'The Working Conditions Bill –' he gulped from his claret glass, setting it down with clattering emphasis, '– is neither here nor there. I have the whole of the paper to devote to the news of the day, and I'm sure our Westminster correspondent will give it his attention if the matter warrants it. As for the readers of "The Ladies' Page", I fail to see how it could interest them.'

She regarded him evenly. 'To begin with, Mr Healy, not all the readers of my page are ladies. I proposed a new title for that very reason, as you may recall.'

'What title?' he said. '"The Evening Companion"?'

'That was your suggestion, Mr Healy, and I'm afraid it has a disreputable connotation. Mine was "The Spirit of the Age".'

He flapped his lips in contempt, shaking his head as he returned to his beef.

'In any case,' she continued, 'it isn't only the season's fashions that concern them, or the fitting out of Mrs Fitzherbert's barouche. They are exercised by political questions, and by the social ills that we must all confront.'

'Dear me, Miss Hillingdon. Is it any wonder that I am remiss about our appointments? You are not at one of your lectures now, and I should rather like to finish my dinner without being subjected to an improving course of instruction. I will certainly not have you hectoring the ladies of Mayfair from a soapbox. There is no shortage of advertisers, you know. That page of yours might easily be put to other uses.'

Octavia rose and smoothed down her gown, at which the porter who loomed near her chair withdrew by a fraction. She raised her chin as she addressed Mr Healy. 'I need hardly remind you, sir, that my grandfather is still your employer.'

'Your grandfather – for so we must refer to him – was always a man of great decorum. If he were still in his senses, he would rein you in himself. And he would take a dim view of this little spectacle.'

Felix Hillingdon had thought of children late in life, and on adopting Octavia and her brother, he had chosen not to style himself their father. To do so, he later explained, would have been to claim a youth and vigour he no longer possessed, even if he had affection still in abundance. It was a question that never troubled the family in the slightest, and one that was alluded to by no one else but Mr Healy.

'My grandfather knew a story when he saw one, Mr Healy, until his affliction. He would have paid no attention to ridiculous tales about stealing souls in Whitechapel, but he would have found it curious, as I did, that Lord Strythe seemed so thoroughly satisfied with a bill that hardly imposed a single obligation or penalty on any employer that did not exist before, and that his only stated concern, in sending it back down, was with the funding of institutions such as his own. My grandfather would have found all that peculiar, and would have wondered at any newspaperman who did not.'

And her grandfather, she might have added, would have found Lord Strythe himself peculiar. Octavia had observed him carefully from the gallery, and he had seemed to her a vain and aloof figure. She had passed him in the lobby as he was helped into his cloak, and though his gaze had settled on her for only a moment, she had never felt so closely examined. A cold fish, her grandfather would have said, though Healy would no doubt dismiss the notion. A devilish cold fish.

'A moment, Miss Hillingdon.' Mr Healy detached his napkin and settled back in his chair, raising a hand to keep the porter at bay. 'Do not trouble yourself, Flett. The lady will be leaving presently, and I will see her to the door myself.'

Octavia seated herself again, and for a moment she and Mr Healy confronted one another in silence.

'Very well, then,' he said at length. 'Here is my offer, Miss Hillingdon, since you will give me no peace until I make one. I draw the line at suffragist claptrap, as you very well know, but I am not so benighted as you suppose. I will consider the thing if it is done in the right way. If Lord Strythe is to be honoured for his good works, as you say, then the moment may be right to give the reader an impression of the man.'

'But that is just what I propose, Mr Healy.'

He held up a plump palm. 'An impression of him, I say, but one that takes account of his standing. He is not much in view for a man of his station, and the reader may therefore be interested to learn how he diverts himself. Has he a fondness for the opera, let us say, or does he keep a lodge in the Highlands for shooting at grouse? That is what is wanted.'

'Well, perhaps, but I do think—'

'What is not wanted, Miss Hillingdon, is sniping and insinuation about the fellow's politics, or any pot-banging about the inequities of our social order or the plight of the working poor. If you can bring yourself to keep within that gauge, then perhaps I will begin to see your true promise. If not, it will be the last time you stray from your little paddock. Is that plain?'

An answer came to Octavia that she chose to suppress. She gave a brief nod.

'Furthermore, you may nurse whatever private opinions you see fit, but I will not have us continually outdone in this Spiriters business. You have a marvellous knack for finding things out, when you are moved to it, and it will not cause you any mortal agony to put it to more general use. Take yourself down to Whitechapel or Spitalfields, or to a seance, to hear what talk there may be among the spiritualists. Fellows who would go out stealing souls may well be known in such circles. Begin your appreciation of Lord Strythe, by all means, but do not think of bringing it to me unless you have something on the Spiriters in your other hand. Have we a bargain, Miss Hillingdon?'

Octavia looked down for a moment at her lap. It was hardly a resounding victory, yet it was a good deal more ground than Mr Healy had ever yielded before.

'We have,' she said at last.

'Splendid,' said Mr Healy, rising. 'Now, if you don't mind, I should like to take my coffee in peace. And as for you, Miss Hillingdon, it seems to me that you have work to do.'

III

At Ashenden House, Octavia was more discreet in disposing of her bicycle. The possession of a bicycle, to Lady Ashenden's guests, might be considered tolerable or even charming in the abstract, but they would not expect to confront the physical article as they descended from their town coaches. Whatever her private sympathies, Octavia was obliged for now to ingratiate herself in such circles, and doing so required that she maintain certain appearances.

It required, too, that she keep up cordial relations with people of influence, even those who shared none of her convictions. She counted some of these as friends, after a fashion, and seldom wanted for company on occasions of this kind. Indeed, she had hardly been announced when Charles Elphinstone, the Marquess of Hartington, broke off a conversation to greet her, relieving the other party of two bumpers of champagne. 'You toddle back for more, Findlay,' he said. 'You will profit from the exercise, goodness knows, and poor Miss Hillingdon looks quite parched.'

He kissed her lightly on each cheek. 'Wavy, my darling,' he said, 'how captivating you look, though you are quite blue from the cold. Surely you haven't been careening about on that preposterous bicycle of yours on a night like this? One might as well be in Nova Scotia, or some such accursed place. Christ, how I loathe the cold.'

'Hello, Elf,' she said, accepting a glass. In her articles, he was Lord Hartington or, on great occasions, The Most Honourable the Marquess of Hartington. Among friends, at his own insistence, he was simply Elf. 'Are you suffering terribly? You don't look it, you know. You're positively tanned.'

'Hmm?' Elf raised his glass to a passing acquaintance, mouthing something of mischievous significance. 'Oh, yes. I spent most of last October in Paris, where I was supposed to be learning about their innovations in policing. I'm on a select committee, you see. Only they were having the most glorious Indian summer, and the Bois de Boulogne was simply Arcadian. You can't imagine the picnics. I've been back for months, though, and all that *joie de vivre* is steadily leaching away. I'm positively ravenous, too, which doesn't help. I do resent balls that start late. One never has time to dine acceptably, and one is offered nothing but trifles. Legs of honeyed pullet, if you can credit that. What good is a leg of honeyed pullet to anyone but a sickly child?'

'Goodness, how you have suffered,' said Octavia. 'Still, it's a relief to learn that you do have some public function. Speaking of which, I hope you did the right thing in the vote this evening. I couldn't pick you out from where I was sitting.'

Elf downed his champagne with a pained expression. 'Good Lord, was there a vote? What on, old thing? I do rather avoid the place when I can. The House of Commons has all but declawed us now, and the tail is very much wagging the dog, though I'm afraid that's a horribly muddled metaphor. At any rate, *sic transit* and what have you. But what on earth were *you* doing there, Wavy? Furthering one of your causes, I suppose?'

'I was forming an impression of this evening's guest of honour. That was my intention, at least, though he now seems more of a puzzle than ever. He didn't seem much concerned with the

Working Conditions Bill, beyond his own interests. It all seemed rather peculiar.'

'Yes, well, he's a peculiar chap, Strythe, yet he can't seem to put a foot wrong. Fancies himself as Home Secretary, I'm told, when we finally dislodge these Liberals, though quite why anyone would covet that dismal office passeth all understanding. You must tell me when these causes of yours are getting an airing, so that I can make a point of being in attendance. But enough of all that, darling. Have you met Jemima Beausang? You really must. She was staying with the Lyndsays, you know, when Sir Clive came down to breakfast in his natural splendour.'

'You don't mean that he was naked?'

'Utterly and gloriously so. He sank two hundred thousand into a hole in the ground in Minas Gerais, and what does he have to show for it? Not enough gold to fill a tooth. It's taken rather a toll on the poor chap's state of mind. Terribly sad, really, but marvellous fun all the same. No one dared say a word, of course. I mean, what *could* one say? He'd finished his kippers and got through most of *The Times* when the nature of the thing appeared to dawn on him. You can't print a word of that, of course, but I'm sure Jemmy has all sorts of other *morceaux*.'

Octavia followed Elf to an adjoining room, where various intimates of his had gathered, using the shelter of an immense potted palm to defame their fellow guests in comparative safety.

'Well, now,' said Mrs Beausang when Octavia had been introduced. 'So, this is the Miss Hillingdon you're forever eulogising. One sees why, of course. Look at her here among us, like an orchid in a bog. But she's much too wholesome for you, dearest. You'll have to give up all your vices, starting with that repugnant tobacco of yours.'

'What, these?' Elf held up his cigarette. 'They're from Paris, you know, where I rather acquired a taste for them. The aroma is agreeable, don't you think? They put in sandalwood, or some such thing.'

'Agreeable? It's perfectly detestable. Like a fire in a eucalyptus grove. But you've reminded me to ask. What on earth were you up to in Paris? The stories I've been hearing are very odd indeed.'

'Oh, it was all rather dull,' Elf replied. 'Official business, mostly, to do with policing methods. I've just been telling Wavy.'

'Well, *I* heard –' Jemima laid an accusing finger on his lapel, '– that you'd been keeping some rather colourful company there, and that you were seen at the salon of that frightful Madame Blavatsky.'

'What perfect nonsense,' said Elf. He had been distracted by someone entering the room, or wished to give that impression. 'Madame Blavatsky is dead, for one thing.'

'Yes, well.' Jemima gestured carelessly, almost spilling her champagne. 'I'm misremembering the particulars, perhaps, but it was someone of that sort. A spiritualist, or whatever they call themselves now. Oh, don't say it isn't true, Elf. I so enjoyed imagining it all.'

'Really, Elf?' Octavia said. 'That doesn't sound at all like you.'

'Good Lord, no. We were entertained by the *comtesse* of something at one point, but she doesn't keep a salon, unless you count her dachshunds. A very ancient creature, and splendidly mad, but hardly an exponent of the occult. I'm afraid you've been toyed with, Jemmy.'

'Yes, but it would explain so much,' Jemima persisted. 'Like your youthful appearance, for instance. You haven't aged a day in fifteen years, and here I am, a perfect hag at thirty-seven.'

'Moderate habits, my darling.' Elf made a theatrical gesture. 'A life of purity and self-denial.'

He looked away again, and this time Octavia saw the man who

had drawn his attention. He might have been invisibly ordinary in other surroundings, but here he was made conspicuous by his plain brown suit. He stood apart from the crowds, silently turning away the waiters who approached him, and his demeanour was both purposeful and curiously at ease. He met Elf's gaze with a slight inclination of his head, but otherwise made no overt gesture.

'Do you know that gentleman?' Octavia said. 'He seems to know you.'

'Hmm? Oh, vaguely. A Whitehall functionary of some kind. I can't think what he's doing here.'

'Perhaps he knows where Lord Strythe is,' Jemima said. 'No one else seems to.'

'What do you mean?' Octavia said. 'Isn't he here?'

'Oh, didn't I say? He's been held up or called away, or goodness knows what. Lady Ashenden is wretched with embarrassment.'

'How awful for her,' Octavia said. 'Called away by what, do you know? Something at Westminster?'

'I'm afraid I wasn't paying attention, dearest. Lord Strythe is so unfailingly dull, you see. One never hears of his doing anything. And then that young pianist passed by, and I was quite distracted. What *is* his name, Kitty, the Austrian gentleman with the good legs? Is it Klemser or Klein?'

But Octavia was no longer listening. Taking hold of his cuff, she drew Elf aside. 'We have to find out what's happened. Can you help, do you think? I'd do it myself, but you have better connections with Lady Ashenden's set.' He glanced over his shoulder again, but the man in brown had been obscured for a moment by an animated cluster of guests. Rumours of Strythe's absence had no doubt begun to circulate, and those who might know more were being discreetly sought out. 'Elf, are you listening? I'm sorry to impose, but it's rather important.'

'Hmm? I'm sorry, darling, what's important? Not the ball, surely?'

'The ball, yes. It will be talked about, you know, if the guest of honour fails to appear. People will want to know why. That is what I do, you know, and in this case I really do want to discover the truth. Something has happened, clearly, and it must be something out of the ordinary. A man like Strythe wouldn't forgo all this adulation over a broken carriage wheel. Something has happened, Elf, and I mean to find out what.'

He considered this for a moment. 'Perhaps you're right, darling, though I fear you'll be disappointed. Strythe is much duller than you might suppose. Still, I shall do all I can. You yourself must remain in the offing, though, so that no one suspects I'm doing your bidding. Her Ladyship is no great friend to the fourth estate, as you may have heard. She was very much aggrieved by her father's obituary, which slighted his Governorship of Ceylon and, what was worse, understated the size of his estate. It sounds ludicrous, I know, but lesser grudges have propped up centuries of strife. Look, they're serving ices in the blue drawing room. Wait for me there, won't you? I shan't be long, I promise.'

Octavia watched as he slipped away into the crowd, but did not see him leave the room. He had a gift for stealth, she had often noticed, and seemed at times to appear and disappear at will. In the blue room, she stationed herself with some reluctance on a sofa, but abandoned it again a moment later. She paced the fringes of the room, refusing the sorbets she was repeatedly offered. She watched the clock. Ten minutes passed, then fifteen.

'Where is Lord Strythe?' she demanded, approaching a serving boy. Even as she spoke, she had hardly a notion of her own intentions, or of exactly what pretence she was adopting. 'I was to be sent for at once when his plans were known.'

'If you please, miss,' he said. 'I shall pass word as quick as you like, but it's Mr Maitland sees to the comings and goings of Her Ladyship's guests.'

'Nonsense,' said Octavia. 'You have been to and fro with your ices since I came in, and must be passing through the kitchens. You don't mean to tell me, surely, that there is no talk below stairs of my uncle's situation. His Lordship will expect that arrangements have been made for me. You did not think he would leave me to traipse home alone in the snow?'

The boy looked anxiously about the room. 'Well, since it's your uncle, miss, I expect there's no harm in saying. Only you mustn't say as it were me who told you, or Mr Maitland will skin me. His Lordship has been called away, miss. He'd hardly got here when the word came. He's been took below to leave by the back of the house. Her Ladyship said it must all be done without a fuss.'

'Called away by whom?' Octavia said. 'My uncle is not on a casual social call.'

Again the serving boy looked about him in discomfort. 'Look, miss, His Lordship was most anxious to light out directly, that's all I can tell you. He's most likely waiting for you now, since his carriage couldn't hardly have been took in to the stables. Shall I send word that I've found you, miss?'

'No,' said Octavia at once. 'No, it is very good of you, but I must get along. I should be obliged if you would show me the way, but without a fuss, just as you say. We must do nothing to add to Lady Ashenden's embarrassment.'

She moved quickly below stairs, meeting no one's eyes until she came to the draughty passageway that gave on to the stable yard, where a flask was being passed around while a footman gave a bawdy account of an incident in a fortune teller's tent.

The servants fell silent at her approach. 'Oh, good heavens,' she cried, with slightly more theatrical emphasis than was needed. 'Oh, I pray I am not too late. Where is Lord Strythe? I must see him before he leaves.'

The groom who had the flask held it half hidden in his cupped hand, uncertain whether deference was required. The footman appraised her for a moment before he spoke. 'Steady on, miss,' he said. 'There's a fuss. His Lordship mustn't be detained. He's been called away on—'

'On urgent business. Yes, yes, I know all that, but there is—' She cast about for a moment in desperation. 'There are donations, you see, that must be lodged to the account of the foundation. The gentleman from Coutts is on hand, but nothing can be done until His Lordship has signed the instrument. Quickly now, where is his carriage?'

'Which it just this minute turned into the lane from the stables. I am sorry for it, miss, but you will not catch him now unless it is by pelting after him as you are.'

'Then that is what I must do,' said Octavia, pushing past him. The lane outside was almost in darkness, but at its end the lights of Piccadilly could be seen, and against them the silhouette of the carriage as it laboured over the poor cobbles. On her bicycle she might easily have caught it up, but she had hidden it near the gates of Green Park, and even at a run she could not hope to close the distance now on foot. The carriage had gone some two hundred yards already, and when it reached the better paving of Piccadilly, the horses would be brought to a trot. She was too late.

'Miss,' the footman called to her from the doorway behind her. 'It's a dog of a night, miss. One of the lads will run out for a cab so as you can follow after him. Come along in, miss, or you'll catch your death.'

And then it came.

Distantly, she felt herself lurch, and knew that she had grasped a railing. The vision was fragmented and indistinct, as if a magic lantern were playing upon rags of muslin. She saw a dark interior, some unknown room. Two figures were in shadow, upright or crouched, but intent, always, on the one who lay between them. She was pale and still, and illuminated faintly, as if by moonlight.

That was all, there was never more. It was almost nothing, like the vestige of some long-ago dream, but it left her weak and shaken always, as if she had witnessed some unspeakable thing and stood by in helplessness.

She clung to the railing as it passed, putting a hand to her chest to soothe her breathing. It was a trick of the imagination, nothing more, brought on by a lack of rest. She ought to seek out a tonic of some kind. She heard the servants calling, and their footsteps as they approached. She ignored them, turning her attention again to Lord Strythe's carriage, which had halted now just short of the corner. A gauze of fog had settled about it, and the thin snow was a greyish smut in the uncertain air. For a moment she saw nothing, then a figure resolved itself. A man had come forward from the shadows, his movements fluid and assured, and when he reached the roadside he did not trouble himself to flag the carriage down. He made himself seen, then simply waited.

The door of the carriage was flung out and a step briskly lowered. The man on the footway approached then paused, seeming to confront the occupant before slowly shaking his head. He looked up finally, as if searching the heavens, but perhaps it was only that he had noticed the gathering snow. He climbed inside, rapping sharply on the frame before pulling the door closed behind him. At this the carriage drew sharply away, turning into Piccadilly in a swirl of mist and horse breath, and in moments even the clatter of wheels and hooves could no longer be heard.

IV

The snow had died away in the night. Where it had lain on the ground, it survived only in smutted brackets, and in the roads the tainted slush was churned under wheels to a running filth. It was early still, not yet fully light, but Soho was thronged with men and women of all walks, with omnibuses and carriers' carts and the dozens of horses that drew them. Gideon lurched among them in a greyish stupor, veering aside at intervals to support himself against a wall or a lamp post, or to bring up a thin but scalding vomit. He could taste it still, the resinous sweetness that had darkened his senses. It was on his breath, and in his sodden lungs. He felt it when he moved his head, encumbering his wits and shrouding his very spirit.

Miss Tatton was gone. Of that much he was certain. He had known it somehow while he still slept, feeling her absence even before the cold. His first thought, when the sexton roused him, had been to look for her. He had writhed free as he was dragged to his feet, had scrabbled at the cold stone, only half-seeing, for some trace of her, some sign that she had been real.

He found the damp and filthy rag first, and near it a small thing that he might have overlooked if he had not felt its buckled edge under his palm. A keepsake. She had kept it, after all. He closed his fingers about it as he was hauled again to his feet, and could do no more before he was marched from the altar, his shoulders gripped by a pair of tobacco-stained talons.

Gideon struggled and twisted still, looking about the church in desperation. 'The young girl,' he cried. 'Please, sir, the poor young girl who was here – did you see her leave? Did you see her taken?'

'A girl, is it?' the sexton snarled, his breath reeking poisonously of gin. He was an aged and misshapen creature, but possessed of a surprising fierceness. 'There's a whippet for you. He don't stop at trespassing, this one. He comes here whoring, and he wants his trollop's comings and goings kept in the parish register. Get to fuck, you filthy pup.'

Gideon was spun about and goaded once more along the aisle, the barb of a thumb driven into the soft flesh above his hip. 'You mistake me, sir,' he said, staggering. 'I am taking holy orders myself, and we are on consecrated ground. The young lady I found here was ill or injured, and I kept her company only until other help could be found. But there was foul play of some kind, sir. I was put out of my senses, but learned first that the girl was in danger. We must do all we can to find her, sir. Surely you see that it is our Christian duty?'

The sexton paid no heed. He kept up his coarse talk as he drove Gideon from the church, and if he believed a word of his account it left him unmoved. He shoved him into the alley, delivering a sharp kick to his right haunch, and when Gideon turned again to plead with him, he took up a discarded trotter and hurled it at his face, bawling a final oath as he slammed the door.

In Shaftesbury-avenue, Gideon picked his way among the laden drays and the heaped barrows of the costermongers, threading a path between the wheels of two stalled and heaving omnibuses. He struggled still to bring order to his thoughts, and to form some clear notion of what he might do. Miss Tatton had fallen prey to some wickedness, he was convinced of that much, and he must seek help for her without delay, but who could he turn to now for aid or guidance? His recollections were imperfect still, and he had not made sense of all she had told him, but insofar as her words touched upon his uncle, there could be no mistaking her meaning.

They took him first.

He would seek him out, even so. Miss Tatton had been in earnest, without doubt, but might herself have been deceived. If she had been drugged, as he believed, her conviction might have been born of some delusion. He would make his way first to his uncle's lodgings, having nowhere else to go in any case, and perhaps he would find him at home after all. Perhaps they would take a restorative breakfast together, his guardian attending calmly as Gideon recounted the events of the night before, and seeing at once what ought to be done.

It was a warming prospect, but there was a dread in Gideon that he could not easily shake. If it was true – if the reverend doctor had indeed fallen victim to those she had spoken of – then he must prepare himself for the worst.

Gone now. He's gone.

Neuilly was his only living relative, however peculiar their relations had been, and no doubt the burden of such a loss would be felt in due course. In the meantime, if his fears were borne out, he must keep his wits about him. He must give an account of these bewildering circumstances that would secure his position until his claim could be proven, yet must ensure too that no time was lost in searching for Miss Tatton.

He would go to the house in Frith-street, then. He would present himself to his uncle's landlady and persuade her, if he could, of his honest intentions. If Neuilly proved to be missing, or worse, he would ask to be admitted to his rooms, where some plainer intelligence might be found of what it was – of *whom* it was – that his guardian had feared. If nothing else, Gideon might come upon some evidence of his own standing, and on the strength of it be shown a measure of hospitality.

He was much preoccupied by these thoughts, and when he felt his shoulder roughly grasped he came about in considerable alarm, only to be confronted by a sallow and ill-shaven young man who did not seem entirely steady on his feet. He wore what appeared to be a shabby uniform – his tunic did not match his trousers, and was missing several of its buttons – and when he addressed Gideon his speech was laboured and indistinct.

'Here, mate,' he said, resting a hand again on Gideon's shoulder. 'Give you a turn, did I? Sorry about that, chief.'

The man pitched forward a little, and on his breath Gideon again caught the sour taint of gin.

'Sorry about that, chief,' he repeated. 'But don't you worry yourself, I'm a poleef—'

He lurched slightly and broke off, righting himself with Gideon's support.

'I'm a police. Off. A poliff – I'm a sergeant, innit.' He let out an escalating sequence of belches. 'Sorry, chief. Bit of a late night is all.'

'I see.' Gideon held himself stiffly under the man's weight, not welcoming this new intrusion. 'How may I help you, Sergeant?'

'Which I—' The young sergeant paled for a moment, then averted his face and retched. It was a moment before he recovered himself and resumed. 'Which I'm wanting directions, is all, and you had the look of a chap who knows where he's going.'

'Well,' said Gideon, 'I'm afraid my own knowledge is—'

'What it is,' the sergeant continued. 'What it is, right, I'm support – I'm supposed to report to some inspector who lives hereabouts, and I ain't got a fucking notion where I'm going. I'm down the King's Cross-road, usually.'

'I should be glad to help,' Gideon said, a little coldly, 'but I'm afraid I—'

'"Number six, Frith-street," the guvnor says, like that's any use to me. I says to him, I been a Finsbury man since I was took in. I says, you send me up to Soho, mate, you might as well be sending me to fucking Wales. So, do us a favour, chief, and point me the right way.'

Number six, Frith-street. Gideon stared for a moment, and the idea came to him in the same moment as the recollection. *That copper*, she had said. Bella, the woman last night. *He ain't that copper, is he?*

A policeman – the very policeman this sergeant was looking for – had his lodgings at the same address as his uncle. That policeman's sergeant would have a ready reason to call on him at home. He would have his inspector's ear, if he should have witnessed sinister events that warranted investigation. And he might – it was a more practical point, but not without an urgency of its own – have some small expectation of being fed and watered in the course of his duties.

Gideon drew himself up and cleared his throat. Already his reservations were gathering force – his senses were far from fully restored, and he was some way from trusting his own judgement – yet he felt that a moment of providence had presented itself, and that he must act before it was snatched away. 'Why, certainly,' he said, pivoting from under the drunken sergeant's arm so as to bring himself face about. 'You have gone a little astray, I'm afraid, but you will make up the time if you hurry.'

In truth, the man was hardly a hundred yards from his destination, but Gideon pointed now in the opposite direction entirely.

His knowledge of the neighbouring streets was crude, and he was half in fear that some passer-by would denounce his deception. The directions he gave were somewhat faltering in consequence, but they would – if they could be followed at all – bring the sergeant not to the home of his superior officer but to some uncertain place in the vicinity of Leicester-square.

It was a shabby turn to do any fellow, no matter how low a sort he might seem, and the shame Gideon felt only deepened his general sense of misery. Yet he reflected, as he watched the drunken policeman totter away, that he was put to such lengths by dire need, and that the means he had chosen, however dishonest, were justified by an honourable end. He had a duty now to Miss Tatton, and indeed to his uncle, and must keep that in sight even if it was at some small cost to his conscience.

Yet it occurred to Gideon, as he drew near to the house, that he had little notion even now of what that duty might be. He had first encountered Neuilly as a boy of six or seven, when he had been sent by his ailing father to visit him at the rectory he then occupied. He remembered almost nothing of his time there save for the very last day, when he had been conducted alone to the reverend doctor's study, perhaps to pay his respects before returning home.

His uncle had been occupied, Gideon recalled, with a number of butterfly specimens that he had gathered. His hands, when his young nephew entered the room, were enveloped by a bag made of fine dark cloth. From it he produced a peacock butterfly, whose lavish wings blinked in panic as he held it out for the boy to see, then all at once grew still.

'There,' his uncle said. 'As if it were enchanted. To subdue a specimen for fixing and mounting, it is necessary only to hold its thorax like so, between finger and thumb, and to apply certain precisely moderated pressures. It requires practice, naturally, but no more than might be expected.'

Gideon had offered no response that he could recall, and perhaps none had been expected. His uncle had not appeared forbidding, exactly, but there had been an untouchable remoteness about him even then, as if he were a fixture of some observable but vastly elevated sphere. If Gideon had formed any distinct impression, it was that a puzzle was being set before him, and one that he was not yet equipped to solve.

'*Inachis io*,' his uncle intoned. The insect's Latin name, in those days, had meant nothing to him, but the particular splendour of its sound – like an incantation, almost – had remained with him. 'First described,' Neuilly continued, 'by Linnaeus himself, whose works you will naturally come to know. A common creature, but miraculous for all that.'

Again it seemed to Gideon that this was no idle observation. Something had been agreed upon that he had no part in. Something was now expected of him, even if its nature was all but hidden. His father, when he returned home, had given no explanation that he could now recall, but matters became plain soon enough. By the time of his father's death – he lived for eight or nine months more – Gideon had been sent, by his uncle's good offices, to a school at Ashfell in Cumbria where boys who were not quite born to that station (these were the words of his first master in that place) were prepared for Cambridge and for holy orders, and where, on the last day of term, he was summoned to the rooms of the dean. On that occasion, and each of its kind thereafter, a brief communication was read to him.

'The reverend doctor is not dissatisfied with your progress.'

'Thank you, sir.'

'The reverend doctor is content for your instruction to continue.'

'Thank you, sir.'

'The reverend doctor is obliged by his particular ministry to keep no fixed abode, and to make do instead with various temporary accommodations. These are wanting in the comforts and amusements that a young boy naturally seeks, and he commends you therefore to the care of Mr and Mrs Strachan until the commencement of the new term, the groundskeeper's cottage being near at hand and having a room that has been unoccupied since that family was visited by tragedy.'

'Thank you, sir.'

So it was that Gideon's education had proceeded in those first years, and so it was that he had been kept from want and warned away from unsuitable distractions. When he had left Ashfell for Cambridge, he had exchanged its melancholy yards and creaking gutters for handsome quads and untouched swards, for lanes where blossom spilled from every wall and the cobbles seemed always to be lit by careless laughter. His own existence, however, had hardly changed. In place of the dean at Ashfell, his uncle's communications came to him by way of a firm of solicitors in the Newmarket-road, with hardly a word of them altered from Michaelmas Term to Easter, whatever small inquiries he might make.

'When might my uncle be less occupied, so that I might visit him and convey my gratitude in person?'

'We have been given no instruction in that regard.'

'Does he speak well of me? Does he say that I am bound to distinguish myself just as he has?'

'We have been given no instruction in that regard.'

'What is to become of me, when I leave this place? What am I to do in the world?'

'We have been given no instruction in that regard.'

It was not until Gideon's second year at Cambridge that he and his guardian had entered at last into correspondence, and even that was of an intermittent and peculiar kind. Neuilly insisted that it be conducted by way of his solicitors, a cumbersome practice that delayed his letters by weeks or months, by which time he was apt to have moved to new lodgings. For this reason, the reverend doctor explained, it would be fruitless to give out his present address, and Gideon was therefore obliged to send his replies by the same circuitous route.

It was a tedious and discouraging business, but Gideon refused to be deterred. Though his uncle's letters were often terse and elliptical, Gideon filled his own with dutiful reports of his progress, and with deferential but increasingly pointed expressions of his hopes for the future. He ventured to wonder, too, if he might not one day convey his respects in person, and as he grew bolder in these entreaties it appeared at last to dawn on Neuilly that his nephew could not be kept at bay forever. Finally, as May Week approached and Gideon had again resigned himself to a Long Vacation spent in dismal solitude, his uncle had relented.

'The reverend doctor will be pleased to receive you in the summer.'

In the summer, that was all. Weeks had passed before a date in August was fixed, and even then he was told nothing more. He was to present himself at Liverpool-street Station, at which point further arrangements would be made. After his visit – and his first encounter with Miss Tatton – Neuilly had retreated once more into silence and isolation. There had been nothing, not a word, until his unexpected letter. Gideon drew it out as he approached the doorway. Even now, having glimpsed at first hand the dangers Neuilly alluded to, it seemed an almost miraculous intervention.

His uncle had written to him, unprompted and in his own hand, had elevated him, at a stroke, from banished ward to

trusted confidant. And he had done something else, Gideon realised, that was quite without precedent and, it had now proved,
marvellously provident. He had volunteered his present address.
Gideon repeated it inwardly, as he had done for much of the journey from Cambridge. There was some small comfort in it, even if
the circumstances now seemed utterly changed.

Number six, Frith-street.

Number six, Frith-street.

Number six, Frith-street, Soho-square, London.

V

Gideon's knocking, this time, was answered almost at once.
He had turned away, expecting to be made to wait, and
had begun deliberating over the manner in which he might introduce himself when he heard behind him the brisk rattling of a
lock. Coming about and righting his posture, he was confronted
by a tall and amply built gentleman who fixed Gideon with a keen
and interrogatory look and thrust his forefinger with startling
force against the centre of his chest.

'What time,' he demanded, 'do you call this?'

Gideon looked from his sternum to the face of his inquisitor.
The inspector – there could be no doubt, he felt, that this was the
policeman he had been told about – was neatly attired and freshly
shaven. His splendidly dark hair had been treated with some
rich oil, and was combed back with strict uniformity from his
forehead. His strong jaw and pronounced features gave a marked
sternness to his appearance, and from beneath his dark brows he
fixed Gideon with a look of singular intensity.

'I beg your pardon, sir, but—'

'Greenwich Mean Time, boy. That is what we observe, as a rule.
Are you familiar with Greenwich Mean Time? Did you think it
was some class of miracle that enables the stationmaster at St Pancras to predict the arrival of the eight twenty-one from Ramsgate?'

'Sir, forgive me, but—' Gideon was by no means practised in

deception, and had been in a state of considerable anxiety even before the door was opened. He began to wonder now if he should not abandon his plan entirely, since there could be no subterfuge devised by man, surely, that might withstand this policeman's scrutiny for long.

'Ah, but perhaps I have it wrong. Perhaps you don't observe Greenwich Mean Time. Perhaps you are an Irishman, and you set your watch by Dublin Mean Time to remind you of home. Or are you a homesick Frenchman, lately returned from Ceylon, who forgot to adjust his watch when he sauntered down the gangplank? Is that it? *Is that it*?'

To lend emphasis to this last bit of rhetoric, the inspector again thrust his finger against Gideon's chest, which stirred him at last to give a more spirited reply.

'I arrived, sir, from no further afield than Cambridge, where I assure you the general fashion is for Greenwich Mean Time, and my train came into Liverpool-street, not St Pancras. That is to say—' Gideon realised his mistake with a surge of consternation. 'That is to say that I have arrived *just now* from the King's Cross-road, that being my usual place of employment, but I had *recently* returned from Cambridge. Just yesterday, in fact.'

The inspector withdrew his finger by a fraction, but remained otherwise entirely still. His countenance, though still fearsome, wore a look of candid amazement, as if Gideon had claimed to have been deposited upon the dome of St Paul's Cathedral by a phalanx of seraphs.

'Cambridge?' he said. 'Liverpool-street? What earthly business had you in Cambridge? Does the writ of G Division run in that place now? What blackguard sent you out into the countryside when I had expressly asked that you be assigned to me? Was it Pendleston?'

'Well, sir—' Gideon was by now seized by outright panic. He had not had the presence of mind, he now realised, even to ask the drunken sergeant for his name. The inspector would surely ask for it at any moment, if only to confirm his suspicions.

'Was it Inspector Fenwick? Eh? Was it on his orders? That anaemic little quisby has had his knives out for me ever since I flushed him out of a knocking-shop at half past three on Christmas morning. That is the stripe of that man. With a wife at home in Camberwell, and a youngster who had been promised a rocking-horse. That is the nature of that specimen. That is what you are up against with the Divisions, day in, day out. You cannot tell which ignoramus will receive your request, and you have no notion what class of a creature he will send you when he does.'

Gideon brightened at this. If the inspector had been given no name, the immediate danger might have passed. 'It was not Inspector Fenwick, sir.'

'No?' The inspector lowered his face towards Gideon's. 'You are quite sure?'

'I am quite sure, sir.' Gideon was sure of nothing, but felt that he must make up a good deal of ground. 'On that point, at least, you may put your mind at rest. And I do see now how my recent arrival from Cambridge might have struck you as irregular. I introduced the matter very badly indeed, and it is no wonder that you became suspicious. I assure you, though, that I was sent to Cambridge on irreproachable authority, and I will be delighted to give you a full report – you will not think me rude, sir, if I take a step back so as to give you more room – yes, to give you a full report of my business there, duly filed and correct in all particulars and what have you, but I have detained us for long enough. We must be about our – well, that is to say, once you have taken your breakfast, and I should be happy to step in and keep you company, since in my eagerness to—'

The inspector struck Gideon with scarcely credible force, causing him to reel backwards into Frith-street, his hand clamped against the livid heat that engulfed his right ear and the neighbouring part of his jaw.

'Shut your trap, like a good man.' The inspector shook his head in vexation. 'There is a torrent of nonsense to be confronted with at this hour. It is either insolence or drunkenness, and I have no patience for either.'

'Sir, I give you why—' Gideon straightened, but found that the blow had impaired both his clarity of mind and his diction. 'That is, I give you my word—'

'Hark at him, the boozy whelp. Not even nine o'clock in the morning, and he presents himself to a superior officer addled with drink. Well, there's an end to it. I got along well enough with no sergeant this fortnight and more, and I daresay I will battle on a week or two longer. Better no sergeant that some babbling ninny who staggers here from the King's Cross-road full to his ears with piss and notions. Get along back to your station, there's a good fellow. Tell them Inspector Cutter has no use for the enclosed imbecile and returns him unmarked, or nearly so. Tell them he will attend the scene at Half Moon-street on his own.'

He was still considerably dazed and contended now with a buzzing sound in the ear that had been struck, but Gideon saw that he must seize what remained of his chance. He realised too that he must curb his more scholarly habits of speech if he was to allay the inspector's doubts.

'Inspector Cutter, sir.' Gideon had laid out in his mind the components of a sentence, but saw at once that he must pack them into fewer and stouter boxes. 'On my word of honour, sir, I have not had a drop to drink.'

Inspector Cutter, who had retreated into the hallway of the house to fetch his overcoat, gave Gideon a sceptical look as he put it on. He turned away again, making no reply, and put his head inside the doorway. 'I am away, Mrs Coombe,' he called out. 'There is no sign still of old Nelly, I believe, so you may wish to throw the bolt.'

Old Nelly. It was his uncle, of course, that the inspector referred to, and his remark did nothing to put Gideon's mind at rest. Cutter pulled the door to and descended to the street, setting off at a brisk pace in the direction of Shaftesbury-avenue. Gideon hurried after him.

'Sir, if my mode – if the way I spoke was peculiar, it may be owing to my visit to Cambridge. I encountered a good deal of peculiar talk, sir, in the course of my duties there.'

'Is that right?' Inspector Cutter halted without warning before a stall, where he called for coffee and a cut of bread and butter, folding the latter item when it was presented to him into a package that he ingested in a single instalment, chewing with grave deliberation. Gideon looked on with fervent longing.

'Yes, sir,' he said. Again, he worked at a reply in his mind until he was satisfied that he had filed it down to a satisfactory smoothness. 'Talk of that kind is very much the custom there. It is not remarked on as being out of the common way.'

'Indeed?' Inspector Cutter resumed his progress, beating the crumbs from his coat as he walked. 'Were you there a long time, then? That would be somewhat out of the common way, for a sergeant of the Metropolitan Police.'

Gideon made haste to catch up. 'Not an unduly long time, sir. In fact, I was able to conclude my business there rather sooner than I had anticipated. And I do hope—'

Here Gideon was brought up short by the appearance in

his path of an eel vendor's barrow. They had turned again into Shaftesbury-avenue, and Inspector Cutter went before him at a remarkable clip. He seemed in no way impeded by the great press of traffic, sidestepping all obstacles with practised agility or, when that could not be accomplished, shouldering them aside without a backward glance.

'And I do hope,' Gideon continued, when at length he regained his place in Cutter's wake, 'that you will not count our earlier mis-understandings against me, and will allow me to assist you at the scene in Half Moon-street, which, if I may say so, I would regard as a singular—'

'There he is again with his drunken blathering.'

'Yes, sir,' said Gideon, now somewhat out of breath. 'Or rather, no, sir. I assure you again that I have taken nothing to drink. I have not even breakfasted, sir, if the truth be known. But your point is well taken. I shall confine myself to—'

As they approached the Lyric Theatre, Inspector Cutter veered without warning across the street, raising a commanding arm to a cabman who duly brought up his horse to let him pass. 'What am I to call you?' he barked over his shoulder.

'Sir?'

'I was given no name, when I sent for you. I trust you are equipped with one, or are you somewhat irregular in that respect also?'

'Ah, of course, sir. That is, no, sir. I am Gideon Bliss, sir, and it is a great honour to—'

'I have no use for your Christian name, man, if that is what it is. Gideon Bliss. There is a Hebrew ring to that. It is all the one to me, mind you. There is a goodly number of Hebrew fellows to be found in Bethnal Green and such places, and they are no great cause of disturbance.'

'Oh, it is indeed a Christian name, sir, though it is true that it was a Hebrew one first. Gideon was a righteous man, sir, who destroyed the idols and heathen altars of the Israelites, and delivered them to their true God, though of course we know Him to be our God now.'

They entered what Gideon took to be Piccadilly Circus, which was so densely crowded and obscured by vehicles as to appear all but impenetrable. Inspector Cutter, however, did not so much as break his stride, and Gideon struggled to keep him within sight and hearing.

'Their true God, is it?' Cutter called back. 'I hear enough of that kind of talk from mad-eyed fellows with pamphlets. I have no more time for it than I have for drunkenness. I hope you do not go in for that carry-on, Bliss. You will not be called upon to destroy any idols in Bethnal Green.'

'Goodness no, sir. That is to say, I am devout, sir, but very much in the ordinary way. I have no ambition to be a destroyer of anything, sir.'

'I am glad to hear it.' Inspector Cutter came abruptly to a halt, surprising both Gideon and the driver of an omnibus in whose direct path he now stood. He turned to Gideon, and subjected him to considerable scrutiny. 'Well, then, Sergeant Bliss. I expect we shall see about you. But for goodness' sake, man, you must learn to keep up.'

VI

The house in Half Moon-street was large and commanding-
ly handsome. Gideon made a remark to this effect as they
waited on its doorstep, but was immediately inclined to regret it.
Since setting out from Frith-street, Inspector Cutter had encountered no obstacle, be it man, beast or human invention, that had
impeded his progress in any measurable degree. Since ringing the
bell, however – he had done so twice – he had been robbed of his
forward momentum for well over a minute, and it was clear that
the change of pace had not suited him. He cast a look of displeasure over his shoulder.

'In the first place,' he said, 'we are in Mayfair. Maybe there's a
Mayfair up Cambridge way, where you seem to spend so much
time, and maybe that Mayfair is a shanty town where a fellow
can hardly turn around without tripping over an orphan or the
carcass of a donkey.'

'No, sir. I meant only that—'

'In the second place, we are now at the scene of what may
well prove to be a crime. Now, I am of a middling temperament,
I believe, and in the general run of things I am inclined to give
a sergeant a bit of leeway. But a crime scene is another matter.
While we are about our business here, I will thank you to stop up
your blowhole until directed otherwise.'

Gideon looked down at his shoes, which had been in poor repair even on leaving Cambridge and were now caked to the uppers with filth. A great deal weighed on his mind still. He was by no means certain that his deception had any hope of succeeding, and the inspector seemed continually irritated by his shortcomings, but perhaps it was a dimly hopeful sign that he should be thought of as occupying the office of a sergeant at all. 'Yes, sir,' he said, his eyes still downcast. 'I beg your pardon, sir.'

As he spoke, Gideon caught sight of a bright sliver of glass, lodged in a crevice a little way from the doorstep. It might easily have been overlooked – and must have been, indeed, for by the looks of it the footway before the house had recently been swept clean – but in the low winter sunlight a fine tracery was picked out on its surface. Stooping, he levered it carefully from its place, examining it as he rose.

A few moments passed in silence. Inspector Cutter drew out his watch, issuing a concentrated snort of impatience as he returned it to his pocket. 'It is a handsome enough house,' he said at length. 'It is the residence of Lord Strythe, if that puts your wonderment at ease.'

'Ah,' said Gideon carefully. 'Yes, sir.'

Inspector Cutter drew back his head a little way so as to glare at the windows. He took out a leather-bound notebook and looked into it briefly before putting it away again. He rasped his knuckles against the underside of his chin.

'You do not know who Lord Strythe is, Bliss.'

'I must own that I do not, sir.'

Cutter let out a long breath. 'When we have the leisure, Bliss, you must draw me up a list of the things you do know. I will give you a stamp or a matchbox, and no doubt you will cover every bit of it. Then I will know what respite I am to have from giving you instruction morning, noon and night. Perhaps it will come out that you already know the price of a pound of sugar, and then I may take a day's leave in good conscience.'

'Yes, sir.' Gideon turned the shard in the light, revealing an intricate pattern of incisions.

'What have you there?' Cutter said.

'A piece of glass, sir. It is cut crystal, I believe, but more finely worked than any I have seen before. I found it lying at the edge of the footway.'

The inspector narrowed his eyes. 'Give it over,' he said.

Gideon deposited the fragment carefully in his outstretched palm. 'Is it of interest, sir?'

Cutter made no reply as he scrutinised the shard, and when the door was opened he enveloped it with a smooth movement in a handkerchief and concealed it in his coat. A servant of grave and corpulent appearance came into view, whom Gideon supposed to be the butler. His acquaintance with households of the better sort was slight.

'There now,' said Inspector Cutter. 'There is some life in this place after all. Tell me, had you a long way to come to reach the door? I hope I did not put you to the trouble of digging a tunnel, or of clambering up from a well?'

The servant appeared dimly troubled by these notions. 'I do beg your pardon, sir.'

'As well you might,' said Cutter. 'What am I to call you, if I am forced to do so?'

'Carew, sir. Of Lord Strythe's household. And may I inquire—'

'I will thank you not to. I am Inspector Cutter, of New Scotland Yard. This is Sergeant Bliss. I am informed of an incident on these premises.'

'Indeed, sir,' said Carew. 'If you will be so good as to come in, I will make you and the sergeant comfortable in the kitchen while I relate the particulars to you.'

The prospect of being made comfortable in the kitchen seemed very agreeable to Gideon, but Inspector Cutter was not of the same mind. When they had been admitted and Carew had closed the door behind them, the inspector made no move to go further.

'Did the incident occur in the kitchen?' he said.

Carew turned to him with great solemnity. 'No, Inspector. It was in another part of the house. But perhaps you will take some refreshment while I—'

'We have no business in the kitchen if no incident occurred in it. We are not the butcher and his boy. Where did it happen?'

'In an upper part of the house, sir.'

Inspector Cutter glanced at Gideon, then approached Carew more closely. The fearsome intensity with which Gideon was now familiar had returned to his expression, along with a pronounced incredulity, as if he had been told that the incident had occurred in some region of the faery kingdom. 'An upper part?'

'Indeed, sir.'

'Tell me this, Carew. Do you oversee the serving of His Lordship's dinners?'

'I oversee the whole of His Lordship's household, sir.'

'Well, then. Have you ever informed His Lordship that he was to dine on the upper part of a cow?'

'Certainly not, sir.'

'Or that his breakfast came from the lower part of a chicken?'

Carew shifted his bulk, as if to relieve some interior discomfort. 'I have not, sir.'

'No, I should think not,' said Inspector Cutter. 'Now, will you be an obliging fellow and show us to the particular room in the upper part of the house where this misfortune occurred. It was a room, I take it, and not a chimney or a nest in the eaves?'

'Very good, Inspector. But I hope you will refrain from any

further levity, for you find us all greatly saddened at what has occurred.'

'Levity?' Inspector Cutter's face darkened, and he clamped his hand for a moment over his jaw. For an instant, Gideon imagined that some predatory creature lurked within him, and might burst from him at any moment like an unhooded hawk from its perch. 'Levity? Will you tell me, Carew, do you keep an eye to the newspapers at all?'

'On occasion, sir. As my duties permit.'

'Did you ever read of the case of the children of Dr St John?'

'The Slaughter of the St Johns?' Carew's eyes widened, but he checked himself almost at once. 'I believe I saw some mention of it.'

'And do you recall how many children the St Johns had, and what their ages were?'

'Not to an exactness, Inspector. I would not have had the leisure to—'

'Five. There were five St John children. The eldest was Anthony, a boy of thirteen, and the youngest was Matilda. Matilda was a babe of fifteen months, and was still nursed at the time of her death. Do you know how it is that I come to know that?'

'No, Inspector. How could I?'

'You could not. And I will do you the kindness of keeping it from you, for I assure you it is a thing that would never leave you. But I will tell you this much. I know their names and their ages. I know the colour of each one's hair, and I could give you a litany of every scrap of clothing that was on them. I know these things because it was I who came to that house after what was done there, and it was I who tended to them when they were beyond any other help. It was I who spent two days in that room, and who saw to it that no one set foot in it until every speck of dust was accounted for. It was I who made the photographic plates that were shown to the jurors, since the Frenchman we depend upon in the normal course would come no further than the head of the stairs. Did you know, Carew, that the adult teeth of a small child are formed in her jaw long before the milk teeth are lost?'

'I did not, Inspector.'

'Yes, it is a remarkable thing. They are hidden away until they are called for, in a tiny and perfect array. The workings of nature are a puzzle, and I suppose I have been fortunate to have glimpsed them as others have not. But you may be certain of this much, Carew. If I had any great store of merriment when I went into that house – and I suspect I had not, if the truth be known – then it was gone from me entirely when I came out, and it has never troubled me again.'

Throughout this address, Carew had stood warily apart, as if he might at any moment be obliged to lumber away or ward off a blow. He relaxed his posture now, and cleared his throat at some length. 'I am sorry to hear it, Inspector,' he said. 'I meant no slight to you, sir. I read only a little of that sad business, and I must confess that your name had not stayed with me.'

The inspector did not immediately reply. He raised his arm a little way, and for a giddy moment Gideon believed that he meant to deliver a clout to the side of Carew's head. But Cutter was merely gesturing towards the staircase.

'This "upper part" of the house,' he said. 'If we are to make our way to it, I believe we will be obliged to make use of the stairs.'

'Of course, Inspector.' Carew turned to lead the way. 'And when you have finished in the workroom, I expect you will want to examine the unfortunate Miss Tull herself, or her mortal remains, as I suppose we must say.'

Inspector Cutter had fallen into step behind Carew, but now

brought himself up short. His shoulders rose, and he clamped a hand across his brow. 'A moment, Carew, if you please,' he said.

Carew came ponderously about. 'Inspector?'

'Now, Carew,' said Cutter. 'You have told us precious little since we arrived, though it was not for want of talking, and here you are now telling us a good deal all at once. I ought to be thankful for it, but I cannot say that I am. I have shown uncommon patience until now, but if you are not careful I will show you something else altogether.'

Carew's face showed the stirring of indignation. 'Inspector, I really must—'

'What you must do is give me plain and simple answers to my questions, and no more of your upper parts. Bliss, you will make note of his answers like a good fellow.'

'I should be delighted to, sir, but I regret to say I find myself in want of certain necessary items.'

Cutter bowed his head and released a long breath. 'Certain necessary items,' he said. 'Do you mean that you have no notebook or pencil?'

'I fear not, sir.'

'You may use mine for now. You may keep them, in fact, since I am no great man of letters and make little use of them. Have you a passable hand, at least, so that you may be put to that use if no other?'

The inspector passed his notebook and pencil to Gideon, still without turning. 'Oh, indeed, sir. It has been remarked on as commendably graceful.'

'Commendably graceful,' Cutter repeated. 'Sweet Jesus.'

He lowered his head again, as if he felt a great burden. Carew looked away uneasily, and Gideon could not help but do likewise.

'Very well,' Cutter said, when he had regained his composure.

'The first question, Carew. What was the forename of this Miss Tull?'

'I believe it was Esther, Inspector.'

'It is a woman's name, Carew, not the promise of eternal salvation. Do you believe it, or do you know it?'

'It was Esther.'

'Good. And was this Esther Tull in service here?'

'She was a seamstress, Inspector, who was engaged only on occasion.'

'A seamstress?' Cutter said. 'Lord Strythe is a bachelor, I believe, and it is no long march from here to Savile-row. What use has he for a seamstress? Has he no maids employed who might mend a few stockings?'

'His Lordship is particular about such things, and Miss Tull was said to be very skilful. She cared for an older sister, who was ailing, and His Lordship was good enough to put her in the way of what work there was.'

'Have you taken that note, Bliss?'

'Yes, Inspector.'

'Put a query by it, for I wish to return to it. Now, Carew, we come to the meat of the matter. No, but that is a poor word to use. Do not put that in the notes, Bliss. We come to the . . .'

Gideon cleared his throat. 'To the crux of the matter, sir?'

Cutter's shoulders rose again, and a moment passed in silence. 'Thank you, Bliss,' he said presently. 'Yes, to the crux of the matter. This seamstress, Miss Tull – she met her end, I take it, in the "incident" that occurred?'

Carew joined his fingertips before his chest and lowered his chin amongst his jowls. 'I am sorry to say so, Inspector.'

'And the incident occurred in an upstairs workroom last evening?'

Carew nodded gravely.

'At what time did it occur, as nearly as you can recollect?'

'I would say that it was a little after nine o'clock.'

'A little after nine o'clock?'

'Yes, Inspector.'

'Were Miss Tull's dressmaking skills often called for after nine o'clock in the evening?'

'Not often, Inspector. But Miss Tull was always most obliging, being mindful of her good fortune.'

'Of her good fortune? What good fortune was that?'

'Why, the good fortune of being employed by a notable household, which even a woman of the finest character might envy.'

Cutter cocked his head at this. 'Am I to take it from that remark that Miss Tull was not of the finest character?'

Carew lifted his jaw from among its folds. 'I do not wish to be indiscreet, Inspector.'

'Do you not, indeed? Well, you are falling short of your own aspirations, I am sorry to tell you. What fault had you to find with her?'

'Well, since I am put to it, Inspector, I understand that she was given to thievery, in her youth. She was born to it, as you might say, her father being in that line. But His Lordship, being a man of charity, was prepared to overlook a good deal.'

'Do you hear that, Bliss? There is uncommon generosity for you. He was prepared to overlook a good deal, you are telling me, if Miss Tull was prepared to be obliging.'

'Now, Inspector, I did not say—'

'Put a line under that, Bliss. Tell me, Carew, was the incident of a violent nature?'

'Yes, sir, it appeared—' Carew halted and began again. 'It was, Inspector. Most violent.'

'And was there another party to this most violent incident?'

'There was not, Inspector.'

'Be sure to note, Bliss, that this last answer was given with great certainty. How is it that you are so certain of this point, Carew? Were you present in the workroom when Miss Tull met her end?'

'Of course not, Inspector. You do not think, surely, that I would stand by and allow such a thing?'

'I am some way from thinking anything surely, Carew, but it seems you are far ahead of me. How is it, tell me, that you come to be so sure if you were not with Miss Tull at the time? This is a house of a fine size, and you have a parlour of some kind, I expect, that you may go to after nine o'clock in the evening if you are not wanted. Miss Tull might have been going great guns on a trumpet and you would not have known it.'

'The top floor is a quiet part of the house, Inspector, and out of the way of things. A woman working up there alone might be troubled by her nerves, being mindful of which, I kept close by.'

'You kept close by?'

'I found some occupation for myself on the top floor while Miss Tull was at her work, so as to give her the comfort of knowing that she was not all alone.'

'Do you hear that, Bliss? That was very handsome of Carew, was it not?'

'Indeed, sir. It was most gallant.'

'Put a star by that observation, Bliss. What is the proper name for those little fellows?'

'An asterisk, sir?'

'There, you have it. Put an asterisk by that, for I hardly know what to make of it. Now, Carew, you have come up very much in the standard of your answers, and I hope you will keep that high mark in your sights as we near the finish, for there is one more question I must put to you. If Miss Tull met a violent death by her own hand in the workroom on the top floor, I would expect to find her mortal remains, as you put it, in that very place. Yet you gave me the impression, as we were about to go up the stairs, that her remains are in some other place. Will you solve that little riddle, like a good fellow, before I lose command of myself?'

'Now, Inspector, there is no cause for agitation. I have been forthcoming from the very first.'

'You have been no such thing, Carew. When you sent word of what had happened, you said only that an "incident" had taken place. You had the good sense to send word to the Yard, mind you, and not to the local lackeys, but you told them no more than you must.'

'His Lordship was not at home last night, Inspector, and when he had not returned this morning I felt I must act on my own author-ity. However, I did not like to say too much. He would not thank me for leaving out scraps that might be fed to newspapermen.'

'Fed to them by Scotland Yard? Make a note of that disgraceful suggestion, Bliss, and make a note, too, of His Lordship's absence. We will return to that, but will you kindly tell me first where the body is and how it came to be there?'

Carew looked aggrieved, but with effort he composed himself. 'Well, Inspector, the fact of the matter is that Miss Tull's remains are not in the workroom because of the manner in which she took her life. She got onto a ledge outside the window, and from there she leapt to her death. I found her remains not far from the front steps. Now, sir, I hope I have given you satisfaction.'

Inspector Cutter worked over his jaw with fingertips. He put his hands on his hips and allowed his gaze to rove over the finely moulded ceiling. Then he turned away from Carew and paced for a few moments in a small circuit. At length he confronted him again. 'Have you given me satisfaction? For my breakfast this morning, Carew, my landlady was good enough to prepare a poached egg. I made no complaint, mind you, she being a lady of a nervous disposition, but when I looked down at that egg, as God is my witness, it was like looking into the eye of a dog that was rabid and is two days dead. Yet that same egg gave me considerably more satisfaction than you have managed to do.'

'But I have told you all, Inspector.'

'Told me all? *Told me all*? Here is the sum total, Carew, of what you have told me. You have told me that a seamstress was called to the house of an unmarried gentleman at nine o'clock at night, and that she was put to some work upstairs while you skulked outside with your lug to the door. That is all I got from you, for all your wheezing and foostering. And it only now comes out that when you found the same woman dead in the street, you shovelled her up and took yourself off to bed and did not trouble yourself to report the matter to Her Majesty's police until this morning. I have never heard the likes of it. Bliss, have you ever heard the likes of it?'

Gideon looked up in some distraction from his notebook. The Inspector had been speaking at a considerable rate, and he had filled up four or five pages already. 'I have not, sir, but I have recorded the particulars.'

'Very good, Bliss. Now, Carew, you mentioned that Lord Strythe was not at home. Where is he, if you please, and when will he return?'

'Lord Strythe was at Ashenden House last evening, where he was the guest of honour at a gala. His Lordship is a man of great charity, as you may know, and he has endowed a new institution. It was to be a very fine affair, with even the Prime Minister in attendance.'

Cutter passed a hand over his eyes, and raised the other in imitation of a flapping mouth. 'Was His Lordship to remain over-night as a guest?'

'Not to my knowledge, Inspector.'

'Is it not unusual, therefore, that he has not returned home?'

'Somewhat so, Inspector. His Lordship is regular in his habits.'

'Is there any other place where he might have spent the night?'

Carew considered this. 'His Lordship lives in a modest way, sir, for a man of his position. When he is not at Westminster or about his charitable works, he is content by and large with his own company.'

'Not even a club, or a house he might have frequented to play at cards and suchlike? Was there no special companion, who might have received him at odd hours? You need not tie yourself up in knots with discretion, Carew. We have no interest in the gentle-man's private affairs if they have no bearing on the present case.'

'No, sir, nothing of that nature. I have given it consideration, being anxious to speak with him myself, but I can think of no-where, other than a house in Kent that is given over to his sister, Lady Ada. Lady Ada has been in poor health for many years, and the air at Vesper Sands gives her some ease. His Lordship is most attentive to his sister.'

'Do you hear that, Bliss? When our business here is finished, you may be striking out once more for the countryside. We may have a call to make at this house on Vesper Sands.'

VII

Notes made by G. Bliss (Sgt.), attending residence at 15 Half Moon-street, Mayfair, in company of Insp. Cutter

Pursuant to discussion in hallway of residence, shown to kitchens in rear by Mr Carew. Again offered tea and refreshments by Mr Carew, but same were declined with some force by Insp. Cutter.

The housekeeper (a Mrs Thorpe, of 51 yrs) confirmed that Mr Carew had remained outside the work-room to her knowledge, and that she had gone up at approx. 8.55 p.m. to serve him tea and plum cake.

A male servant aged approx. 13 yrs was dispatched to the home of Dr Carmody, police surgeon, the latter being requested to attend the scene with all poss. haste.

Insp. Cutter again remonstrated with Mr Carew for improper removal of remains from scene. Mr Carew again defended actions on grounds of delicacy and consideration for nearby residents. Mr Carew further volunteered that remains were in 'unholy state' on

cobbles, w/ considerable qty. of blood visible
on same.

Insp. Cutter inquired as to why no blood
visible on our arrival, to which Mr Carew
replied that great efforts had been made with
scrubbing brushes, carbolic soda, &c. Insp.
Cutter lodged forceful objection in re <u>wilful
destruction of evidence</u> (this last underlined
per instruction of Insp. Cutter).

Insp. Cutter demanded to know whether
remains of Miss Tull were still on the
premises. Mr Carew stated that same had merely
been removed to a proper place pending the
arrival of the undertakers.

Insp. Cutter wished to know what business
undertakers had with remains, when deceased
had not been examined and pronounced upon by
surgeon. Mr Carew stated, to the contrary,
that Miss Tull examined soon after her expiry
by Prof. Caldicott of Univ. College London,
the latter being the family physician and
great friend of Lord Strythe.

Insp. Cutter responded that Prof. Caldicott
might have treated Her Majesty's own piles,
but had not attended on the deceased prior to
death, which must therefore be notified to the
coroner.

Mr Carew produced certificate of death,
which was found to give the following cause:
'Catastrophic trauma subsqt. to misadventure'.
Insp. Cutter pronounced this unsatisfactory

and expressed view that same would not be acceptable to the registrar, remarking further that it might be put to an unmentionable sanitary purpose.

Mr Carew reminded Insp. Cutter of Lord Strythe's absence and protested that he was under duress to act beyond his authority. He further requested that proceedings be delayed until the following morning to allow for return of Lord S.

Insp. Cutter remarked that lawful processes had already been retarded and must be held up no longer. Carew then directed a porter (?) of approx. 16 yrs to fetch the solicitor for Lord S., but this servant was prevented from doing so by Insp. Cutter, who [*remainder stricken through very heavily and no longer legible*].

Dr Carmody arrived and was in v. genial humour, notwithstanding the disturbance to his breakfast of kedgeree, a dish he encountered while serving as a naval doctor in the subcontinent and recommended as an exemplary source of vitality.

Carew then conducted the officers present to a cold store which was reached by an exterior door. The remains of Miss Tull were observed wrapped in tarpaulin on the floor. This room was windowless and by no means suitable for a medical examination, and the two younger servants were directed to carry the remains to the scullery. The remains of Miss Tull were

placed on the work table and the tarp. was
[*illegible*].

**Notes resume following a brief lapse of
consciousness on the part of the present
officer, this being due to his having gone a
considerable time without food or drink.**

Proceedings were halted for a short time,
Insp. Cutter having been kind enough to call
for beef tea w/ bread & dripping, these being
known to be restorative.

Proceedings were resumed at 9.38 a.m.
by Insp. Cutter's watch, and the present
officer was provided with a chair. Dr Carmody
positioned himself so as to obscure the upper
part of the deceased from the view of all but
himself and Insp. Cutter. Dr Carmody then
began his examination and made the following
observations.

Female subject, aged approx. 35 yrs.

Marked calluses on the fingertips of the
right hand. Moderate curvature of the spine
and features suggesting chronic compression of
the lower organs, these being consistent with
the stated profession of the deceased.

Below average weight and somewhat spindly
appearance. Dentition somewhat better than
average, and likely preserved by moderate
habits. Evidence of two extractions, one of
them poorly executed and leaving a fragment

in place. Decay in varying degrees in four locations.

Rigor mortis advanced but incomplete. Marked lividity in the intact region of the face. Death likely occurred at some time between 6 p.m. and midnight last evening.

Dr Carmody called for scissors. When these were produced, he positioned himself as before and a portion of the deceased's hair was shorn away. Dr Carmody then made the following further observations.

Catastrophic and widespread fracture encompassing the better part of the left hemisphere of the cranium, extending proximally to the left occipital ridge and the upper maxillofacial (sp?) region on the same side.

Extensive rupturing of the dura mater visible, as was substantial contusion and impaction of the cerebellum, with portions of same expelled upon impact and presumed deposited at the scene.

Very pronounced haematoma in the tissue surrounding the fracture, this being characteristic of unusually forceful trauma.

Dr Carmody then covered the head of the deceased and announced that he would now examine the remainder of her person. He directed that the room be emptied save of those not present in any official capacity.

Mr Carew protested on two counts: first,

that the cause of death had already been determined, and that no further indignity was necessary; second, that a representative of the household must remain to ensure the fair conduct of the proceedings.

Dr Carmody replied that he did not recall stating any cause of death and would not be instructed in his professional conduct by a domestic servant. He further remarked that a thorough examination was required by law, and was called for in any case, since the front of the dress showed evidence of bleeding from beneath that was not consistent with the principal trauma. He allowed that it was proper for one representative of the household to remain, but insisted that the two younger servants must vacate the scullery.

These instructions being complied with, the door was locked. Dr Carmody proceeded to cut away the clothing of the deceased, and made the following further observations.

Extensive but highly regular area of haematoma on the area of the upper abdomen immediately distal to the breasts.

Highly regular formation of puncture wounds considerably obscured by congealed blood, which was swabbed away to allow the inspection of the injuries.

Dr Carmody paused in his examination to express his surprise, and remarked on the singular nature of what he now observed, same being without precedent in all his years of practice. Insp. Cutter concurred, and directed the present officer to approach the table so as to ensure the fullness and accuracy of the record.

Dr Carmody then gave the following description, which the present officer can vouch for as correct in every particular.

Highly regular formation of puncture wounds extending distally from below the breasts approx. halfway to the navel, and approx. 10—11″ from left to right. Puncture wounds caused by the sewing into the flesh of a coarse red yarn to the apparent depth of the dermis, showing a degree of skill that would be no disgrace even in a surgeon. This sewing might conceivably have been effected by the deceased herself, but would, absent analgesia, have occasioned very severe pain, both during and following the act.

The arrangement of these sutures was such that a sequence of letters was plainly legible, just as if a sampler had been embroidered upon the victim's own skin. The words thus formed were the following.

MY SOUL DOTH MAGNIFY THE LORD

III

DIES IRAE

VIII

By morning, when Octavia presented herself at Strythe House, Mr Healy had entertained second thoughts about their agreement. His message had arrived before she came down to breakfast, and while it stopped short of revoking his offer altogether – even he had that much decency – it made plain his view of how her efforts ought to be apportioned.

'Strythe can wait,' his scribbled card had read. 'Get down to Whitechapel first. More talk of Spiriters about town, and a tip-off from a duty sergeant in Leman-street who has been sound in the past. Girl missing from a boarding house for unfortunates.'

He gave the address, and such other scant particulars as he had come by, and it was not that she dismissed the matter lightly. It would be troubling to find that such a girl had indeed gone missing, but she was doubtful for now and suspected him of playing upon her sympathies. She knew too that the girl's fate would interest him only if it satisfied his appetite for sensation, and that no account of it would be printed unless it were filled with wild talk of black magic.

The events of the night before, meanwhile, had only deepened her own preoccupations. To begin with, there was the matter of Lord Strythe's conduct, which seemed no less peculiar in the light of day. It was not only that he had left in such haste, or that he had been at pains to do so unobserved. In this much, at least, he had not succeeded, and since witnessing his encounter with the man at the corner of Piccadilly, she had thought of little else. Strythe had expected to find him there, plainly, or had not been surprised when he did, but beyond that she could not guess at the nature of their relations and it was this that would not allow her to rest.

Octavia had spent years observing men and women of influence. She knew how they comported themselves, whether at the height of their pomp or in their unguarded moments. Even the slightest inflections of posture, she knew, could signal the utmost deference or the deepest contempt. Although she had observed the two men for no more than a few moments – and had glimpsed no more of Lord Strythe than the arm he threw out to open the carriage door – she had seen enough to be sure that something out of the ordinary had passed between them.

She passed Mr Healy's note to Georgie at the breakfast table, since she could not very well disregard it entirely. Her brother was awaiting a long-promised naval commission, and was ill-suited by temperament to periods of idleness. He was glad to be of use, if a little puzzled by the development.

'Well now, sister,' he said, clapping the crumbs of toast from his hands before accepting the card. 'What has it come to if you're letting me put my oar in?'

He had offered his help before, but she had found gentle ways of refusing it. 'Georgie, darling, you've met some of the people I write about, and you know how dull they are. Dull or poisonous, or both. This is different. This is—'

She gestured loosely, and Georgie raised an eyebrow. 'This is off your beat, you mean to say. Not that I'm sorry, mind you. I'd as soon not have you wheeling about the back alleys of Whitechapel, though I know you won't thank me for saying so. But what good will I do, for that matter? Surely you set no store by this talk of – what is it? – this talk of Spiriters?'

'Of course not, Georgie. But Mr Healy is susceptible to all sorts of notions, especially when he thinks there is money in them. Grandfather would turn blue if he knew of it. Just see what you can find out. You're good at it, though you don't realise it. You have an easy way with people who, well . . .'

'Who aren't the right sort. It's all right, sister. I'm not the right sort myself, which makes matters easier. I'll put my head in to a few gin shops. I might see if I can rouse out this duty sergeant, too. What about you, then? What's so important that you're ducking orders from old Healy?'

'I don't know yet, Georgie.' Octavia raised a fingertip, examining a tea leaf she had teased from the rim of her cup. 'I honestly don't know yet.'

Lord Strythe's residence was in Half Moon-street, hardly three minutes by carriage from Ashenden House, and while she could hardly expect to be received there at this hour, Octavia hoped at least to discover whether he had returned home. His butler, a dour and slow-footed character named Carew, would say only that His Lordship was not at home to callers. He held the door only part way open, and his attention even as she spoke seemed taken up by the street behind her. Lord Strythe was not receiving guests, perhaps, but it was plain that someone was expected.

When she was sure that she was not observed, Octavia made her way instead to the mews at the rear of the house, reflecting that she might do just as well in these inquiries by dispensing with front doors altogether. Nor had she long to wait, for within ten or twelve minutes she had waylaid the household's messenger, a quick-limbed creature in a cloth cap whom she mistook at first for a boy.

For the sum of ninepence, paid out in solicitous instalments, she learned that the girl – who would not on any account give her name – had earlier been dispatched to the telegraph office with a message for Vesper Sands in Kent. Mr Carew, the girl confided, had got his dander up something fierce, and he hoped to find word there of the master of the house. Lord Strythe was not at home, then, and by the girl's account he had not been seen since the day before. He had been sent for, right enough, and was known to have left Ashenden House, but there had been no sign of him even by morning.

Beyond that the girl knew very little, and Octavia began to wonder if she had paid above the odds. Neither the girl nor anyone else below stairs had been told why the master was wanted. They had been packed into a cellar for above an hour, she said, while Mr Carew saw about some private business upstairs. He was in a lather of sweat when he got back, and as dirty a humour as the girl had ever seen, but they had known better than to ask any questions.

Octavia had drawn on her gloves and picked up her bicycle when a final question occurred to her. Lord Strythe himself had not returned home, but had anyone else come? After all, his departure from Ashenden House had attracted a good deal of notice. Had he no particular friends who might have thought to inquire after him? At first the girl insisted that there had been no one. His Lordship was not one for callers, she said. Or at least, he was not one for friends. But something seemed to occur to her then, prompted perhaps by her own words. Octavia held out another coin, turning it in her palm.

Devlin's, the girl said. The man from Devlin's had come.

It was a scrap, nothing more, but there was a thread in it at least that might be tugged at. Devlin's proved to be a firm of carriers in St Thomas's-street, engaged by Lord Strythe for some years. A man had come after midnight with a team and a cart. It was not unheard of, the girl said, even at that hour. The master was a great collector, and something was always coming or going, but last night the man from Devlin's would not say whether he had brought a load or expected to carry one off. He would speak to no one but His Lordship, and went on his way when he found he was not at home. The girl knew no more than that, she said, and if she stopped out any longer Mr Carew would be calling for her skin. She bid Octavia good morning and took her leave.

The day was grey and cold, but the snow was thinning on the streets and the going was hardly worse than usual. Octavia paid a brief visit to the offices of the *Gazette*, gathering certain items that might prove useful in her inquiries, then set out without further delay in the direction of London Bridge. She had no clear notion still of what it was that she hoped to discover, but she was surer now that her curiosity had some foundation. If nothing else, she had an errand that might prove fruitful, and even in such foul weather there was a small satisfaction in simply having somewhere out of doors to go.

The premises of Devlin & Sons, however, were not easily found. There were a good many other carriers' yards in the vicinity of the station, most of them in the service of the railways, but Octavia called at three of these before encountering a foreman who had heard of the firm she wanted. He directed her to a narrow lane under the arches of the station, where she came at last to a shuttered and silent yard. On its gate was a blackened plate that might easily have gone overlooked, giving the following particulars and no more.

DEVLIN & SONS
BY APPOINTMENT

Octavia hammered at the gate for a time, but no one came. The yard was hidden by a high fence of corrugated iron, and not a sound could be heard from behind it. She had mounted her bicycle and turned away in disappointment when it occurred to her that her journey might not have been entirely wasted. If Lord Strythe had indeed travelled to Kent, as his butler thought possible, he would have departed from London Bridge Station. Such things could be found out, if one was sufficiently determined. There was almost always a way.

She made her way to the station office, where she ingratiated herself with a young clerk of amenable disposition. He took a keen interest in the sporting life, as young men of his sort often did, and having made provision for just this kind of encounter, Octavia was able to supply him with a report – due to appear in the midday edition of the *Gazette* – of the racing conditions at Portsmouth. While he was taken up with these, the clerk mused, a person might well turn over the whole of the office and he should be none the wiser. There was a science to be made of racing conditions, if a fellow only applied himself.

Five trains had departed for Kent during the hours in question, and Octavia looked over the passenger lists of every one. Lord Strythe's name appeared on none of them, and on reflection she was not altogether surprised. If he had left for Vesper Sands at all – if his butler had not been merely clutching at straws – he might have gone by second or third class, leaving no name on any list, or travelled by some other means entirely.

But where might he have gone, if not there? Why had he not returned home, if the private matter that had arisen there was so urgent? Could it be that word of what had happened had not reached Lord Strythe, or that the message had not called him home at all, but warned him away or directed him to some other place entirely? Had the news given him cause for alarm, or even for fear? Was there someone from whom he wished to hide?

Octavia returned north of the river, where she could at least make use of certain trusted lines of inquiry, and by midday she had discounted the most obvious possibilities. Lord Strythe was not a member of All Souls or the Conservative club, or indeed of any of the better clubs in St James's. Nor did he frequent any of the lesser-known establishments where gentlemen of means might play at cards and keep company with women. Octavia knew of a number of such places, and knew that they kept no rolls of membership, but she was acquainted with a private detective in Smithfield – he had built his practice on the engineering of profitable divorces – who could recite the name of every man who passed through their doors and the sum, down to the last penny, of the debt that each had run up at the whist table. He had never heard of the Earl of Maundley.

When all else had failed, Octavia resorted to the method she knew best. She would encourage the right sort of people to say the wrong sort of thing. She set out first for the home of Lord Hartington in Grosvenor-crescent. Elf had often been of use in such cases, and his intelligence might prove especially valuable today. She was curious, too, having rejoined the party the night before to find that he had disappeared. This was not altogether unusual, since he often had several engagements in the same evening, and she could hardly complain, having left without an explanation herself. Still, she was keen to find out if he had learned anything useful from Lady Ashenden. But Macken, his valet, seemed amused by the very idea that his master might have been at home.

'Why, Miss Hillingdon,' he said. 'It is hardly lunchtime, and he was abroad last evening. You know his habits. We'll not see hide nor hair of him before six o'clock.'

She left a calling card – with nothing on it but the vexed scribble of a question mark – and as she bicycled away she contemplated the options that remained. On a fine afternoon in spring, she might have counted on any number of casual encounters, but in this weather no one of consequence would dream of promenading in the parks. Still, one was often obliged to make do.

In the two or three hours that followed, Octavia visited a number of houses, choosing with care among the dozen or so ladies who entertained at this time of day. During each of these visits, she took care to conduct herself with lightness and gaiety, joining the company without a fuss and taking up whatever subject it was occupied with. When the course of the conversation prompted it, she might dispense some harmless morsel of gossip, giving no sign that she wished for any particular confidence in return, least of all the one she hoped for. She did not once introduce the subject of Lord Strythe, much less the question of his mysterious disappearance. She did not even mention that she had been a guest at Lady Ashenden's ball. There was no need, if one was patient.

For all her patience, though, she learned almost nothing of worth. There was talk of the gala ball, of course, and of Lord Strythe's abrupt departure. Lady Ashenden was spoken of in sympathetic terms, and while judgement was otherwise reserved for now, there was agreement that His Lordship must put about some satisfactory account the same day if the affair was not to become an outright scandal. As to what this explanation might be, she met no one who even ventured to speculate. Lord Strythe was a man of considerable standing and powerful connections, yet there seemed to be almost no one who knew him directly. It was a singular thing, in Octavia's experience, and it left her feeling oddly defeated. Uncovering secrets had always come easily to her, however boring or distasteful she might find it, and she took a certain furtive pride in her skill, yet now – when it seemed at last that the outcome might matter – all her ingenuity had come to nothing.

It was after four o'clock when she bicycled wearily home, and the sky above Smith-square was darkening. There would be more snow, she felt sure. There was that peculiar lull that comes before it, that sense that the air is silently encumbered. She let herself in by the back gate, as always, stowing her bicycle in the woodshed to keep it out of the weather. Finding the kitchen pleasantly deserted, it occurred to her that she had taken nothing but tea since breakfast time. She looked into the pantry, and after a few minutes of idle rummaging, she had assembled a serviceable meal.

Shoving her sleeves to her elbows, she settled in a chair – disturbing Juno, the household's elderly cat – and set out her food. She had found a monolithic heel of bread, a pot of crabmeat and a fine pair of Cox's Pippins. It was nothing that might be called a luncheon or a tea, but she tucked into it with quiet delight. She cherished these secret, childish feasts, and never more so than when she had returned from long hours in refined company.

Juno pawed at her skirts, having scented the crabmeat, and looked up at her in jaded supplication. Her appetite had begun to fail, and she did not much bother with mewing any more, but some small scrap was still expected by way of tribute.

'How did you pass the day, Juno?' Octavia tossed her a pink shred of meat. 'I hope *you* caught something, at least. I did myself no credit at all.'

The morning's newspapers had returned, still folded, from her grandfather's rooms. He scarcely recognised his *Gazette* or his *Times* these days, but the ritual was never overlooked. Octavia spread them out before her as she wolfed down her sandwich, and spent perhaps a quarter of an hour in the utmost contentment.

She hardly minded when Georgie came in, since it was his habit to seat himself quietly and wait to be spoken to. He took up a crust that she had neglected and poured himself a mug of tea, helping Juno into his lap and scratching her absently behind the ears.

'Now, here is a thing,' she said, when they had sat for a time in companionable silence. 'A fellow is accused of stealing a noted stallion, and the whole of the case seems to turn on whether a horse might be concealed on a barge.'

It was a moment before he replied, and when she looked up he seemed unusually preoccupied. He had taken a chair by the range and was staring into the banked embers.

'Well now, sister,' he said at length. 'I fancy it would be a tricky business even to get him aboard in the first place.'

'Why, Georgie,' she said. 'How hopeless I am. I had quite forgotten about your expedition to Whitechapel. Did you turn up anything at all? Can I tell Mr Healy to set aside this ridiculous obsession of his?'

Georgie examined the back of one broad hand. Discovering a nick, he raised it thoughtfully to his lips. 'Why, as to that,' he said, 'the truth of it is that I hardly know. I mean to say, I know what I was told, but I hardly know what to make of it.'

Octavia folded her newspaper and put it aside. 'What is it? What did you learn?'

'Well, I hadn't much of a notion how to go about it, not being in that line, but it seemed to me I would do best by speaking to all sorts. When you speak to all sorts, you hear all sorts.'

'And?'

'Well, I went into some rough places, and there was a deal of drunken talk, as you might expect. I paid little mind to most of it. It is all the same the world over, even if there is some gossip stirred into it that a fellow has heard third-hand. But it was not all of that kind.'

Georgie frowned and passed a hand through his untended hair. There was a plainness in his nature, and he had no great gift for dissimulation. Something had unsettled him. She said nothing, only moving her chair nearer to his. He would come to it in his own time.

'I met a woman,' he said, 'in one of the gin shops. She was the worse for drink, to be sure, but not as bad as some I saw. She had not been at it for long, she said, and I was inclined to believe her. She was well enough kept still, and did not have that look about her. Worked hard all her life, by her own account. But then her niece was taken, she said, a niece she had reared as her own, for her mother went when the girl was a babe in arms. Cholera, she said it was. Her niece was taken, and she hasn't been right since then.'

'Taken,' Octavia said. 'What did she mean by "taken"?'

Again Georgie hesitated. 'That's where her talk took a peculiar turn,' he said. 'Now, you may make of it what you will or think me foolish, but there was something in it. She may have been addled from the gin, but in her mind what she was telling me was gospel. The girl worked in a laundry, she said, and in such places the hours are cruel and the heat is worse. She wasn't made for it – there is no one made for it, to hear the stories this woman told me – and she took sick last summer. It was her breathing that went, and in the end she came down with something very like consumption. As good as bedridden, she was.

'Now, this the woman took very hard indeed, since she had not only the worry of it, but a wage gone from the house, and before long she was working nearly twenty hours in the day, so she said. It got that bad she was seeing things, by her own account, but she swears to what she told me next. They were being watched, she said, or the girl was. Being watched by these Spiriters – she said the word before I ever uttered it, mind. A priest warned her, she said. Some reverend. They looked for a special kind, he said – and remember, sister, I am only giving you the woman's own words – a special kind whose souls were very bright. What she meant by that I cannot tell you. Maybe it was only that they had a goodness in them beyond the ordinary. Not all could see it, he said, but they could and so could he. And the more she sickened, the brighter it became until . . .'

Georgie grasped at the air, as if it held the word he wanted. Octavia waited, her breathing quiet and careful.

'Until the end, I suppose. And that is how she came to the queerest part of her story. The woman came home one night, half-dead from tiredness, and looked in as she always did to the back room, where a bed had been made up for the girl. She found them standing over her. Two men, she said, all in black. There was not a light burning in the place, so she could see nothing of their faces. Well, I say no light – the girl herself was laid out, the woman said, in a dress she had never seen. A fine white gown, she said, fit for a princess to marry in. And a light was coming from her – do not look at me so, sister – a light was coming *from within her*.'

Octavia pressed her hands flat in her lap, not speaking until she could be sure of doing so calmly. This, exactly this. It was what she saw when the visions came.

'Go on, Georgie,' she said quietly. 'I don't know how I looked, but it wasn't what you thought. I don't doubt you at all. What else? What else did she say?'

'Well, sister, she was knocked to the ground, or so I understood, and put out completely. They were gone when she woke, and the girl gone with them. Gone, and never seen again. The thing was very raw with her still, and worked her up a good deal.

She took to shrieking – which is all you can call it, not to slight the woman – about how they came and went as they wanted, how they took these girls, body and soul. The company in the place took no notice, being used to her ways, but it was more than I could sit still for, I'm afraid to say.'

'Her name, Georgie. Did she tell you the girl's name?'

'Aye, she did. Felicity Hardwick. Eighteen years of age was all she was. And before you ask, I went straight to the peelers with it – to Leman-street, where the woman had gone herself – and spoke to a sergeant at the counter there. Blake was his name, a straight, civil kind of man who had a bit of time for me once I told him I was in the Service – a fellow officer, as you might say. In any case, he had heard it all, this Blake. It had been looked into, he said, and had come to nothing. The case is open still, and he keeps an eye out, on account of he has daughters of his own.

'Now, I did not like to ply this Sergeant Blake too hard, when he had already said more than he might, but I was mindful of your Mr Healy and the girl who was supposed have gone missing from the boarding house. So, I asked the sergeant was there anything to it, and now he closed up a bit and looked at me askance. There had been a report, he said, but it had come in only this morning. How had I got word of it, he wanted to know, when the ink was hardly dry in the crime book?

'Well, I am no hand at any kind of ruse, as you know, so I did not risk spinning a yarn. I said only that I had spent half the day in Whitechapel, and that such stories were the talk of the place, which was true enough. I said I had been straight with him, and had made no false representations. I said that the woman's story had moved me, and that she had made me promise not to forget it, and to do all I could to uncover whatever wickedness was at the heart of it all. I said nothing false, mark you, though I left out a good deal, and maybe that was what set him at his ease again.

'Whether or no, he told me a little of the latest case, if that is what it is. The girl is a flower-maker, and she was reported missing by the mistress of a boarding house for orphan work girls up Finch-street way. A Mrs Campion, her name is.'

Octavia had found a pencil and was jotting notes in the cramped margins of *The Times*. She looked up. 'Was there anything else?'

Georgie reached for his mug, pushing it away when he found that it had gone cold. 'There was,' he said after a moment. 'There was, sister, though perhaps you will think it is nothing – and if it is not nothing, perhaps you will not thank me for it. Sergeant Blake looked about the place and leaned across the counter, so as not to be overheard. There were certain elements, he said, who had seen to it that the case of the Hardwick girl kept no one up at night. It was done in a careful way, he said, and no marks had been left, but it was plain that the thing had been put on short rations and left to die. He would say no more than that, but I could see it had left him wary.

'As to the new case, he said, he could not be too free with the particulars, which were scarce in any case, but already there were things he did not like. The new girl was of near enough the same age as the last. She was an orphan, too, but with no kin she might turn to like the other girl had. She had sickened from her work, though she was not as bad. That much is common enough, you might say, but the last thing struck him more particular. The girl had been brought to the boarding house by a clergyman. There had been unwanted interest, he said, that he had wished to keep her from. He said no more than that – which, perhaps it was in his mind that if he said too much, this Mrs Campion might turn her away altogether – but it was Sergeant Blake's view that he said just enough, and I am inclined to agree with him, for what little that is worth.'

Georgie yawned and leaned back in his chair, working his thick fingers through Juno's shabby and greying fur. 'Well,' Octavia said, straining for lightness in her tone. 'For a man who is not in this line of work, you have a good deal to show for your first day's efforts. If Mr Healy discovers your talents, he will dispense with me altogether.'

Georgie gave her a cautious look. 'You do not mean to say that you will tell him? There is not enough in it for an article, surely?'

'Not yet, perhaps,' Octavia said. 'It's just that – some of what you told me, Georgie – there is something I—'

He leaned towards her, laying a hand gently on her forearm. 'What is it, sister? Are you all right?'

She patted his hand briefly, but pushed her chair out and stood without replying. 'We must go back there, Georgie. We must see what else we can discover. We can begin with the boarding house near Finch-street, which can surely be found. We can speak to this Mrs Campion.'

Georgie looked up. 'What, now?'

'Well, of course. A girl is missing, at the very least, and I have accomplished nothing else today. What is her name, Georgie? Did you think to ask?'

'Why, certainly, sister. I put it all in a notebook, since I knew you'd ask, but that much I remember. Tatton, her name is. Angela Tatton.'

IX

*A*ngela Tatton. Gideon smoothed out the letter on the counterpane. Scarcely touching the page, he traced the shape of her name. *Miss Angela Tatton*, his uncle had written, *with whom you became acquainted at my former rooms.*

He was perched on a narrow and creaking cot in the mean storeroom where he had woken shortly before. Its window offered a curtailed view of Frith-street, which he took to mean that he had been brought to the inspector's own lodgings, yet he had no memory of arriving there. He had called out, on first waking, but no answer had come. He had tried the door but found it locked, and hammering at it did no good. The rest of the house, as far as he could tell, was deserted and silent.

Having nothing else to occupy him, Gideon had turned his attention once more to his uncle's letter. He was preoccupied still with Miss Tatton's insistence that she and Neuilly had fallen victim to the same villainy, and it had occurred to him too that something in her account might shed light on his guardian's own words. He hoped to find in them some clue, obscure to him until now, to the nature of the menace they had faced.

He returned to the beginning of the paragraph.

You will recall the nature of my ministry, nephew.

Gideon frowned at this. When he had seen him last at St Magnus-the-Martyr, his uncle had said something to the same effect, and on that occasion too it had struck him as puzzling. If Neuilly had indeed confided in Gideon about his work, or indeed about anything of consequence, he was quite sure that he would not have forgotten it. Nor would his uncle, surely, having taken pains for so long to reveal almost nothing. He put the thought aside. His uncle had been greatly troubled when he composed his letter. The strain might have taken a toll on his clarity of mind.

You will recall that those I cared for were susceptible to certain dangers, and that I strove to place them beyond the reach of harm. For some of my wards, I hope, I accomplished that much, but I fear I did not serve them all well. Miss Angela Tatton, with whom you became acquainted at my former rooms, was one such. I have hopes for her still, and have taken great pains to improve her prospects, but I fear it will not be enough. She is marked out, so to speak, in a way that the others were not. It may be more than I can do to alter her fate.

At this Gideon rose in agitation, still clutching the letter. He paced the floor for a time, then crossed again to the door. Finding it locked still, he struck it in fury with the flat of his hand, but it was not his confinement that troubled him most.

How had it escaped him all this time? He had read the letter countless times, yet until now the starkness of his uncle's words had made no impression. Gideon could not have guessed the *nature* of his fears, but he ought surely to have understood their *gravity*. When Neuilly alluded to peril, he had not been thinking merely of poverty or ill health. He had not meant, as Gideon had blithely assumed, that Miss Tatton was marked out by her circumstances.

'Fool,' he said aloud. 'What a fool I have been.'

He read on, slumped against the door frame.

I will not abandon her, even if I must endanger myself for her sake. Those who would thwart me will not reveal themselves, but I am not without allies in this – the seamstress is one such – and have reason to hope that they will be undone. In the meantime, their eyes are ever upon me. Even my letters, I have cause to believe, are seen before I open them myself. I warn you, therefore, as I have warned others, to send no word by reply that may aid them. You will soon be here, God willing, but until then I cannot freely speak my mind.

Gideon bowed his head, but was roused from his despondency by a scuffling beyond the door, followed by the rattling of a key in the lock. He straightened hastily, passing a hand over his hair and beating the coarser dust from his clothing.

The woman who entered, having worked the door open with some effort, was diminutive and somewhat aged, but her demeanour was very fierce. Fixing him with an accusing look, she advanced upon him without a word.

'Good morning to you, madam.' Gideon gave a slight bow. 'My name is—'

She raised her walking stick, a gnarled length of varnished blackthorn, and thrust it against his chest.

'There he is,' she said. Her voice, like her stick, had a hard and spiny character. Gideon withdrew by a step, but she came nearer, forcing him to retreat to the cot. She adjusted her cane and prodded again at his sternum.

'It's all right, he says.' She jerked her free thumb towards the door, indicating that she referred to the absent inspector. 'Don't you worry, he says. That's just the new sergeant what took a funny turn while we was out on the job.'

The new sergeant. For a time he had almost forgotten. What had possessed him to attempt such a thing? He must make a clean breast of it at the first opportunity. Cutter would see, surely, that he had acted in desperation and confusion. If his uncle was no longer here – if something really had befallen him – Gideon had his letter to vouchsafe his claim. Might he not then ask for a period of grace while his uncle's affairs were looked into?

Gideon tried to sit up, but the woman's stick held him back. He squinted, propping himself up on his splayed elbows. 'Madam,' he said, 'I wonder if I might—'

 She silenced him with a look. 'New sergeant, indeed. I says to him, you know your business, Inspector, but I'll tell you this much. I says, that boy in there no more looks like a sergeant than I do. You could put him on a donkey's back come Christmas time, and he'd pass for the Blessed Virgin.'

Gideon tried to edge sideways, but again found himself firmly pinned. This woman could only be Cutter's landlady, surely, who had been described to him on the night he arrived in London. She did not appear to be deaf, as Bella had suggested – indeed, she seemed to find it objectionable when he spoke – but she fitted the description in all other particulars. He could not for the life of him recall her name.

'I says, I'll take you at your word, Inspector. You ain't never given me a day of trouble, unlike some, so I must give you a bit of credit, but I'm particular about who I let in, as you well know. I gave that vicar a chance, and now he's up and vanished. If that boy don't turn out bona fido, I says, you and me is going to have words.'

Vanished. Was it true, then? When she withdrew her walking stick at last, he ventured to respond. 'You are quite right to be vigilant, madam. There is a good deal of wickedness abroad. But the vicar you mentioned, do you mind if I—'

'Wickedness, is it?' The woman raised her stick and swung it now in a menacing arc. 'Of course there's wickedness abroad, boy, and that's where I like it. That's why I keep my doors locked night and day and don't open them to no strangers. I wouldn't have opened them to you neither, but the inspector said you was taken ill. Inspector Cutter and that doctor fellow had to hump you out of a cab like you was a knock-off carpet.'

Gideon remembered none of this, but began now to apprehend the depth of his humiliation. His last clear recollection was of Miss Tull's remains, of the solemn quietness in the scullery when the words on her skin were uncovered. He had fainted, then, and in the very midst of an investigation. Perhaps he need not concern himself with revealing the truth, since the inspector would surely dismiss him at the first opportunity. 'If I may, madam. How long have I been asleep?'

'Long enough, boy. They brought you back before lunchtime, and it's gone three now. That's more rest than I get most nights, so there ain't no excuse for you. You take that bit of broth now and get yourself right. The inspector's off about his business again, but when he gets back I expect him to take out what he dragged in. You needn't take it amiss if I lock you in again in the meantime.'

She withdrew her stick, and Gideon sat up warily. On a low trestle by his cot he found a chipped cup patterned with butter-flies. A thread of vapour rose from it, as did an irregular aroma. Reaching for it, he glimpsed a livid whorl of egg yolk, trailing greyish tatters of albumen.

'You are very kind indeed, madam,' he said, putting the cup discreetly aside. 'I am most grateful for your hospitality. My name is Gideon Bliss, in case the inspector did not mention it. Sergeant Bliss, that is to say, though of course you may—'

'Some of us has wash days,' she said, rapping at the floorboards as if to adjourn the proceedings. 'The inspector's vests will be boiled away to strings.'

He slept again, for all his agitation, and it must have been above an hour before he woke again. The narrow chamber had grown dim and the window showed a meagre scrap of sky, its colours deepening now to foxglove and umber. He lay for a time in disconsolate silence. It was not only his humiliation that he now contemplated, or the fresh uncertainty of his circumstances. Though his exhaustion was unrelieved, he had slept through the better part of the afternoon. Nearly a whole day had now passed since he last saw Miss Tatton. Nearly a whole day, and he had not even begun to look for her.

He stirred at a noise from the adjoining room, lurching to his feet at the oath that followed it. The inspector had come back, and in an ill temper by the sound of it, yet he felt a modest stirring of his spirits. He might now be released from his little cell, if nothing else, and if he was not at once sent on his way, he might be put in the way of a nourishing meal at last, and given one more chance to prove himself of use.

The door had indeed been unlocked, but could not be dislodged from its frame without a good deal of effort. When it finally yielded, Gideon stumbled into the room beyond, having flung the whole of his weight against the obstacle, and very nearly lost his footing. Inspector Cutter – who had been standing in his shirtsleeves before a long workbench – turned to him with a severe look.

'What is all that racket about, Bliss?' he said. 'It's no use having a burst of energy now. You are not battering down the door of an opium den.'

'I do apologise, Inspector. I did not mean to disturb you at your work. I tried to come in quietly, but the door defeated me. The architrave is considerably askew, I fear.'

Cutter cast his eyes up at this and turned again to his work-bench. A small case lay open by his elbow, and before him was an array of unfamiliar implements. He examined one of these minutely, then scrawled a note in a ledger.

'I see that you were kind enough to put me up in your own rooms, sir. I hardly know how to thank you.'

Cutter held a hooked needle to the light, testing its sharpness against the pad of his thumb. 'There is not much, Bliss, that you do not know how to say. It is more in the shutting off of the valve that you are inclined to struggle. Did Mrs Coombe fetch you up a mug of her broth?'

'She did, sir. And I am glad you reminded me of the lady's name, for she was reluctant to give it herself.'

'And did you drink it off, Bliss? You complained of a powerful hunger, as I recall.'

He hesitated. 'I did not manage quite the whole of it, sir. It was a remarkable sort of a broth, and seemed to fill me up almost at once.'

'You are not trying out for the diplomatic corps, Bliss. It was like a scoop of bathwater with an egg in it, was it not?'

Gideon shuddered. 'Very much like, sir. And the egg had a peculiar look to it.'

'Mrs Coombe is a great believer in the nourishment that is to be got from eggs, but she is dead set against waste. It would be a rare thing to see her boil a kettle twice in the same week. She maintains that a good swirl of a hot poker is all that is needed to cook an egg.'

'That is a practice I have never encountered until now, sir.'

Cutter gathered his papers into an unruly sheaf, fixing them in place with what appeared to be a pair of leg irons. Nearby, nestling in a fold of velvet, Gideon glimpsed the fragment of crystal he had found at Strythe House. Cutter parcelled it up, noticing his gaze, and stowed it out of sight.

'That item, sir,' Gideon said. 'Did you happen to give it further attention?'

'I did not,' the inspector said. 'But a man who knows about such things did.'

'And what did he tell you, sir, if I may ask? Is it of interest?'

'Never mind all that now,' Cutter said, clapping his hands together. 'You will not depend on Mrs Coombe for your dinner, you will be relieved to hear. We will venture out to Leggett's, which is an establishment I am fond of. Have you ever been to Leggett's?'

'I cannot say that I have, sir.'

'No? Well, you will come to know it tolerably well, for I do a good deal of my business there. A fellow is obliged to have dealings with all kinds, in my profession. They are bad specimens, some of them. And the worst of them – did you ever kill a rat with a knife, Bliss?'

'Kill a – no, sir. I have never killed a rat by any means.'

'Well, think of a rat, in any case, but a rat that would stand up and take the knife off you and eat it. He would eat the knife and shit it out, and *then* he would stab you with it. That is the class of fellow I mean. Mrs Coombe would never stand for them coming here. Come, put on your coat. It is a sharp evening, you will find.'

Gideon followed the inspector unsteadily from his rooms, descending with him by a gloomy staircase to the hall, where Cutter paused to put on his own hat and coat. From the front door, he turned and called out – just as Gideon had seen him do the morning before – that he was off out about his business. No answer came from the darkened quarters at the rear of the house, and Inspector Cutter did not seem to expect one.

Mrs Coombe took most unkindly to disturbances, it appeared, and regarded most of humankind with deep distrust. It was a thought whose implications troubled him. If he were to confess his deception, he reflected, he would not only be throwing himself on the inspector's mercy but on Mrs Coombe's as well. He would be asking her, having admitted to masquerading as a police sergeant, to accept almost entirely on faith that he was the nephew of a tenant who had recently disappeared.

No, it would not do. If he was to have any hope of keeping a roof over his head, he must stay the course for now. No doubt he would be exposed soon enough – it would not be long, surely, before the real sergeant reported once more for duty – but in the meantime he would do all he could to win the inspector's confidence. Then, when the right moment presented itself, he would introduce the disappearances of Miss Tatton and his uncle. He would persuade him, if he could, that the full might of the Metropolitan Police must be brought to bear on the case.

They set off along Frith-street once more, and Inspector Cutter led the way at his habitual clip. Gideon tried for a time to catch up, but he was far from fully recovered and could not match the older man's pace. He fell into step a little way behind him, breaking now and then into a panicked run when the inspector threatened to disappear from view.

He kept this up until they turned into Warwick-street, where the inspector came to a halt at last before an unmarked door. Athwart it stood a pockmarked fellow very near to seven feet in height, who issued in greeting a guttural rumble that Gideon could not interpret.

'This is Sergeant Bliss, Sweeney, who has been inflicted upon me by the fellows in G Division. He is not much to look at, but I must make do with him for now. Will you let him in whenever you see him, like a good fellow, for I may not always be with him.'

One of Sweeney's eyes was set awry, and he adjusted the bulk of his head so as to bring the serviceable one to bear. 'You won't get much wear out of that fellow,' he said. It was meant in jest, perhaps, but Sweeney's voice was not an instrument of levity. It might have been produced by an injured bull that had been flung into a well.

Gideon shrank by him warily, but Cutter only laughed, clapping a familiar hand to the man's great unshaven jaw. 'Not all dogs are bred for fighting, my friend. Will you give my compliments to Mrs Sweeney?'

'I will not, sir.' Sweeney replied. 'She is a ferocious bitch and a disgraceful cut of a woman. She has me nearly in my grave.'

'She will succeed yet, Sweeney, and then I will give her my compliments in person. Now, Bliss, it is this way. Get along in, man. It is not a cave full of adders.'

Leggett's proved to be a public house of uncertain character, whose interior was so dim that Gideon was obliged in places to feel his way. The inspector led him through a sequence of cramped and low-beamed chambers, where patrons kept for the most part to the shadows and did not raise their eyes. Those who did greeted Cutter with nods and murmurs of deference, but Gideon was looked on with surly scepticism. He might have been a show dog that had entered upon its hind legs, and which might presently provide a moment's amusement by toppling over.

He was greatly relieved when the inspector led him into a secluded parlour at the rear of the premises, where a modest fire burned in the grate between a pair of dilapidated armchairs.

Cutter hurled his overcoat onto one of these and directed Gideon to the other.

'The finest seats in London, Bliss,' he said, planting himself in front of the fire and beating his hands together. 'And reserved, as you might say. There is no shortage of rogues in this place, but you will find those chairs empty at any hour of the day or night. I get better value from them, I fancy, than the Queen does from her box at Ascot.'

Cutter had crossed to the door before Gideon could reply, and bellowed at some unseen functionary that chops and cordial were wanted.

'No doubt you would sooner have a mug of ale, Bliss.' The inspector turned to him, having warmed himself for a time before the fire. 'Or is a glass of sherry more in your line? In any case, you must fall in with my habits while you are under my command, and I cannot abide drunkenness. You must make do with peppermint cordial, which is sovereign in clearing the muck from a fellow's pipes. Here we are now. What kept you, lad? Had you to cuddle the lamb to death?'

The serving boy put out their plates – on each was a brace of chops and a potato the size of a navvy's fist – and Gideon fell upon his at once, with a swell of gratitude that very nearly moved him to tears. 'I take this as a singular kindness, sir,' he said between mouthfuls. 'I am temporarily embarrassed, I'm afraid, since a sergeant's pay goes only a little way in the metropolis, but I will gladly return the favour on another occasion.'

'Yes, yes,' said Cutter, who had not yet joined him at the table. He had taken up a newspaper instead, and was giving keen attention to an article that had caught his eye. 'We must feed you up a bit. We will not make much headway with our case if you are forever keeling over in sculleries.'

Gideon swallowed a morsel of his chop. 'I am mortified to think of it, sir. I am afraid I put you to a good deal of trouble. It was very much out of the ordinary, I assure you, and you need not fear for the soundness of my constitution. If you will allow me to continue in your service, sir, I will do my utmost to recover your confidence. You have my word upon it.'

Cutter looked up from his newspaper. 'There's a fit of oration, Bliss. You must be feeling yourself again. And you need not worry, I will not be packing you off back to the King's Cross-road just yet. You proved yourself useful enough, in your way, before your fit of the vapours.'

Gideon put down his knife and fork, having scoured the plate quite clean. 'Useful, sir?'

'Oh, I should say so,' Inspector Cutter replied. 'Those notes of yours were as handsomely done as I have ever seen. There was a good lot of guff, mind you, that could have been done without, but you have the knack of noticing the right things all the same, and not a letter out of place. It would pass muster before a judge, which is the main thing, and more than can be said for many in the Yard. Why, there are chief inspectors with twenty years behind them who could hardly spell out a list for the grocer.'

Gideon wiped his mouth and straightened his posture. 'It is no more than I might have done, sir, but I am very glad to have your good opinion.'

Cutter folded his newspaper under his arm and scrutinised Gideon for some moments. 'Well and good, Bliss,' he said. 'Well and good. But do not write home with your news just yet. I have certain reservations as to your fitness.'

'Again, sir, I must stress the exceptional nature of what occurred this morning. I am no prize wrestler, I do not pretend that, but I am in excellent health.'

'That is not what I meant by fitness. I had only to look at you on the doorstep this morning to know that I would not be putting you in among the brawlers of Putney on a Saturday night. I am more concerned with your – what is the word I am thinking of, Bliss, for the quality a fellow has when he is straight with you?'

'Candour, sir?'

'That is the very one. Your *candour*, yes. I have reservations about your candour, Bliss.'

Gideon bowed his head.

'And I am bound to say, Bliss, that you are doing very little to put my mind at ease. For it is not only the quality of your report that is remarkable. There is all that fine talk of yours, which is just as if you were reading aloud from *The Times*, only it is all done without effort. I put it down to drunkenness this morning, but I know to my own satisfaction that you have not taken a drop since then. And I will tell you another thing. I have twenty-two years of service, and I have never before encountered a sergeant of G Division or any other who could have given me the word "candour" as readily as you did just now. And I have not even mentioned the Cambridge business.'

Gideon could not bring himself to look up.

'You are no sergeant at all, Bliss. You will not deny it, surely?'

'No, sir.' He could hardly trust his voice. 'I will not deny it.'

Gideon had witnessed Cutter's wrath, though he could not say that he had seen the full extent of it. He braced himself in dread, seeing the inspector approach his chair, but when Cutter put out his hand, he did so only to take hold of Gideon's chin and scrutinise his face. He did not raise his voice when he spoke.

'When a fellow tries to pull the wool over my eyes, I generally know the how and the why of it in short order. If I do not, I let him pay out his line for a while until I have his measure, and then

I kick his arse for him, or I bring him up before a judge who will kick his arse for him. But this caper I cannot size up. What would possess you to try such a thing, Bliss? You are an educated fellow, that much is plain. Surely you knew what might come of it?'

Gideon lowered his head. 'I did, sir.'

'Well, then? What do you have to say for yourself? I want the truth of the matter, Bliss. Every bit of it, do you hear me?'

'Yes, sir.' Gideon took a moment to compose himself. 'The truth of it, sir, is that I acted in desperation. I came to London from Cambridge, that much was true. I came because—'

'Wait now, we will come to that. What did you do in Cambridge?'

'I was a student of divinity, sir.'

'Well, that explains a good deal. Had you not a great future before you, then? You must have been a favourite of the masters there, with all your fine talk.'

'Well, sir.' Gideon fidgeted with his cuff. 'I applied myself, since it was my duty, but I did no more than that. As to my future, well – it was somewhat uncertain, sir.'

'Oh? And why was that?'

'Sir, if I may – this has nothing to do with the account I meant to give you. It is not the reason I left Cambridge.'

'No, but it may be the reason you do not go back. I want every bit of the truth, Bliss. Every bit of it.'

'Yes, sir.' Gideon took a long draught of his peppermint cordial. He put his hands on his knees and cleared his throat a number of times.

'I fell out of favour, sir, with the Master of Selwyn College.'

'Did you now?' said Cutter. 'And what was at the root of that, I wonder?'

Gideon clutched at his knees. 'The Master had been attentive to me, sir. I took his attention for a recognition of my merits, and I welcomed it. But that was not the nature of it, sir. The nature of it was improper, sir.'

'Here now,' said Cutter gruffly. He looked uneasily about the dim parlour. 'Do not upset yourself, man. You sent him away about his business, did you? There is no shame in that for you.'

'Thank you, sir. I did, sir, but he did not take kindly to it.'

'Well, that is the way of such fellows. But what of that? I fell out of favour often enough with my own masters. I was still obliged to see out my schooling.'

'Yes, Inspector. But the Master of the college is the man who presides over it. He is a bishop, sir, and a man of great standing.'

Cutter grunted. 'A man in that position has much to lose if it is brought to light that he has been lifting some young fellow's shirt.'

'He did not – I did not allow any lifting. It is a painful subject, sir, and I hope we need not dwell on it. In any case, the Master's conduct did not trouble me so much as the doubts it revealed in me. Even before I was called here, the certainty of my vocation had begun to desert me.'

'Very well,' said Cutter. 'Go on with your story. How was it that you fetched up on my doorstep? You did not take to your studies, but that is not the end of the world. Why did you not go home to your father and mother and take whatever medicine was coming to you?'

Gideon had discovered a tear in the knee of his trousers, and he worried at it now with the tip of his index finger. 'My father and mother are no longer living, sir. I came to London at the request of my uncle, by whose generosity I was educated. I had a letter from him, and since the matter seemed urgent I came straight away. But when I arrived last night I did not find my uncle at home. It was a bitterly cold night, as you may recall, and due to my temporary embarrassment – that part was true also – I was obliged to take shelter in a church. When I presented myself at your doorstep this morning, I had come directly from that place, and had not taken so much as a mouthful of tea since leaving Cambridge.'

Inspector Cutter drew himself up with a grunt of ambivalence. He worked one of his shoulders about in its joint, studying Gideon with great thoroughness as he did so. Then he paced for some time about the cramped parlour, stopping at intervals by the fire to pick his teeth with a matchstick.

'Well, it is a sorry tale,' he said at last, flicking his matchstick into the coals. 'But most tales are, in my experience. And you have not come to the point of it yet. Why was it my door that you came to, of all the doors in London?'

Gideon shifted in his seat. 'Well, sir, that is the easier part of my explanation. My uncle lives at the same address, or he did until these last few days. I have reason to believe that he has met an unhappy end.'

Inspector Cutter left off his pacing and turned to face him. 'You are old Nelly's nephew?'

'The Reverend Doctor Herbert Neuilly. Yes, sir, I am. I have his letter, if you wish to see it. And there is a firm of solicitors in Cambridge you may send to. They will bear out my claim.'

Cutter studied Gideon with a vexed look, working with his thumb at a knot in his jaw. 'Well, this alters the complexion of the thing,' he said at length. 'It is a sorry bit of news, though I did not know the man well. In Mrs Coombe's house, as you have seen, we are inclined to keep to ourselves. He was a great fellow for good works, by all accounts. Forever ladling soup into orphans and that kind of carry-on.'

'Yes, sir. At least, that is my understanding. I came to know a little of my uncle's work, but no more than that. He provided for my education, but he did not encourage any great intimacy between us. No doubt it would have been a hindrance to his ministry. Still, it is a comfort to know that he was well thought of.'

Cutter cleared his throat gruffly. 'Well, no doubt he wished to do right by you in his own fashion, but found that his calling left him time for little else. I daresay it is like my own in that way. But let us return to the point, Bliss. You are not off the hook just yet, for you have given no account of the deception itself. Impersonation, no less, which is fraudulent in the eyes of the law. What put such a thing into your head? Why did you not simply state the case as it was, since you had some proof to offer of who you were?'

Gideon shook his head, and with a small groan he lowered it into his hands. 'Sir, it was an act of—'

'Here now,' Cutter put in. 'This will not do. Sit up and look me in the eye, like a good fellow. It is not a confession if you do it staring at your boots.'

Gideon brought himself warily upright. 'Forgive me, sir. It is only that you have at times a rather forbidding aspect.'

'A forbidding aspect?' Cutter made himself rigid, at which Gideon was seized with anxiety, but the moment seemed to pass. 'A forbidding aspect, indeed. Perhaps you are right, Bliss. It is a thing a fellow must cultivate, if he is to be of any use in this profession. Not that you need to concern yourself with such things any longer, since you have given up your bit of foolishness.'

Gideon blinked. 'But I have not given it up. I had hoped, sir, that by explaining matters to your satisfaction I might have some hope of redeeming myself. And of continuing in your service.'

'Of continuing in my what?' Cutter gave him a look of stark incredulity.

'But I fear it is impossible,' Gideon said quietly.

'Well, now. As to that, few things are impossible. You are no great physical specimen, it is true, and that would count against you if you were put forward in the usual way. There are ways and means, however, and I am long enough around the Yard to know my share of them. No, that need not hinder us. But you have mystified me again, Bliss. Why would you want to keep up such a thing, when it will mean trotting after me into every foul lane and tenement in London – for it is not all grand tragedies in Mayfair, I assure you – and enduring my temper day and night. An educated fellow like you might apprentice himself to a QC, or to a firm of clerks at the very least. Why would you persist with it, Bliss?'

Gideon lowered his head. He gave his answer softly. 'Because I must, sir.'

'You *must*?'

Gideon steadied himself. 'Sir, I mean to give a full and truthful accounting of my actions. I will omit nothing, and on my honour I will not utter a single false word. If at the end of it you still find fault with my conduct, I will thank you for your indulgence and leave you in peace. But if you find it satisfactory, sir, may I ask for something in return?'

'Something in return?' The inspector spluttered, upsetting his cordial as he put it down. 'You are in no position—'

'I believe you want to know, sir. That you *need* to know, in fact, and that you will not rest until you do, even though it is a matter of almost no consequence. I believe that is in your nature, sir, if I may make so bold.'

Cutter said nothing, but looked at him as if he had sprouted wings.

'Will you let me serve on probation, sir, if you are satisfied? Will you keep me on, unless you find some other cause to dismiss me?'

The inspector looked about him in dissatisfaction. He worked a kink from his neck and scoured his palm against the underside of his jaw. He fixed Gideon at last with a look of stark menace. 'This,' he said, 'had better be good.'

X

I t was the better part of half an hour before Gideon had given a
full account of events, from the moment he entered St Anne's
church to his arrival at the inspector's own door. By the end of it,
he was pacing the floor just as Cutter had done, too much agitated
to keep still. While he took care to omit nothing – relating even
his shameful encounter with the drunken sergeant – he gave emphasis to certain features of the case, returning more than once
to Miss Tatton's disappearance and speaking with an urgency he
could not conceal.

Cutter remained seated throughout, having turned his attention to his own supper. He did not interrupt at any stage, or give
any sign that his sympathies had been provoked. Gideon surveyed
him anxiously as he resumed his seat, but the inspector was not
moved to any immediate reaction, only inclining his head con-
templatively as he chewed over the last of his chop.

'Well, now,' he said at last, setting down his glass of cordial and
swiping his tongue over his upper lip. 'That was a colourful bit of
business, I must say. And you have a way about you with a story,
I will give you that. You are like a fellow on the verge of a poem.
But I am at a loss, Bliss. Leaving aside your little deception, which
we will come back to shortly, what has any of this to do with the
Metropolitan Police?'

Gideon stared for a moment in incredulity. 'There is a missing person, sir. Indeed, it is very likely that there are two. And that may be the least of it, if one takes a certain view of Miss Tatton's words.'

'We will return to that in a moment,' said the inspector, taking a more easeful position in his chair. 'Who is the first missing person, tell me?'

'Forgive me, sir. Perhaps I was not clear in my account. Miss Tatton was lying before me when I was put out of my senses by some malefactor. When I awoke she was gone. Angela Tatton is the missing person, sir.'

'Is that so, Bliss?' The inspector drew himself up, his sternness returning. 'Who has reported her missing?'

Gideon hesitated. 'Why, I have, sir. That is the whole import of my story – that this poor girl has disappeared in unaccountable circumstances, and may now be at risk of greater harm than she had already suffered.'

'You, Bliss?' The inspector regarded him balefully. 'No, that will not do at all. How can you report her missing? Before you came across her in that church, you had never set eyes on that girl in your life. You might just as well tell me that you encountered a pigeon in Trafalgar Square, and that you woke from a doze to find it missing.'

'You are making fun of me, Inspector. And in any case—'

'I am giving you a dose of instruction, and one you are sorely in need of. You may give a great account of yourself in trigonometry or Latin verbs, but there are trollops in Houndsditch not three weeks on the job who know more of police work than you do. You cannot report a stranger missing, you empty-headed Canary-bird. For all you know, Bliss, the same girl creeps into that church every night of the week to be out of the cold, but has the good sense to creep out in the mornings before anyone is stirring. She might be about the streets even now with her cart of oysters, or returned to some tinker's camp. She might be a day's sailing from Southampton, bound for New York.'

'She went nowhere of her own accord, sir, that much I am certain of. She was in no fit state to leave by herself, and was plainly in fear of those she believed were returning for her. In any case, sir, she was not a—'

'Bliss.' The inspector approached him, laying a hand on his shoulder. The heft of it was considerable, though the gesture was kindly meant. 'You are a tender-hearted soul, I see. Your uncle was the same, no doubt, and saw only innocence and virtue in all he met. Now, that is fine and well for a fellow going into the God-fearing racket, but it will do you no good in my line of work. This Tatton girl had an ungentlemanly companion, no doubt, who used her ill and put your lights out when he found you with her. It is a sorry tale, but believe you me, it is not a hundredth part of the misery that is doled out in a single night in any square mile of London that you care to name. And do you know what portion of that misery we concern ourselves with, in the Metropolitan Police?'

'I have an approximate conception, I think. But, sir—'

'The portion that we cannot avoid, Bliss. The portion that must be put in the crime book because the fellow who reported it is not himself a drunkard or a maniac. The portion that has been looked into by the newspapermen, or that has got up the dander of some Right Honourable Member. The portion that has been declared a great social ill by some Quaker with notions, or which the Assistant Commissioner has seen all but stamped out in Paris. We concern ourselves with what we must, and no more, or we would very quickly wear ourselves down to stumps.

'It is not that we never act according to conscience, Bliss, but the Yard has a fixed view of things, and no great notion of charity. Why, even this business at Strythe House may not put us much in favour if we cannot winkle something more out of it than a lunatic seamstress. I do not like the look of that affair one bit, but that is neither here nor there. You cannot go turning over the mattresses of a peer of the realm without good cause, and we have nothing yet to answer that description. You must put this missing match girl from your mind.'

'*If you would let me finish, sir.*' Gideon struck the table, regretting the outburst immediately and folding his arms to prevent a recurrence. 'If you will permit me, sir, what I have been trying to tell you is that I *had* set eyes on Miss Tatton before – that she and I were formerly acquainted.'

Cutter closed his eyes and brought his hand to his brow, caressing it as if to relieve some sudden discomfort. It was a moment before he could bring himself to continue. 'You knew the girl, is that what you are telling me now?'

'Yes, sir.'

'I see.'

The inspector's tone seemed reasonable, but his expression had darkened considerably. Gideon thought it best to say nothing more until he was called upon to do so.

'That, Bliss, is what might be called a salient fact. Do you know what a salient fact is?'

'I believe so, sir. It is from the Latin *salire*, meaning "to leap". A salient fact, I suppose, is one that leaps out.'

'From the Latin.' Cutter closed his eyes again. 'Would you say that this particular fact leapt out of your account, Bliss?'

'Perhaps not, sir.'

'Perhaps not.' The inspector drummed softly on the arm of his chair. 'We will pass over this, I think, while I still have command of myself. This former acquaintance of yours, Bliss. How did that come about, then? Was Miss Tatton at Cambridge too? Is she a doctor of divinity?'

'No, sir. I met her in London, while visiting my uncle at his previous residence. She was one of those he aided in his charitable works.'

'Is that right? And did you aid her too? Did you give her comfort? Was that the nature of your acquaintance?'

Gideon got up from his chair and crossed to the parlour's single grimy window. The glass was a good deal obscured by grime, but he rubbed at one pane until he had a constricted view of Warwick-street. 'I spent only a few days in Miss Tatton's company, sir. My uncle had found new lodgings for her, and I myself was obliged to return to Cambridge. Even so, I came to know her tolerably well. I was shocked, Inspector, to find her as I did. Her circumstances were not fortunate, it is true. She had known hardship. But with my uncle's aid she had been striving to better herself. She would not have kept low company, sir. She was not brought to that state by any fault of her own.'

'All right, Bliss.' Cutter spread his fingers in conciliation. 'All right. You are fond of the girl, and you would not have it said. It is natural enough. And she was not a stranger, at least. But when had you seen her last, before the encounter in the church?'

'Sir?' Gideon did not turn from the window. It was now fully dark outside. He watched as a woman passed from one interval of darkness to the next then lingered by a street light. She shivered, drawing a poor shawl about herself as she surveyed those who passed. A cocoon of gauzy light surrounded her, crowded at its edges with gentle smudges. The snow had returned. It would be another cruel night.

'The girl, Bliss. When had you last seen her?'

'August, sir. I remember it to the hour.'

'Six months ago,' Cutter said. 'And nothing since then? No letters between you?'

'No, sir. No letters.'

'And had you word of her from anyone else? Had you any cause to fear for her?'

Gideon bent his head to the window, resting it against the sash. He had tried to keep the woman in view but saw now that she was gone, his eyes deceived by shadows in the slow tumult of whiteness.

'Bliss? Had you any cause to fear for her?'

Had he cause? For a short while, since leaving Frith-street, he had managed to put his uncle's letter from his mind, but he could escape his failure no longer. He had cause, almost from the beginning, but he had failed to see it. He stared, only half-seeing, into the patient absolution of the snow.

Miss Tatton. Miss Angela Tatton.

Gideon scratched her name on the slate, practising the shape of it, then effaced it hurriedly with his bundled cuff. He spoke it softly to himself, whispering it at intervals while he waited. Miss Tatton ate below stairs, though Gideon was troubled by this arrangement, and he did not think it his place to send for her. When she appeared at last he started from his chair, seized with the fear that she had overheard him. She was followed by Mrs Downey, the housekeeper goading her from the doorway before seating herself with a piece of lacework to observe the proceedings.

Miss Tatton offered him an unpractised curtsy. Gideon bowed in turn, but with such awkward haste that he feared he had startled her. 'The master said I might come up after supper,' she said after a moment's hesitation. Her pinafore was freshly laundered, and beneath its starched cuffs her knuckles showed, hard and narrow against the yellowed linen. 'That you might read to me and such.'

'Yes, yes,' he said with too much eagerness. 'That is, I should be delighted. Will you not have a seat?'

She regarded him with uncertainty. He had indicated the head of the table. It was Neuilly's place, when that gentleman was at home.

'Please,' he said, gesturing again. 'My uncle has been called away on business. He mentioned a seamstress, though I cannot think what he might want with one.'

Miss Tatton clamped her lips together, suppressing a surge of merriment, and Gideon flushed again. The joke had been unintended, though it was true that Neuilly gave little attention to his manner of dress. 'At any rate, he is not expected for some time. Do please feel free.'

'Yes, sir,' she said, taking her seat. 'Thank you, sir.'

'I do wish you would—' Gideon coughed and began again. 'I hope you will call me Gideon, miss. We are very nearly the same age, I am sure.'

'Could be,' she said evenly.

Gideon blinked. 'Well,' he said, turning to the books he had laid out. 'Perhaps we ought to—'

'No one ever told me my birthday,' she said. 'So, I picked the seventh of May. Seven's lucky, so they say, and May's the prettiest.'

'Then it is certainly yours by right,' Gideon said, regretting his choice of words at once. Why could he not keep from babbling in this way? 'And you, miss. You will not mind, I hope, if I call you Angela?'

The housekeeper gave a forthright cough. He would do well, her look made plain, to proceed with whatever business was in hand. 'I have put out a primer,' he said, indicating the book at

Miss Tatton's end of the table. 'We might begin with some pieces of verse, I thought. I shall be glad to assist you, if there is a word you have not encountered.'

She looked down at the book, but did not take her hands from her lap.

'But perhaps it is too simple a book, in which case I beg your pardon. I'm afraid I don't know the extent of your schooling. My uncle did not have time.'

'Yeah, well.' She raised her chin, fingering the spine of the primer. 'It wouldn't take long.'

Gideon shifted, clutching at his cuffs. 'Well, then,' he said. 'We might begin instead with the alphabet, if you have had no instruction at all. I have a slate on which you might practise your letters.'

She looked at him without a word. He had sought out her face compulsively, since her arrival, but a stillness came over it now that he could not confront.

'Forgive me, miss,' he said quietly. 'I'm afraid I have spoken thoughtlessly. I would not have injured your feelings for all the world.'

Mrs Downey rose abruptly at this. Crossing to Angie's place, she stooped briefly to her ear then lurched in disgust towards the stairs. He waited for Miss Tatton to follow, persuaded that his disgrace was complete, but she did not stir.

'Well, you're a one,' she said at last. It was a moment before Gideon recognised the tremor of amusement about her lips.

Gideon blinked again. 'But Mrs Downey,' he said.

'You're harmless, she reckons.' Miss Tatton pressed her lips together. 'Well, that weren't the word, exactly.'

Gideon slumped, a heat rising again to his cheeks. His eyes would redden too, as they often did in such moments. Perhaps he could bolt from the room before she saw. Perhaps he would be in time still for the last train to Cambridge.

But there was a gentleness in her voice when she spoke. 'You could just read something, maybe.'

He looked up cautiously.

'A story, not a lesson. I'd like that.'

Gideon searched her face. 'Of course,' he said, coughing when his voice faltered. 'Of course, I should like nothing better. The library will be closed at this hour, but among my uncle's books, I'm sure – if you'll excuse me for just a moment. Will you excuse me?'

Miss Tatton only laughed.

But Neuilly's shelves proved to be poorly stocked, due perhaps to his itinerant manner of living. He had works of theology, as might be expected, many of which seemed to touch on the nature of angels. There were a number of field guides (Gideon had forgotten his fascination with butterflies), as well as volumes on natural history, treatises on the plight of the poor and works on more arcane subjects (Gideon had no notion, for instance, what 'spirit photography' might be). Neuilly seemed to have little interest in novels, however, and Gideon's own acquaintance with fiction was slight. He was growing anxious, too, at keeping Miss Tatton waiting, and settled without a great deal of deliberation on Mr Richardson's *Pamela*.

Gideon was by no means accustomed to reading aloud, and was soon persuaded that he had no great gift for it. He hesitated and cleared his throat a good deal, and when he glanced at Miss Tatton he was apt to lose his place. Even so, she listened contentedly enough for a time, exclaiming mildly now and then at some new intrigue or revelation. But after twenty minutes or so, when he had read out half a dozen of Pamela's letters, Gideon saw that Miss Tatton was growing impatient.

'I'm afraid I'm a dull reader,' he said, lowering the book.

'It ain't you, sir—'

'Gideon, please. Do call me Gideon.'

'It's her, that Pamela. Such a mug I never seen. Don't she see what he's about, that Mr B? His mother's not long dead, and here he is making free with her maid, telling her she writes with a pretty hand and all the rest of it. Ain't she got eyes in her head?'

'Yes, well.' Gideon felt his colour rising. 'Perhaps you are—'

'And now he's giving her all these presents. One minute he wants her to keep up her reading, and the next he's slipping her silk stockings.' She glanced at the book in his hands, her expression faintly mischievous. 'Maybe the reading is how it starts.'

Gideon gave a laboured cough and shifted in his seat. 'Pamela may write for guidance to her mother and father, at least. They perceive her situation more clearly, I think.'

'It's just as well someone does,' Miss Tatton said. She studied him for a moment, and there was something in her look that he could not decipher. 'Perhaps I ought to learn my letters, then. So that I may write away for guidance when I am in my new situation. Not that I have anyone to write to, mind.'

'No, miss.' Gideon hesitated for a moment. 'We are alike in that, at least.'

Her gaze settled on him again. 'Is that what you think, young master? That we are two little orphans? That we are two peas in a pod? You had your uncle, when yours were gone, to send you off to Cambridge. Do you know what I had?'

'Forgive me, Miss Tatton. If I speak without thinking, it is only because—' He lowered his head. 'Well, I do so at the best of times, if the truth be known, but this evening I find that I am hardly equal to thinking at all.'

'Is that right?' Her indignation had passed. 'That'll never do, will it? I'd best keep away, or you'll be no scholar at all by the end of the week.'

Gideon looked at her shyly as he measured out what he might say. 'That might do more harm than good, miss.'

Miss Tatton rose from her place. 'You ain't been reading a good long while. Harmless or not, her below will be stirring. She's off out tomorrow afternoon, though the master don't know it. Her old fellow owes money on a cockfight, and he ain't being let home until someone pays it. I shall be cooped up for long enough after you're gone – wiring flowers all day, most like, then back to some boarding house that's near enough to a prison. I'm going out, young master. Old Nelly says I mustn't because it ain't safe, but I'm going out.'

'Gideon. Call me Gideon, I beg you. Why isn't it safe?'

'Four o'clock at the back steps onto Fish-street Hill.' She paused at the doorway, half in the lamplight and half in darkness. 'Goodnight to you, young master. I shall leave you to your thoughts.'

At first Cutter could make nothing of what Gideon had said. Returning shamefacedly to the fireplace, he had intended to put the case plainly. He would produce his uncle's letter, regretting that he had not done so before, and would admit his fault in failing to heed its warnings. Such were his emotions, however, that he struggled to keep to a direct course.

'I mistook my uncle's meaning, sir,' he said, lifting his head from his hands. 'Or I passed over it entirely. I did myself no credit in any case.'

'What meaning is this now?'

'You asked if I had cause to fear for her, sir, and the answer is that I had. My uncle had made it plain enough in his letter, but I did not see it at first. Miss Tatton saw it herself – just as she perceived the dangers to Pamela – but I lacked the wits. I'm afraid there was a great deal that I missed.'

'Wait now, who is this Pamela, in the name of God?'

'Forgive me, sir. She is only a character in a novel. It was an example that came to me just now. But I ought to come to the matter of the letter.' He drew it from his coat and unfolded it carefully. 'I mentioned my uncle's letter, I believe, urging me to come at once to London. He seemed preoccupied by some downturn in his affairs, but at first I thought no more of it than that. It was Miss Tatton's account that forced me to reconsider his words.'

'What she told you in the church, you mean? But she was drugged, you said. She was rambling.'

Gideon shook his head forcefully. 'She was weakened, sir, but she had her wits. And there was no mistaking her conviction. She had been in fear – of who or what I do not know – and my uncle had tried to protect her. His letter hinted at dark misgivings, but until now I failed to heed them.'

'Hark at him with his dark misgivings,' said Cutter, casting up his eyes. '"A character in a novel" is right. Here, give over this letter of yours. If I wait for you to tell me what is in it, we will be here half the night.'

Gideon slid the letter towards him, looking on in apprehension as the inspector digested its contents. He read quickly, grunting now and then or raising an eyebrow, but otherwise passing over its pages with an air of impatience. He returned it with a weary look, yawning strenuously as he sat back in his chair.

'I will say one thing for your uncle, Bliss. He is not far behind you when it comes to larding the pudding.'

'Yes, sir. But you see the cause of my agitation, I trust? You grasp the import of his words?'

'I saw a good many words, but not much that a fellow could grasp.'

'But he speaks of his fears for Miss Tatton, sir. He worries that she is marked out.'

'He feared for her prospects, as he did for all such creatures. Have we not spoken already of his calling?'

'No, sir, that was my mistake. The truth was more sinister, I fear. Look again at this passage. He fears for her, and he speaks of those who would thwart him. They will not reveal themselves, he says, but he has allies who can expose them. Do you see, sir?'

'Do I see *what*, in the name of God?'

'Sir, you spoke of winkling something out, so that we might be given more licence in these matters. I believe we have hit upon that very thing.'

Cutter raised his eyes, resting his boot heel on the coal scuttle. 'Have we indeed? I will polish up a pair of medals.'

Bliss spoke with urgency. 'The two matters are bound up, sir, I am sure of it; the incident at Strythe House and the fate of Angie Tatton – they are bound up.'

'Bound up? How are they bound up?'

'My uncle mentions allies, sir, and his hopes for the undoing of his enemies. But he goes further – he names one of them.'

'One of his enemies?'

'No, sir, one of his allies. Look here.' Gideon pointed out the line in question. 'He says that "the seamstress is one such". The *seamstress*, sir.'

'And what seamstress might that be?'

'Why, Miss Tull, naturally.'

'Miss Tull? What hand did she have in anyone's undoing but her own?'

'I will return to that point in a moment, sir, but we know at least what she wished to reveal.'

'Do we indeed?' Cutter enclosed his face with his fingers, working gently at his brow. 'And what is that?'

'The words that were stitched into Miss Tull's skin, sir – do you recall them?'

'My soul doth – what is it now? My soul doth something.'

'"My soul doth magnify the Lord", Inspector. It is from the *Magnificat*, one of the oldest of our hymns. It is the song of praise that was offered by the mother of Christ herself.'

Wearily, the inspector lowered his hands. 'You will have to draw out the connection for me, Bliss,' he said. 'You are the only scholar among us.'

'But no scholarship is needed, sir. We need only consider the facts of the case. Miss Tull was driven by what she knew to end her life – by something she had been made a party to – but she had the consolation of knowing that in doing so she was bearing witness. To those who knew no better – to those she feared – it would appear to be no more than a pious woman's last act of expiation. But to one who knew her intentions, the meaning of it is plain.'

'Is it, indeed? Well, I am glad it is plain to someone.'

'*My soul doth magnify the Lord.* Her immortal soul, sir, which is all that was left to her in the end. In the prayer, the soul of the Virgin is said to magnify the Lord – to give tribute to his glory – but even a pious woman, surely, would not go to such pains to leave only those words behind. They must have some other meaning. What if she meant not to glorify the Lord, but to magnify something as a glass does, to reveal it beyond mistaking? And speaking of glass, sir, it occurred to me also that Miss Tull might have done more than merely bear witness.'

'Did it now?'

'Yes, sir.' Gideon shifted in his chair as he chose his words. 'If I may, sir. The fragment of crystal I found – it was lying near to, well, to the place where poor Miss Tull's remains must have come to rest. You mentioned that you had it examined, sir, and since we have a moment of leisure—'

'Do not think to distract me, Bliss. This notion of yours must stand on its own legs. *My soul doth magnify the Lord.* What was it that Miss Tull meant to magnify, when she stitched those words into her own skin? Or who? God himself, is it? I will send word straight away that he is to be brought in for questioning.'

'Not God, sir. Again, the true meaning is less exalted. Another Lord. Her employer.'

The inspector drew in a long breath. His expression assumed a severe cast, and he took again to kneading his brow, as if to relieve some interior pressure. 'I will say this much for you,' he said, after a long silence. 'You are not one for starting in a small way. Are you sure you missed nothing out, now? Is there not a secret agent who comes into it somewhere? Or a dragon?'

Gideon coloured and looked down at his feet. 'It sounds outlandish, sir, but Miss Tull's act was outlandish in itself. It was never likely, surely, that such a thing would have a commonplace cause.'

'You would be surprised, Bliss, at what people will do for ordinary reasons. And in any case, you have some distance to cover yet with this grand theory of yours. Why did Esther Tull not simply leave a letter, as suicides commonly do? She need not have left it at the scene, where it might have been destroyed. She could have left it at home, or posted it to your uncle earlier in the day.'

'Well, sir, it may be that she had reason to be fearful, that she believed herself to be under suspicion. It may even be that she felt herself to be illiterate in the usual sense, though in her embroidery she could reproduce letters with prodigious skill. My uncle described such a woman to me once, and it struck me as a most poignant thing. But here again I suspect there is a simpler explanation. If her revelation was indeed intended for my uncle, a letter might have been intercepted before it reached him. He says here quite plainly that he feared as much. What puzzles me still is the question of how my uncle was to have received the message she chose to leave. He would have learned readily enough of Miss Tull's death, especially if he had feared it was imminent, but how was he to decode a message he had not seen – a message that was, well, intimately concealed?'

'He would have read it in the papers, Bliss, as will anyone else who takes the slightest interest.'

'In the papers, sir? But how would such a thing come to be known?'

'The police surgeon examined the remains, and he will give out his findings at the inquest, where the gallery will be near to bursting with newspapermen waiting to take them down. *The Times* will use the Latin words, but the rest will choose their own. No, Bliss, there are a great many faults to be found with this flight of fancy, but that is not one of them. Whatever her fears and whatever her reasons, Miss Tull intended her bit of needlework to come before the public, and so it will in due course. Now, listen to me, like a good man. You have gone a long way on very little steam, but now you must give your engine a rest. I will not be given much leeway in looking into the Strythe House matter, and I mean to try the more usual methods first.'

The inspector drained his glass of cordial. Scooping out his watch, he glanced in the direction of the passageway.

Gideon gave a small cough. 'Forgive me, Inspector, but I am not sure I have understood you. Do you mean to extend your investigation to the events I described at St Anne's Church?'

Cutter appeared distracted. 'I have not yet spoken my mind on that point, Bliss. I will give it due consideration.'

'But we must act quickly, sir, if we are to act at all. Almost a whole day has passed since Miss Tatton was last seen. She and my uncle may be in the gravest danger. We cannot simply leave them to their fates.'

The inspector only frowned at his watch, giving no sign that he had heard. Crossing with a vexed air to the doorway, he peered out into the passageway. At length he appeared to catch sight of someone.

'Fox!' he called out. 'There you are, Fox. Good man, good man. I had nearly given you up for lost. Come in for a moment while we make ready to leave.' He ushered in a sad-eyed fellow with a wilting moustache, clapping him on the shoulder and steering him to the fireplace. 'This specimen here – get up out of that armchair, Bliss, and show a bit of smartness – this specimen here is to serve as my sergeant until better can be found. Bliss, this is Inspector Fox of J Division.'

Gideon leapt upright. 'Delighted, Inspector,' he said. 'I beg your pardon if I seemed discourteous. I'm afraid I've been rather unwell.'

Fox thumbed one nostril closed and then the other, snuffling back the contents of each as he did so. He hawked the resulting matter into the coky fire, where it gave out a viscous sizzle. 'Where'd you pick that one up?' he said, turning to Cutter. 'Stage door, was it?'

Cutter ignored this, reaching for his overcoat and hauling it on. 'Fox has been good enough to look into the late Miss Tull, Bliss. He has turned up her lodgings on his patch, down Bethnal Green way. She lived there with a sister of hers who might have a good deal to tell us. You may take a note of that, Bliss, in your new book. That is a bit of real police work for you.'

Gideon reached for his notebook, but realised as he did so that the inspector's observation was rhetorical. 'Yes, sir,' he said. 'That is a valuable piece of intelligence, of course. But if I may, sir – surely we might have got it from Mr Carew at Strythe House without troubling Inspector Fox?'

Cutter exchanged a look with Fox, who applied his tongue to his teeth and expressed a thin whistle. Inspector Cutter leaned towards Gideon and clasped his shoulder. 'We might have done so, Bliss. We might indeed. And then Mr Carew might have passed word of it to whatever wig represents His Lordship's interests, and before I knew it I might have found myself hauled in to the Yard to give an account of myself.'

'Of course, sir,' Gideon said quietly. 'I shall endeavour to be of use, in any case.'

Inspector Fox stared at him for a moment, then shook his head with some force, as if to clear his ears of an obstruction. 'Best be off, then,' he said. 'One of my lads is out in the wagon with a loon that done a runner on us. Picked up outside the Palace, he was, bollock naked and threatening an anarchist revolt.'

Fox slouched after Cutter, who had marched already to the door. 'You ever wrestle a naked anarchist to the ground, Priss?' he said, glancing over his shoulder.

'Bliss, sir. And no, I cannot say that I have.'

'No?' Fox smoothed down the limp extremities of his moustache. 'Well then, this might just be your lucky night.'

XI

Notes made by G. Bliss (Sgt.), attending residence at 23 Charlotte-street, Bethnal Green, together with Insp. Cutter (CID) and Insp. Fox (J Division).

Boarded a police carriage in the command of Insp. Fox in Warwick-street, in which vehicle we encountered Sgt. Knowles, who was endeavouring to restrain an unclothed lunatic.

On entering the carriage, Insp. Cutter gave assistance to Sgt. Knowles, and was obliged to administer a [*stricken out*] to the suspect's [*stricken out*]. The prisoner quietened considerably, and was covered to the point of decency with a feed bag.

7.10 p.m. Arrived at Bethnal Green police station, where the lunatic was with some difficulty removed.

7.38 p.m. Arrived at Charlotte-street.

Insp. Fox observed that the dwellings in the street were weavers' cottages, these being characterised by a large window set into the upper storey so as to admit the abundant light called for by that profession.

Upon presenting ourselves at No. 23, it was found that no one could be brought to the door, though Insp. Cutter knocked with considerable energy for two minutes or more.

A woman emerged from a neighbouring dwelling in a state of some agitation, and demanded to know the cause of the racket. When the officers present identified themselves, said woman's demeanour became coarse and unwelcoming and officers were invited after a brief exchange to 'fuck off out of it' [*sic*].

Insp. Cutter directed the woman to disclose her name, which she gave as Mrs Kiss-My-Arse [*sic*], whereupon Insp. Cutter announced that he would search her dwelling and would leave it looking like a [*stricken out*]. The neighbour was induced to give her name as (Mrs) Ginnie Reston.

Mrs Reston was questioned as to the whereabouts and habits of the occupants of No. 23. She identified these as Miss Esther Tull and Mrs Mamie Hanley, the latter being the elder sister of the former and widowed a good twenty years.

Mrs Reston further volunteered that the elder sister had been for some years 'laid up'. Mrs Hanley was dependent upon the care of Miss Tull, who put it about that she worked as a seamstress, while keeping the hours (this being Mrs Reston's own private view) of a tart. In the light of the foregoing, she

suggested that the officers present return in
the morning. Mrs Reston was then directed to
return indoors, and was advised that her views
on the conduct of the present investigation
would be sought if they were wanted, this
eventuality being understood to be unlikely.

The officers present then conferred for a
time on the necessity of seeking a warrant if
a forced entry were to be made to Miss Tull's
former home. Insp. Cutter and Insp. Fox then
stood apart and spoke privately.

This discussion being concluded, the
inspectors asked the present officer if he
had heard a scream coming from within the
dwelling. The present officer expressed
uncertainty, but following a period of
reflection concurred with the view that an
exclamation of distress had indeed been heard.

Insp. Fox then produced a suitable implement
from the carriage, and immediate entry was
effected in the interests of safety. Insp.
Cutter gave out a loud announcement and
called on any person concealed within to
show himself. When no answer came a lamp was
brought from the carriage and the officers
began to look about the lower rooms.

The parlour and kitchen were both found
to be empty and unheated. The grate was
quite cold. Both rooms were in a state of
considerable disarray, with pots and pans,
items of crockery, &c. having been scattered

from their places, and a good deal of breakage
was observed. The larder had been emptied
out and provisions were likewise found to be
strewn about the floor.

All present then made their way above
stairs, entering first the room whose large
arched window had been observed from without.
A bedstead and nightstand occupied one corner,
but the greater part was in use as a workroom.
Garments in varying states of completion were
hung neatly upon a rail, but others had been
cast about the room. Items of piecework had
likewise been swept from a bench, but some
had been left untouched and were carefully
ordered still. A scrap of butcher's paper was
pinned to each, showing the particulars of the
commission in a neat hand.

A Singer sewing machine had been upset,
and was found lying on its side. Insp. Fox
examined it and pronounced it undamaged. It
was a handsome article, he said, and one that
spoke well of Miss Tull's skills, since it was
by no means cheap. Insp. Fox explained that
his own wife takes in needlework to supplement
their living, but does not profit enough by it
in a whole year to make such an investment.

The covers had been torn from the bed in
the corner, and its mattress had been hauled
aside. A nightstand had been overturned, and
near it a Bible and one other book were found,
which the present officer was moved to examine.

The Bible was found to be unremarkable, but the other volume — an annotated edition of the Book of Common Prayer — was taken into evidence for later examination.

Insp. Cutter took a wastebasket from beneath the workbench, and removed from it a quantity of oddments. An opium bottle was recovered, but its label had been scoured away and the dispenser could not be identified. Also found were wads of gauze, saturated in varying degrees with blood.

The officers present went next to a room of modest proportions at the rear of the house. Like the other parts of the dwelling, this room was observed to be in a disordered state, and a woman was found on a bed there who could not be roused by any means. A window had been left open, and the room was inhospitably cold. Insp. Fox was for shutting it at once, being susceptible to pleurisy, but Insp. Cutter advised against it on the grounds that evidence might be disturbed.

Insp. Fox brought his carriage lamp to the bed, where the woman lay supine, and Insp. Cutter made a brief examination of her person. Finding no pulse, he desired Insp. Fox to fetch Dr Carmody in his carriage.

Insp. Fox expressed some dissatisfaction at this request, noting that he had gone out of his way as it was. He took the view that J Division need render no further assistance in the matter of 'some old dear who got herself smothered by a burglar', and that the police surgeon should not be troubled.

Insp. Cutter took a moment to confer with Insp. Fox at the head of the stairs. A discussion took place, during which Insp. Cutter [*stricken out*] and a good deal of [*stricken out*] was heard. The matter was resolved to the satisfaction of both parties.

When Insp. Fox had taken his leave, Insp. Cutter directed the present officer to document the scene as faithfully as he might, since the expense of engaging a photographer would not be countenanced by the Yard in the present circumstances. The following observations were made between 8.06 p.m. and 9.03 p.m., when Dr Carmody arrived to begin his examination.

The wrought iron bedstead had been dragged from the wall and left at an irregular angle. A number of boxes kept beneath it had been opened or tipped over. The nightstand had been upset and a chest forced open, with items of clothing and bed linen from same left heaped on the floor.

A window pane had been smashed from the outside, leaving a qty. of glass scattered about the floor, and the lower sash had been raised to a height sufficient for a man to enter. The roof of an outhouse in the yard below was seen to offer a route by which an intruder might have gained access to the upper storey.

A sheet that had covered the remains of the deceased was drawn back, though they were not otherwise disturbed pending the surgeon's arrival. The lady's night attire did not appear to have been disturbed. She had been clutching at the bedclothes prior to her death, but her posture was otherwise unremarkable and the inspector noted that there were no obvious signs of struggle.

On closer inspection, the skin of the woman's face was found to be discoloured to a striking degree. The mouth was fixedly open, and the lips were contorted as if they had been arrested in the midst of some urgent utterance. The eyes were protuberant and markedly bloodshot. They remained open and staring, as if fixed on some lingering apparition that was visible only to the dead.

XII

Octavia made the journey to Whitechapel by cab, since the weather had worsened and Georgie had no bicycle of his own. He had often offered to accompany her when she went out in the evenings, and until now she had always declined, but she could hardly refuse him when he had gone to such trouble on her account.

'I will keep out of your way, sister,' he said, by way of a concession. 'You will hardly know I am about. But it makes me easier in mind, I must say, for there is no telling who might have had a hand in such a thing, and who might be about the place yet.'

In fact she was content to have him with her. The day had left her oddly dispirited, and Georgie's natural diffidence made him an undemanding companion, even when she herself was distracted and silent. The carriage was musty and cramped, and their progress seemed intolerably slow. In Whitechapel High-street, a brewer's dray had pitched over, drawing a crowd that blocked the way, and when they had stood for nearly ten minutes without so much as turning a wheel, Octavia could bear the confinement no longer.

'We will do as well by walking, Georgie,' she said, gathering her belongings. 'We might be sitting here for an hour at this rate.'

He followed her without protest, pausing only to pay the driver for his trouble, but ventured to suggest, as they turned into Osborn-street, that they might keep by the shopfronts on the better-lit side. 'Not to tell you your business, sister, which I keep from as much as I can, but we are not in Mayfair now. There are streets hereabouts I would not wander into even with half a ship's company at my back.'

They were watched, as they passed, from the shadows beneath the stained awnings. A few men whistled, or let out coarse exclamations. Georgie kept close to her, and she noticed the ease with which he carried his bulk. He did not strut or puff himself out, but there was no trace now of the shambling and clumsy youth he had been.

They passed the gates of an iron foundry, where a sparrow was snared in a rut of cooling pitch. A small boy stooped to seize it, trapping its panicked wings and tearing it from its legs. Georgie lunged at him, moved to an unaccustomed fury, but Octavia took hold of his elbow.

'To harm a little bird.' He gave a low growl of disgust. 'A little bird, sister, not two ounces in weight. I keep myself to myself, by and large, but in Malta I laid a fellow out for trapping a plover.'

She led him away, meaning to cross the street, but at that moment a police carriage rattled from the gloom, obliging her to step back. It came close enough, as it passed, that for a moment she met the rather fearsome gaze of one of the officers within. The driver loosed his whip then, and the carriage continued at an alarming clip in the direction of Brick-lane.

'Coppers are in a hurry,' Georgie remarked. 'I wonder if we'll see them where we're going.'

'We ought to lodge a complaint,' Octavia said, oddly unsettled by the policeman's scrutiny. 'Driving like madmen when the road is so poorly lit. They might have killed us. Which way is it, do you know? I don't care for the man in the flat cap who is keeping abreast of us on the far side.'

They turned into Old Montague-street, and from there into a narrow thoroughfare whose name Georgie did not know, but which would allow them – or so he hoped – to cut across to Finch-street. It was a mean and filthy place, hardly more than an alley, and pools of fouled rainwater stretched in parts to almost its full width, obliging them to keep flat against the walls as they passed. It was deserted too, save for a woman in a shuttered doorway who had squatted over a blackened bucket to void herself. They heard screeching behind them as they hurried past, and as the bucket was tipped out, the rasp of iron and the lush slap of filth on the cobbles.

The boarding house stood in a narrow and lightless court, reached from Finch-street by a passageway beneath the eaves of a foundry. The woman who came to the door opened it by a cautious fraction, keeping her shoulder to it as she surveyed the shadows behind them.

'Mrs Campion?'

'Who's asking?'

'Forgive me, Mrs Campion. I am Octavia Hillingdon, and this is my brother, Lieutenant George Hillingdon.'

Mrs Campion studied Georgie, disregarding Octavia's extended hand. 'Gentlemen ain't admitted,' she said.

'Yes, of course, I do understand. That's all right, isn't it, Georgie? You shan't mind waiting?'

Even when Georgie had withdrawn, touching his hat glumly and searching in his coat for a cigarette, Mrs Campion was wary. Octavia introduced herself, but made no mention of the *Gazette*, alluding only to an advantageous position, and to the influence of certain like-minded friends. She had heard of Miss Tatton's disappearance, she said, and wished only to lend whatever aid she could.

'We get all kinds of do-gooders,' Mrs Campion said. 'Not many of them do any good.'

'I had thought of beginning with a donation,' Octavia said, reaching for her reticule. 'I have already made out the cheque. And of course, if more is needed—'

'Don't take that out here.' Mrs Campion looked about the lane again, then shook her head wearily and stood aside. 'You'd best come in for a bit.'

Mrs Campion showed her to a small parlour, where she offered a terse introduction of her own. She had served for some years in the Salvation Army, she said, but had come to the view that while soup and soap were well and good, salvation might just as easily be done without.

'The younger ones get lessons, since it occupies their minds. They are up there now, learning their kings and queens with Mr Critchley. I'd just as soon keep them to the settled way of things, after all the upset.'

'Of course,' Octavia said. 'And if there is anything else that can be done for them, perhaps you will let me know.'

Mrs Campion greeted this with a certain weariness. 'I will put your money to good use,' she said. 'That I can always do. But I must ask, miss. What affair is it of yours? Why should you put yourself about for this of all places, or for our missing girl over all others?'

It was a moment before Octavia could answer. She thought of revealing her own origins, of confiding that she herself, if not for an accident of benevolence, might have led a life much like Miss Tatton's and been left to the same fate. She thought of confessing that her own good fortune was a burden on her conscience; that she tried, almost daily, to persuade herself that she would surrender all she had if not for the hope of putting it to good use; that she tried, but never quite succeeded. But no, she could not bring herself to say these things, and even if she did, she would not have answered the question. Why this girl?

'I simply feel—' She faltered and looked away. 'I feel that I must. That I must *do* something.'

Mrs Campion folded her arms stoutly. She seemed satisfied to have taken Octavia's measure, even if it did not alter her opinion. She named a sum that might relieve certain difficulties, if it could be depended on once a month.

'You might have a seat, miss,' she said, when that much had been agreed upon. 'Though I haven't long to talk, which you must excuse.'

Octavia looked about the parlour, much of which was given over to storage. Canned goods were stacked in the brownish shadows, and cast-off clothing spilled from stacks of orange crates. No fire had been lit, and there was only a single armchair. 'You are very good, Mrs Campion, but I will do very well standing.'

'As you wish, miss.' The woman pursed her lips, her hand straying to her watch pocket.

'I shan't keep you long,' Octavia said. 'You have a great deal to think of, I'm sure, and I don't mean to waste your time. When I spoke of my connections just now, and of certain resources, it was not idle talk. Finding things out is what I do, Mrs Campion. I want to find Miss Tatton, to see her returned safe and well.'

'The police are looking for her, miss. The matter is in hand.'

'The police won't look very hard, Mrs Campion. Not for a missing work girl. You know it as well as I do. But I don't give up so easily. Please, let me help you. Let me help her.'

Mrs Campion considered for a moment, then shook her head in resignation. 'What is it you want to know?'

'When was Miss Tatton missed? Let's begin there.'

Mrs Campion drew a battered ledger from her housecoat. 'That I can tell you exactly, for I am particular about times and such. The girls must be kept to steady hours, if there is to be any hope for them. Now, what is today? The third, is it? No, the second. Yesterday was the first, then, and a working day. Angela Tatton – Angie, as she was known to us – Angie had been found work as a flower-maker. Up Spitalfields way, it was, near the Black Eagle brewery. Flower-making was her mother's trade, while she was living, so the child was born to it, as much as she was born to anything. She made something for my hat, when my sister was married.' Mrs Campion softened a little at the recollection. 'A little spray of quince blossoms, in just the right shade. They might have opened an hour before, to look at them.'

'How lovely,' Octavia said. 'Angie is of good character, then? She has given you no trouble before?'

'She was quick with her tongue, at times, and blew hot and cold, but she was a good-hearted girl. Did her share about the place. Used to sing her little songs, on laundry days and the like.'

Octavia gave an uneasy smile. 'You talk as if she were never to return.'

Mrs Campion studied the wallpaper, where a small deposit of soot attracted her notice. She rubbed at it with the pinched extremity of her sleeve. 'We live in hope, miss. We live in hope, I'm sure.'

'I'm afraid I interrupted you,' Octavia said. 'You mentioned that Miss Tatton had been at work yesterday. When was she expected?'

Mrs Campion pressed her lips together and returned to her ledger. 'Angie worked until eight in the evening, save for Saturdays, and returned here directly most days, but yesterday was a Wednesday, which was Angie's day for an outing. You must give them that much, or you will lose them entirely.'

'Where might she have gone, Mrs Campion, on these outings of hers? Who might she have seen? Did she ever say?'

'She didn't say, miss, and I didn't ask. I have eight girls under this roof. A dozen, if you count the little ones. I will keep them out of the gutter, if I can help it, but I am not fitting them out to marry parsons. As long as they come in that door by half past ten, they may step out with whoever they please.'

'But she didn't, did she? Miss Tatton, I mean? She didn't come back.'

Mrs Campion shook her head. 'I knew it for an ill sign. If it had been one of the other girls, I should hardly have turned a hair. A true stray will never keep to your lap for long, but Angie – I had hopes for her.'

'So, you went to the police?'

'For all the good it will do. As you said yourself, miss, the peelers won't be turning London upside down for a flower-girl. But I did what I could, if only for my conscience.' A clock struck the half-hour somewhere in the house, and the sound it made was thin and dissonant. Mrs Campion glanced about the room, smoothing out a ruck in her apron with the heel of her hand.

'Had Angie any particular friends, Mrs Campion, among the other girls? One or two who might know her ways, to whom she might have confided things?'

Mrs Campion reflected for a moment. 'She had a fondness for Liz Barnsley, one of the little ones. Used to brush her hair, she did, and sing her to sleep. Made a baby of her, you might say, which girls will do sometimes when their own mothers ain't long gone. But she kept to herself, mainly. She was learning her letters, she said. You'd see her sitting in some corner with a book.'

'And the other girls, Mrs Campion? How have they taken the

news? Has it upset them? There must be talk, surely, of what might have become of her?'

Mrs Campion wrung her lips in vexation. 'There is talk, miss, as there might be anywhere. The girls read the papers, them that can, or look at the pictures anyway. They hear stories, as we all do. As you have yourself, I'm sure.'

'And you, Mrs Campion? Have you heard stories?'

The woman crossed her arms again, and her expression hardened. 'I've heard all kinds, miss.'

'But the stories about the Spiriters? You have heard those?'

Mrs Campion looked away, as if something distasteful had been said.

'You don't believe them, then?'

'Believe them? Stories about dark arts and magic potions and stealing souls? I told you, miss, I gave up all that carry-on about salvation. I gave it up because I had no faith left of my own, and I could do no good for anyone by making them false promises. I don't believe in angels, Miss Hillingdon. Why should I start believing in devils?' Mrs Campion crossed to the door and held it open. 'I hope you find her, miss, truly I do. But I've seen a good deal of the world, and it's darker than any of them stories. Men need no magic to do harm. If they did, there would be a good deal less suffering in the world. I will bid you goodnight, miss.'

Octavia followed her to the door, keeping silent as they passed the stairs. Somewhere above them, imperfectly, Mr Critchley was beating time, and the children in faint and uncertain chorus were chanting the names of the dead.

XIII

The home of Dr Carmody was in Portland-place, and it was not until well after ten o'clock that he was finally deposited there. He had found Whitechapel a good deal less congenial than Mayfair, it seemed, and his examination of Mrs Hanley's remains had been conducted rather briskly. By the time he had certified her death and consigned her to the undertakers, he had been left considerably out of countenance, and since then his mood had not lightened.

Inspector Cutter, too, betrayed a strained temper, or impatience at the very least. He had been obliged to engage a cab – Inspector Fox having taken his carriage back to the station – and had hardly uttered a word since boarding it. The journey had passed therefore in unconvivial silence, and Gideon had chosen to occupy himself in the examination of Mrs Hanley's *Book of Common Prayer*. Indeed, he was so much absorbed in this that he failed to notice when Dr Carmody got out, looking up only when Cutter rapped on the door frame to order the driver onwards.

'Do we return home, sir?' said Gideon, marking his page and looking about him in momentary confusion.

Cutter was staring out of the smirched window, worrying at his jawbone with the knuckles of his right hand. He broke off, giving Gideon a sharp look. 'Home, is it?' he said. 'When did you come by a home? In any case, we are doing no such thing. We will proceed directly to London Bridge Station, where we might yet catch the last train for Deal.'

The inspector turned once more to the window, and the ochrish gaslight did little to soften his features. Gideon deliberated for some moments before he spoke again. 'You mean to seek out Lord Strythe, then? At the house he keeps in Kent?'

Cutter pulled out his watch. He shook it vigorously and held it to his ear, glowering at it when this proved unavailing. 'Certainly I do.'

'May I take it—' Gideon's voice faltered, lurching as it still did on occasion into a neighbouring octave. He coughed at some length to disguise his embarrassment. 'May I take it, sir, that the circumstances of Mrs Hanley's death have some bearing upon your thinking?'

The inspector put away his watch. 'You may make of it what you wish, Bliss, as long as you hold your peace while you are about it. I am thinking.'

Gideon wished to say more, but restrained himself with some effort. The inspector settled back in his seat and adjusted his cuff, but it was not long before the signs of irritation returned. He thrust his jaw from side to side, and the muscles of his neck bundled and strained. 'Damn it all, Bliss, can you not sit still?'

'Was I not sitting still, sir?'

'Sitting still? You have not stopped fidgeting and scratching since we left Bethnal Green. You are like a fellow with eight hands and a case of fleas.'

'Forgive me, sir. I am preoccupied, I fear. I will try not to disturb you again.'

Cutter grunted and returned to his thoughts, but as they turned into Regent-street it was he who broke the silence. 'Well, Bliss,' he said. 'What is it you're so preoccupied with? Your little match girl, I suppose?'

'I am thinking of Miss Tatton, yes. I am gravely concerned for her. But it is not only that. I have been giving thought to our discoveries of this evening.'

'Have you now?' Cutter arranged himself as if to enjoy a spectacle. 'And what did we discover this evening, tell me, beyond learning that Dr Carmody comes out in a rash if he is made to venture anywhere east of Holborn?'

Gideon straightened and cleared his throat. 'Well, sir, I can give you only my untutored impressions, and no doubt you will correct me where I go wrong. We learned the cause of death, to begin with, which the surgeon gave as mechanical asphyxiation. This seems to put it beyond question that Mrs Hanley was murdered.'

'Yes, Bliss. The lady did not break her own window and smother herself. I believe we are on firm ground there.'

'Yes, sir. And her death occurred, in Dr Carmody's view, at some time between midnight and noon today. That is to say, she was killed the morning after her sister's death at Strythe House.'

The inspector joined his fingertips before him. 'And what do you infer from that?'

'Well, sir, I suppose we must allow that we can infer nothing at all, and that the two events may count as nothing more than unhappy coincidence. But it seems to me that a degree of suspicion is warranted.'

'A degree of suspicion is always warranted, Bliss. I wake up in the morning with a degree of suspicion. I look at you with a degree of suspicion, God knows. But you must have more than that to prove a case. Our friend Inspector Fox takes the view that this was no more than a common burglary. He believes that some local gonoph put a pillow over Mrs Hanley's face so that he might tumble out her drawers in peace. What do you say to that?'

'Well, sir,' said Gideon cautiously. 'The house was left in considerable disorder, as might be expected in such a case. However, it seemed to me that a good many items of value had been left untouched. There was the sewing machine, for instance, which Inspector Fox judged to be of some worth.'

'A sewing machine is a heavy article. A fellow cannot easily heave it over his shoulder.'

'I suppose not. But there was fine clothing in the workroom that might have been taken, and in the kitchen there was a quantity of tea and sugar and other such provisions. A thief broke into my own room at Cambridge, sir, and made off with all I had in the way of tea and sugar. I was obliged to go without for some weeks afterwards, and it is a thing that has stayed with me.'

'You have passed through a vale of tears, God help us. Anything else?'

'Well, let me see—'

'Begin where the killer began. Where did he begin?'

'Begin, sir?'

'Where did he come in, Bliss?'

'Why, he came in by the bedroom window, surely, which we found broken.'

'No, Bliss, he came in by the front door. The victim's sleep was not disturbed until he was upon her, which tells us that he came in quietly. Coming in quietly means coming in the front door, since there is none to the rear. In any case, it was the wrong window.'

'Sir?'

'He broke the wrong window. A thief is like running water, Bliss. He follows the easiest course. A man standing in the yard would have had the kitchen window directly before him. Why would he haul himself up onto the outhouse? Out of an adventurous spirit?

No, it was the wrong window. Not only that, it was the wrong pane. If you are trying to come in a sash window, you break a pane near the centre, the better to reach the lever. But no, our man put in the bottom left pane. That is what you do when you are standing inside with the sash raised, reaching out with your hammer. A nice gentle tap he gave it, too, so as not to do himself an injury.'

To demonstrate his point, Cutter worked open the window of the carriage, reaching out and rapping at the glass from the other side.

'Goodness,' said Gideon, starting a little at the brisk influx of night air. 'That is an admirable bit of deduction, sir.'

Cutter gave a grunt, still tapping absently. 'I do not like it, Bliss. I do not like it one bit.'

'No, sir. It is a sad business.'

The inspector stared at him. 'I am talking about the particulars of the crime, you witless coot.'

'Of course, sir.'

'I do not like it, Bliss. I didn't like it to begin with, because I had been hoping to find Mrs Hanley safe and well, or as near to well as a bedridden woman may be. I had been hoping she would tell me, after a bit of wheezing and blubbing, that her poor sister had been at her wit's end over money or a married beadle, that she was in pain day and night from a tumour or heard voices in her head. I did not mind about the ins and outs of the thing, in all honesty, as long as it was bad enough for Miss Tull to fling herself from a height.'

'But you were given no satisfaction in that regard, sir.'

'No, Bliss, I was not. I was given no satisfaction at all. I was given another dead woman. What is worse, I was given a murderer who knew his business, but who did just enough wrong to niggle at me.'

'Why do you say that he knew his business, sir, when you have pointed out his mistakes?'

'It is no easy matter to kill a person, Bliss, even an ailing woman. It is not like the penny shows, where a fellow gets a clout or a jab in the ribs and keels over without a fuss. People struggle and thrash. They make you work at it. And to smother a woman where she lies, so that the bedclothes are hardly disturbed – that is another thing again. The fellow who did that is a black-hearted bastard, but he knows what he is about.'

Gideon considered all of this. 'There is something I do not follow, sir. How did he come in quietly by the front door? Did he pick the lock, do you suppose?'

'It cannot be ruled out, certainly. In other circumstances, I would be leaning towards that explanation. But in this case, there is a simpler one. Who would have had a key to the front door, Bliss?'

Gideon sat up. 'Miss Tull, sir.'

'There you are. Miss Tull had a key to her own front door, we may be sure. And yet there was no key among her personal effects, which I got from our friend Mr Carew during your fit of the vapours. You will find everything present and correct, he said, which would be well and good if I had asked him. I had not asked him, however, and when a fellow volunteers a thing like that, you may take it as a certainty that something is missing. I took the trouble to make an inventory, therefore – I was at it when you woke up this afternoon, as you may recall – and I found all manner of implements, but not a single key.'

'Mr Carew, sir – you don't suppose that he—'

'There is not much I like about Carew, Bliss, but he could not rise to the likes of this. The man can hardly climb a flight of stairs. No, he may well have procured the key – that is more in his line – but if he did he left it to others to make use of it.'

'To Lord Strythe, sir? To his master?'

'Or someone acting for him. To a man, at any rate, who was in the way of making things happen promptly. To a man who did not care a great deal for what Esther Tull might have confided to her sister, as long as her sister could confide it to no one else, and who was anxious, perhaps, to know what might have been concealed in their home. We cannot say yet whether His Lordship answers that description, but we have grounds enough for wishing to speak with him. Since no trace can be found of him here in town – and I have had reliable people looking, you may be sure – I believe we will try his house in Kent.'

Gideon fell silent for a time, gazing out at the darkened streets as he gave thought to all the inspector had said. He had not taken his bearings for some time, and he felt a jolt of alarm when he caught sight of the Monument, rising stern and singular among the slow veils of snow. Straining to look ahead, he glimpsed the lamps of London Bridge and felt a mournful throb of remembrance. These were the very streets they had walked, he and Miss Tatton, only the summer before. Just around the corner – not two minutes away, if he were to get out and walk – was the church of St Magnus-the-Martyr, where he had first seen her.

'No,' he said, somewhat startled by the abrupt resolve in his own voice. 'We cannot leave yet.'

Cutter regarded him with frank amazement. 'Come again?'

'Forgive me, sir, but we cannot leave London yet, not without looking for Miss Tatton. Or if you insist on continuing, you must do so without me. I will leap from the cab if I must.'

'You will what? I have shown a good deal of patience, Bliss, but this goes beyond all. Have you not a teaspoonful of wits? Have you no notion at all of your good fortune in being taken in as you have?'

'I am in your debt, sir, and I mean to repay your confidence, but surely you see that I am bound in honour? Miss Tatton has no one else in the world. I cannot simply turn my back on her.'

'You cannot turn your back on me either, you maundering little weasel, and if you do I will kick your arse. We are in the middle of an investigation. I will not be distracted from it.'

'But finding Miss Tatton is not a distraction from the investigation. On the contrary, it is essential to it. Lord Strythe is mixed up in something, sir – something he fears will come to light now that Miss Tull's death has brought his household under scrutiny – and someone, it appears, is willing to go to great lengths to keep his secrets safe. Miss Tatton is in danger, sir. My uncle knew it, and he protected her for as long as he could, but he never learned who his adversaries were. That was left to Miss Tull to reveal, and though she gave her life to do so, it came too late to help him.'

Cutter shook his head in dissatisfaction. 'It is speculation, Bliss. There is a flash of style about it, I will grant you that, but it is speculation all the same. There is not a shred of evidence to support it.'

Gideon turned the book over in his lap. Dusting it with his sleeve, he passed it solemnly to the inspector. 'I believe there is, sir.'

'What is this now?'

'It is the *Book of Common Prayer*, sir, which I found by Miss Tull's bed, along with her Bible. I took it into evidence, and made a note to that effect. I hope I did not do wrong.'

'That depends, Bliss, on what you found in it.'

Gideon cleared his throat. 'I have marked a page, sir, in the Order for Evening Prayer. You will find that a line has been underscored, and an annotation made in the margin.'

The inspector put a broad fingertip to the page. He considered it for a moment in grave silence, then looked away in thought.

'The same words,' he said at length. 'The words from that prayer of yours.'

'From the *Magnificat*, yes. And the words in the margin, sir – you see their significance?'

'"For H.N. – Because I cannot write."'

'For Herbert Neuilly, sir. My uncle's name was—'

'I know what his name was, you chattering streak of gannet's shite. What does it mean?'

'Why, it bears out what he told me in his letter – that he feared his post was being opened, and if he believed that to be the case, he would surely have warned the allies he mentioned. It means, sir, that because Miss Tull could not write to him, she resolved to leave her final testimony by some other means. You said yourself, sir, that the man who broke into her home likely wished to know what Miss Tull might have concealed there. We do not know what else he may have found, but it seems he did not trouble himself to examine this book. For that much we may be thankful, I think.'

'Neuilly knew her, then, this Esther Tull? She was the seamstress he spoke of?'

'I am convinced of it, sir.'

'But how? How would he have come to know such a woman?'

'I cannot say with certainty, but it is not so difficult to imagine. Suppose that she had come to suspect the nature of her employer's activities; that foul acts were being committed against young women, and that she herself had been made a party to them, if only in a small way. She was a pious woman, plainly. She might have confided in a clergyman – the priest of her own parish, let us say – who might in turn have directed her to my uncle. My uncle told me little of his work, but it was well known to others, it seems. She hinted at her predicament – that much we know from his letter – but was too much in fear to reveal all she knew. And perhaps it was not only that; perhaps she was resolved already to act as she did – to end matters as she did. In any case, she gave him to understand that she would find a way. And she did, it seems. She found a way.'

Cutter tapped at the page for a moment longer, then slapped the book closed. 'Blast it!' he said, tossing the volume back to Gideon. 'Blast it to hell.'

Gideon shifted in his seat.

'It will not do if we ever come to stand before a judge, but it is more than we can overlook. What a cursed nuisance you are.' He drew in a breath that might have filled a weather balloon, emitting it again with effortful evenness. 'Very well, damn it. We will go and inquire after your match girl, though I ought to be clapped into a strait-suit for allowing it.'

'Inspector, I cannot begin to—'

'Oh, you can begin right enough. It is leaving off that seems to tax you. In any case, you may stow away your sermon for now. We will inquire after your match girl, Bliss. We will begin at the church, in case there is any trace to be found of her there, and we will spend the night at it if we must. If there is any word to be had of her, for good or ill, we will find it out, on that you may depend. But come the morning, we must be on the first train to Kent. Do you hear me? No matter what we have learned of your little crossing-sweeper, you will be required to conduct yourself at last like an officer of the Metropolitan Police. From now on, you will do your duty like any other sergeant or you will be hauled up for insubordination. Do you hear me, Bliss? Do I have your solemn undertaking?'

Gideon sat up and straightened his lapels. 'You do, sir. My most solemn undertaking.'

'Very good.' The inspector studied him for a moment longer, then thrust his head once more from the window. 'Driver, turn around and go back over the bridge, will you? We are obliged to make a detour.'

XIV

The driver set them down in Wardour-street and was given an hour to take his supper before returning. Inspector Cutter had engaged him for the remainder of the night, since their inquiries might lead them to a good many other places, but he had struck the bargain in a spirit of considerable rancour.

'A shilling and sixpence for the night,' Cutter said, as they stepped down. 'For that price I might have the company of one of Mother Goulding's girls instead, if I went in for such things. And Mother Goulding's girls are a cut above, let me tell you. They are forever reciting sonnets or playing at the harp. I will get my money's worth from him, by God, whether he is needed or not. I will drag him up and down the Caledonian-road, where it is all cobbles still, until the teeth are rattled from his head.'

The inspector continued in this vein for a time, and Gideon allowed his attention to wander. They had come to a long stretch of ironwork palings, and behind them the ground rose in a steep bank to a crest jagged with broken stone. At first Gideon could make nothing of this scene. The street lamps were feeble, and the shapes of things were altered by the soft pervasion of snow. It was only when they turned in at the gate and began climbing the steps that he saw above them the looming bulk of the church tower.

'What is the matter, Bliss?' said Cutter, noting his distracted gaze. 'You are not having a vision, I trust?'

'Forgive me, sir. I did not know the church at first, having entered it by another way, but of course it stands to reason. I passed along an alley that led from Shaftesbury-avenue, and came into it from behind, as it were.'

'Did you, indeed?' Cutter strode ahead, holding up a carriage lamp he had taken from the cabman. 'That seems to be the custom among churchmen. We will come at it by the usual way, though at this hour it will be locked up in any case. We will have to call at the rectory and rouse them from their beds. What was his name, by the way?'

'Pardon me, sir – whose name?'

'The sexton who flung you out, you halfwit. Did you think we came here to ring the bells?'

'He did not give it, sir. He was of a surly disposition, as I believe I mentioned.'

Cutter grunted, and Gideon looked about him with unease. At any time this place might have had a melancholy appearance, but the snow made it seem otherworldly. It had grown insistent now, swooning from the darkness above the bell tower and deepening in patient surges among the broken monuments. He had not considered it before, the way the solid world was made strange by snow, the quiet secrecy it brought to ordinary things.

The church itself was indeed shut up and silent, but beyond it they came to a low annex where a door stood open. A man stood by it, bearing a light of his own. He came forward when he saw them approaching and planted himself in their path.

'What business, there?' he called out. 'Parish ain't open to callers.'

'Cutter of Scotland Yard,' bellowed the inspector in reply. 'State your own business, or I will crack your skull for you and have my sergeant search that boneyard behind us for a hole to put you in.'

The man swung his lantern aside and squinted into the darkness. 'Fuck me if it ain't,' he said. 'Begging your pardon, Inspector Cutter, sir. Constable Canning, sir, here from Little Vine-street with Inspector Warnock. Which it was the inspector posted me here, sir, even though it's a night to take the skin off your bollocks – saving your presence, sir – and gave me orders to let nobody in.'

'Warnock, is it?' said Cutter, coming even with Canning and taking up an easy stance. The constable shifted a little way to the side, casting an uncertain glance at the doorway behind him. 'What is Jack Warnock doing in a church at this hour? He is no great carol singer, to my recollection.'

Canning gave him a keen look. 'You ain't been told, sir?'

'Told what, Canning? Out with it now, and do not try my patience. I have had a whole day of fellows talking in riddles, and I am sick to the gills of it.'

'Yes, sir. Only I thought you was here about the sexton, is what it was. The Yard is known to get across the odd case of ours – which, no disrespect, sir, not being my place.'

'The sexton?' There was a marked asperity in the inspector's tone. 'What does Warnock want with the sexton? I am not a man to make a nuisance of myself among the Divisions, but if he has queered the ground before I speak to him, I will not be accountable for what may follow.'

'Speak to him, sir?' Here Canning glanced at Gideon, as if seeking some assurance that he had not misheard.

'Good Christ,' said Cutter. 'Speak to him, yes. Speak to him. Is there any man left alive in London who can conduct ten minutes' business in plain English?'

'Yes, sir,' said Canning. 'And begging your pardon, sir, only there must have been a mix-up. Maybe it's a different sexton as you was wanting, sir, but this one ain't going to be no use to you.

He was found by the rector this morning with his head bashed in. Sir? Hold up, sir, or I'll catch hell. Inspector Warnock gave the order most particular, sir.'

Cutter was striding towards the door and did not look back. 'This way, Bliss,' he called. 'We need only follow the smell of smoke. Warnock is partial to his cigars.'

Gideon followed the inspector inside, where he paused before a door at the end of a musty passageway. 'You may leave your note-book in your pocket tonight,' Cutter said in a low voice. 'Observe all you can, but make no show of doing so, do you hear? And do not put your oar in on any account, no matter what you hear me say. If this bit of business has anything to do with our case – and I say *if*, mark you – we must give this ignorant mongrel no sign of it. Do you hear me?'

The room they entered was in a disordered state, but it had the appearance of a vestry. In the midst of it stood a stout chest on which the body of a man had been stretched out. A surplice had been draped over his face, but Gideon had only to glance at him to see that he had suffered a death of singular violence. His limbs lay askew, and a gash in his clothing revealed the flesh of his belly. It was bloated and richly bruised, and what survived of his shirtfront was sodden with blood. A sour fug of spirits hung in the air.

Inspector Warnock, identifiable by his cigar, was taking his ease on a dilapidated pew. He squinted at them through a lazing ripple of smoke, but appeared otherwise unconcerned. A younger officer, propped against the opposite wall and gnawing at a heel of bread, regarded them with dull curiosity.

Cutter set down his carriage lamp and clapped his hands to-gether for warmth. 'There you are, Warnock,' he said. 'Looking fit and well, I see. You are a stern cove, I must say, to put a fellow out on post on such a night. Half his face is black with frostbite already, and we must hope it was uglier still than what he is left with. Our friend here was given a fine send-off, I see.'

'What's got you down here on my heels, Cutter?' Warnock said. He leaned briefly aside to expel a shred of tobacco, but made no move to rise. 'We got matters in hand. Me and Sergeant Colley done our spadework here, and now we're just waiting on the surgeon. We had to call for him or the rector would have made a song and dance about it. Ain't nothing fancy about this one, if that's what you're thinking. Some character come in for whatever was in the poor box, I reckon, and this punter here got in the way. Pissed drunk, it looks like. It's plain as day, this one. Ain't getting nobody's name in the paper.'

'You may rest easy, Warnock. I am not coming trampling on your pansies. Take care there, Bliss, the floor to that side is a mire of blood. No, our paths have crossed in innocence, you see. This sexton of yours – what was his name, by the by?'

'Merton,' said Sergeant Colley curtly.

'Merton,' Cutter repeated. 'I am obliged to you, Sergeant. Yes, this Merton was to assist me in a small matter, and I had come here to speak to him. I chose my moment badly, it appears. That is all there is to it, and we will be out from under your feet presently. You will not object if we warm ourselves for ten minutes, though? It is a sharp night out.'

Warnock ground out his cigar against the seat of the pew, pocketing the stunted remainder. He stood, thrusting up his blunt chin as he straightened his tie. 'What's this small matter, then?'

Cutter made a sauntering circuit of the room, keeping his distance from the body. He rested his bulk against a sill, knocking absently at the panelling with his boot heel. 'A bit of paperwork,' he said, consulting his watch as if in idleness. 'I wanted to look over the register of births, to test a claim that a fellow has made in an investigation of fraud. The rector directed me to his sexton. What have we there now, on the floor beneath the victim's head?'

'Load of gin bottles.' Warnock made his reply without looking. 'Our boy here, he'd had a few, like I said, so the bottles was handy. Used them to bash his head in, it looks like. Broke a couple, and all, so watch out for the glass. This rector, then. He tells you to talk to his sexton, but he don't give you a name?'

'Three, if I am not mistaken,' said Cutter, surveying the floor. 'Three broken, that is. And nine remaining. I am not a drinking man myself, but a fellow with that much gin on board would surely never have stirred again, never mind given anyone trouble, and yet he was orderly about lining up his empties. Do you see that, Bliss? There is a tidy bit of work for you – I am trying to instil a bit of neatness in this fellow. You need only look at him to see why. In any case, the rector gave me no name, Warnock, for I took him aside just as he was about to officiate at a wedding and he could spare me only a moment.'

Warnock adjusted his waistband as he considered this, then delivered himself of an emphatic belch. Sergeant Colley, having disposed of his bread, made a mournful examination of his knuckles. Cutter crouched for a moment and took up a corner of the victim's coat, lifting it briefly to his nose.

'Your murderer was not one for half measures, it seems. Half measures, what? And they say I am without a sense of humour. He had – here is another one for you – he had no shortage of bottle. But he must have been thorough enough, all joking aside, if you covered this poor creature's face while you set about your supper.'

Colley looked up, a sourness in his slack features. 'Common decency is all it is. Don't bother me none. I seen as bad as anyone.'

'Good man, Colley,' Cutter said. 'A sergeant should have a good thick hide on him. I only wish this whelp behind me was more like you.'

It was said only to produce an effect, but Gideon felt his colour rise and could not keep from the blinking that he was prone to. He looked down at his shoes.

'Will we give him a look?' Cutter continued, resting a hand for a moment on Colley's forearm. 'Will we see if we can stiffen his spine for him?'

'The surgeon's expected,' Inspector Warnock put in. 'I don't want no poking around the remains until he's done his bit.'

But Colley had already taken up the hem of the surplice. 'He won't touch nothing. Ain't that right, Little Miss Apple-Cheeks? Come over here and let's see about you.'

Gideon looked up, finding all eyes fixed upon him. He approached the chest, the splay of ruined limbs. He averted his gaze, as Colley raised the surplice, and waited for his breathing to settle. Then he looked.

When the inspector emerged from the vestry, Gideon had spent perhaps a quarter of an hour in the company of Constable Canning. For all his officiousness on their arrival, the constable had proved an amiable companion. He had watched with a pitying expression as Gideon staggered from the doorway and braced himself against a plinth, but he had not made sport of his discomfort.

'Get your head down good and low, mate. A few minutes in the fresh air will set you up lovely. I ain't got the stomach for that carry-on myself, and I don't care who knows it. These old bastards let on like it don't take a feather out of them, but you talk to their old ladies – them as still has them, I mean, not like your guvnor – and they'll tell you. Wake up at all hours, they do, screaming fit to bring down the house.'

Gideon looked up. 'My guvnor?' he said. 'Do you mean Inspector Cutter?'

Canning squinted at him, huffing for warmth into his chambered hands. 'Ain't you been told? About his wife? Proper bit of frock, she was, so they say. Which, fuck knows what she ever saw in him. Anyway, she took ill not long after they was married, and your guvnor come home one day to find her stretched out dead. Only it weren't the sickness took her.'

'Not the sickness? What was it, then?'

Canning glanced again in the direction of the rectory. 'Case weren't never solved,' he said, leaning closer and lowering his voice. 'Weren't even a case to solve, some say. But old Cutter maintains he come home one night and found her all tricked out in some fancy white dress he ain't never seen before. Pale as a ghost, she was, but laid out all prim and proper, like she was having her picture taken. Same as them Spiriters do, if you can believe all that bollocks.'

'Spiriters?' Gideon stooped again to retch. 'Who are the Spiriters?'

But Cutter emerged from the rectory before Canning could reply. 'Nah, mate,' he said, straightening and raising his voice again. 'You give me a bit of sentry duty any day. Might be a bit nippy, but I don't mind the cold. The cold don't give you fucking nightmares.'

Gideon brought himself unsteadily upright and hurried after the inspector. Cutter made no mention of his discomfort, much to Gideon's relief, even clapping him on the shoulder in gruff encouragement as he boarded the cab, where the driver – who seemed more amenable since taking his dinner – had set a warming pan beneath their seats and furnished them with a small bottle of brandy.

'There now, Bliss,' the inspector said. 'You know my views in the matter of liquor, I believe, but you might do worse than to take a mouthful or two, in the circumstances.'

Gideon accepted the bottle without meeting Cutter's eyes. He weighed it in his hands for a time, then worked the stopper free and took a cautious draught. The spirit was coarse and scalded his throat, but he welcomed the gentler surge of warmth that spread from his belly. He managed not to cough, and his eyes watered only a little. The inspector passed a hand over his mouth, but kept himself otherwise in check.

'You will last the night, I daresay,' he said at length. 'And you have not had the best medicine yet. Wait until you hear what I squeezed out of our friends from Little Vine-street.'

Gideon turned to the inspector at this, his alertness returning. 'Does it touch on Miss Tatton, sir?'

Cutter settled back with a look of satisfaction. 'Was that not our business in coming back here? I did not put on that little show for the good of my health, you know. Indeed it does, Bliss, though I began with no great hopes, and I had even less when we tripped over Warnock and Colley. They are not much troubled by diligence, as you may have gathered, and what they lack in that department they make up for in suspicion. It was a job and a half to persuade them that I was not coming to put my oar in.

'But once I had them halfway softened up, I inquired a little into the circumstances of Merton's death, though you had only to look at him to form a general notion. He may well have had a few, as they put it, but a church sexton does not buy his Gordon's by the case, surely, or keep his stock in the – what is the name for that part of a church, Bliss?'

'The vestry, sir.'

'In the vestry, yes. That man had taken more than a few, as

anyone could see who had eyes in his head. Every stitch of clothing on his body was drenched with it. And did you mark his swollen belly? The surgeon will find more gin in it, I will wager, than any man ever willingly swallowed. And then to set about him with the empty bottles? There is no shortage of lunatics creeping about these streets, but there are not many who would go to so much trouble over the contents of a poor box.

'In any case, here is what I got from Warnock and his booted monkey of a sergeant. The rector, a fellow by the name of Nathaniel Cusk, came upon the body at about six o'clock this morning. He is an elderly fellow, this rector, and Warnock did not hope for much, but it seems he is a spry customer. I got the gist of his account from them, and he had a good deal to say that interested me, particularly about the evening before the murder.'

'About last night, sir? It was last night that I discovered Miss Tatton in the church.'

'Yes, Bliss, I believe you made mention of it. Well, this Cusk was asked if he had observed anything out of the ordinary last night, and our friends could hardly have wished for a better witness. He is orderly in his ways, it seems, and it is his practice to make all ready for the morning service before retiring. When he set about this last night, he found that Merton – who was usually put to use at such times – had not made an appearance. The rector was obliged to do for himself in the way of hassocks and what have you.

'Now, that was no great calamity, you might think, but it put Cusk's hackles up. This Merton spent half his life propped up in gin shops, by all accounts, and this was by no means his first offence. Cusk went to his quarters and found them locked up, but he took to hammering at the door all the same, having come to the view that Merton was within. Sure enough, the sexton piped up before long, pleading a bout of dysentery or some such thing, and begged leave to keep to his room. The rector did not like this one bit, but he was not minded to drag the man from his pot, only giving Merton warning that he would have more to say in the morning.

'Cusk took himself off to bed, and there matters might have rested, but he was troubled by an abscess on his hip and could not get off to sleep. At some time after eleven, having got up to see about a mug of milk, he chanced to look out into the churchyard, and who should he see, beating a path to the *Seven Bells* across the way? Our friend Mr Merton, large as life, and no more troubled by dysentery than I am myself. Well, Cusk was put on a war footing, as you might imagine. He resolved to turn Merton out for good and all, and to put a sober and dependable fellow in his place.

'Beyond that, Warnock was not inclined to be forthcoming, and I had the distinct impression that there were details he would sooner keep to himself. I have not yet fathomed out his thinking, but whatever it was, he had not taken his sergeant into his confidence, for Colley found his tongue then. But sir, he says, fit to burst, you have not given him the best of it, and by the time Warnock got an elbow to him the damage was done. The rector had his own key to Merton's quarters, Colley said, and once he had caught him out, he marched on them in a fury, intent on packing up the man's belongings and dumping them in the yard before he should think better of it. And so it was that he came to look into Merton's room. No, Bliss, you fear the worst, I see, but put your mind at ease. He came upon your little match girl, right enough, and she was on the poorly side, but living still. The Reverend took her off to the Hospital for Women in Soho-square, not a hundred yards from my own lodgings. She is found, Bliss. She is safe.'

Gideon pressed his eyes shut and sank back in his seat. He

ought to offer a silent prayer in thanksgiving, he knew, but he could not summon the words. He could not raise his face to that emptiness any longer, or offer it his devotion. He drew his sleeve over his cheek and let out a long breath.

'Thank you, Inspector,' he said simply.

Cutter only nodded and lifted his palm.

'But how did she come to be there, sir, in that creature's room? Did Warnock and Colley offer any opinion?'

The inspector shook his head. 'None. And I could not press them much more, since my interest had to seem idle. But you may put your worst fears to rest, I think. He did not harm her, I believe, though I doubt he did much to help her either. My own belief is that he took her there at the bidding of others, and was to confine her until other orders came. It must have been done after he put you out – I found the rag he used, by the by, and he took no chances with the chloroform. It is no wonder you were green about the gills for a while.

'When he had done that much, it seems his thirst got the better of him, for he took himself over the road and did not trouble to remove you until he returned the next morning. By then we may suppose that those he answered to had returned, only to find the girl sprung from her cell and Merton missing from his post. They lay in wait for him, I expect, and when he put in an appearance at last, well, it seems they gave him a bit of a talking-to. Now, much of this is supposition, as you yourself might call it, which in the normal course I would keep to myself, but since the matter touches you personally I make an exception. There is a good deal we do not know, Bliss, but we are not finished just yet. We will speak to your little paramour shortly, and she will give us her own account of all of this.'

'Yes, sir.' Gideon looked away as he contemplated this encounter.

'Yes, sir, I very much look forward to it.'

Cutter's expression took on an unusual mildness. 'Are you sure, Bliss? You are not having second thoughts now, surely, after all your pining?'

Gideon sat up. 'Oh, no, sir. There is nothing I wish for more. I was only thinking of the last time I saw Miss Tatton. Not in the church, I mean, but before that. There were certain matters that I – that is to say, there were things I might have—'

Cutter drew up an eyebrow. 'There was unfinished business between you, is that it?'

Gideon inclined his head. He spread his hands on his knees and plucked at the poor cloth of his trousers. 'Yes, sir,' he said quietly. 'There were things I should have said. It will surprise you, perhaps, since I am apt to say too much – it is a failing you have remarked on yourself – but there were times when my fault was to say nothing at all.'

XV

On the last day, when Miss Tatton came out onto the back steps, Gideon had been waiting for almost an hour. It was foolish of him, he knew, since she could not leave before the housekeeper did, and it was while they were within the precincts of the church that they were most at risk of discovery. At any moment, he felt sure, his uncle might come into view at the corner of Thames-street, though Gideon had scarcely seen him since three nights before. He might chance to look out from some upper window, having returned by another way, just as Gideon and Miss Tatton stole away.

When at last she appeared, he was in a state of considerable anxiety. He sprang from behind a pamphlet-seller's stand, causing Miss Tatton to start in fright, and hurried away at once in the direction of London Bridge-wharf, urging her in a sharp whisper to follow him.

'Why, young master,' she said gaily. 'There's a fuss over nothing. Anyone would think you was wanted for murder.'

Gideon glanced nervously over his shoulder, but kept up his pace. 'Will you not pull up your shawl, miss? We might be seen by anyone. I will not feel easy in my mind until we are a good way from the church.'

Miss Tatton laughed aloud. 'I'll do no such thing. It's not a shawl neither, it's a muslin scarf. What do I want a shawl for on a day like this?'

'Scarf, then,' Gideon said, with more abruptness than he had intended. 'Only do please cover your face.'

'Now, you just stop your gallop,' Miss Tatton called after him.

Gideon turned to face her, berating himself already for his want of composure.

'You see this scarf?' she said.

Gideon nodded mutely. They had crossed the street so that she was in sunlight, and he could not think how he had paid her no attention until now. She wore an afternoon dress of primrose yellow with a pretty and intricately fashioned shirtwaist. The scarf was a delicate ivory-coloured thing, folded about her shoulders so as to catch the bright spill of her hair. These were finer clothes than she could have afforded, he knew – finer, certainly, than his own – and no doubt she had gone to some trouble even to come by them for the day.

'I spent half the morning starching this scarf,' she said. 'And the rest of this lot. Half the morning. And it weren't like I had nothing else to do. You may take no notice if you like – and Lord knows you lollop about the place in a daze – but you ain't dragging me straight off into the shadows. We're going this way, if you please. If you're going to step out with a girl, the least you can do is take her to the market and buy her an orange.'

Gideon might have been stricken with panic at this, having come near to penury as the week drew to a close. He had not made bold enough to raise the matter with his uncle, but he had recognised nonetheless that he must make some provision. That morning, though it had filled him with shame and apprehension, he had taken Mr Richardson's *Pamela* from his uncle's shelves. He had wrapped the volumes in a flour sack and lugged them all the way to Cecil-court, where a bookseller had examined their gilt-ribbed spines and – with a look of penetrating contempt – had counted out the sum of eight shillings and sixpence.

It was no great fortune, but he had often subsisted on less for a fortnight. He felt a painful want of experience in such matters, but it would be enough, surely, to keep him from outright embarrassment. And so they went first to Billingsgate Market, whose arcade was lined with traders of all kinds. From a Spaniard whose baskets were brilliant with samphire and limes, Gideon bought a plump pair of tangerines. When they had eaten these – Miss Tatton first scratched the skin with a thumbnail, breathing the zest with a delighted swoon – they wandered about the great market hall itself, emptying at this hour, and found a nook in the basement where cockles and periwinkles could still be had, served in blunt cornets of newspaper and smelling brightly of the sea.

From the market, with no object in mind, they set out westwards, passing at an easy pace along Cannon-street and lingering by the cathedral, where a gentle apricot light touched the dome and the colonnades. The evening was warm and mildly reeking, but a light air could be felt even at this remove from the river. In Fleet-street a flower-seller stopped them, declaring that the lady must have a posy, for shame. In his embarrassment Gideon handed over sixpence for a spray of blooms he hardly glanced at, and such was his haste to be away that he very nearly tumbled into the open cellar of a pub.

Miss Tatton did not laugh openly, and when she covered her mouth she pretended that it was only to bring the flowers to her nose. Gideon trudged on in abject silence, keeping a little way ahead so that she could not see his face.

'Here,' she called after him. 'You should see them, at least, since you paid such a fortune for them.'

There was gaiety in her voice, but not unkindness. He stopped and turned, keeping his face a little averted. The heat had not yet faded from his cheeks.

'Come and have a sniff,' she said, gently now. 'Such a treat, sweet-peas are. Nothing nicer, except for jasmine, maybe. Here, come in close.'

She held out the blossoms, sheltering them with her free hand. Gideon approached shyly, bowing in hesitant increments to the well of fragrant air.

'Oh,' he said softly. The petals were pretty – deep blush and indigo – but the scent had its own colour, almost, a hidden milky glimmer. Unthinkingly, he raised his own hand to hers, and in the same moment she inclined her head. A slip of her hair fell, soft and intricate against his wrist.

'See?' she said, almost whispering. 'Nothing like it.'

Gideon took a slow breath. He tried to be still, to alter nothing in the world.

Miss Tatton came upright, and took a moment to pin the sweet-peas to her dress. Gideon recovered his wits as he waited, and grew mindful once more of keeping the appearance of propriety. A man stood watching them, or so he fancied, from a little way behind. The street was a good deal obscured by steam, since the doors of a printing works stood open in the heat, but beneath the clock of a newspaper office a figure had halted, his brownish silhouette made faint by the vapour. Gideon glanced at Miss Tatton, who now stood waiting, and when he looked back the man was gone.

They carried on towards the Strand, and Gideon must have looked back more than once, for presently Miss Tatton nudged him with her elbow. 'You looking out for the coppers again?' she said. 'Don't you worry, young master. I'll tell them you couldn't have done it. I'll tell them you were with me the whole time.'

She elbowed him gently, and Gideon could not help but laugh with her.

'Don't you worry about your uncle,' she said. 'Old Nelly's up Whitechapel way, I'm told, seeing about lodgings. That's where I'm to be sent, he says. Can't stay where I was no more.'

He considered this in silence for a moment. 'And why is that, miss, if I may? Is it because he believes you are not safe?'

She tutted impatiently, quickening her step a little.

'Miss Tatton?' Gideon hurried after her, skipping clear of a sweeper's brush. 'Forgive me, but what is it that he wants to keep you safe from?'

'Safe?' Miss Tatton glanced at him, but kept up her pace. 'Ain't much that's safe, young master, when a girl must work for a living.'

'It grieves me to hear it,' Gideon said. 'Truly, it does. But I believe you meant something different, miss, or my uncle did. Did you not say, when we spoke last evening, that he did not want you to be seen walking abroad? What is it that he fears?'

She glanced at him, and her look was quick and measuring. 'Your old uncle,' she said, after a moment. 'He means well, as far as I can tell, and he's done right by me. He has some peculiar notions, maybe, but he keeps me in clean lodgings, and puts me under honest masters, which not every girl can say. I don't know why he bothers, if you want to know the truth. It's the work he was put here to do, so he says. You stop wondering about the why of it.'

Gideon puzzled over this, and was about to pursue the matter of his uncle's 'peculiar notions', but Miss Tatton chose at that moment to cross the street, gathering in her skirts and skipping lightly from the kerb. She darted behind a tinker's cart, and for a moment he lost sight of her. When he caught up, on the far side of the road, he was disconcerted and a little out of breath.

'Miss Tatton?' he called after her. 'I did not give any offence, I hope?'

She half-turned as she walked, raising her face to the mild light. 'We're going to the duck pond,' she said.

Gideon hurried to her side. 'The duck pond, miss?'

'It's my day out, young master, in case you've forgotten. I want to feed the ducks, while it's still nice and light. I'm fond of ducks. You ain't going to tell me you're not fond of ducks?'

She looked at him from beneath the brim of her bonnet, and there was more in her look – slyness and resolve, a testing levity – than he could easily disentangle.

'Oh no, miss,' he said, finding himself flustered again. 'I hold them in the highest regard.'

Miss Tatton's duck pond, it transpired, was a grand body of water in the grounds of St James's Park. They stopped on the way to buy a loaf of bread and, keeping half for the ducks, they passed the remainder between them as they went along, talking easily of his uncle's peculiar table manners, or of the likely fate of his housekeeper's husband. Gideon watched Miss Tatton when he could, guardedly and at cautious intervals. There were habits of hers, small gestures that he came to recognise. Her way, when she was bored, of swinging her arms in loose arcs, or of raising her wrist – inflected just so – when something moved her to laughter. In all of this there was a strange charge of giddiness. It occurred to him that even this faint intimacy was unfamiliar, that in all his life he had never paid such close attention to another living soul.

They turned for home at seven o'clock, returning by way of the river. The sun was declining as they passed through Victoria Embankment Gardens, kindling the tired willows and glazing the flanks of the birches. Before them on the footpaths their shadows splayed and crossed.

They spoke freely now, after a fashion, having come to it by accidents and false starts, and although they talked of inconsequential things – of fashioning petals from scraps of cambric, or of the perils of sneezing in a cathedral – it seemed to Gideon that their conversation was directed by hidden means. Miss Tatton did not prompt him to say when he might return, but he found himself brought to that subject by a sequence of disconnected remarks. Likewise, when he spoke of the prospects of a young churchman, and of his likely circumstances if he were to secure a small living, he could not tell what had led him to it.

The sun was setting when they came at last to London Bridge, and although they knew they must shortly return to his uncle's lodgings, they turned and lingered at the parapet. Looking out over the river, they watched its surface cleave and fold in the slow wake of the barges, turning from copper and violet to rosewood and pewter, syrup and ash.

'Perhaps I'll learn my letters after all,' Miss Tatton said after a long silence. 'Just in case.'

'I do hope so,' Gideon said, deliberating over his words. 'Not that it is any failing, of course. I mean, that is, if circumstances prevent it.'

'It won't matter, though.' She glanced down at the foreshore, where a gaggle of children roved, combing the broad expanse of mud that the tide had uncovered.

'Why do you say that, miss? It can only be to your advantage, surely.'

Miss Tatton squinted, her eye drawn to some glimmering place on the shore. 'I meant it won't matter to us. It don't happen overnight, does it. That Pamela had her whole life to learn. I won't be writing letters any time soon. Or reading yours.'

'Scripture teaches us patience,' Gideon said, unable to think of anything less feeble to say. 'Jacob served seven years for Rachel, but to him they seemed but a few days because of his . . . well, because of the nature of his feelings.'

She looked at him keenly. 'You're not like him, young master. You're not your uncle, and I like it better when you don't pretend to be. You were put on this earth for other things. For better things. Ain't that so?'

Gideon took off his hat. He studied it for a moment before meeting her eyes. 'I believe so, miss. I believe you are right. And yet – well, I should not complain of my lot, I know, but I am not as free to choose as you might suppose. Such prospects as I have depend on doing as I am bid.'

'I know that much,' Miss Tatton said. 'I know what your uncle wants for you, and what he don't want too. And if he thought you had any notions to the contrary, I know what he'd tell you.'

'Yes, miss.' He passed a hand over his hair, finding it disordered from the heat of the day. 'I know what he would tell me. But I will not always be so beholden. A time will come, perhaps, when I may . . .'

He extended his free hand towards the water, describing a vague arc of liberty, and as he did so a cry reached them from the shore below. Miss Tatton leaned out to look, and a ruck in her hem disclosed a stockinged fraction of her calf. Gideon fidgeted with the brim of his hat, crushing the felt against the heat of his palm. In an instant of panic, he realised that she had spoken.

'Pardon me, miss,' he said, coming to her side. 'Is something the matter?'

'He's got something,' she said, pointing to the foreshore. 'Something for us, he says.'

Gideon stared in puzzlement. Below them, ankle-deep in the mud, stood the ragged figure of a boy. He was perhaps ten or eleven years old, though he was so much obscured by filth that it was hard to be sure, and he held something aloft. 'Who is he?' he said in bemusement. 'Who are these children?'

Miss Tatton gave him a quick and pitying glance. 'Mudlarks,' she said. 'They go about the shore when the tide is out, rooting in the mud.'

'Rooting for what?' Gideon said, half-disbelieving still.

'Anything that'll fetch a few coppers. Coal, mostly, or bits of rope, but sometimes they get lucky.' She made a funnel of her hands. '*Bring it up here, then! Let's have a look!*'

The boy called back in answer, but Gideon could not make out his words. 'We'll have to take it off him,' Miss Tatton explained. 'If he's to come all the way up.'

Gideon blinked, uncomprehending.

'You never know, young master.' She cuffed him lightly and raised her face to his, gilded softly by the low sun. 'It might be nothing. Or it might be treasure.'

She turned back to the boy and waved him ashore, watching eagerly as he climbed to the wharfside. Gideon was glad of the returning lightness in her mood. He felt a furtive gratitude, too, at the timeliness of the distraction. He did not know quite what it was that he had begun to say, or how he might finish it with any credit.

The boy scurried along the bridge, slowing as he drew near them and coming to a halt a yard or two off. He was a diminutive and wary creature, but with a decorous way about him for all the squalor of his appearance. 'I'll stop here,' he said, 'for I don't smell too handsome. I'll leave it here once you put down the price of it.'

'The price of what?' Gideon said.

The mudlark opened a blackened palm, showing the dull gleam of a misshapen coin. 'Crooked sixpence, sir. Which it looked like you was wanting a token.'

Miss Tatton raised her wrist, but withheld her laughter.

'A token?' Gideon repeated the words in frank bewilderment. 'A token of what?'

The boy looked to each of them in turn, his soiled face inscrutably creased. 'Ain't you making your promises? You and the young lady? What else you stood here for in your courting clothes?'

'Courting clothes?' Gideon said dully.

The boy turned to Miss Tatton. 'He all right, is he? Tell him he's got to take it now, one way or the other. That was the bargain.'

'Yes, very well.' Gideon stepped forward, anxious to bring this fresh embarrassment to an end. 'How much do you want for it?'

'Sixpence, innit,' the boy said. 'Like for like, when they're in good nick. Which, I'm actually going easy. Little beauty, that one is.'

'*Sixpence*?' Gideon was incredulous, but it was clear now that he must appear either foolish or miserly. He put down a bright new coin, and in an instant the boy had replaced it.

'Gentleman,' he said, touching his sodden cap. 'Might as well use it as not, you ask me. She's a pretty one, and the likes of you will do no better. Give you joy of it.'

With that the boy darted away, and when Gideon snatched up the token he did so only out of an unthinking urge to have it out of sight. It was hardly a creditable way to bring the matter to an end, but he could see no other course that would not deepen his humiliation. He returned to Miss Tatton's side without uttering a word. Still clutching the coin, he leaned on the parapet and stared out in dejection at the declining colours of the evening.

Gently, impossibly, her fingertips grazed his knuckles. 'Well, young master. It's getting late.'

He turned to her slowly. She did not look up at once, and when she did her expression was both teasing and solemn. He hesitated, then turned his hand under hers, carefully uncurling his fingers. 'Will you not call me by my name at last, and let me call you by yours?'

She pressed her lips together. 'You ain't caught on yet, have you?'

'Forgive me, caught on to what?'

'Oh, God bless us all. You're meant to give that to me.'

'The sixpence? But it's crooked, and filthy besides. Surely it's worthless?'

'Well, it ain't worth sixpence, I can tell you that much. There's a lot they don't teach you up in Cambridge, young master. It's a token. It's what people give – you know, when they ain't got the price of a ring.'

'Ah.' He blinked, a heat flourishing in his chest. 'Yes, of course. I'm afraid I didn't quite—'

'You never do, do you?' She traced a circle on his palm, not yet touching what he held. 'Well, Mr Gideon Bliss? What is my name to be?'

She held his eyes, and he could no longer pretend that he did not understand. He would be worthy soon, he hoped, would offer her everything. But until then he could not give the answer she wanted.

'Not Angela?' he said. He felt a sour shame now that thickened his speech. '*Angela mea.* "My angel", it means. It is Latin.'

Her gaze was steady and searching still, but she smiled a little. 'You're a funny one,' she said. 'One minute you can hardly get a word out, the next you're saying it all. And still saying nothing.'

He flushed again, and made an indistinct sound.

'It's all right,' she said. 'It's nice. But everyone calls me Angie. Angie Tatton in ribbons of satin. It's what my – when I was little. It's what they used to say.'

'Angie, then,' Gideon said. 'May I call you Angie?'

'Well,' she said. In the heat of his palm, her fingertip traced a dwindling volute. 'I suppose it'll have to do.'

XVI

Soho-square was no great distance from Wardour-street, yet the journey seemed interminable. The carriage laboured through the mired streets at hardly more than walking pace, and in the thickening snow the life of the place seemed strangely lulled, its ashen somnolence slowing all movement almost to stillness.

But when they reached the hospital at last, Gideon was like a man set free from a prison. He leapt from the cab before the driver had set out the step, skidding a little in the slush of the gutter but righting himself at once and surging towards the steps. He presented himself to a porter, not even turning to see if Cutter was behind him, and announced their purpose firmly, asking to be shown at once to Miss Tatton's bedside.

He paced the floor as they waited, while the inspector – who had come in quietly and seemed content for now to let him make the running – took his ease with a newspaper in the porter's own chair. It was Gideon who greeted the doctor in attendance when he appeared, and who demanded to be taken up to the wards with all possible haste.

The doctor drew out his spectacles, fitting them after some fumbling to the bridge of his nose. He was pale and thin, and somewhat disordered in his appearance.

'You must excuse me,' he said. 'The porter did not give me your names.'

Cutter rose from his place at this. 'Inspector Cutter of the Yard,' he said. 'Sergeant Bliss here is the soul of politeness, as a rule, but he's taken a good rattling.'

Cutter extended a hand, and the doctor clasped it briefly. 'Usher. Dr Samuel Usher.'

'You must forgive the lateness of the hour, Doctor,' Gideon said, offering his own distracted handshake. 'There is a young girl in your care, we believe, who may be of assistance in a police matter – in a police matter of considerable urgency.'

'Indeed?' said Dr Usher. 'Such things cannot be avoided entirely, I am afraid. We open our doors to those of all walks, you see. If you give me her name, I will have her brought down. She will forfeit her place, naturally.'

'You have the wrong end of the stick, sir,' said Cutter. 'The girl in question is wanted on no charges. She is the victim of wrongdoing, if anything. Her name is Tatton, Angela or Angie. It was the Reverend Cusk of St Anne's parish who brought her in.'

'Miss Tatton?' Usher blinked at each of them in turn. 'You believe *she* can assist you?'

'Is there cause to think otherwise?' Cutter said.

Dr Usher let out a weary breath and considered them for a time in silence. The vestibule was poorly lit, and his face was half in shadow. 'Come with me,' he said at length. 'See for yourselves.'

The hospital was a dim and sprawling place, bigger by far than it appeared from without. Usher led them up several flights of stairs, then conducted them through a warren of dismal passageways. The wards were hushed at this hour, and they hardly glimpsed a single soul. They climbed still higher, into the lightless upper reaches of the building. The air was cold here, and tainted with the sad must of abandoned rooms.

'God help us, Doctor,' the inspector called out at last. 'Have you consigned the poor child to an attic?'

Usher glanced over his shoulder but made no reply. He reached into his coat, and presently he came to a halt before a door, bending in the gloom to rattle a key into the lock. The ward they entered was orderly in its appearance, but it seemed entirely desolate. A dozen bedsteads were arranged about a broad aisle, each flanked by a nightstand and set apart from its neighbour by the same precise interval. Above the bare tables where nurses might have been stationed, great lamps hung unlit on their sturdy chains.

But there were no nurses in sight, nor any patients to be tended to. The ward was silent, its beds unclothed and empty. Gideon turned to the doctor, meaning to demand what he meant by this, but Usher put a finger to his lips. He took an oil lamp from a stand and lit it, indicating with a small motion of his head that they were to follow him. At the far end of the ward, they came to a curtain that had been drawn across its entire width, keeping a portion of the room out of view. Here Usher paused and again raised his finger for silence.

The sound of singing reached them. It was faint and abraded, as if it came from a phonograph, but it was her voice. Her voice, but strange now. Paler somehow.

'She is here!' Gideon cried, and lunged forward, but the doctor raised his arm, barring his way.

'A moment, Sergeant.'

'She is here,' Gideon repeated, confronting Usher with an unthinking fierceness. 'We must speak with her. Did we not make it clear that this is police business?'

Usher relaxed his arm, bringing it to rest for a moment on Gideon's shoulder. His expression softened a little, though perhaps it was only in weariness. He was unshaven, and the lamplight gave him a jaundiced and ill-nourished look.

'You will speak with her,' he said. 'But before you do, I must make plain to you certain particulars of her case. There are things you must know, since you are to take charge of her.'

This drew a sharp look from Inspector Cutter. 'Take charge of her? We mean only to question the girl. In any case, you cannot mean to discharge her yet, surely? She was brought here half-dead, by all accounts.'

'Half-dead,' Usher repeated. He looked away for a moment and let out a frigid laugh. 'It is strange that you should choose those words. Listen to me, both of you. This institution is a place for the sick, for women and their general and particular ailments. We are far from richly endowed, but we do our utmost. There are limits, however, to what modern medicine may accomplish.'

Cutter agitated his shoulders beneath his coat, in a manner Gideon had come to find familiar. 'Here is another fine orator,' he said. 'You would give young Bliss here a run for his money.'

'My point, Inspector, is that certain conditions are beyond the province of science, which is to say nothing of the moral and ethical considerations. We must preserve certain essential virtues if we are not to leave our institution open to condemnation. And we must think of our nurses, for that matter, whose good offices we could scarcely do without. They are good Christian women, as befits their calling. And the papists, the Irishwomen – they do not like it one bit. They are simple-minded creatures, and very fierce in their resentment of the unnatural. They will not even enter the ward, Inspector. What is the time, by the by?'

'Nearing midnight,' Cutter said. 'What of it?'

'I have tended to her alone since morning, and had not slept as it was. I have taken nothing but black tea. I have tried to keep a professional countenance through it all. But this—' He glanced wearily at the curtain. 'One encounters certain rumours in my profession. In yours too, perhaps. But one is never quite prepared.'

'Prepared for what?' Cutter said. 'What are you saying, man?'

Usher looked away. When he turned to them again, Gideon saw the pewtery shadows in the hollows of his eyes. As the doctor searched Cutter's face, his own took on a despairing cast. 'It was only my exhaustion, perhaps, but when you asked for her – but no, you don't know, do you? You haven't seen it?'

'Seen *what*, damn it?'

But Gideon had already pushed past him, unable to master his impatience, and Cutter followed a moment later. Usher joined them, but kept a little apart.

'It may not be readily apparent,' he said quietly. 'It was some hours before I observed it myself. It waxes and wanes a little, but progresses slowly all the while. It is most pronounced when she is distressed.'

'What have you done to her?' Gideon demanded. 'Look at her, she is as pale as a ghost. Why is she locked in this frigid attic? She must have warmer blankets. She must be given nourishing soup.'

'I do not know what she needs, Sergeant,' Usher replied. 'But I know it is not soup.'

Gideon ignored him. He approached the bedside hesitantly. 'Miss Tatton?' he said, moving to her side. 'Angie? It is Gideon. Forgive me, I came as quickly as I could.'

She looked at him, or seemed to, but only for an instant. Her gaze was languid and remote, seeming to pass through what was before her, and her demeanour was strangely tranquil. If she suffered still, there was no sign of it.

She began singing again. Her voice was gentle and ragged, hardly more than a whisper. It was no longer laboured, as it had been in the church, but something in it troubled him. It made him think of dust. He knew the song, though he could not think from where.

'*Western wind, when wilt thou blow?*
The small rain down can rain.
Christ, that my love were in my arms
And I in my bed again.'

He turned to Usher, who stood now at the other side of the bed, observing the scene with something approaching distaste. 'You have drugged her,' Gideon said. 'She is not in her right mind.'

'I assure you not,' Usher said. 'She has refused all we have offered her, even food and water. I am sorry for it, Sergeant, but I fear she is beyond our aid.'

'Beyond your aid?' Gideon's voice was now openly raised. 'What manner of doctor are you? Surely you can see how frail she appears? And why does she not answer, if you have not drugged her? Is she delirious?'

Usher shook his head slowly. 'You have not seen it. Perhaps you will understand when you have seen it.'

'I will say it once more, Doctor.' Cutter had taken up a position at the foot of the bed. His manner was grave and intent. 'When we have seen what?'

Usher approached the bedside and gave a small cough. 'Miss Tatton, if you will permit me.'

Her singing continued. She gave no sign of having heard. Usher took hold of her right arm, which lay folded over her left on the bedspread. Supporting it at the elbow and the wrist, he extended it fully. His touch was practised but fastidious, as if the limb he held were gangrenous. He manoeuvred it towards the candle on the nightstand, bringing it so close that Gideon started in alarm.

'What is this?' he demanded. 'I will not see her harmed.'

Usher replied softly. 'The candle is only to help you see. Stand by the inspector, if you would. It may be necessary to crouch. Position yourself so that Miss Tatton's hand is in alignment with the candle flame.'

Gideon turned to Cutter. 'This man is no better than a charlatan, sir. He exhibits her as if she were some curiosity at a fairground. Surely there is a statute prohibiting such malpractice.'

Cutter ignored him. He looked at Usher in wariness, as if he expected to be shown a familiar trick. Then he lowered himself, spreading his thick fingers on his thighs, and peered for a long moment at Angie's outstretched hand.

'Christ,' he said.

Gideon looked in wonder from him to Miss Tatton. He went to the foot of the bed, and the inspector moved aside to let him take his place. Gideon positioned himself just as Cutter had done, adjusting his stance so that Angie's palm was immediately before the light.

Then he saw.

The palm of Angie's hand, or a portion of it, had faded to translucence. The missing part was perceptible still and continuous with the rest, but so faint in appearance that it might have been sculpted from smoke. Behind it, as if seen through a dusty window, the flame of the candle dipped and quickened in the dark.

IV

SANCTUS

XVII

'Ladies and gentlemen,' said the voice. 'Ladies and gentlemen, the darkness is complete.'

Octavia settled uneasily in her chair as the oil lamps were doused and the light faded from their wicks. A deep gloom had settled, if not quite the perfect darkness the speaker had announced. She could make out the shadowy bulk of the curtained cabinet and, when her eyes had adjusted, the faces of those seated nearest to her. From the far side of the circle, animated whispers could be heard.

'Silence,' the voice said again. 'Silence, ladies and gentlemen, I pray you. Silence is the twin of darkness. One is handmaiden to the other.'

Octavia was distracted for a moment by the faults in this figure of speech, but her attention settled once more on the centre of the circle, where the speaker could now be faintly seen. It was the voice of the medium herself, she supposed, whose ethereal quality was due to some contrivance of showmanship. The effect was remarkable even so, and more than a little disquieting, as if a small chorus of voices were speaking at a slight remove.

Whatever trickery she might employ, it was Octavia's view that Miss Callista Bewell was little more than a charlatan, of the kind that often practised on well-to-do but credulous society ladies. Indeed, she had it on good authority that even Callista Bewell's name was an affectation, and that she had been born Caroline Bellew, the daughter of a Wolverhampton cutler.

Mrs Florence Digby, who had convened the gathering, was particularly susceptible to flimflam of this sort. She was devoted to spiritualism of all kinds, which was hardly unusual in itself, but her considerable wealth – amassed by her late husband in the manufacture of medicinal tar soaps – allowed her to indulge her passion on a far grander scale than most. Her lavish and highly theatrical 'spiritual evenings' were talked about widely, and often attracted guests of considerable distinction.

Octavia found such occasions tiresome, regardless of who was in attendance, but Mr Healy had been insistent. She had encountered him that afternoon at the offices of the *Gazette*, where she had hoped to confer with Mr Sewell, who corresponded on matters before the courts, and whose informants among the ranks of the police might prove useful in her investigations. Mr Sewell had been attending an inquest, however, and on hearing of her inquiries in Whitechapel, Mr Healy had ushered her into his excessively upholstered office – a rare occurrence in itself – and had kept her there for almost an hour.

He had been delighted to hear the particulars of the disappearance, and quite untouched by the thought that a real girl was missing and might have come to harm. He was persuaded that it gave substance to all his outlandish talk of Spiriters, and that it needed only a little more in the way of evidence before a great splash could be made of it. In any case, as he had reminded her with particular satisfaction, it was just the sort of thing she had agreed to look into when they had made their bargain.

Octavia had conceded the point, though not without reminding him of his own undertakings. She would go to Mrs Digby's seance, where an 'especially gifted' medium was to appear and a number of distinguished guests were expected. She would give a flattering impression of the gathering for the society page, but if she did discover anything of substance about the Spiriters – and she would almost certainly discover it elsewhere – her account of it would be given a more prominent position in the paper.

It was a relief of sorts, even if she held out no great hopes. She had Miss Tatton's disappearance to occupy her now, as well as Lord Strythe's. This arrangement would allow her to continue looking into both, at least for a time, but only if she kept alive Healy's hopes of a sensation while making no mention for now of the earl.

It could be managed, though she would find herself thinly spread, but it was not the effort involved that troubled her most. She had been thoughtless in acting as she had, in rushing to Whitechapel and gaining someone's confidence on false pretences, and she feared that her foolish promise to help find the girl had only made matters worse. She meant to keep her word if she could, but surely it would be ghoulish even in that case to make use of Miss Tatton's story for her own ends. These doubts had begun to oppress her, and when the medium resumed – she had been standing for some time with her eyes closed and her fingertips pressed to her temples – Octavia almost welcomed the distraction.

'Ladies and gentlemen,' Miss Bewell now intoned. 'We live, we are told, in an age of discovery, in a time of marvels. Every day we read of some new miracle that men of science have accomplished. Men who are separated by a mile or more may converse by means of wires as if they were seated in the same room. The voices of those now dead have been etched into foil so that we may hear them as if they were still living. Men have made light, not with fire or gas, but with nothing more than electricity. Let there be light, men have said.'

The drawing room was in near darkness still, but Miss Bewell could be seen to fling out her arms as she uttered these last words.

'But there are other marvels, ladies and gentlemen, that reveal themselves not in the harsh light of the laboratory but in the ancient sanctity of shadow. There are wonders, though it is not commonly known, that do not surrender themselves to men. You will recognise the truth of what I say, I trust, and you will not find it presumptuous or unbecoming. I do not deny the genius of men, or seek to trespass in the domain for which God has fitted them alone. I am not one of those boisterous agitators who deny the natural order of things.'

Here Miss Bewell's voice took on a mellifluous character, though it was altered still by the same mysterious mechanism. Octavia shifted impatiently in her chair.

'But even the gentlemen present,' she continued, 'will surely grant this much. They will allow that our sex, being disposed by nature to gentleness and quiescence, is granted a stillness of mind and a fineness of perception. These feminine gifts, however modest, are not allotted equally, any more than the dominant sex exhibits its defining virtues without distinction. For myself, ladies and gentlemen, I make no claim to genius, but such gifts as I have I now place at your service. I will guide you, if you are willing, to the very extremities of nature, but no further. Others may boast of their skills in the dark arts, but I do not meddle with witch-craft or necromancy. Such power as I possess was bestowed on me by nature, for nature encompasses all. Only by admitting her supremacy may we be admitted to her deep and final mysteries. Ladies and gentlemen, the darkness is complete.'

And now the feeble light that remained was indeed extinguished by some unseen hand. Miss Bewell's face vanished entirely, and a murmur of disquiet arose among the guests. A lady seated to

Octavia's left gave a nervous exclamation, and there was a good deal more in the way of coughing and fidgeting before someone – Octavia took it to be Mrs Digby herself – issued a stern shushing.

'Ladies and gentlemen,' Miss Bewell went on, 'I will now withdraw to the manifestation cabinet. I will be occupied there for some time, how long exactly I cannot say, for I depend on the whims of ungovernable forces. The other element, the immortal substance of our souls, is constituted with an unimaginable delicacy. Think of a drifting filament of spider silk, disturbed by the merest breath, or the frail tissue of a butterfly's wing. The stuff of the spirit is more fragile still, and it must cross an unimaginable distance if it is to be urged before our sight.

'As for the identities of those who will come before us, those are more uncertain still. I have certain familiars, as do all of us who practise this art, and doubtless you will see one of those first. My familiar will perhaps say more, for it is they and not I who are in proximity with the other realm. After that, I cannot tell who may speak or be seen. No doubt some of you have come tonight in the hope of conversing with those you have lost, and I am glad to say that I have brought about such happy communions in the past. But you must not fix your hopes on that prospect, I beg you. Our cries are heard, more often than not, merely by those wanderers who happen to be near. I will say no more, ladies and gentlemen. The next words you hear, whatever their nature, will not be mine.'

Octavia, relieved that this rather tedious preamble had come to an end, heard a momentary disturbance as the drapes enclosing the cabinet were parted, and what sounded like the scuffing of bare feet on boards. After that, a silence fell, or the nearest approximation of it that could be managed by a dozen or more grown men and women who had been perched on dining chairs in varying states of discomfort or boredom for almost half an hour.

Some minutes had passed – and Octavia had allowed her mind to wander – when a slight noise recalled her to herself. A guest who had entered the room unheard now settled into the vacant seat to her right, which gave out a jarring squeak. Having murmured an apology to the company, this person leaned towards Octavia and gave a discreet cough.

'I say, is that you, Wavy? I shall be quite mortified if I've taken the wrong seat after going to all this trouble.'

This drew an indignant rebuke from Mrs Digby, and Octavia allowed a moment to pass before whispering her reply. 'Elf?' she said. 'How on earth did you manage to slip in? It's like being sealed in a tomb.'

'Oh, you know me, my darling. No drawing room in London is impervious to my wiles. Macken said you'd been to see me while I was out, which I felt wretched about, but I mean to make it up to you. I've come by some intelligence, you see, that concerns—'

He was cut off by a strenuous shushing from the assembled company, and the silence was restored. Ten minutes passed, or twenty. Octavia could not tell. The effect of the silence and the darkness was strangely dislocating. She felt as if she were a passenger in a windowless train, sensing only the continuous unspooling of unmarked distances. A slight brushing sound came from the curtained booth, then nothing again. Not even the ticking of a clock.

He seemed quite near to her, Elf, in the darkness. She was aware of a faint emanation of heat and scent. It was odd, she thought, that he should have gone so much out of his way. Mrs Digby's gatherings weren't at all his sort of thing. And how had he known to find her here?

A light appeared at the centre of the circle. It stuttered at first, then persisted, a peculiar column of radiance whose source could not be seen. It was not especially bright, but its purity of colour was remarkable. Lesser shafts mingled and shimmered at its core, but the limits of the whole were perfectly fixed. It was quite unlike any light she had ever seen. She could not take her eyes from it.

'I am Psyche.'

A new voice spoke, or the first had been disguised by some altered mechanism. It was multiplied, as before, but projected now so that it seemed to come from all around her. It was chilly and precise, faintly exultant.

'I am Psyche, and you must listen.'

In the midst of the light, a face could now be seen. It was bodiless, as if suspended in a void, and its features seemed formed from some diffuse and insubstantial surface. The apparition waxed and waned, shifting and indistinct.

'I was beauty itself once, coveted and pure. I was adored as none before me. But I lived among men, and no man can rest while there is fault to be found in a woman's virtue. Condemned by my own father, I was given in sacrifice to the underworld. I was cast out onto the peaks, abandoned to the winds and whatever demons they carried. Do not ask me what trials I passed through, for I will no longer speak of them. I am sanctified once more, and belong now to love itself. It is my light that you must carry into the palaces of the night, if you would know it and have it know you. But behold, someone approaches. There is someone who wishes to speak.'

In another part of the drawing room, a second column of radiance flickered into being, serene and quartz-like, and rippled with lazing dust. No doubt it was some concealed apparatus that produced these illusions, but it was done with a singular skill.

'Who comes to us?' said the voice of Psyche. 'Do not be afraid to speak. You find yourself among friends.'

In answer, there arose a violent surge of noise, as if a great many disparate sounds had massed together: a roaring sea, a bow wrenched over slack strings, the grinding of some immense engine. A woman clutched her husband's arm in frank terror, and a number of other guests looked about them for some reassurance that all was still in hand. Then, after ten or fifteen seconds – and just as abruptly as it had begun – the noise died away.

What followed resembled silence, at first, but soon a pattern unfolded. A pulse of whispers formed, a susurration. It shifted, gathered itself. It was a voice. Someone was speaking. 'Ain't you ain't you ain't you oh ain't you yes you.'

'There,' said Psyche, a gentleness now in that strange, ramified voice. 'There, you must not be frightened. Tell us what you came to say.'

'Ain't you oh ain't you the pretty one will you be pretty one.'

'Yes. Yes, tell us.'

'Will you be the first pretty one will you will you oh little pretty one will you be my first.'

'Were you little, our visitor? Will you say your name?'

'My sister talks of you, little Alice, says you're pretty as the day.'

'We welcome you, little friend. When did you go, Alice? Is there someone living you wish to speak to?'

The child's voice spoke again. 'Oh long, long all gone in that cold, long will you be long, will you little be my first.'

'Who do you remember, Alice? Whom do you wish to be remembered to?'

There was silence, for a long moment. Alice's light guttered and faded. An anxious muttering arose in the room, but Psyche simply waited, her spectral face impassive. The noise returned briefly – a tangled, metallic shrieking – and for a moment the light flared with a new intensity.

'The black water,' said the child's voice. 'He said I was bright, but the black water filled me up. Little brightness, he said. Where's your little brightness now?'

The room fell silent, and Alice's light was gone.

In the lull that followed, Elf spoke to Octavia again.

'What can you be doing, Wavy, old thing? Surely you're not taking all of this down?'

She stared into the darkness, distracted still, and it was a moment before she realised he had spoken. 'I'm sorry,' she said. 'I'm sorry, what did you say?'

He nodded towards the notebook in her lap. 'I noticed you were making notes, and I was wondering what on earth for. You don't put any stock in this nonsense, surely?'

'Mmm.' Octavia stared again at the place where Alice's light had been. *Little Alice.* It was a performance, no more than that, and the words had been disordered and nonsensical, yet it had made her dimly uneasy. 'Well, no, of course not. It's all perfectly idiotic, but even so, our readers will want to know what was revealed. It gives the thing colour, I suppose. But never mind all that. What on earth are *you* doing here? And how did you find me?'

'Mr Healy was good enough to share your whereabouts, since he knows how indispensable a friend I am. Oh, and he mentioned that you're now carrying more than one brief, so to speak.'

'Did he really?' She spoke with a measure of irritation now. 'What did he say, exactly?'

'Oh, he was quite vague, really, and perhaps I inferred more than I should have, but it seemed to me that I might be of some assistance. You mustn't be cross, darling.'

She looked away for a moment. 'What do you mean by assistance?' she said. 'What is it you think you can help with?'

He peered about the drawing room, lit once again by a single pillar of light. Psyche had fallen silent, though her lips moved now and then as if in soundless incantation. Mrs Digby's other guests, awaiting the medium's next pronouncement, had fallen into low but animated talk as they speculated on the nature of what they had seen.

Elf folded his legs, and pivoted smoothly towards her. 'Well, the fact is that I have become privy to certain matters. To matters that may concern you, given your new interests.'

Octavia tried to scrutinise his expression in the gloom. 'Are you being serious, Elf? I can never tell.'

He laid his hand across his breast. 'Upon my word, old thing. I have been drawn into what I will call deliberations, in my official capacity, concerning certain police matters.'

'What *is* your official capacity, exactly? Do you sit on a committee of some sort?'

'Oh, I sit on several, and they are all of them unbearably tedious, but no, I mean another official capacity. I am attached to the Home Office, after a fashion, and have a modest function concerned with the conduct of Her Majesty's constabulary as it pertains to cases of special interest of one kind or another.'

'What sort of cases? What do you mean by "special interest"?'

'I must be somewhat circumspect, as you will appreciate, but in certain matters your curiosity may intersect with the public good. I understand that you're looking into this Spiriters business, for instance.'

Octavia regarded him carefully. 'I've been making inquiries, yes, and I've encountered certain rumours, but nothing more than that. *Is* there more than that?'

Elf considered this for a moment. He was about to reply when a surge of dissonance announced the resumption of proceedings. 'I shall tell you more afterwards,' he said. 'Are you sure you wouldn't like to slip out before the end?'

But another voice was heard before she could answer. This one belonged to a child named Rosalind, whose diction and manner – she made several scolding appeals to 'Nanny Jojo' – suggested more fortunate circumstances. Like Alice, though, she was given to repetitive babbling and her monologue sputtered out before anything else had been revealed.

A third presence announced itself, this time without the slightest prompting. Its column of light appeared, in another part of the drawing room, almost as soon as Rosalind's had vanished. This time, it was not a child who seemed to speak, but a young woman.

'How'd you get in?' the new voice said. 'He always locks up, I says to them. He's careful that way, being in his line of work. Don't you know who he is, I says? He'll have your skins.'

'Welcome to our gathering, friend,' said Psyche. 'Will you tell us your name, so that we may grasp the import of your words? Are they addressed to someone here present?'

'And you newly married, says one of them. To be laid low like this, and you only newly married. What a shame it is, says the other. Will you not let us ease your suffering? And I knew, I knew. Did they think I had the wits of a child?'

'Tell us your name, dear one, or the names of those you speak of. If some wrong was done to you, you must help us to bring it to light.'

But the speaker carried on, quite unheeding. There was something laboured in her voice, as if her illness troubled her still, but there was a fierce resolve too. She meant to give this account, whatever it signified, and would not be deflected from her purpose. 'You will answer to him, says I. If any harm comes to me, he will make you answer. And where will you be then, with all your strange talk? Take that away, I says. It has a foul smell, and it makes me light in the head.'

The noises returned, in a low undercurrent at first, but rising in pitch and intensity until they began to obscure the sense of the woman's words. A massed screeching arose, like the racket of agitated starlings, and beneath it a slow and laboured sawing. 'Take it away, damn you. *He will find you, you creeping, black-hearted cowards! Don't you know who he is? He'll not just put you away! He'll not rest until you're sent to hell!'*

The woman seemed to call for someone by name, but the noise had reached a disturbing intensity, and Octavia could not be sure she had made it out. She wrote it down, but put a question mark against it.

'For whom did you call, my dear?' Psyche's voice grew shrill as it contended with the din. 'Say his name again, and your own, if you can find the strength.'

Psyche repeated this entreaty twice more, but soon her voice too was engulfed by the swelling cacophony. When it receded at last, the new light had faded too.

Another soon appeared, and by the end of the evening's proceedings Mrs Digby's guests witnessed five further apparitions of this kind. All those who spoke were girls or young women, and although each was distinct in certain particulars – muttering a certain scrap of verse, perhaps, or fretting about some flower show – it seemed to Octavia that they were more alike than otherwise in their walks of life. One had worked in a cotton mill, or so her wandering testimony suggested, and had come by some injury beneath its machinery. Another had been a blind crossing-sweeper, if such a thing were possible, and seemed to convey that she had fallen under the wheels of a carriage. She could not see the men who came to her as she lay dying, but knew the blackness of the vapour by its smell.

The last two visitors appeared together, their lights side by side, and gave their jumbled account by turns. They had been sisters, it appeared, and had shared some occupation requiring the mixing of colours. Years of this work had poisoned them, and they had been taken, in the end, to 'the sick house'.

'That's where they found us,' the one called Agnes had said. 'Weren't no more colours then. You get black when you mix them all, and that's what it was like. Half-blind from it, we were, and all the colours going.'

The noises abated too, after the sisters had fallen silent. After a time even Psyche's light dimmed, and her face grew indistinct. Octavia shifted discreetly. She had been confined to her chair for over an hour, yet it was only now that she took notice of the discomfort in her limbs. Her companions were stirring too, taking the performance to be over, and a low thrum of talk returned to the room.

'Most diverting,' said one gentleman. 'Most diverting, Mrs Digby. We are always assured of that.'

This was met with a low murmur of assent, but it seemed the sentiment was not shared by all. 'One might have hoped,' ventured an unseen lady, 'for one or two visitors who were known to someone present, that being the usual practice. But of course it was very prettily done, Mrs Digby, and may I compliment you again on the very agreeable bit of trout.'

'*Was* the trout agreeable?' Elf whispered.

'I wasn't hungry.' Octavia was silent for a time. 'I'm sorry, Elf, I'm a little distracted, I'm afraid. And this evening's performance – and it was a performance, I do realise that – well, it was rather unsettling, didn't you find?'

'Well, it was a creditable bit of theatre, to be sure. Mr Boucicault himself could not have done better in the contrivance of the illusions.'

'And they said things, some of those who spoke – there were certain particulars that seemed familiar. But that's how it works, isn't it? And one pays attention in spite of oneself, because these are just the sort of stories one expects. But the truth is always plainer, isn't it? And always uglier. What was it that Mrs Campion said?'

'Mrs who?'

'Oh, no one.' Octavia suppressed a shudder. 'I was thinking of all this talk about Spiriters. But those are just stories too, aren't they?'

'Well, it rather depends on which stories you mean. As for Miss Bewell's confections, well, she has a certain flair for all this, it must be admitted, but goodness me – she belongs at the end of a pier, darling.'

'But there isn't anything to it, is there? I mean, these Spiriters aren't real, surely?'

He paused, lowering his eyes. 'As for the name, it emerged from certain quarters of the press – not your own, of course, but the lower sort of rag. But yes, they exist, as nearly as we can tell. There have been disappearances, that much is true, and certain patterns have emerged. Sickly work girls, that sort of thing. But one can never be sure in such cases, especially when there aren't any – well, when there aren't any bodies. Forgive me, Wavy, but it's rather a grim business.'

'Well, you needn't think of sparing my feelings. I know it's a grim business. Women are missing – real women, not just bodies, who may still be found. Is there something else, then? Have there been other clues?'

He made a delicate gesture. 'I am constrained, you understand, in what I can discuss.'

'What about all this talk of dark arts and potions, and so on?

And those lurid illustrations in the papers? Has anything been found? Is there any truth to it?'

'A little, perhaps. Certain details, here and there. Residues have been found, for instance, though I don't know about potions. And scraps of cloth, oddly enough. Fine stuff, embroidered and what have you. But as for dark arts, well, people develop peculiar notions, don't they? It's all this Ghost Club nonsense that's going about. That nitwit Doyle has a good deal to answer for.'

A surge of noise was heard again, and Psyche's light stuttered and flared. A moment later, a second aura appeared. It was brighter than the others, and almost unwavering.

'Speak to me,' said the voice of Psyche. 'Speak to me quickly, for I am almost spent.'

'Lucy.' The voice was small at first in the receding noise. 'Lost her.'

'Lucy?' answered Psyche with some eagerness. 'Is that your name, Lucy?'

'Lucy Locket.' There was a hardness in the voice, though it was still faint. Light but hard, like zinc. 'Lost her pocket.'

'Please, young friend—'

'Kitty Fisher found it.'

'No rhymes, young friend. Please, there is no time.'

'. . . a penny was there in it, only ribbon round it . . .'

'We must leave you, dear one. The weariness after so much effort – you cannot imagine it. I must bring this to its end.'

'. . . only ribbon . . . ribbons of satin . . .'

'Goodnight, young friend. You have all our blessings.'

'. . . Tatton, in ribbons of satin . . .'

Octavia lurched to her feet. 'Wait!' she cried. 'Ask her to wait! Is it Angie Tatton? Ask her, please.'

'Be seated, madam,' said Psyche. 'We ask that those in the circle make no intervention unless they are called for. It is late, in any case, too late.'

'No!' Octavia stumbled, and Elf took hold of her arm. 'Please, forgive the interruption – I do apologise, Mrs Digby – but it is a matter of great urgency.'

The visitor's light flared all at once to a searing intensity, and her voice rose to an abrasive screech. '*You tell them I'm coming!*' she shrieked. '*They can't touch me no more, but I can touch them! You tell them, you tell them! I'll show them brightness!*'

'Angie!'

'*I'll show them the fucking dark!*'

The voice was gone then, and Psyche too had fallen silent. The light went out, and this time no others appeared in its place. The darkness was complete.

XVIII

By morning the train had carried them as far as Deal. Gideon had slept for a time – he and Cutter had each taken a watch while the other rested – but felt little the better for it. A coarse sleet scoured the platform and the taunting of unseen gulls filled the grey air. While Inspector Cutter saw about engaging a driver, Gideon shepherded Miss Tatton to the waiting room. There he tried, as he had done for much of the night, both to engage her in conversation and to keep her from drawing the attention of strangers.

For all that it troubled him privately, the appearance of her hand was not his most pressing concern. Before he would consent to remove her from the hospital, Inspector Cutter had insisted that she be fitted out not only with a pair of gloves – these were of fine grey kid – but with all that a young lady of middling station might be expected to wear while travelling at this time of year. If he knew anything of her condition he did not reveal it, but he seemed anxious to keep its symptoms hidden from view.

For much of the time, then, she attracted no particular curiosity. Indeed, when they entered the waiting room, the two young military men who stood to bid her good morning did so with open admiration. Gideon glared at them in indignation, but this seemed only to amuse them, and Miss Tatton herself passed them by as if they had been quite invisible. He kept by her side and made what discreet efforts he could to lead her away, for if her appearance seemed ordinary at first, it was an impression that could be quickly dispelled.

Although she was silent for much of the time, she was given to occasional outbursts of speech or song. These utterances had a strange and elliptical quality, and it was often impossible to tell what prompted them. Her pallor, too, had drawn curious glances. It was not that she appeared sickly – she did not have the etiolated complexion and sunken features of the consumptive – and indeed she seemed in many respects to be preternaturally restored. Her face, though deathly white, had about it a look of serene contentment, so that she was apt to appear conspicuous even when she was quiet and perfectly still.

He chose a table in a quiet corner, where she would be partly concealed by a chimney breast, but she simply stood before it, transfixed by a lozenge of sunlight that trembled on the roughly plastered wall. Keeping his back to the room, and shielding her as well as he could manage from view, he urged her gently to a chair.

'Miss Tatton,' he said, glancing about him as he took his own seat. The two young officers had resumed their conversation, so he felt that he could safely resume his efforts. 'Angie, do you—' He lowered his voice. 'It is Gideon, Angie. It is Gideon Bliss. You do remember, don't you?'

She smiled faintly, but when he leaned towards her he saw that her gaze was averted by a fraction. Turning, he saw that her attention had been drawn now to a table near the window, where the air held a slow flux of cigar smoke.

'The black,' she said softly. 'It came out in the washing water. Swashes out, I said, when I was little. Swash for wash.'

'Swash for wash,' Gideon repeated, straining for a tone of levity. He cast a nervous glance about the room. 'It has a charming sound, certainly. But what was the black, Miss Tatton? Can you tell me?'

Angie gave no sign that she had heard, and Gideon felt a bleak fatigue settle on him. He was almost relieved when Inspector Cutter appeared in the doorway.

'Bliss!' he called out. 'Look lively, will you. You haven't all morning to be cooing at her. The driver is waiting.'

He turned his back with a scowl and marched outside. His disposition had darkened since leaving London, and Gideon was puzzled by his attitude to Miss Tatton. Dr Usher had been adamant that she must be discharged, and Cutter had seemed to accept the wisdom of this. He would not reveal his thinking, but it seemed to Gideon that he felt conflicting impulses. He wished to keep Angie with them, or felt that he must, but made it plain that he did so on sufferance. He made it known, too, that it would fall to Gideon to tend to her needs, and to keep her as much as possible out of the inspector's way.

'Damn it all, Bliss,' Cutter said, when he had succeeded at last in guiding her to the carriage. 'Could you not at least have kept her from making a spectacle of herself in the waiting room? Have I not told you we must pay this visit quietly? We are some distance from London, and I am a good way from acting on proper authority.'

'I am doing my utmost, sir, but there are certain—' He glanced at Miss Tatton, who sat placidly in the next seat, absorbed now by the hail against the window. She was perfectly indifferent still to everything that was said, but it seemed indecent even so to speak of her as if she were not present. 'Well, sir, she is hardly amenable to instruction. I kept her from view as well as I could.'

Cutter only grunted, and when they had climbed into the carriage he turned to the window and folded his arms, his manner making it plain that he wished for no further conversation. Once

they had left the town behind them, they travelled in dreary silence, relieved now and then – if relieved was the word – by Miss
Tatton's inscrutable chatter, her snatches of eerie singing. They
made their way north, by a narrow but tolerably even road, and
passed through farmland that gave way in time to wan and scrub-
by flatlands. Beyond these the sea could at times be glimpsed, iron
dark under low swags of cloud.

It was some time before Gideon ventured to speak. 'Since we
have a moment's leisure, sir, I wondered if we might return to the
subject of the crystal.'

Cutter had been tapping at the face of his watch, which he now
returned to its pocket. 'Were we on that subject, Bliss?'

'You mentioned that you had sought the opinion of an expert.
I am eager to hear it, sir, and to understand how it might help us.
It was I who found the item in question, as you may recall, and it
would be most gratifying to know that—'

'Yes, yes.' The inspector brought up his hand. 'God help us, Bliss,
if I had any notion of your skills as a torturer, I might have made
use of you in the cells. I had it looked at, your bit of glass, and it
seems it is a rare bit of craftsmanship. Nothing like it is produced
in England, my man says. It may be Flemish-made, though he
cannot be certain of it. Beyond that, he could say very little, except
that it was meant for more than decoration. The vessel it came
from, he said, was made for strong stuff.'

'Strong stuff, sir? Brandy and the like?'

'No, Bliss. Chemicals, he meant. A "volatile agent", whatever
that may be.'

Gideon considered this. 'I have no training in the natural
sciences, sir, but a volatile substance, I believe, is one that lends
itself to evaporation, and which may therefore be inhaled to some
rapid effect. Like ether, for instance.'

'Is that so?' Cutter nodded and looked away, but it was Gideon's impression that he was being humoured.

'Am I right in supposing, sir, that you have some notion already of what the vessel may have contained?'

'I have all kinds of notions, Bliss, but it takes more than notions to put a fellow in the dock. You know my ways by now, surely?'

'Yes, sir.' Another thought came to him, which he sought to suppress by sitting on his hands.

Cutter caught sight of him and cast up his eyes. 'Out with it, Bliss, before you rupture your hydraulics.'

'Forgive me, sir, it is just that I was reminded of something.' He glanced at Angie, but she seemed entirely absorbed by her own thoughts. 'When I came upon Miss Tatton in the church, she spoke of a "black air". I mentioned it to you, I believe, when I gave you my account of what had happened. It was how she described it, sir, the drug she was given.'

'Is that so?' said Cutter again.

Gideon drew in a long breath. 'Sir, I know you are right to be cautious in your hypotheses, but I have begun forming a theory of my own. All I ask is that you indicate your opinion of it. If you think it foolish, you need only shake your head.' When Cutter said nothing, he was emboldened to continue. 'A "black air" or vapour answers the description, it seems to me, of a "volatile agent". If a substance of that kind had been kept in vessels at Strythe House – and if Miss Tull had come to guess at its purpose – might not her conscience have demanded that she destroy them, since she was bent already on destroying herself? You need only shake your head.'

The inspector's expression remained comparatively mild. He scratched at his lower lip with a thumbnail, but made no other movement.

Gideon let out a sigh, and a gentle elation took hold of him. 'Do you recall, sir, the undertaking I gave you?'

Cutter did not immediately reply. He had turned again to the window, and was gazing at the sullen landscape. 'Undertaking?' he said at length. 'What undertaking was that, Bliss?'

'I pledged, sir, that if you allowed me the opportunity of finding Miss Tatton, and of keeping my promise to her, I would give you my diligent service as a sergeant thereafter, and apply what little learning I have to the peculiar case that confronts us.'

The inspector's gaze remained fixed on the window. 'That undertaking,' he said. 'Yes, Bliss, I do recall it. Do you wish to retract it?'

'On the contrary, Inspector. I wish to reinforce it. I am at your service, even if my duty to Miss Tatton encumbers me somewhat.'

Cutter gave a low snort, and his expression darkened, but he said nothing in reply.

'May I speak frankly, sir?'

The inspector detached his hand from his jaw, splaying three fingers in weary assent.

'It is an inconvenience that poor Miss Tatton must accompany us in her present condition. I am sure she would not wish it herself if she were – if she were quite in her senses. But you would not have permitted it, sir, if you had not some notion of her usefulness, if you did not believe, as I do, that she has some connection with that melancholy business at Strythe House, and perhaps with what happened at Bethnal Green. We know now that Miss Tull's last message was meant for my uncle, who had been trying to protect Angie. We know that it was Lord Strythe she meant to identify.'

Cutter stirred in his seat, gathering his coat about his bulk. His eyes narrowed but did not leave the window.

'And if I may, sir, it is my belief that you know something of Miss Angie's condition, of the appearance of her hand, or rather its disappearance. What we saw last night – well, I scarcely know how to describe it, and I am distrustful still of my own senses. Whereas you, when we were presented with this . . . with this phenomenon – well, you seemed to me, sir, to be no more than a little put about, as if you had seen nothing out of the common way.'

Now, at last, Inspector Cutter turned from the window, folding his arms in deliberation. Gideon cleared his throat at some length, working the heels of his hands into the greasy cloth that covered his seat.

'Other officers have alluded to your work on "special cases". Inspector Fox made mention of it, when he took you aside at the house in Charlotte-street, and Constable Canning said something of the same kind. They seemed to suggest, sir, that you are called upon when the circumstances of a crime do not appear altogether natural.'

The inspector yawned and worked a knot from his shoulder. 'If you have a question to put to me, Bliss, will you come to the end of it, like a good fellow?'

Gideon glanced at Miss Tatton, who had plucked a cobweb from the window frame and was teasing it into a skein on the spindle of her gloved fingertip. He leaned towards Cutter and addressed him in a whisper. 'Ghosts, sir. Do you investigate ghosts? Is that what Miss Tatton has become?'

'Not yet, Bliss.'

'Not *yet*, sir?'

Cutter leaned forward in his turn, confronting Gideon with a look that was at once weary and intent. Without warning, he reached for Angie's hand, drawing it towards him without ceremony and tugging it from its glove.

'Sir!' protested Gideon.

'You need not fear for her, Bliss. Look at her, she is scarcely sensible of our presence.'

It was true. She had not so much as turned to see who it was that held her wrist, only straining forward a little to clutch at the wisp of cobweb that had slipped from her grasp. Cutter took up a newspaper that an earlier passenger had discarded. Folding it across his knees, he laid Miss Tatton's hand on it, pressing it flat. Gideon looked stiffly away, as if from some scandalous display of intimacy.

'Look, Bliss,' Cutter commanded. 'Look at it.'

Gideon obeyed. The newspaper was a recent issue of *The Kent and Sussex Courier*, whose front page was given over to advertisements of various kinds. Against this background, he saw that the translucent portion of Miss Tatton's hand had grown larger, engulfing almost her entire palm as well as three of her fingers. As before, its substance appeared almost entirely absent, its contours dissolved, like syrup in warm water. Beneath it an irregular patch of newsprint could be clearly seen.

The inspector pointed. 'Read it,' he said.

Gideon gave a small cough, glancing towards Miss Tatton as if to ask her leave. 'The finer type cannot be made out, sir.'

'Read what you can, damn it.' Cutter stabbed at the page with his forefinger. 'The name of the merchant is not in fine print. Read that.'

'He is a Mr T. Wagner, sir.'

'And where is he established?'

'At 66 and 68 Calverley Road, sir, in Tunbridge Wells.'

'Opposite the Town Hall.'

'Just so, sir. Opposite the Town Hall.'

'And what does this Mr Wagner advertise, Bliss?'

'A great sale of unredeemed pledges, sir. He is a pawnbroker, I believe.'

'What has he to offer in his great sale? Perhaps we might put ourselves out of our way to look in.'

'Blankets and sheets, sir. Quilts and counterpanes. Warm shawls.'

'Warm, is it? I suppose that is a virtue in a shawl. What else?'

'I hesitate to mention the other items, sir, in the presence of a lady.'

Inspector Cutter enveloped his face with his hands, letting out a long breath as he drew them away. 'A word that you hesitate – God help us, Gideon Bliss, if you are not entirely helpless in the sight of the world. You are reading this pawnbroker's advertisement through your little flower-maker's hand, and here you are worrying about the demands of propriety. Read it out, you miserable piss-puddle.'

Gideon coughed again. 'Yes, sir. It refers, sir, to underclothing and baby linen.'

'Very good, Bliss,' said Cutter. 'That will do.'

The inspector set about replacing Miss Tatton's glove and, with some gentleness now, settling her arm once more across her lap. 'I am obliged to you, miss. Now then, Bliss, you ask if I look into "special cases", and whether I am an authority on ghosts, if that is indeed the right word. What I do, Sergeant, is no more than what you have just done yourself. I look at what is before me, and I get on with the business of learning from it whatever is there to be learned. As for the likes of Miss Tatton, I do not pretend to understand their true nature, though it is not for want of puzzling over it. I have made certain observations, nothing more. I do not trip over her kind every night of the week, and I am heartily glad of it.'

'But what do you mean, when you talk about Miss Tatton's kind? What has happened to her, sir? What *is* she?'

Cutter folded his arms and fixed him with a solemn look. 'Be careful what you ask, Bliss. You may not like the answer.'

'Please, sir. I must know.'

'She is a half-shade, Bliss, or that is how I think of them. Perhaps there is a proper term.'

'A half-shade? What does that . . . what does it mean?'

'It means, Bliss, that she is passing from the world. She is slipping away from herself, as we do in our dotage, leaving only what we remember from the first – songs and rhymes, and what have you. But her mind is not gone, as a dotard's is. It is elsewhere. She is passing from the world, but she has some business in it still. People talk of fearing ghosts, but it is not ghosts they should be afraid of. It is the likes of this poor creature.'

Gideon looked at Miss Tatton in disbelief. She had arranged her gloved hands in her lap, and gazed out in her vacant way at the greyish margin of the coast. 'Afraid, sir?' he said. 'You cannot believe, surely, that she is capable of harm?'

'You needn't worry, Bliss. She will not trouble you or me. Her business is with those who brought her to this. I have seen it for myself.' The inspector broke off for a moment, working with one knuckle at the corner of his mouth. 'The worst of men, a slaughterer of children, brought to his knees. Brought to his knees, Bliss, without a word being uttered, before a creature who in life was not yet ten years old. I wrested the gun from his mouth myself.'

'Are you speaking of the St Johns, sir? Was that how you came to—'

'Never mind what cases I am speaking of. I have said all I mean to say about them. But it is some comfort to you, maybe, to know what preoccupies her. She seems miles away, and so she may very well be. She sees things we cannot see, and she has a long reach. But her time is short.'

Gideon stared, a coldness spreading in his chest. 'What does that mean, sir? What will happen to her?'

But Cutter only shook his head, and at that moment the carriage rattled to a halt. They had turned into a narrow lane shadowed by a dark lace of elms, and the place seemed enveloped by a strange quietness. Gideon started when the driver opened the door.

'Begging your pardon, sir,' the driver said. 'Guvnor said I was to pull up short of the gates and keep it good and quiet.'

'The gates?'

'The Strythe place, sir. Them trees is part of the boundary, and the gates you can just about make out at the next bend. This is where the guvnor asked for, sir. This is the house on Vesper Sands.'

XIX

The house was not large, for a family of such means, but its isolation gave a stark grandeur to its appearance. It rose from a promontory overlooking the dunes, and might have served at one time as a seaside villa. There was a faded elegance still about its arches and mullions, but it had fallen into neglect. Years of salt air had roughened its stonework, and its gables were discoloured by lichen and rust.

The sleet had yielded to a cheerless drizzle, giving a dismal air to the unkempt grounds. They passed a disused greenhouse, its panes mottled and crowded by vines, and glimpsed a tennis court beyond an untended hedge whose net slumped into a drift of blackened leaves. Cutter strode ahead as always, while Gideon trudged by Miss Tatton's side, keeping her beneath the inspector's tattered umbrella when he could and urging her onwards when she fell into her trances.

As they drew near the house, he looked up to find Cutter waiting. His expression was bleak. 'Show a leg, will you?' he called out. 'You are not strolling the botanic gardens with your sweetheart.'

'Pardon me, sir,' said Bliss. 'I am doing my utmost, but Miss Tatton seems to grow more distracted. She caught sight of an old summerhouse just now, and it was all I could do to keep her from wandering away.'

Cutter shook his head in exasperation. 'Come,' he said. 'We will try the servants' entrance first. I want to know who is here before our presence is announced, and whether anyone is lately arrived from town.'

When Cutter rapped on the kitchen door, it was flung aside by a serving woman of dour appearance with a shotgun braced under her arm.

'What's your business here?' she demanded. 'We ain't expecting no callers.'

'We are police officers, madam,' said Cutter. 'Will you put down that firearm, please, before I relieve you of it?'

'What police? I ain't never seen you before, and I know every constable from here to Ramsgate.'

'We are not with the Kent Constabulary, madam. I am Inspector Cutter of the London Metropolitan Police and I have papers on me to prove it. But I say again, put down that shotgun before I am obliged to do it for you. I have had a good many guns pointed at me in my time, and it has rarely ended well for those doing the pointing.'

The woman gave him a surly look, but broke the shotgun with a practised movement and let it hang by her side.

'You might give me your name, madam, since I have given you mine.'

'Cornish.'

'A very good day to you, Mrs Cornish. We hope to speak to the lady of the house, or to His Lordship, if he should happen to be present.'

'We don't see much of His Lordship,' Mrs Cornish said. 'What business you got with either of them?'

'No business I intend to discuss with you. Now, madam, I have traipsed a good way in this weather, and I am standing here in a wet overcoat and a sour mood. Will you do me the kindness of showing us in?'

Mrs Cornish eyed them for a moment longer before standing aside. 'Who's the young miss? Looks like death, she does. You ain't going to tell me she's a police officer and all?'

'You are right there, Mrs Cornish,' Cutter said. 'I am not going to tell you.'

They were shown to a musty drawing room whose French windows overlooked the dunes and the sea beyond. Miss Tatton was taken at once with the view, drifting to the window and refusing to be led from it even when Mrs Cornish returned with tea.

'Ain't no fire lit,' the housekeeper said, setting down a rack of charred toast. 'Lady Ada keeps to her rooms till near enough six o'clock most days, and she don't much feel the cold. I've told her you're here, but I can't say when she might appear. You'll have to put up as best you can. You may go at the bookcase if you've a mind for all that. Lady Ada is forever at the books.'

The inspector swallowed a mouthful of tea. 'Did you mention that we are police officers?'

Mrs Cornish folded her hands on her apron. 'I said who you was, but it won't signify. Lady Ada ain't the most regular in her thinking, God bless her. You could be Prince Albert himself, sir, and not be sure of seeing her until I put out the drinks tray in the evening.'

Cutter took up a position by the vacant fireplace, tugging in agitation at his damp collar. 'It cannot be helped, then,' he said. 'We are obliged to you, Mrs Cornish.'

The housekeeper paused at the door, her attention drawn once more to the window. A kestrel hung intently above the dunes, and Angie's attention was fixed on it. She had become still, clutching the frills of her cuffs. Her lips moved, as if in some silent recitation.

'She all right, the young lady? She may take her ease in the day room if she's feeling poorly.'

Gideon rose from his chair at this, but the inspector intervened before he could speak.

'You need not trouble yourself,' he said, crossing the room and placing himself in front of Miss Tatton. 'We are obliged to you, Mrs Cornish.'

In the event, they had waited for hardly more than an hour when Mrs Cornish returned to announce her mistress, a lady of striking appearance who strode immediately to the centre of the room, planting her cane before her and scrutinising each of her guests in turn.

'We will take some sherry, Mrs Cornish, and some fruit cake, since you can subject that to no further indignity. Be pleased to bring me a dish of sardines also. I am conscious of some diminishment in my constitution.'

When the housekeeper had withdrawn, Lady Ada turned again to the company. She might have been above fifty, but was vigorously erect in her posture. She wore a splendid cape of some exotic ivory-coloured fur over jodhpurs and a weathered pair of riding boots.

'I haven't the slightest need for a cane,' she remarked, as if in response to some inquiry. 'I play at tennis every day of the week, you know, even if it is quite dark when I come to think of it. The housekeeper's boy can scarcely return a ball, but I pelt them at him all the same. And when I am not holding a racquet, I keep my stick about me. It was impressed upon me at an early age that one ought never to be without some sturdy implement.'

Gideon drew out his notebook, in case Lady Ada's remarks proved to be of interest, but Cutter rebuked him. 'Put that away, Bliss. We are here as Lady Ada's guests.'

'Nonsense,' Lady Ada said. 'I am never without a notebook myself, especially in the field. Let the boy take his notes, if it keeps him from fidgeting.'

Cutter adjusted his stance as he absorbed this. 'As you wish, madam. Pardon the interruption.'

Lady Ada took a cigar from an imposing silver box. She struck a match, and let loose a startling profanity when it sputtered out. 'You interrupted me by coming here, yet you have done so without compunction. Why *did* you come, Inspector?'

'I am anxious to speak to your brother, madam.'

'You don't look at all anxious, Inspector. What do you want to speak to him about?'

'An unfortunate incident, madam. He was not at home when we looked for him, but we had reason to believe we might find him here.'

'But you have not found him here, have you? And yet you have dragged me from my bed.'

Cutter cleared his throat. 'I regret the disturbance, madam, but you may be able to assist us. We will not keep you long.'

Lady Ada gave him a sceptical look. 'What about these companions of yours?' she said, gesturing with her cigar. 'You yourself could not be mistaken for anything but a thief-taker, but your understudy was not made for such things, if I am any judge. As for the little miss who has so enraptured him, and who is at this moment lost in the contemplation of those cloud formations – they are nimbostratus, child. I have a splendid cloud atlas somewhere about the place. What is her purpose, would you say? And how does a policeman come by such an uncommon creature?'

Cutter looked troubled at this. Miss Tatton wore her gloves still, and her appearance – leaving aside her pallor – ought not to have seemed remarkable. 'The girl has come to us in unhappy circumstances, madam. I will not trouble you with the particulars.'

Lady Ada made no reply to this, choosing instead to join Miss Tatton at the window. Stowing her cane in the crook of her arm, she unscrewed the lens cap from a brass telescope and stooped to adjust its focus.

'Come, child,' she said. 'Clouds are all very well, but I have something better for you. Come, look at this.'

Gideon rose from his chair in alarm. 'If I may, madam,' he said. 'You may find that she—'

'Hush, will you,' Lady Ada said. 'What is the girl's name?'

'Angela Tatton, madam, but I believe she is commonly known as Angie.'

'Angie, indeed. I do not hold with diminutives. It is bad enough that so many young girls must be named after blossoms and virtues – after pretty trifles of no consequence in human affairs – all that is bad enough without lopping off the extremities of those few poor names we are granted. Angela was the name she was given, and Angela she shall be called. Come, Angela.'

Gideon looked on, clutching the arms of his chair, but in a moment his apprehension gave way to wonder. Miss Tatton turned slowly, hearing herself addressed. She glanced at the telescope, her expression uncertain, but made no move to touch it.

'Come, child,' said Lady Ada. 'There is no great mystery to it. Simply put your eye to it here, as I do now. It is already in view. If you disturb nothing, you will see it directly.'

Angie crouched above the instrument, clutching herself as if she feared it might injure her. For a moment she was silent and motionless, then she let out a gentle gasp. 'Up she rises,' she said softly. 'Up she rises.'

'You see her, then?' said Lady Ada in triumph. 'But she does not rise, alas, and never will again. The mast you see, and the spar that clings to it, are the only visible remnants of the *Persephone*, which was lost in fifty-two.'

'Lost,' Angie repeated.

'Just so. She has been claimed by the sands now, save for what you see, but she foundered in open water. She belonged to a clockmaker named Hartnell, if memory serves, who bankrupted himself in pursuit of a perpetual timepiece. He sank her for the insurance money, I gather, but drowned in the attempt. It was all done for love, of course, like the greater part of the foolishness that has been visited upon the world.'

Lady Ada directed this last observation to Gideon, who shifted uneasily in his seat. Miss Tatton gave no sign that she had understood. She had seemed to pay attention, but it was difficult to tell. She blinked after a moment, setting her head to one side in slow consideration.

'Tick-tock?' she said. 'Tick-tock?'

'Yes, my dear,' said Lady Ada. 'You understand more than you let on, I believe. You know about clocks, don't you? And about time?'

Here the inspector gave a discreet cough. 'Speaking of time, my lady, I wonder if we might return to the matter at hand? You are anxious to be rid of us, I'm sure.'

Lady Ada turned to him distractedly, as if she had forgotten he was present. 'Oh, there will be plenty of time for that, Inspector. Angela is to be my guest, I have decided. I seldom have visitors, and it has been a long time since I encountered someone – well, someone quite of her kind. You might as well stay too, since she has you in tow.'

The inspector cleared his throat gravely. 'It is very civil of you, Lady Ada, but our business is rather pressing. Since Lord Strythe is not here, we must return to London as soon as possible.'

'What is it you are investigating?' Lady Ada turned from the window, taking her stick from under her arm and planting it before her. 'You have given me no satisfactory account of it, you know.

What is it you want with my brother? And with me, for that matter?'

Cutter knotted his brow, as if he felt an unfamiliar discomfort. 'It is a delicate matter, madam. I hoped to spare your feelings.'

Lady Ada laced her fingers about the pommel of her cane. 'I have known rather more unpleasantness than you may credit,' she said. 'I will thank you to proceed, and no more of this mimsy circumlocution.'

'*Mimsy*?' The inspector's expression grew even more congested. 'Very well, then, madam, let me be direct. A woman was found dead at your brother's home in Half Moon-street. When we were called to the scene, we found that His Lordship was not at home. We were given to understand that he may have travelled to Vesper Sands. Believing the matter to be of some urgency, we followed him here, so as to interview him at his earliest convenience.'

'What woman?' Lady Ada spoke more quietly now, though she was no less intent. 'How did she die?'

'A Miss Esther Tull, madam. She was employed in Lord Strythe's household, we gather, as some manner of seamstress. She fell to her death from an upstairs window.'

'Fell to her death?' Lady Ada drew her lips taut. 'It can hardly be common for people to fall from windows to their deaths. They either leap from them, I should have thought, or they are pushed.'

Cutter's unblinking gaze met hers. 'That is very much the way of it, in my experience.'

'And what do you make of the present case, Inspector, given your experience? Did she jump, this Miss Tull, or was she pushed? Do you wish to charge the fourteenth Earl of Maundley in a murder? Is that the urgent matter?'

'The case is unusual, madam, that is all I may say, but I have reached no conclusion. I am aware of His Lordship's position, you may be sure. He was Miss Tull's employer, and as such he may know something of her circumstances, of what may have brought her to this. I am informed that he was not present at the time of her death, and that he was expected later that night but did not return. We should like to establish that he is safe and well, in the first place, and we should like to speak to him so that he may give us his own account of all this and send us on our way. That is the position, my lady, as plainly as I can lay it out. I hope I have given you some satisfaction.'

Lady Ada looked away for a time, as if in contemplation. 'Indeed,' she said at length. 'Indeed you have, after a fashion.'

She bowed her head, standing for a moment in thought before returning to the window. Angie had perched on the window seat, having tired of the telescope. She looked up as Lady Ada approached, her gaze unusually intent, and seemed to wait for her to speak again.

'You have given me satisfaction, Inspector,' Lady Ada resumed, keeping her back to the room. 'And if what you tell me is true – if it betokens what I believe it does – then I believe I may do the same for you. Young man, will you be good enough to ring the bell for Mrs Cornish? I will ask her to prepare your rooms.'

'Forgive me, Lady Ada,' said Cutter. 'Did I not make it plain that we must return to London?'

'Why, yes, Inspector. I am quite unimpaired, you know. You wish to return to London to seek my brother there, but you may spare yourself the journey. I know little enough of my brother's affairs, goodness knows, but I have made certain observations. He is a creature of habit, whatever else he may be, and has only ever had a single recourse when he finds that the world cannot be bent to his will. It is a spectacle I am always made to witness. You need not seek my brother in London, Inspector. My brother, unless I am much mistaken, is on his way here.'

XX

When Georgie knocked to announce a visitor, Octavia assumed at first that she had simply misheard. She turned from her dressing table as he put his head around the door.

'I'm sorry, darling, *who's* downstairs?'

'That Lord Hartington. I'd hardly have known him, mind you. Not a frill or a carnation in sight.'

'Honestly, Georgie. How old-fashioned you are. Elf is a little flamboyant, that's all. It's the fashion. It can't be him, though. It's only half past eight in the morning.'

He nodded, indicating the window. 'See for yourself. Won't even come indoors to wait. Urgent business, he says.'

On social occasions, Elf was driven in his town coach, a grand affair bedecked with armorial bearings and attended by at least two footmen. The carriage waiting below was no more than a common growler, drawn by a tired and mismatched pair. Elf was pacing the footway alongside it, with an idleness that seemed affected. He wore a sombre and unremarkable coat, and his hat might have belonged to a commercial traveller. When Octavia emerged, perhaps half an hour later, he greeted her with faint embarrassment.

'Why, Elf,' she said. 'I should hardly have known you. What on earth brings you out at this hour?'

He said nothing until he had shown her aboard, signalling to the driver with a rap on the roof. 'You see me in my official capacity, my darling, which calls for a certain restraint. Still, it is not all bleakness. Here, have a swig of this against the chill.'

He held out a pocket-flask, which she declined, looking on as he took a decorous swig. 'There is no disgrace in drinking from a flask,' he said, 'as long as one's entire person is aboard a moving vehicle. I have it on Her Majesty's own authority.'

'What's this about, Elf? It's lovely to see you, of course, but I'd quite like to know. Where are we going?'

He smiled at this, looking away out the window as they turned into Millbank-street. The glass was imperfect, and had the ochre taint of tobacco smoke. In the street outside the office workers shuffled towards Whitehall, and against their dark umbrellas she saw the hesitant smudges of returning snow.

'How dreary it must be,' he said. 'Simply making one's way every day. Trudging to the same stool before the same counting desk. Improving one's lot by sheer dint of industry.'

'Elf,' she said again. 'Why are you here?'

'I've been thinking, Wavy, about your chosen profession. And you have *chosen* it, haven't you? You don't *have* to work for a living, goodness knows.'

'Grandfather always felt that one ought to.' Something in her flinched at this. The words did not seem entirely her own. '*I* feel that one ought to. I wasn't born to this, as you know. Things might have been different.'

'Yes, well. Sterling chap, old Felix. Such a shame about his ...' He gave a perfunctory grimace. 'How *is* he, these days?'

'Elf.'

'I'm sorry, darling. I'll come to the point. I've been thinking, you see, since my conversation with Mr Healy at the *Gazette* – he really is quite unpleasant, isn't he? I'm afraid I've neglected you rather. I mean, I've fed you titbits of gossip, but you can get those from dozens of people. And besides, it's not what you really want, is it? You want to turn your mind to serious subjects, to matters of public importance. Which I applaud, by the way.'

She waited, regarding him evenly.

'Yes, I've been a poor friend to you, I'm afraid.' He looked out as they turned into Parliament-square, gesturing negligently in the direction of Whitehall. 'These scurrying labyrinths, Wavy. You really can't imagine. They found an assistant secretary dead, you know, in an attic at the India Office. He'd been gone three years, and the vague impression had been formed that he'd popped out to Bengal to modernise the post offices. And yet it creaks on, the entire cumbrous and dilatory apparatus of Empire – someone said that, I can't remember who. Somehow the defence of the realm is sustained. And when one enjoys a certain proximity, one comes to detect certain currents, and – well, there is a tide in the affairs of men, and what have you.'

'Which affairs in particular?'

'Well, I am somewhat constrained, as I've mentioned. One has a duty of discretion. And this new Official Secrets Act, goodness me. A chap can be broken on the wheel for divulging the shipping forecast. But there are other duties, aren't there?' He gave a soft cough. 'The bonds of affection, and that sort of thing.'

She offered him a brief smile and brushed something from her cuff. It had been over a year since his strange little declaration. He'd been terribly embarrassed, at the time. He had taken too much champagne, that was all. She had thought it kinder not to mention it again.

'At any rate,' Elf resumed. 'The thing is, I've come to believe I can help you, my darling. I can direct your steps, as it were, in certain matters of public interest. Matters whose significance even Mr Healy can't fail to recognise.'

'This Spiriters business, you mean?'

'There's that, yes.' He looked out again. 'Birdcage-walk, wavy. You could do worse than start here, you know, if it's secrets you're after. The fellows who have undone themselves, keeping assignations behind these trees.'

'There are certain things I won't stoop to, Elf. Besides, I know most of those secrets already.'

'Of course, dear heart, and I wouldn't dream of insulting you with tattle of that kind. I meant only that one must look in high places as well as low.'

'Which high places, exactly?'

'Oh, you don't need my help with that, Wavy. I rather suspect you already know.'

'Honestly, Elf. Must you be so infuriatingly cryptic?'

'Forgive me. A habit of my profession. When we spoke last night, after that ridiculous seance, you mentioned that you'd gone to Whitechapel quite late the day before, and only after first dispatching your redoubtable brother on a mission of reconnaissance.'

'Did I really say all that? I knew I oughtn't to have had a second glass of madeira.'

He smiled, stroking one arched eyebrow. 'Oh, you were admirably guarded otherwise. Wouldn't say a word about where you'd been that morning. As it happens, though, I wasn't relying entirely on your confidence. I'd been making certain inquiries of my own. You weren't the only one who was curious about where Lord Strythe had got to.'

She stared at him in silence for a moment. 'How did you know?'

He spread his hands, mockingly aggrieved. 'Why, Wavy,

darling. You haven't forgotten, surely? You had already confessed to a certain curiosity at Lady Ashenden's. And when he failed to make an appearance, I was the one you sent to find out why. And off I went in unquestioning gallantry, doing your bidding behind enemy lines.'

'Except that there aren't any enemy lines, not where you're concerned. You can be sure of safe passage anywhere in London, can't you?' She looked away, drumming at her reticule in irritation. 'And of finding anything out, it seems. Yes, I went to Strythe House on the morning after the ball, as you seem to have been informed already. Shall I just assume, from now on, that you can account for my every waking hour?'

'Dear me,' said Elf. 'I'm afraid I'm making rather a hash of all this. I wasn't informed, old thing, I simply guessed. I was curious, yes, but I haven't had you followed by footpads. Goodness, how sinister you must think me.'

Octavia studied him for a moment. His wounded air was plainly affected, but that was hardly unusual. As with all his affectations, it seemed to invite the suspicion that a truer sentiment lay beneath it, bravely withheld. 'Well, in any case,' she said, relenting a little, 'why did you bring it up? Is that how you mean to help me? By saving me the trouble of finding Lord Strythe? Are you going to produce him triumphantly and take a bow? Is that why we're here?'

He gave a measured sigh. 'Look, old thing, you've got the wrong idea. I'm not doing any of this to spoil your fun. If I've taken a keen interest in our friend Strythe, it's because he and his household have begun to attract an unwelcome degree of attention.'

'What do you mean? What sort of attention?'

'My connection is to the Home Office, as you may remember. I have oversight of, well, certain police functions.'

'The police? Lord Strythe has come to the attention of the *police*? What on earth for?'

'A suicide at his home, to begin with. And then he went missing, which was a little disobliging of him. And now, this morning – well, you'll see when we get there. You'll want to see everything, I'm sure, for the purposes of accuracy.'

'Accuracy? What are you talking about now?'

'I'm talking about the account you're going to write for the *Gazette*.'

'Of what, for goodness' sake? Elf, this is absurd.'

'Of a sad event that will attract a good deal of public notice.' He glanced out again. 'Look, we're turning into Piccadilly. There isn't time to explain everything now, so I must ask you to trust me. This is what you wanted, isn't it? A worthier subject? Secrets that are worth uncovering? Trust me, Wavy, and I promise you, there will be more. Not just Strythe, but the rest too. The Spiriters. The missing girl. All of it.'

She had been about to speak, but now she could only stare. She shook her head slowly. He leaned towards her.

'Don't ask how I know. It's not the right question any longer. You do want to find her, don't you? Perhaps you've even promised to. You really needn't say. I do too, you see, even if it's for slightly different reasons. Please, just trust me for now. This is what you can do for me. Afterwards, there will be much more I can do for you.'

Octavia drew back, considering him. Elf reclined too, opening his hands as if to welcome her scrutiny. She shook her head again. 'Healy won't print it.'

'Oh, he'll print it, dear heart. If he doesn't, he will be beaten to it by half the papers in London. He might even be inclined to put out a late edition.'

The carriage paused at the corner of Half Moon-street, where a small crowd had gathered in spite of the weather. A pair of police vehicles had been drawn together to block the way, and before them a loose rank of constables stood glowering at the onlookers. A man in brown moved unobtrusively among them, muttering occasional instructions. He was watchful and unhurried, and his hat and coat had a borrowed drabness about them, just as Elf's did. When he caught sight of their carriage he gave a signal, at which the barricade parted and the constables began clearing a path. The man in brown looked on wordlessly as they passed, only raising a desultory finger to his hat brim. Elf, who seemed to have looked for him as they arrived, gave a languid salute in acknowledgement. It was only then that Octavia recognised his face.

'That man,' she said. 'We saw him at Ashenden House. You said you knew him vaguely. Who is he, Elf? A policeman?'

'Not exactly, old thing.'

She studied him again. It was not only his clothes. In the greyish light, even his skin had an unfamiliar pallor, as if his habitual colour had been carefully suppressed. 'Honestly, Elf,' she said. 'I feel I hardly know you at all. And if you can engineer all of this, why bring me into it? I'm quite sure you can have something reported on in the papers without my help.'

'Look, Wavy.' He faced her again, and now his manner was confiding. 'Don't think I don't understand. I know this isn't quite what you'd have wanted. You'd much rather have made your name with a scandal you'd ferreted out for yourself, but the circumstances that come to define us are almost never of our own choosing. Fate is a fairy tale, my darling. In life, there is only opportunity and advantage.'

She waited, keeping her expression neutral. She knew there would be more.

'And there is something else you must understand, Wavy. This is an opportunity, yes, but it is also a necessity. I can't explain exactly what I mean – not yet, at any rate – but we must take these steps first if there is to be any hope of our finding the missing girl. There are other interested parties in all of this, who will almost certainly frustrate our efforts if we do nothing. This will win us time – not a great deal of time, perhaps, but it may be just enough. Well, what do you have to say, Miss Octavia Hillingdon? Is this to be your opportunity?'

She sighed in resignation. 'You're pretending I have a choice. It's kind of you, I suppose, in a way.'

He pulled on his gloves and gave an equivocal smile. 'Splendid,' he said. 'Now, then. I haven't been given all the details yet, but they wouldn't have gone to all this trouble to keep the crowd back unless there were something pretty ghastly for them to gawk at. I know you're not the frail sort, and no doubt you see all manner of things as you bicycle about the meaner districts. But even so, I'm afraid you must prepare yourself.'

'Prepare myself? How?'

He drew his pocket-flask from his coat again and offered it to her. 'Well, to begin with,' he said, 'you really ought to reconsider that drink.'

Mayfair Gazette

February 4, 1893

ANOTHER FATALITY AT STRYTHE HOUSE

A SECOND UNEXPLAINED DEATH HAS OCCURRED AT STRYTHE HOUSE IN HALF MOON-STREET, MAYFAIR, THE LONDON RESIDENCE OF LORD STRYTHE, 14TH EARL OF MAUNDLEY. The fatality follows the death of MISS ESTHER TULL, 37, a seamstress, who met her end in strikingly similar circumstances late in the evening of the 1st inst. These are to come before an inquest at a date to be announced by MR A. BRAXTON HICKS, Coroner for the South-Western District of London and Surrey.

The deceased in the present case was a male person aged approximately 55 years, whose death was in apparent consequence of falling or jumping from an upper part of the residence. His remains were discovered in the early hours of this morning by JOHN WARNOCK, an inspector of police, C Division, who was in the vicinity on unrelated police business and granted an interview to a correspondent of the *Gazette*.

The dead man had occasioned grievous injuries to the face and upper body, which the present correspondent was permitted to observe at close quarters. No identification had yet been made, and the police surgeon had yet to attend the scene. Insp. Warnock would not enter into speculation, but affirmed that the age of the deceased was consistent with that of Lord Strythe.

Asked whether adult males other than His Lordship were ordinarily resident at Strythe House, Insp. Warnock said that to his knowledge there were none, with the exception of the household staff, and remarked that the deceased did not appear to be clothed in the manner of a domestic servant, but rather in the evening attire of a gentleman of rank.

The present correspondent sought the testimony of other members of the household, but none was forthcoming. Callers are discouraged from presenting themselves at Strythe House, and no statement is expected from His Lordship's representatives until such time as the proper Authorities have made an official determination.

XXI

Gideon was woken by a quietness in the weather.

He had felt it as he slept, this lull, and his dreams had grown uneasy. He had seen his mother and father, faceless now in his memory. They had left him behind, on a rutted track in some colourless fenland. He had called to them from where he stood, but his voice had failed in his throat.

His mother looked back once, raising the crook of her hand to shade her whited face, then trudged onwards at his father's side to a place in the road where a laden cart was waiting. A hawk crossed the vacant sky, and the cart lumbered slowly away. Nothing else stirred, and the soundlessness troubled him. Perhaps it was like that, in the end. Perhaps a silence came.

Gideon woke to these unravelling thoughts, and to a peculiar sense that something in his surroundings had been altered. He lay still for a moment, then sat up abruptly, as if to catch sight of some stealthy intruder. There was no one, and no sign that anyone had come in while he slept. His water glass stood undisturbed at his bedside. His clothes hung just as he had left them on the chair by the washstand. The curtains were not quite fully drawn, leaving an interval of darkness where the moon had been before he slept.

Nothing had changed, or nothing that he could name, but his conviction persisted. Some subtle transfiguration had occurred.

It was in the stillness of the air, in the spill of cold light at the doorway.

Gideon stood with no clear intention, confronting himself in the dressing mirror, a borrowed nightshirt hanging loosely about his meagre frame. He flexed his feet, looking about him in wariness. The boards were dry against his soles, and minutely fissured, like the ridges of seashells. He crossed to the window, drawing back the curtains so as to let in what moonlight there was. A stalled wind stirred faintly among the fringes of the dunes. Where it met the darkness, the skin of the sea had the greenish pallor of lichen.

There.

To his left, at the margin of his vision. It had crossed the door-way, the quadrant of pale light from the landing beyond. If he waited. If he hid the thought from himself, or looked away until it receded. If he waited, he would turn and see nothing. He would admonish himself, sighing with fond relief as he returned to his bed.

And so it was. He turned. *There, you see.* He turned, and he saw nothing.

But it was not so.

There.

He pressed his eyes closed. When he opened them, his senses were sundered, adrift. He saw her and he did not.

'Angie? Miss Tatton?'

She was fading. He had seen her only hours before, yet he was shocked by how far advanced the changes seemed. He approached her, surveying her anxiously. Perhaps it was her clothing, at least in part. She had been a good deal covered up, and now she wore only a yellowed and threadbare nightgown. The vanishing had crept from her extremities on the right side. Her right arm had faded now almost to her elbow, and from just below the knee her right leg was reduced to the same spectral translucence. Yet there was a delicate wholeness still to what remained of her. The taut hollow of her throat, the stark clavicle enclosing its scoop of shadowed softness.

'Oh, Angie.'

'Hush,' she said. 'Hush-a-by, rock-a-by.'

On the landing, a pale light flickered and brightened. It was chilly and pure, and came from some unseen source. He thought of an opal he had been shown once, by a chap at Selwyn whose father had been in the Colonial Office. It had been mined in Zanzibar, and it had looked, even against a clammy palm, like a phial of Arctic sunlight.

Gideon ventured closer. 'Angie?' he said. 'Is something the matter? Did something wake you?'

But it came to him even as he spoke the words. She had not been sleeping. He had not seen her sleep since taking her from the hospital. A half-shade, Cutter had called her. She was not yet a ghost, perhaps, but there were needs she no longer felt.

Yet perhaps she had been disturbed, even so, by this strange quiescence in the weather. It was passing now, he thought, and the air was astir once more. At the windows, in ragged pulses, he heard the returning rain.

Miss Tatton had been pacing the floor, silent and distracted, but she halted now, suddenly alert.

'When the wind blows.' Her voice was vacant and desiccated. 'Lord have mercy.'

'Angie?'

She seemed agitated, in her distant and unknowable way, and he felt the urge to comfort her. He reached for her hesitantly, meaning only to touch her arm, but she hissed and spun away.

Her face, for an instant, was cold and feral.

'Miss Tatton?' He drew back. 'Miss Tatton, forgive me. I did not mean to—'

But the moment passed. She grew distracted again, looking uneasily about her as the rain gathered force against the eaves.

'Angie?' He spoke gently, fearful still that she would turn on him again. '*Angela mea.* Is that what you are becoming, an angel? We are taught to distrust such notions, but Augustine himself might have entertained it. When we speak of angels, he said, we speak of the office they hold, not of their nature. In nature, they are spirits.'

She paid no attention. She raised her face to the air, as if to catch the thread of a scent.

'Miss Tatton?' But he knew it was useless. He shook his head ruefully. 'I believed I was in awe of you once, but I had forgotten the first meaning of that word, that there was terror in it long before there was wonder. I had forgotten the angels in scripture, who are not always seraphs. There are angels of destruction too.'

She glanced at him, or through him, her face avid and fierce.

'Forgive me,' he said. 'I cannot keep from babbling. I was helpless from the very beginning. Do you not remember, Angie? Those first days, in the summer? Do you really not remember?'

She took a step towards him, her bare soles soundless on the boards. Her gaze flickered about his face, as if seeking out a resemblance in a portrait. He made himself still.

'Angie?'

'One for the master,' she whispered. When she raised her hand, or the ghost of it, he could not tell if her fingertips had touched his cheek. 'And one for the dame.'

'Yes.' He whispered too, afraid even to disturb the air. 'Young master, you called me, though I wished you would say my name.

And how I wish it now. It is me. It is Gideon.'

But she looked away even as he spoke. She had grown intent again, as if she were certain now of something that had eluded her. She stared into the darkness, her attention fixed on something he could not guess at. The landing overlooked the entrance hall two floors below, but the wall she faced was windowless and dark. She crossed to the stone parapet that joined the banister at the head of the stairs, skimming it with unseen fingertips as she peered out into the shadows.

'Angie?' he said. 'Miss Tatton?'

She was still for a moment, hunched and alert. Then – silently, and with unnatural ease – she mounted it and stood lightly upright. Gideon clapped a hand to his mouth, as if to keep his breath from disturbing the air. She craned outwards into the darkness, intent on something only she could see.

'Angie.' He spoke in the faintest possible whisper. 'Miss Tatton, please. The drop must be thirty feet. Come down, I beg you.'

The parapet was eight or nine inches wide, and her toes – those he could see, at least – extended a little way beyond its outer edge. She flexed them gently, testing the surface of the stone. He wondered if she had lost sensation in her faded limbs. If she could still feel pain. From outside, at some distance still, he heard the first low rupture of thunder.

'Rock-a-by, baby,' she sang faintly. 'On the treetop.'

'Angie.' He crept towards her. 'Angie, please.'

'When the wind blows, the cradle will rock.' She swayed gently as she sang, but her gaze never wavered. 'When the bough breaks, the cradle will fall.'

'Angie! Oh, Jesus Christ!' He lunged, grasping in desperation at the hem of her nightgown. She turned for a moment, glancing over her shoulder as if at the source of some faint irritation. She spread out her arms, and spoke the last words in a whisper.

'Down will come baby.'

Lightning. In the stutter of brightness he saw her, crouched and hawk-still, then she was gone. He felt it as she vaulted clear, her fierce cold quickness. He heard the slicing air, the snap of cotton. He hung there then, stretched above the vacant darkness. For a moment he could not be sure if he had closed his eyes, and in the devouring silence when she was gone, he could not tell at first that he had screamed.

XXII

The man who waited for them at London Bridge Station was by now familiar. The train for Deal had been due to depart some minutes before, and an agitated conductor now hovered at his elbow, but the man in brown was unperturbed. He watched Octavia and Elf approach from the door of the first-class coach, keeping one foot on its step and the other on the platform, and he made it plain by his bearing – even as the steam gathered about him – that he would not be moved until he was ready.

Octavia had seen it in him at Strythe House, that air of stolid assurance, the way he had of seeming indifferent while observing everything. Inspector Warnock had been in notional command of the scene – a ludicrous, preening oaf with a reeking cigar – but it was this man whose quiet directions had been heeded. It was this man, too, who had drawn back the sacking that covered the body, whose unblinking gaze she had felt while she mastered her breathing and made her notes.

When he was obliged to speak – to explain, for instance, that he would deliver her finished article to the *Gazette* while she returned home to pack her things – he made the smallest possible concessions to civility. Even now, as Elf stood aside to let her board first, the man in brown greeted her with no more than a fractional nod.

'Dear me,' said Elf, as they settled themselves in their compartment. 'We do find ourselves in sadly reduced circumstances, don't we? All this humping from one dreary coach to another. I'm afraid I have dragged you rather a long way from our usual milieu. But perhaps even the South Eastern Railway may stretch to a bottle of champagne to steady our nerves.'

Octavia studied their unnamed companion. He had taken the seat opposite hers, folding his arms and turning with equanimity to the window. The train slipped its cowl of steam, shuddering eastwards under a decaying mass of grey cloud. They passed a vinegar works and a brewery. Beneath them, against the dingy bricks of Bermondsey, the snow persisted in meagre scatters.

'In our usual milieu,' she said, 'the gentleman and I would have been introduced by now.'

Elf looked at her in mild distraction, folding away his greatcoat and signalling to a porter that he would sooner keep it by him. 'Why, yes,' he said. 'I suppose that is rather irregular. My colleague shares my habit of discretion in official matters, though we are much too dull, goodness knows, to warrant such excesses. Allow me, then, to present – let me see – Mr Brown. Mr Brown, this is Miss Octavia Hillingdon. She is the granddaughter of Felix Hillingdon, the great newspaperman, and now a journalist in her own right. I am pleased to think of Miss Hillingdon as a particular friend.'

She studied him at some length, taking note of his coarse tobacco-coloured suit, his freshly clipped moustache, the tiny comma of dirt beneath his thumbnail. When she turned back to Elf he smiled blandly. The deception was a minor courtesy. She was not expected to believe it, but she was expected to spare them the awkwardness of pointing it out.

'Mr Brown,' she said curtly. He inclined his head and nudged the brim of his hat. 'You also serve in some official capacity, I suppose?'

'In a modest capacity,' Elf interjected. 'Rather like mine. Our sort are ten a penny in Whitehall.'

'I find that hard to believe, Elf. And does Mr Brown also – how did you put it, exactly? Does he also have oversight of "certain police matters"? Without being a policeman himself?'

Elf beamed. 'We are fortunate to have cordial relations with Her Majesty's various constabularies. And yes, we lend them our assistance in certain matters.'

'It rather appeared to me,' Octavia said, 'to be the other way around.'

Elf reclined in his seat and studied her with faint amusement. 'How do you mean, old thing?'

'I'm not an imbecile, Elf. You brought me to Strythe House because there were things you wanted me to see. Did you expect me to notice *only* what you wanted?'

'Touché,' he said. He had taken his gloves off and clutched them now against his chest. 'I'm afraid I rather deserved that.'

'You asked me to trust you, Elf, and I have. But there are limits. Strythe House is one thing, but I'm not about to trot behind you all the way across Kent with nothing more than your assurances. This train is for Deal, which isn't far from Lord Strythe's seaside residence. I have been looking into his affairs, you know, and I've tried to be thorough. I take that to be something more than a co-incidence, but I have no intention of puzzling out the rest on my own. Unless you explain all this to my satisfaction, I'll be getting off at the first stop.'

Elf let out a languorous sigh. 'Well, Brown,' he said, 'it looks as if the game is up, old chum. We shall have to be more forthcoming, if we are to remain in Miss Hillingdon's good graces.'

Mr Brown thumbed the corner of his mouth. 'Looks that way,' he said.

'Miss Hillingdon has always been devilishly sharp,' continued Elf. 'I have relied upon it, in fact, and always intended to be frank with her when the time was right. These little adventures are splendidly diverting, of course, but one is obliged to conduct oneself according to certain methods. Very well, then, Wavy. Where ought we to begin?'

'We ought to begin with why. Why are we going to Vesper Sands? His Lordship's household sent for him there, but he wasn't to be found.'

'Goodness, you have been thorough, haven't you? We're going there because I promised to help you. When we spoke last night, you had a great deal on your mind. You'd been preoccupied as it was, what with our friend Strythe and his irregular doings, and then you'd been thrust into the Spiriters business, which turned out not to be entirely the product of Mr Healy's daydreams. Your cup has been fairly running over, lately. And then there was the matter of this missing girl, of this . . .'

'Miss Tatton. Miss Angela Tatton.'

'Miss Tatton, yes. You wanted to find her, naturally, and for the noblest of reasons, but you couldn't bring yourself to put aside these other mysteries. And why should you? Chances like these don't come along very often. But what if you didn't have to choose? I'm not sure about the Spiriters – not yet, at any rate – but what if I were to tell you that you could look for Miss Tatton *and* find out more about Strythe? And that all you had to do was stay on this train?'

'What? But why would the missing girl be in Kent?' Mr Brown cocked his head at this, as if he too were curious. 'You aren't suggesting that Lord Strythe—'

'Steady on, old thing. No, nothing of that kind. As for the girl, well, the circumstances seem rather peculiar, but we shall return to that in just a moment. The police have been sniffing around Strythe all right, but only because people keep plunging from his battlements. They were first called to the house on Thursday morning, after the seamstress was found.'

'Her name was Esther Tull,' said Octavia. 'Aged thirty-seven years, of Charlotte-street, Bethnal Green. That dreadful Inspector Warnock had all the particulars at the ready, though I'm not sure he'd got them first-hand.'

'Well, no. Warnock has his uses, but when there's a delicate bit of business at the home of an earl, well, he's not the sort of chap you'd send. No, it was a man from the Yard, and the thing seems to have aroused his curiosity.'

'He suspects foul play, you mean? But Lord Strythe himself was not at home.'

'So I gather. As to the circumstances of the death itself, the coroner must have his say in the first instance. In the meantime, the fellow who was sent to the house has begun making discreet inquiries. And this is where the missing girl comes in, curiously enough. Now, I have only the sparsest of intelligence as yet, but this policeman seems to have turned her up, and in circumstances we haven't yet accounted for. It may be that he was looking into the Spiriters too, although it wouldn't be entirely regular if he were. That's being investigated by local chaps in Whitechapel, where it hasn't really gathered any steam. As far as they're concerned, it's just a spate of missing persons cases. Of course, it may be that this fellow simply stumbled upon the Tatton girl quite by chance, but in that case I'd have expected him to hand her over to the boys at Leman-street. Instead, he seems to have taken the rather bewildering step of keeping her with him. He and his sergeant took the first train for Deal this morning, Miss Tatton in tow.'

'But why? Why would this policeman keep her with him?'

'Well, it's a puzzle, as I say. Again, it may simply be that he has more than one iron in the fire. But even so, it can hardly be convenient. If he's going to go poking around in Lord Strythe's affairs, the last thing he ought to do is draw attention to himself.'

'I don't understand,' said Octavia. 'If he suspects some wrongdoing, then surely he is acting within his powers?'

'Well, it rather depends, you see. It's a question of proper grounds. As things stand – or rather, as they stood – nothing more than an unexplained death had been reported. A sad case, of course, but one that might well prove to be nothing more than a doleful little suicide. Scotland Yard is not in the habit of making work for itself. It is certainly not in the habit of provoking scandals involving peers of the realm unless they cannot in all decency be avoided. No, our man has got a sniff of something, but no more than that. Until he has built a case like the hull of a dreadnought, he is on his own.'

'Even peers of the realm are subject to its laws. And to the scrutiny of the press, for that matter. What do you know about this policeman? Is he likely to be proven right?'

'You may well ask,' said Elf. 'He is Inspector Henry Cutter of the CID. A well-regarded chap, if rather more feared than loved among the ranks. He made his name with the investigation of a rather gruesome and distressing case, though I imagine it was before your time. In the pages of the tawdrier publications, it was known as "The Slaughter of the St Johns".'

'I've heard it mentioned,' Octavia said. 'Wasn't there some connection to a cabinet member?'

'To the Home Secretary, no less. Dr St John was his brother-in-law. Yes, it was a thoroughly nasty affair, and took a good deal of unpicking. There aren't many who could have made a go of it as he did, and he's been given quite a bit of leeway ever since – rather too much, in the view of some. He has a weakness for certain exotic cases, you see, and his methods tend towards the unorthodox. Still, even Cutter is not given free rein. Indeed, I have it on good authority that until this morning he was on the point of being called in for a talking-to.'

'What do you mean, "until this morning"? What was it that changed their minds?'

'Why, the most recent tragedy at Strythe House, of course. Since it now appears that Lord Strythe himself may have met an untimely end, they must be seen to spare no effort. Inspector Warnock is hardly fit to investigate a break-in at a henhouse, but he need only mind the shop until Cutter returns. Inspector Cutter, meanwhile, has taken himself off to Kent to ask impertinent questions, and there's no reason now to haul him back.'

'As long as one assumes,' Octavia said, 'that the remains we examined belonged to Lord Strythe.'

Elf studied her for a moment. 'Well, quite,' he said. 'One must keep an open mind, after all. I must say, Wavy, you have quite the gift for intrigue.'

He was about to say more when they were disturbed by a rattling at the door. A man in a drab black coat entered, uncovering his head with a diffident flourish. 'Do excuse me,' he said. 'The mechanism proved troublesome – the door handle, that is to say – though perhaps the fault is in my own creaking apparatus. The indignities of age, you see. But never fear, I shall be as quiet as a mouse once I have taken my seat.'

The passenger turned from the door, making a shuffling bow to the company. He removed his scarf – revealing a clergyman's collar – and was on the point of unfastening his overcoat when Mr Brown interrupted.

'That seat is taken.'

The clergyman greeted this with a look of mild perplexity, blinking above his spectacles at each of them in turn. 'I beg your pardon?' he said.

'That seat.' Brown pointed to it. 'This compartment. They're taken. You're in the wrong place.'

'Oh,' said the clergyman. 'Oh, dear. What a dreadful muddle.'

He was in his middle fifties, Octavia judged, and had about him the genteel shabbiness that is tolerated in churchmen of a certain age. 'You must forgive me,' he continued, buttoning his coat again. 'The porter guided me almost to the very door, yet I have contrived to go astray. At my age, you see, one navigates a perpetual fog.'

Elf opened the door for him. 'My associate is a little brusque in his manner, I am afraid. It is only that we are transacting some private business. Otherwise we should have been very glad to have the pleasure of your company.'

'Not a bit of it, not a bit of it.' The clergyman bowed as he retreated to the passageway. 'I should never get on in business, I fear, being so much occupied with the eternal. I must wait rather longer for my rewards.'

He paused in the doorway and studied each of them in turn. His expression was benign, in the practised manner of clergymen, and curiously immobile. His features, once he had arranged them as he wished, might have belonged to a waxwork figure. 'Goodness me,' he said, glancing at the window. 'How the snow hastens the gloom. It is hardly more than two o'clock, yet the darkness is all but complete.'

Elf closed the door behind him and stood for a moment in thought. As he moved to return to his seat, he caught sight of something and stooped to pick it up.

'How tedious,' he said, rising. 'Our absent-minded friend

seems to have dropped something. Brown, old fellow, would you be awfully obliging?'

Elf held out what appeared to be a small and unmarked medicine bottle. Mr Brown studied it for a moment, then glanced in the direction of the passageway. He raised an eyebrow.

'I didn't notice either,' said Elf, as if in reply. 'We were distracted, perhaps, and it is rather a tiny article. In any case, it seems the gentlemanly thing to do. Return it to him, will you. With my particular compliments.'

'Your particular compliments?'

'Just so.'

Mr Brown seemed satisfied by this. Retrieving his hat, he excused himself with a perfunctory nod and stepped neatly into the corridor.

'Yes, a curious fellow,' Elf mused. 'And faintly familiar, it seems to me, but perhaps my imagination has been stirred by all this excitement. Now then, I find I have quite lost the thread of our conversation.'

'We were talking about the death of Lord Strythe,' said Octavia. 'Or the appearance of it, at least, which will put this Inspector Cutter on a longer leash.'

'Yes, precisely. And whatever the truth of the matter, it will do Cutter no harm if that appearance is kept up for a while. The longer he has a free hand, the more you yourself may discover. I ought to have explained things a little better before bundling you aboard this frightful train, but I've had your best interests at heart. You do see that now, I hope?'

Octavia looked away in weariness. They passed the dockyard at Woolwich, where some scaffolded hulk loomed in the grey air. 'And what about you, Elf? What about your interests? You do have some continuing interest in the matter, I take it? You and Mr Brown aren't taking a holiday by the sea?'

He smiled faintly, extending one hand to examine his finger-nails. 'We shall keep a watching brief, nothing more.'

'Really, Elf? I still have no clear idea of what it is you do, but I've seen you and Mr Brown around policemen. Scotland Yard may not be interfering any longer, but how can I be sure this Cutter will be allowed to do his job?'

'Cutter is his own man, I assure you. If he weren't, I'd know a good deal more about what he's up to. He's certainly not the sort to make himself amenable to fellows like me. I shall be obliged to keep a certain distance while you and he become acquainted. Of course, you'll have to ingratiate yourself with Strythe's sister first. Did you know about Lady Ada? Rather miserable sort of existence she's had, by all accounts, and I'm not sure it's left the old girl entirely untouched. In any case, I'll remain in the offing. The man we found this morning will be examined by the surgeon, and his identity will be confirmed, one way or the other. It will be at least a day or two, I imagine, before word reaches us, and in the meantime, well, gather ye rosebuds, as it were. All I ask is that you keep me informed, and that you do nothing for now to dispel the impression that Strythe is dead. Dear me, what's all this now?'

The train was shuddering to a halt amid a violent clamour of chains and shrieking metal. Soon the whistles of the guards could be heard, and a commotion of raised voices.

'Good Lord,' said Elf, releasing the arms of his seat 'Are you all right, Wavy? I fear you were thrown about.'

'I'm fine,' Octavia said. 'They were braking hard, that's all. Go and see what the matter is.'

He crossed to the door and put his head out. 'You there,' he called. 'I say, you there, guard. What the devil is all the fuss about? Why have we stopped?'

Octavia joined him at the door, where a guard stood with his cap under his arm. He was no more than fifteen or sixteen, and breathless and grimy from some heavy work. 'Which there's been an accident, sir,' he said, casting an anxious glance along the passageway. 'I'd best get on, sir, begging your pardon. All hands is wanted.'

'What sort of accident?' said Octavia. 'Is anyone hurt?'

'I'd as soon not say, miss, if you won't take it amiss.'

A sooty grease obscured half the youth's face, so that at first Octavia had paid no attention to the remainder. She saw now how pale it was, and how grave and sunken his eyes appeared in his boyish face.

'You've had a shock,' she said. 'But I had seen a dead man before you had your breakfast this morning. Tell me what happened.'

'Well, miss, sir.' The boy took his hat from under his arm and began worrying at its peak with his thumbs. 'We passed the train for London a ways back, when we was just out of Woolwich. Only the London train don't stop there, no more nor this one does, and so it were running all out – upwards of forty mile an hour, easy. And it seems a gentleman put out his head for a nip of fresh air at just the wrong moment. Must have been hard of hearing, Mr Downes reckons, or he'd have heard it coming.'

'Where is he?' said Elf, who spoke now with evident agitation. 'You must take me to him. How severe is the injury?'

The guard began to speak, but hesitated. 'Sir, we ain't found – we ain't found everything yet.'

'Everything?' Elf looked at him as if he were raving. 'What are you talking about, boy?'

The youth looked in discomfort from Elf to Octavia, lodging his hat under one arm. 'Which, sir, the trains was both at full speed.

The gentleman's head was took off his shoulders, and it must have been carried a good way, for we ain't found it yet.'

It was after eight o'clock in the evening when at last the train arrived at Deal. It had stood on the track outside Woolwich for over an hour while the grim business of the accident was attended to, and had been made to wait a further half an hour outside Faversham, where the platform was occupied by a goods train from Whitstable.

Octavia had gone with Elf to inspect Mr Brown's body – she had insisted upon it, though he grew strangely vehement in his objections. It was official business, he said, turning and barring the passageway when he saw her following. Mr Brown's death had occurred in the service of Her Majesty's Government, and was now a matter of the utmost sensitivity.

'Is that why you kept his real name from me?' Octavia said, finding a hardness in her voice. 'And wasn't he on official business this morning, too, when he showed me the body at Strythe House? You were quite content to have me witness that.'

The carriage had been emptied of other passengers, and one of its doors stood open to the cold. Mr Brown's body was slumped in front of the other, at the far end of the corridor. It puzzled her at first, the lapsed mass that remained. Only when his feet came into view could she begin to make sense of it. There. She saw where the heaped parts were curtailed, how they had folded helplessly upon themselves.

She put a hand to her mouth.

And the blood. It was lavish almost, how much there was to be expelled. It had reached even the ceiling, leaving great looping flourishes on the walls and windows. So much had pooled on the floor that they had put down sand, covering it in turn with sacking so as to make the corridor passable.

Octavia supported herself against a bulkhead, refusing an offer of tea. Certain practical matters were discussed. The railwaymen had formed the view that the police could be called only when the whole of the body could be produced. It wouldn't reflect well, Mr Downes maintained. Another porter remarked that head office wouldn't like it.

Head office, he repeated, until his joke was understood. He was sent out to rejoin the search. Even the driver was out on the tracks, they were told, and the boilerman was beating up and down the banks.

The question of identifying the remains was mentioned, though it seemed somehow ludicrous. Mr Brown had left the compartment and had not returned. There could be no mistaking that glum, dun-coloured suit; or those ungainly brogues, upturned now beneath his contorted bulk. Even so, Elf seemed anxious to retrieve some documentary proof, lowering himself to a crouch and straining to keep his feet on the sacking while he searched those pockets he could reach.

He rose at last with a small packet of papers, which he examined with a look of dissatisfaction. 'There are items missing,' he said, addressing the boyish guard. 'Has someone else searched him?'

'Missing? No, sir. Which we was all to touch nothing till the peelers come.'

At this another uniformed railwayman climbed up from the tracks, stamping against the cold and letting out a great cloud of agitated breath. He was ponderously stout, with greying whiskers halfway to his chin, and when he had surveyed the scene he turned sharply to the younger guard.

'What's all this, Parrish? What are you about, letting these two in here rooting and pilfering?'

'You will mind your manners, sir,' said Elf, rising to confront him. 'I am Charles Elphinstone of Her Majesty's Home Office, and this man was my associate. We were on official business. Official business of a confidential nature.'

The elder guard squinted in appraisal. 'Well now,' he said, 'that's fine and well for you to say, sir, but how are we to be sure of it? The driver means to call for the constables as soon as – as soon as what's missing is found.'

'Do you mean the missing papers?'

The guard gave him a look of sour pity, then glanced at Octavia. 'I mean the missing head, sir – saving your presence, madam.'

'Miss,' said Octavia. 'And your meaning was perfectly clear to me.'

'There was a clergyman aboard,' Elf said. 'He came into our compartment a short while ago, and I have reason to believe that – well, that he may have seen something.'

'You must be mistaken, sir,' said the guard. 'Ain't no clergyman on board.'

'How can you be sure?'

'Which, I check the tickets, sir. Every passenger on the train. I looked at yours, as you might recall.'

'I will speak to the driver,' Elf replied. His impatience was evident, but he tried to smooth it from his voice, to summon his customary assurance. 'I have papers about me, of course, and it will be a simple matter to have a satisfactory telegram sent when we reach Deal. Then I will see to it myself that the proper authorities are notified. This is not a matter for some flat-footed country constable, do you hear?'

The railwaymen exchanged looks, but no one else spoke against him for now. When it was recovered at last, Brown's head was returned to the train, thickly bundled in sacking. It was deposited with great solemnity by his body, as if it were an item he might want upon waking. Elf spoke in turn then to every man who ventured an opinion, measuring his tone and choosing his words so that each was persuaded by slightly altered means. Octavia had witnessed this before, at grand receptions and occasions of state; the way he had of gliding without effort between guises, his gift for *seeming*. It had been charming then.

Afterwards, when they had returned to their compartment, their own conversation faltered. He became distant, seeming for once to have exhausted his capacity for performance. He gave terse or elliptical answers to her questions, or simply pretended not to hear.

'I'm terribly sorry, old thing,' he said, noticing her scrutiny after a long silence. 'Bit of a shock, you know.'

Perhaps it was true. She'd suffered rather a shock herself, which seemed to occur to him after a time. He tried once or twice to restore some semblance of ease. He made small remarks about the discomfort of travelling by train in winter, and offered to see the porter about a blanket. Octavia hardly answered. She kept her eyes fixed on the window, though it was now entirely dark and she could see nothing but their own ghostly inversions. When that grew tedious, she simply pretended to sleep.

When they arrived at last at Deal, Elf had much to occupy him. Word had been sent from Woolwich, in spite of his objections, and the stationmaster was waiting with two local policemen. He called to her on the platform, as she looked for a porter. He would not be detained long, he said. He had taken rooms at the *Swan*, and would join her as soon as he could.

'Are you all right, old thing? It's been a grim sort of day, I know.' His composure was returning as he readied himself once more to face the public. 'I shall make it up to you, I promise. We could take some sort of rustic supper, perhaps, if the hotel isn't too dismal?'

The platform was busy, and she was spared the necessity of answering when a porter's trolley obscured her for a moment from his sight. She slipped away to see about a cab, and when her driver appeared she toyed with the thought of deserting Elf entirely, of finding another hotel and shutting herself away. It was not only weariness she felt, but a kind of saturation. She wanted solitude, to empty herself of all she had seen.

But no, that would not do either. They had come to an arrangement, however uneasily, and she could not simply withdraw from it without a word. She had suffered a shock, that was all, and was not thinking clearly. She would feel differently when she had rested. In the morning, her surroundings would not seem quite so strange and unfamiliar. She would no longer feel so very far from home.

V

IN PARADISUM

XXIII

She was gone. Angie was gone.

Gideon stood for a moment at the foot of the stairs and looked about him in bewilderment. The flagstones were smooth and unmarked. Outside the wind and the rain were gathering force, but the grand entrance hall was otherwise silent. There was no sign of disturbance, or that anyone had been here at all. He looked up to make sure of his bearings. The strange bluish light was gone from the landing above – it had vanished when Angie did – but he could pick out the balusters of the parapet. He stared dazedly into the empty air, as if he might find her suspended there.

He turned again, supporting himself on the stair post as he recovered his breath. He tried, as the violence of his panic subsided, to bring some order to his thoughts. Angie was not lying dead on the floor. She had come to no harm – could come to no harm, perhaps – but the thought gave him no comfort. What comfort could he hope for, after all? Wasn't it senseless even to have feared for her in the first place; to care for her still in the common way, given what he now knew?

A half-shade. A ghost, almost.

She was passing from the world, Cutter had said. She was already elsewhere. And yet, had she not recognised him, if only fleetingly? Were there not vestiges of her that might be saved, even now? If she was a half-shade, whatever that might truly mean, then surely she was half human too. What remained was altered, he could not pretend otherwise. She was not as he remembered her, and in truth he was not even certain of what he remembered. It had been unfinished, whatever had passed between them. Almost nothing had been said.

And yet.

He turned slowly, conscious of a drift of cold air. The front door stood open, lurching gently in the rising wind. He crossed towards it, absently at first, but an urgency gathered in him. Angie had left the house, and Cutter had charged him with keeping her from wandering. Nor was that his only duty. It fell to him now to protect her as his uncle had.

He stepped outside, recalling that he was barefoot only when he felt the bite of the gravel. And the cold. The brute shock of it. He ought to go back and dress, he knew. But he had glimpsed her in the distance, or thought he had, and feared he would lose her altogether. He looked back at the house, the wind beating open the flaps of his nightshirt and scouring his chest. Cutter would think him entirely mad if he were to find him in this state, but then Cutter had no great opinion of him as it was.

He pressed on, breaking into a stumbling run as he sought to kindle some warmth in his limbs. When he sighted her again, he was sure of it. Lightning revealed her for an instant, crossing the rough lawn some way ahead, her nightgown whipping about her in the thickening wind. She was perhaps a hundred yards off, her steps quick and purposeful as she approached the massed darkness of the trees. The thunder came, solemn and violent.

'*Angie!*' He ran now at full pelt. '*Angie! Miss Tatton! Wait!*'

An answering cry came, but from the direction of the house. '*Bliss!*' It was Cutter, his voice formidable even in the midst of a storm. '*Bliss! Stand where you are, you witless pup! Stand there till I reach you.*'

Even now, Gideon could not defy him. He waited, though he did so in an agony of anxiety. As he searched the darkness for the inspector, he cursed himself for letting these moments slip by.

'Look at you,' Cutter barked as he came into sight, his resolute stride hardly checked by the wind. 'You are like a ravaged convent girl, God help us. Was that you screaming back at the house? Here, put on this overcoat. The boots belong to the housekeeper's boy. He is nearly twice your size, and built like a side of beef, but perhaps you will grow into them.'

Gideon followed Cutter towards the trees, still struggling with the second boot. 'I know how foolish I must appear, sir, but I was concerned that Miss Tatton might slip away. I woke to find her acting in a most peculiar way. She *saw* something, sir, though she was only staring into empty space. And now, well, it is as if she is sleepwalking, but she is intent on some purpose I cannot guess at.'

Cutter gave him a sidelong look. 'Did I not tell you, Bliss? She sees things that we cannot. As for her purpose, she has only one now. Which way did she go, have you any notion?'

Gideon raised an awkward arm. The coat was cumbersome, being several sizes too large. 'That way,' he said. 'Towards the woods. And she is moving quickly, sir. We must hurry.'

But Cutter was already striding away, his gait as firm and purposeful as ever. Gideon pulled his coat about him as he followed, and managed at last to work his right heel into its boot. He was glad of the warmth, even if his appearance was not much improved.

'It was very good of you, sir, to think of bringing me a coat. I am most grateful to you.'

Cutter grunted, but not unkindly. 'It is as well that one of us is in possession of his faculties. Did your little match girl say anything intelligible, tell me, before she took herself off?'

'I do wish you would not refer to her in that way, sir. She was an innocent in all of this, who fell victim to wickedness we can scarcely imagine. I feel a very grave duty towards her, and the proper fondness of a protector. Surely even you, Inspector, have felt such an attachment at one time. Surely you are capable of that tenderness.'

Gideon's thoughtlessness struck him even as he spoke, and he clamped a hand to his mouth in dread. Cutter halted mid-stride, his back heaving visibly with exertion. He turned a little, as if he were about to speak, but seemed to think better of it. He let out a plume of breath, and squinted into the darkness.

'Forgive me, sir,' said Gideon. 'I spoke without thinking.'

But Cutter had set off again, just as abruptly as he had stopped, and now resumed his questioning in an easier tone.

'Did she say anything of use, your little – your young miss? And while you are about your answer, you might explain what it was you were doing in her company in the dead of night. Was it your proper fondness that had you out of bed? She is a pretty little thing, whatever else she may be. Did that escape your notice, when you first found her in your uncle's keeping?'

Gideon swabbed at his streaming face with one coarse sleeve, casting a fierce look at the inspector's unheeding back. 'Something has disturbed her, sir. She is given to distraction, I know, but this was different. She is acting with some purpose, I believe.'

'But did she say anything, Bliss?'

'Nothing that I could fathom, sir. She spoke in riddles and rhymes, yet she did so with the utmost gravity. And then—'

Cutter plunged into the woods, thrusting aside a hazel branch that whipped back as he passed. Gideon leapt clear, only to stumble into a patch of briars. He spat out a coarse oath, surprising even himself. It was a word he had never spoken aloud.

'Forgive me, sir,' he said, trotting to make up the ground he had lost. 'I injured myself on a bramble.'

Cutter gave a snort of amusement. 'It is rubbing off on you, Bliss. We will make a copper of you yet. And then?'

'Sir?' He sucked a thorn from his palm, tasting a rich dribble of blood.

'And then, you said, before you broke off. You were about to tell me what your – what Miss Tatton did next.'

'Yes, sir.' Gideon hesitated. 'Only, I fear you will doubt me when I do. I can scarcely credit it myself, even after all we have seen.'

'I have been knocking around a long while, Bliss, and I have seen a good deal.'

'Well, sir. We were standing in the passageway when the storm began. Miss Tatton was overtaken by some urge, and before I could prevent her she had climbed onto the stone rail – leapt onto it, really. It was astonishing, sir, the swiftness of it. Like a finch flitting to a branch. I pleaded with her to come down, but she paid no heed. She seemed to have no notion of any danger. She became perfectly still, and then—'

'And then she jumped. I have the gist of it now, Sergeant, you need not make a saga of it. She jumped, and alighted two floors below without a scratch.'

'I confess it seems fantastical, sir.'

'Then she made at once for the front door. Wait.' He halted abruptly again, planting one foot on a stump and pivoting towards the house. 'Which way did she face, from the landing?'

'I'm afraid I lack your easy command of the compass. If I were put to it, I would say that—'

'Towards the front or the back of the house will do, or to the left or the right.'

'Towards the front, sir.'

'North-west, then, or near enough.' He peered through the trees, searching for the lights of the house, and swung his arm in a careful arc, his eye trained as if along the sight of a rifle. 'There, that is our mark. Follow me, Bliss.'

Cutter lunged ahead with renewed vigour. The way he had chosen was through the thickest part of the woods, yet the trees gave him no more trouble than the throngs of Piccadilly. He equipped himself with a sturdy willow cane, and where the growth was dense he used it to beat a path, swinging it before him like a marauding Mongol.

The inspector was as puzzling as he was fearsome, Gideon reflected, and no less of an enigma than he had been from the moment they met. He was given to wrathful outbursts, and had a very small capacity for levity even when he was unprovoked. Yet for all his expressions of impatience, and for all his professed indifference in the matter of Miss Tatton, here he was doing just as he had done in Soho, flinging himself into her pursuit with all the astonishing energy he possessed.

Cutter paused at the brow of a bank to check his bearings, peering away to the left at something Gideon could not discern. 'There, look,' he said at length. 'We are closing with the boundary, do you see? We will come to the gate shortly, and we must hope we have not let her elude us. Ho now, what is that?'

He whipped a finger to his lips for silence. Gideon heard nothing at first, but presently he made out the ragged percussion of hooves, and with it the lurch and clatter of a carriage.

'That is hard driving for this time of night,' the inspector said.

'A coach, perhaps?' Gideon said.

'A coach would keep to the high road. And it would show lights – but there is no sign of those, and we are near enough to the lane to see them.' Cutter lifted his hat to tip the rain from it, shaking his head as he did so. 'Whatever it was, it was drawn away by a good strong pair, and at a fair clip, too, for a poor and unlit lane. What business was so pressing, I wonder? Come, this makes me no easier in my mind.'

Restoring his hat, he surged from the bank. The trees had thinned now, and he broke into a trot wherever a clear run of ground presented itself. When he slowed, at last, it was not for any obstruction. Gideon had seen it too.

'The light, Bliss.'

'Yes, sir. I see it.'

Cutter moved warily. They were nearing the edge of the woods. Shafts of pale light pierced the cage of the elms, making wraiths of his rising breath. At the snap of a twig, a body of crows rose and scattered. The inspector put his hand inside his coat.

'I am drawing out my revolver, Bliss. I have not produced it in your presence, I believe, so I mention it to keep you from taking fright. It is only out of caution.'

'Yes, sir.' Gideon peered through the rain. There was a careful tension in the set of Cutter's elbow, but he could make out nothing of the weapon itself. 'You will take care with it, I trust. You will think of Miss Tatton.'

In reply, the inspector only turned his head, raising his free hand and putting a finger to his lips. He lowered his head for a moment, letting the rain spill from the lip of his hat, then shook himself and strode out into the light.

The man was suspended from the great arch that surmounted the gates, the crude noose made fast to the ironwork of the armorial crest itself. He swung by a little way, like a pendulum that was still but has been disturbed. The wind had caught his cape, spreading it behind him as if in some grand display of ceremony. Angie stood solemnly at his feet. Her arms hung at her sides, and her face was raised in contemplation. Her agitation seemed to have passed for now. She was at peace.

'Quickly, Bliss,' said the inspector, bounding across the drive and taking hold of the man's legs. 'There may be time yet. Here, you must fish out my pocket-knife. I will support his weight until the last possible moment, then give you a leg-up so that you may cut him down.'

Gideon came to a halt with an ungainly skid, keeping his eyes averted as he followed Cutter's directions. Delicately, he patted the outer pockets of the inspector's coat, then drew back his hands and coughed in embarrassment.

'Do you recall, sir, where it was about your person that you placed it?'

'It is in my right trouser pocket. Where else would a man put a pocket-knife so as to have it ready to hand? Get it out now quickly and none of your foostering. What rhyme was she singing, Bliss?'

'Excuse me, sir?' Some moments passed as he fumbled in the inspector's clothing, and when at last he located the knife, he spun away in such embarrassed haste that he immediately dropped it.

'Mother of Christ,' said Cutter. 'I might as well entrust my knife to a showman's monkey. Open it up, like a good fellow, and do your best not to stab me in the eye. You will need the blade at the ready once you are up. That's it. Now, come and stand beneath him.'

Gideon shuffled into position, holding the pocket-knife awkwardly apart from his body. Above him the cloaked hulk lurched in the wind. He fixed his gaze on the rope.

'On the count of three, Bliss,' said Cutter, 'I will let go his legs and take hold of yours. Get a grip on the rope and saw at it just beneath your fist where it will be tautest. Keep your strokes square against the same mark for a clean cut. Are you ready?'

'In all honesty, sir, I cannot tell you if I am or not.'

When it was done at last and Cutter had let him down, Gideon staggered away and retched. The inspector paid no attention. He had retrieved his knife and dropped to his knees, lowering his head to the fallen man's lips as he probed his wrist for a pulse.

Finding none, he paused for a moment in consideration, then began examining the remainder of his person. Gideon saw his expression darken. In agitation, he unbuttoned the man's topcoat, then pressed a hand to his abdomen before raising it to his face to examine his fingertips.

'What rhyme was it, Bliss?'

Gideon shuffled to Cutter's side. 'Sir?'

Cutter only shook his head. Laying open the man's coat, he set about the buttons of his waistcoat. The urgency was gone from his movements now, and he proceeded with grim deliberation. He opened the man's hands to examine his palms, then worked the noose from behind his head. He probed the knot with his thumb, as if to test its strength.

'Riddles and rhymes, you said. Do you remember what they were?'

'Oh. Yes, sir.' A small movement caught his eye, and Gideon looked up to find that Angie had drawn near. She looked on, silent and attentive. 'Perhaps you know it, sir. It is about a baby asleep in a tree.'

Cutter drew a wallet from the man's coat and looked over its contents. He looked up at Gideon, his face strained.

'Of course I know it, Bliss. It's a fucking nursery rhyme.

Rock-a-by, baby. Everyone knows it.' He turned to Angie then. 'When the bough breaks, eh?'

Her gaze flickered for a moment when he spoke. She set her head to one side, as if some distant music had caught her attention. Absently, she took her afflicted hand in the other, tracing its vanished surfaces with her thumb. She made a cradle of her arms and, rocking them gently, she closed her eyes and lifted her face to the rain.

Cutter stood, regarding her warily, then made his way slowly to the gate. He kept his eyes on the ground, and when he was directly beneath the arch, he lowered himself once more to a crouch.

'Narrow enough,' he mused. 'Only a cart, maybe. It was let in, whatever it was. These gates were chained when we got here, but of course he would have had a key. It may be about him still.'

Gideon moved to his side. 'The carriage we heard in the lane, sir?'

'No doubt,' said Cutter, rising. 'The driver had the fear of God in him by then. He drew up here and stopped, for the tracks go no further. And then His Lordship climbed on top.'

'His Lordship, sir?'

But the inspector was not listening. He rasped his chin against his palm. 'He tied his own noose. He was no great hand at knots, but he managed it. And then he gave the word himself, I imagine. She would have made him give the word.'

'The word, sir?'

'To the driver, Bliss. To drive away. To let him drop.'

Gideon turned to Angie, who was watching them serenely. She opened her cradled arms, one whole and one vanished, and let them fall to her sides.

'And baby,' she said softly. 'And baby and all.'

She turned away and started towards the house.

'Get along after her,' said Cutter, rising. 'I will keep watch here. Rouse the servants when you reach the house. Tell Mrs Cornish to send her young lad. There is some heavy work to be done. The remains must be carried to the house, until suitable arrangements can be made. Do not allow Lady Ada to be woken yet, if it can be helped. I would sooner give her the news myself.'

'The news, sir?'

'That her brother is dead, Bliss. That Lord Strythe is dead.'

XXIV

Octavia dreamed of the house on Vesper Sands.

A storm had come and gone in the night, or she had imagined one, and her sleep had been restless and shallow. She had wandered the sands, in the dream, and had seen the house that rose from the dunes. She knew it somehow, though she had never seen it, and she hurried towards it. Behind her the water was rising, and rags of shadow skirted the pale blade of the moon.

She ran, but the tide surged around her and she could not keep her feet. As she sank to her knees, she saw Lord Strythe, and she knew the girl at his side by something other than sight. Angie Tatton wore a bridal gown, its train spreading serenely over the water, and they made their way in calm procession as the sea rose all around them. Octavia called out to her, before the waves overcame her, but Angie did not hear. She glimpsed her once more, in the far distance, a bright wraith that passed out of sight as she buckled under the flooding cold.

She was breathless when she woke, and feverish in spite of the chill. It was not yet light, but she knew that she would not sleep again. She sat up, meaning to bathe her face at the wash bowl, and caught sight of something by the door. An envelope. The night porter must have slipped it under the door, not wishing to disturb her.

She took the envelope to the small writing table near the

window. It was heavy, for a letter. A packet, really. Her name had been scrawled on it, but nothing else. It was not stamped, and bore no postmarks. It had been brought by hand, then, and had come in the night. She went to light the lamp, but something made her wary. At this hour hers would be the only window to show a light. She made do instead with a misshapen stump of candle that she had set at her bedside.

She broke the seal and drew out the topmost sheet. The writing paper was handsome, if not impeccably clean, and the letter was in the same hand as the envelope. It was elegant enough, but betrayed a certain haste.

My dear Miss Hillingdon,

I pray this does not reach you too late.
Be warned of this much first, since he may be near you. (If you are observed, give no sign of what you have learned.) Lord Hartington is not your friend. I have not yet uncovered all, but I am sure of this much. He conspired with Lord Strythe in abduction, murder and other dark acts. He is one of those they call the Spiriters.

Octavia broke off. She stood, breathing slowly. The wind was restless still, and she could not tell if the hotel was entirely quiet. A light had been left burning on the landing, and a dull blade of yellow showed beneath her door. She crossed the floor quietly. The door was bolted, but she wanted to be sure. She took a shawl from her case and wrapped herself in it, then stood for a moment with her eyes closed.

She sat at the table and began again.

I will be brief because I must. Read to the end if you can. I have enclosed certain photographs and documents. I took them from the other man, after what happened on the train. Do not judge me harshly for that. You will understand soon enough that I did only what I must.

Do not take these items out unless you are alone. But do look at them, if you can bring yourself to it. They will show you what I cannot explain. They will show you the nature of those we must confront.

The women, first, and the girls. They were only children, some of them. Only children. I will come to them first, for it is they who have always mattered most. They wanted them for their brightness, Miss Hillingdon. For the brightness of their souls. You will wonder at that, and perhaps you will suspect me of some infirmity of mind, but you of all people ought not to doubt the truth of this.

You ought not to doubt it, because you yourself are possessed of the same brightness. Your being is suffused with it, like the phosphorescence that mariners observe beneath the skin of the sea. I saw it myself when I entered your compartment on the train. You did not notice me, perhaps, but I could not help but take account of you. It has been visible to me always, this particular brightness, and in this it seems I am something of a rarity.

Perhaps you doubt me still, as well you might. I will try to offer you some proof, so that you do not dismiss these as the ramblings of a madman. Do you experience visions, Miss Hillingdon? I imagine that you do, and that they have troubled you lately. It is common in those gifted as you are, especially when others of your kind are in peril.

If I have missed my mark, then by now you will have cast

my letter aside and all will be lost. If not, then I hope I have your trust.

They took the last of my poor girls, Miss Hillingdon. They took Angela Tatton, whom I had cared for longest, the last and the brightest. She is not gone yet, I hope, but she is fading. I want to see her before the end.

And before the end, by the grace of God, she will see justice done.

There is much more to say, but it must wait until we meet. Lord Strythe is not dead, whatever Hartington may have led you to believe. He is gone to Vesper Sands, and that is where you and I must go too. That is where this must end.

Look at them now, Miss Hillingdon. Look, if you can, at these lost bright souls. We will try to honour them, you and I, in the work we must now do.

I am thus, and shall remain, your dutiful servant,

H. Neuilly

Afterwards, Octavia dressed heedlessly. She had brought other things, but could give no thought to choosing among them. She put on the stale travelling clothes of the day before. She lurched towards the door, meaning to go down and ask for a cab, then remembered the envelope. She wrapped it in a chemise and stowed it at the bottom of her case. It was to keep the contents safe, but not only that. She wanted to keep them –

Lottie Hinde (aged 17)

– out of sight. Those photographs. She wanted not to have seen them.

She had bundled them together without looking again, touching them only at their edges, had pushed them away and staggered from the table. She had stood at the foot of the bed, gazing about her in bewilderment. She had clutched herself, as if an ache were welling in her. As if something might rupture.

Tabitha Norton (aged 22) – The life everlasting.

She turned to lock the door behind her, fumbling even as she tried to keep her movements quiet. At the end of the landing, when she stumbled, she saw that she had put on only one shoe, that she was still clutching the other. She paused to slip it on, and to pin up her hair before a mirror. But a moment later, on the stairs, she had no recollection of her appearance. She halted again, putting a hand to her face. Had it been a mirror, or only a picture?

She reached for the banister, feeling herself sway, and her vision swam and darkened. She saw the room, as she always did, and the girl in white, supine and still. The men crouching over her were in shadow, just as before. She tried this time, tried to look, but nothing could be seen of their faces. One of them held something, a flask or vessel, and from it a shadowy vapour rose. The girl's body was jolted by a violent spasm. She arched her back, spreading her arms stiffly, and for a moment she was still. Her eyes opened wide then, and her mouth gaped as if she were screaming. Above her the air was disturbed – for a moment Octavia could make no sense of it – then a smoke poured from her, a slow coil of shadow at first, then a living swarm of black moths that filled the air and became the darkness.

It was gone. Octavia clutched the banister, waiting for the lightness to pass.

'Wavy, old thing. You're up early.'

It was him, of course. Behind her, at the head of the stairs. She heard him descend, his tread deliberate and unhurried. She would not turn. She would not see him.

Johanna Styles (aged 19) – Perpetual light grant unto them, o Lord.

But he had reached her already. He turned on the step below her, looking her over with careful levity.

'How's your room, my darling? Did you sleep well?'

Beneath her, in the entrance hall, the rose-patterned carpet showed a warm spill of light. What was his name?

'I say, Wavy. Are you quite well?'

He was pale and unshaven, his voice not quite airy. He leaned on the banister, his arm slack but blocking her way. The porter's name. He had given it as he brought up her bags. *What was his name?*

'Alfred?' At the root of her throat she felt a small flux of panic. 'Master Alfred! Are you there?'

For a moment Elf regarded her in frank surprise, then something changed in his face. She saw his displeasure. A tremor of contempt. He looked down to the hallway, where a hulking young man had edged into the light.

'Master Alfred?' she said again. But no, the uniform was not right. Surely a night porter would not – the young man uncovered his head, shaking the ropy curls from his face.

'Georgie?' Half a flight of stairs separated them, but she raised a hand, unthinkingly, as if to touch his face. 'Georgie, is it really – but how did you—'

He took another step, so that his face was no longer in shadow. She saw the patient set of his brow, the furrowed attentiveness. 'Well now, sister. It is a tale and a half, but the long and short of it is that I was disappointed of my place on the *Osprey*. I was not as sorry as I might have been. There's been all manner of talk in town about – well, about that business we was looking into. I wasn't easy in my mind.'

'Dear Georgie,' she said. 'But how did you find me?'

'Old Healy at the *Gazette*. I followed by the mail train, though

I didn't trouble to tell the guards they had a passenger. I got here just after four, and Master Alfred here has been uncommon civil. He set me up nicely with a toddy and a sandwich, and he has borne all my talk of the service such as he ought to be sainted.'

Lily Chorley (aged 15) – And ever shall be. World without end.

She steadied herself. For a moment her senses whitened. Georgie advanced to the foot of the stairs, his face showing a plain concern. He took note of Elf, appraising him slowly.

'Octavia?' he said. 'Is something the matter? Master Alfred, might I trouble you for a drop of brandy for my sister.'

Alfred came to Georgie's side, a loping and gangly sort of boy, but obliging in his demeanour. 'Miss?' he said. 'Are you took ill, miss?'

'I am all right,' she said. 'It is only that – would you excuse me, Lord Hartington?'

Elf stared for a moment, then detached himself from the banister, edging aside with a tepid smile. He glanced at Georgie, mouthing a conspicuous yawn.

'It is only that I have had some troubling news, Georgie, and must leave as a matter of urgency. I should be very grateful, Master Alfred, if you would send for a cab. But perhaps it is much too early. I'm afraid I've had rather a shock, and I am not at all sure of the time.'

'It is getting on for seven, miss. The drivers are abroad this hour and more. Should you like to take a bite of breakfast as you wait?'

'You are very kind, Master Alfred, but I don't feel at all hungry.'

'You must go and lie down, Octavia,' Georgie said. 'We might be waiting half an hour for a cab even if Master Alfred sends out. I shall run out myself and flag a driver down between here and the station, where they are most likely to be found.'

'No, Georgie,' said Octavia at once. 'I'm sorry, what I mean is—'

Behind her on the stairs, the timbers complained softly. She turned her head by a fraction, but did not look round. Georgie studied her with concern, then looked beyond her to the staircase. He drew in a long, considering breath and she noticed, as she had often done, how warily he inhabited his own bulk. He had surged into manhood at twelve or thirteen, and had returned from his first six months as a ship's boy seeming twice the size. But he had not coarsened, as she had feared he might, or grown swaggering in his ways. There was a gentleness in him that would not permit it.

'Goodness, Wavy,' said Elf from behind her. 'What is this news you have had? You won't dash off alone, I hope. I'm sure I can be of some service.'

Octavia's eyes flickered aside at the sound of his voice. She made no reply, and still did not turn around. Georgie was again intent on her face.

'Octavia?' he said.

'Master Alfred will see about the cab, I am sure. But you might help me down with my bags, Georgie. And I have – there are some things I must keep about me, things I must keep safe.'

Georgie lowered his face a little way towards hers. He glanced again towards the stairs, then gave her a look of careful inquiry. 'Keep safe, sister?'

Felicity Hardwick (aged 13) – In Paradisum deducant te Angeli.

She felt herself weaken. Georgie took her arm and rested it gently on his own.

'Dear Georgie,' she said. 'How happy I am to see you.'

'You might keep hold of me, sister, as we go up the stairs. In case you are taken light-headed again.'

He led the way, hunched by her side. When they passed Elf on the stairs, she did not look up. Something had been stirred in her.

She felt it as the shock receded. Once, as a child, she had seen an old dog pulled from under an omnibus. Its head had been appallingly crushed and lay open like a hulled fruit. That pale mass, glistening and threaded with pink. She had felt it then too, as she was led away. A tenderness that was also a rage.

'I will trouble you to step aside, Lord Hartington, sir.' Georgie spoke with just enough emphasis, and she felt him straighten at her side. Elf drew back without a word.

'Poor Georgie,' Octavia said, when they had reached the landing. 'I'm afraid I'm impatient with you sometimes, even when you're trying to be kind. Especially then, perhaps. How awful you must think me.'

He halted for a moment, turning to her with a rueful smile. 'Well now, I don't know about that, but who can blame you, if you are? I am a good way off your pace in most things, after all. Still, there's horses for courses, they say. There is cargo to be stowed, and I am to do duty as an escort. Why, it is as good as any commission. Now then, sister, you must show me which room is yours so that we may get on. This is not the worst of places by any means, but I do not like the look of all the patrons.'

It was hardly more than half an hour before they were on the road out of Deal. Their driver, Master Alfred had assured them, was often asked for by name, having bought his carriage out of the service of Lord Sackville himself. It ran along so smoothly, he said, that they would hardly know they were upon the road at all.

Master Alfred had taken them aside, before seeing them aboard, and had spoken to them in quiet confidence. He was a perceptive youth, for all his awkwardness, and he had formed some notion of how things stood. The other gentleman had returned to his room, he said, and had not yet reappeared. When he did, said Alfred, he might find that a cab was harder to come by, what with the London train leaving. He would do his best for him, of course, but the gentleman might be waiting an hour and more.

Georgie kept up his easy chatter when they were under way, though he took care to moderate his tone and kept watch for any sign that Octavia was tiring of it. She smiled now and then, but only half-attended. It was comforting to have him by her, but she could not pretend to be at ease. She tried to keep her thoughts from it, to occupy herself with small and practical concerns. With what she must do.

Ginny Foster (aged 24) – Et perducant te in civitatem sanctam Ierusalem.

Georgie broke off and sat abruptly upright. 'What is it, sister?'

She had started from her seat, she realised, her hands out-thrust as if to shield herself from something. She had seen it again, for an instant. The girl in the shadowy room. The smoke and the moths. She could not escape it now. The darkness was complete.

'Georgie,' she said suddenly. 'When you look at me, can you see a brightness?'

He blinked and passed a hand over his mouth. 'A brightness, sister?'

'A brightness, something out of the ordinary, something – oh, God, I don't even know. I don't even know what I'm saying.'

'Octavia?' He leaned towards her and spoke very gently. 'Can you tell me what the matter is?'

She looked at him helplessly. Could she? Could she tell him? Could she open the packet and show him one of the photographs? Could she show him the picture of Ginny Foster? She had been arranged, like some of the others, on the steps of an altar. She had been dressed, as they all had, in a fine white gown. Hers was especially ornate, with a bodice of intricate lacework that rose to an elaborate ruff about her neck. Its sleeves were of such lavish proportions that they spilled from her outstretched arms to cover three entire steps. All about her, forming a broad and perfect circle, was an extraordinary arrangement of flowers. In the photograph their colours had been lost, but there were freesias and columbines, Octavia thought, and a great many roses and lilies. It had been summer when she was taken. The brightest days of June.

Could she tell Georgie? Could she show him? Taken by themselves, the photographs might seem merely peculiar. It was not uncommon for portraits to be made of the dead, though it was a practice she had always found ghoulish. One saw pallid infants, propped up on frilled pillows alongside their living twins, and hollow-cheeked wives fastened to dining chairs among their children, dutiful even in death. If Georgie was to understand, she would have to show him the rest: the letter from her mysterious informant, and the items of evidence he had provided; the telegrams and memoranda, the pages that had been torn from some hideous journal. She would have to show him everything, and would he understand, poor Georgie, even then?

'It's that Lord Hartington, isn't it?' He spoke gently still, but could not conceal his indignation. 'That Elf of yours. He's mixed up in something, isn't he?'

'Oh, Georgie,' she said. 'I hardly know where to begin.'

'Well, as to that, you might begin with where it is we're off to. We naval chaps do not relish a voyage without we are told something of the destination. Where is this Vesper Sands, and what is it we shall find there?'

'It is a place a little way along the coast, or so I understand, where Lord Strythe keeps a house. Do you know of him, Georgie?'

'Lord Strythe?' He looked at her intently, spreading his hands on his knees. 'Why, I do now if I never did before. The newspaper boys was calling his name from every corner before I left town. The tragedy in Half Moon-street, they're calling it. He topped himself, they say. Flung himself off his own roof.'

'The other papers have taken up the story, then?' Octavia said. 'They were quicker about it than I imagined. And they have larded it with all manner of speculation, I'm sure.'

'You knew about it then? Before it was in the papers?'

'It was our paper that first carried the report, Georgie. I wrote the article.'

'You?' His amazement showed plainly. 'Mr Healy said you was off on some business for the *Gazette*, but I thought it must be a hunt ball or some such. Which, I mean, you being concerned with high society matters, as a rule, and not with—'

'And not with anything of importance. It's all right, Georgie. Have they given his name, then, in the newspapers? God, what a perfect idiot I've been. I told myself I was being careful in my choice of words, but I knew how it would seem. I knew, and I went along with it. Of course people thought it was Strythe. What else could they have made of it? And that was his intention.'

'Whose intention?'

'Elf's, Georgie. Lord Hartington's. He is not what he seems. No, he is not at all what he seems.'

Georgie looked away, with as much severity in his features as his nature permitted.

'You may say it, Georgie, and no one would blame you. You may say that you told me so, that he and his kind were not to be trusted. But I thought I knew better. I thought I could make my way in their world even if I didn't truly belong to it. I thought it was enough to be clever, Georgie, and to make a secret of all I truly cared for. I thought it was enough.'

He reached towards her, seeing her distress, splaying out his fingers a little way short of her arm. 'Now, sister,' he said. 'There now. If you were deceived, it was only down to your own goodness. You played the lady better than a duchess, and yet you never forgot those who came up rough. You never forgot how matters might have stood for us, if not for the luck of the draw. That's why it got under your skin, about them poor lasses in Whitechapel. I saw it in you, when you came out of that boarding house. You were all talk about giving substance to the stories, but all you cared about was getting that girl back.'

She took his hand and pressed it between both of hers, but her eye was caught by the view. They had come to a bend that brought them within sight of the sea. It was half a mile away, or a little less, its surface drab and gull grey, coarsened by the restless weather. The window was quick with wet again, and was battered at intervals by rough pulses of hail.

'Listen now, Georgie,' she said. 'We haven't much time, and there is a great deal that I must tell you.'

XXV

It was still dark when Gideon was shaken awake. He started in fright, not recognising the figure who loomed above the bed.

'Your guvnor sent me.' It was Ned Cornish, the housekeeper's boy. He set a mug on the nightstand, then stood in ungainly silence. 'You're wanted down below, he says.'

Gideon swung his legs out hesitantly. He sat on the edge of the bed, keeping his blanket about him so as to hide the slightness of his frame. Ned was a hulking boy of fifteen or so, and sullen even for his age. The night before, having himself been roused from his bed, he had hauled out a cart that was meant to be drawn by a donkey, and in the hour or more it had taken to bring Lord Strythe's remains to the house, he had hardly uttered a word. When the body had been laid out at last – in a disused still-room set apart from the main house – he had stood for a moment in silence, a steam of exertion rising from him, then he had trudged back out to see about chaining the gates.

'What time is it?' he managed to ask. 'If I may trouble you.'

'Half past six, or near enough.' Ned swung his arms loosely, curling his fingers about his thumbs. 'You're to come down, your guvnor says. Lady Ada has been told the news, and means to go and see him after her bit of tennis. You know how to play tennis?'

Gideon shook his head.

'No more than I do. Still drags me out every day, she does. Fires them fucking balls at me.'

Gideon coughed. 'It must be very trying.'

'You're wanted to take notes, he says. And to keep an eye to the lass. You're to be sure of that, he said.'

Gideon stood up at this and freed himself from the tangle of blankets. 'Is something wrong?' he said, forgetting his nervousness. 'With Miss Tatton, I mean. Is something the matter?'

'Been wandering off, is all.' Ned eyed him with dull pity. 'More than before. Her below found her in the music room in the night, making free with books and papers. Lady Ada has a fondness for her, my mother says, but it won't last if she keeps that up. Lady Ada won't have nobody in among her papers.'

'Yes, of course.' Gideon edged towards the chair where his clothes were folded. 'Lady Ada will forgive Miss Tatton, I hope. There is no wickedness in what she does. It is just that she has . . . that is, it is just that she is not quite . . .'

Ned stared for a moment, his broad features unaltered. 'You best get on,' he said. 'Like I said, you're wanted downstairs.'

He found Cutter in the drawing room. The inspector's mood was sombre, but he was in easier temper than Gideon had feared, making no mention of his tardiness though it was half an hour since he had been sent for.

'I am to take Lady Ada to see the remains.' He had kept his place by the window when Gideon came in, and gazed out to sea as he spoke. 'It is a duty I never cared for, no matter who it is laid out.'

'No, sir,' Gideon said. 'It will be hard on Lady Ada too, I imagine.'

'Lady Ada?' Cutter gave a dry laugh. 'Lady Ada is going about the place like a spring lamb. She is out there now in the rain, lobbing balls at young Ned. It is just as well, too, that she is not senseless with grief. We have a good many questions to put to her now that I would much rather have put to her brother.'

'Yes, sir.' Gideon hesitated. 'If I may, sir, can I take it that the matter is no longer in doubt? That you believe Lord Strythe had some hand in what happened to Miss Tatton?'

'Indeed I do, Bliss, and have for some time. I suspect he had a hand in that and more. Much more.'

'But, sir.' Gideon approached the window. He wished the inspector would turn from it, so that he could see his face. 'But, sir, you did not – when I shared my own suspicions, you did not seem—'

'Did not seem to credit them.' Cutter was following the course of a lone trawler. 'Look, Bliss. It was a bad day to venture out, but he thinks he can keep ahead of the weather.'

'Sir.'

Cutter turned at last to face him. 'I had my reasons, Bliss. It is in my nature to be wary of all such talk. My way is to say nothing until I am sure enough to say it before a fellow in a wig. And in this case I am all the more cautious. You asked me if I looked into special cases. I said nothing then, or as little as I could, because in that line especially I am slow to trust anyone. Yes, Bliss, there are special cases, but I must walk a very careful line when I go near them. In the first place, I must give them a more ordinary appearance if I am to bring them before my superiors, never mind before a court. I would not last long otherwise.

'But it is not only that. In some such cases, I have come up against certain interested parties. Parties who do not welcome my curiosity. Who they are exactly I have not discovered, but they are well beyond my reach. We are not beyond theirs, though. They have their hooks in people. In the Divisions mostly, but there are some in the Yard too. High up and low down. Warnock is one of theirs.'

'Inspector Warnock? The man we came across at St Anne's?'

'Oh, yes. He is no great specimen, mind you, and does not worry me much, but seeing him there told me that they had an interest in whatever business was at hand, and that we must keep our wits about us. But that did not mean that Warnock had any notion of what was before him. On the contrary, he is useful to them only because he never does. That was what made me think of the bottles.' He looked out to sea again, where the fishing boat had changed course. 'He is running for home, look. He does right, I suppose, but I liked him for taking his chances.'

'The bottles, sir?'

'The bottles that were found by the dead sexton. It seemed a plain enough thing, at first. A drunkard had failed his masters, and they dosed him with his own poison. Murderers are inclined to get notions, when they are at it long enough. But the neatness of the thing did not sit easily with me. Why twelve bottles? And why were three of them broken? That little show was not put on for no reason. I was meant to see it. Nine and three. I cannot be certain yet, but if ever a tally can be made of the souls who were lost to these demons, we may have our answer. We may know how many were lost, and how many saved. In any case, it made me think of your bit of crystal, and of what Esther Tull might have died for.' Cutter looked at him, and for a moment something very like amusement showed in his face. 'It was no easy matter for me, Bliss, but it came to me that you might have been right.'

Gideon coloured and lowered his head. 'Thank you, sir. It comes as a great relief to me.'

'Yes, well.' Cutter beat his hands together, and seemed to bring his reverie to an end. 'Do not lose the run of yourself just yet. There will be time enough for giving out prizes. Right or wrong, we are a good way from the finish. I have been hunting these bastards a long time, these Spiriters – yes, Bliss, that is who they are – and it seems we have run one of them to ground. Well, when I say we – your young miss made much of the running. I might have wished her to wait a little longer to settle her account with him, but there is not much that will stand in her way now.

'He was not the only one, though. He did not act alone in all of this. That was my belief all along, but we may be sure of it now. If it had been only him, Miss Tatton's business here would be finished. And we would know, Bliss, if her business was finished.'

Gideon clutched his cuffs. 'How would we know, sir? What would happen?'

Cutter approached him, resting a hand on his shoulder. 'Bliss,' he said. 'You are a tender-hearted creature, as I have said before.'

Gideon swallowed and looked away.

The inspector cleared his throat carefully. 'I do not mean to judge you harshly,' he said. 'You might have done much worse, having been left all alone in the world.'

Gideon scrubbed at his eyes with his sleeve, not trusting himself to speak.

'Do not think me an ogre, Bliss.' Gideon looked up. The inspector spoke softly now, so softly that he hardly sounded like himself. 'I was left alone too, in a way.'

'Yes, sir,' Gideon said. 'I have learned a little of your loss, and I am very sorry for it.'

'Have you now?' Cutter gave him a sharp look.

'Sir, when you lost your—' Gideon looked away. 'When you spoke of hunting them a long time – was it then that the hunt began?'

Cutter was silent.

'Only it seemed to me – pardon me, sir, if I go too far – it seemed to me that if that were so – if you yourself had been so grievously wronged – that bringing these men to justice might offer something more than mere professional satisfaction. That it might bring you peace.'

Still the inspector said nothing. He had spoken too freely. He could not think what had possessed him. 'Forgive me, sir,' he said, turning away. 'It was not my place to say so much. Miss Tatton has been wandering, I gather. I will begin searching in the—'

'The Priory,' said Cutter.

Gideon halted and faced him again. 'Pardon me, sir?'

'The Priory.' He had turned again to the window, and spoke in an absent way that Gideon had not witnessed before. 'There was a house of that name, a mile or so from where I was born. It had been a grand enough place once, but for as long as I could remember it had stood derelict. I cannot say how it came about – it was in probate, perhaps – but by the time I was six or seven, it was overgrown entirely and the doors and windows were all bricked up. It troubled me to think of it, for some reason – to think of all those dark and empty rooms – and when we passed it I would plague my father with questions. It is only to keep out the thieves, he would say. It would be a nest of gypsies in a week, left as it was. But keeping fellows out of it was not what troubled me. What if there was someone in it still, I would ask him? What if someone dwelt there still, unseen and forgotten? He took no notice, of course, but it so happened that my father was called out one night – he was a constable before me, you see – by word of a fire. I went with him in the trap, and when we reached the place the flames had taken a quarter of the roof. We saw the room where it began, high up in one corner, and a window where half a dozen bricks had been knocked out so that someone might leap clear. I can see it still, how pale and fierce the fire burned within. It was only vagrants, no doubt, who had crept in and lain up a while, but at the time it seemed to me that I had been right all along – that the place had never been abandoned, that its fires had been tended unseen. Do you understand me?'

Gideon took care with his words, not altogether certain that he did. 'I believe so, sir.'

'Then we need say no more, I think. We need say no more. But what about you, Bliss? You did not brick up your house, did you? You flung open all the windows and the doors, so that anyone might wander in.'

'Perhaps you are right, sir. I have been too trusting, I fear.'

'I meant no slight. There is no great satisfaction in the alternative, I assure you. And one day soon, I am sure, one of those who wanders in will make a home for herself. And why would she not? You have no great surfeit of common sense, for all your Cambridge education, and you have the constitution of a consumptive poet. But you are an agreeable young fellow, on the whole, with something very like decency in you. Others will come, Bliss. You must try not to cling to shadows.'

Gideon hung his head.

'But I am wasting my breath, I know. There has never been any talking to you where that girl is concerned. Go and find her, then. Mrs Cornish has promised us a bit of breakfast, when I have finished playing the undertaker. We will talk more then. Go and find her, Bliss. We may expect another visitor, as like as not. Maybe more than one. We must be watchful now. Go and find her. Stay near her, while you can. One way or another, this will all be over soon.'

The house was larger than it first appeared. Gideon lost his way frequently among its dim passageways and shuttered rooms, or found that he had looked in the same place twice: a disused parlour, where an abandoned bureau was strewn with damp furs; a billiard room, where he tripped and clutched at a shrouded harpsichord, scattering sheet music and spilling peacock feathers from a crusted ewer.

By the time he heard a clock strike nine, he had hardly covered even the whole of the ground floor. It might take him half the day to search the house, never mind the whole of the grounds. He tried to think as she might, or at least, to imagine what she might do. For she had certain habits, after all, even if it was impossible to know her mind. He had been lurching from one sepulchral room to the next, but it occurred to him that Miss Tatton was not drawn to such places. She had no fear of the dark, certainly, but neither did it seem to hold any fascination for her. She lingered by windows, when she was at ease, watching the changes in the weather, the light on the water. She was drawn to the air and the elements, to brightness.

Descending a small flight of steps, he found himself in another gloomy hallway. But a doorway at its far end disclosed a spill of light, thin and rain-grey. Raising his face in the musty air he caught a faint ribbon of cold.

He knocked gently when he came to the door. 'Hello?' He waited. 'Hello? Forgive me, it is Sergeant Bliss. I hope I do not intrude.'

There was silence. He edged into the room, taking care not to disturb the door.

'Hello?' he said again, but no one answered. Gideon wandered in, blinking in the unaccustomed daylight, and looked about him in fascination. Unlike the others he had entered, this room appeared to be in frequent use. Indeed, it was so richly furnished, and held such a variety of objects, that it was difficult to tell just what use it was put to. It seemed to serve as a study, since there was a bureau on which a great quantity of books and papers were heaped, and a number of mismatched bookcases were likewise filled. But it did duty, too, as a music room – a great honey-hued violoncello was propped up by a music stand – and as a laboratory of some kind. A bench before a window was arrayed with polished instruments, and glass-fronted cabinets held a profusion of minerals and crystals – amethyst and azurite and bright knuckles of quartz – alongside meticulously labelled animal bones, glossy ranks of beetles and countless moths and butterflies.

Gideon had stooped to examine a moth – an enchanting thing with primrose-yellow wings – when a small noise startled him. He straightened, retreating briskly from the cabinet. It would not do to be found rootling about in what must be Lady Ada's private study when even Miss Tatton had been warned against it. He stood for a moment in apprehensive silence.

The noise came again – a shuddering creak – and a small movement caught his eye. The French doors were unlocked, and had swung a little way open in the freshening air. They looked out over a dank lawn and a sombre procession of yew trees. In the distance, half hidden beyond a decline, a weathered summerhouse could be seen. It would be quiet there, with views of the sea, and it occurred to him that he ought to look there next.

A darkness, outside. Quick and oblique, it crossed the flagstones. Then the man whose shadow it was.

'Well, well.' The man was dressed in black, with the poor light at his back. He did not remove his hat, and his face was in shadow. Gideon stared, but he could not bring his senses to bear.

'There you are at last,' the man said, stepping inside. He nodded ruefully as he surveyed the room, as if it were a place he remembered with fondness. He approached a cabinet, caressing its frame with gloved fingertips. 'Do you remember your taxonomy?'

Gideon thought to speak, but the words had not yet formed.

'That is *Gonepteryx rhamni*,' the man said, tapping the glass. 'The primrose-yellow specimen. The brimstone butterfly. Is it not delightful? Our friend Linnaeus designated it *Papilio rhamni*, having granted only a single genus to all the butterflies and moths. We may scoff at him now, having added a great many rooms to his mansion, but before him we all dossed in a cowshed. You have kept up your reading, I trust, in the natural sciences? Or have the doctors of Selwyn College grown intolerant of such things?'

Gideon shook his head feebly. 'Uncle?'

'I am glad to see you, boy. I was not certain that I would again.'

'But you are living, sir.' Gideon was conscious of appearing foolish, yet he could find no other words. 'You are not dead.'

'You have gained some mastery of logic at Cambridge, I see. It is a comfort to me.' His uncle smiled then, and it so altered his appearance that Gideon was quite disconcerted. He could not recall that he had ever seen him do so before. 'Forgive me, nephew. It was my habit, always, to be severe with you. There were reasons, but I fear I was mistaken in those. I'm afraid I have been a good deal mistaken. I will try to account for it all, if there is time.'

Gideon lowered his head for a moment. 'I should be glad to hear all you have to tell me, uncle. But I am glad above all to find that you are well. Inspector Cutter will be pleased too, I am sure. You remember Inspector Cutter, who shared lodgings with you in Frith-street?'

'Indeed. You fell in with Cutter, then, when you found me gone?'

'I hoped to find Miss Tatton with his help. And we did find her, uncle. She is here with us. It was from Miss Tatton that I first heard the dreadful news. She would have been overjoyed, I'm sure, to know that you are safe. But I'm afraid you may find that – uncle, a great deal has happened since I last saw you. A great deal is still happening, in fact.'

Neuilly inclined his head sadly. 'Yes, nephew. We have much to discuss, I think. But perhaps it may wait until we have joined the rest of the company. I am anxious to see Miss Tatton, though I expect she is no longer quite as I remember her. We have met, all of us, at a melancholy hour, and I fear there is worse to come. Each of us holds pieces, I think, of the puzzle that confronts us, and each of us will have a part in what remains to be done.'

Neuilly swayed for a moment, as if in exhaustion. He put out a hand to steady himself, upsetting a framed specimen that had been set apart from the others. Gideon caught it as it tumbled and returned it carefully to its place.

'The ghost moth,' his uncle said, touching the frame. '*Hepialus humuli*. This is the female, of course, as her yellow forewings attest. She is a prettier thing, in life, than this rather drab specimen suggests.'

Gideon put out his hand, then checked himself. Neuilly seemed much changed, but he felt a deference still that was not easily overcome. 'Uncle, are you quite well? Can I aid you?'

'You are kind, my boy. Kinder than I deserve. I will last the day, I imagine. You need not concern yourself. Where is Miss Tatton? She is the one we must look to now.'

'I have been looking for her, uncle. I do my best to keep watch over her, but I'm afraid she has a tendency to wander. It is one of the peculiarities of her condition, and it is worse when something unsettles her.'

'Has something happened to unsettle her?'

Gideon looked away for a moment in discomfort. 'Since you are here, uncle, I take it that you know whose house this is?'

'Oh, indeed, nephew. I came here to find him. Has he arrived yet?'

'Last night, sir.'

'And is Cutter holding him? Does he know the nature of his crimes? That man has a reckoning before him.'

'Uncle, will you not take a seat for a moment? You have suffered a good deal, I fear. The rest can wait until we join the others, but I'm afraid there is something I must tell you about Lord Strythe.'

The cabman could take them no further than the main gates, since these were made fast by a chain. They might go in on foot, he said, since the wicket gate stood open, but he could not say if they would find anyone at home. A madwoman lived here, people said, or had at one time. It was his own belief that the place had been shut up for years.

Octavia looked about her while Georgie took down the bags and settled the fare. It was only a little past nine in the morning, yet the weather had so darkened the day that it might easily have been taken for dusk. The hail had given way for now to a desultory sleet, but it was carried by a restless, slicing wind. The Strythe estate had a forbidding look. A high stone wall and a gloomy mass of elms hid it from the lane. The house itself could not be seen.

Above the gate rose an arch of wrought iron, choked in places with ivy. It had a mournful appearance now, but might once have seemed imposing. From its apex hung a yard or so of coarse rope, whipping idly in the wind.

When he had paid the cabman, Georgie thumped lightly at the frame of the coach to send him on his way. 'Lord, sister,' he said, clapping his hands against the cold. 'What a purgatory you have brought us to. If this is where an earl must come paddling, I am quite content to be a third lieutenant for ever more.'

But Octavia was not listening. She hesitated, uncertain for a moment of what she saw, then advanced slowly towards the gate.

'Now, then,' Georgie went on, occupying himself with the luggage. 'You must put up this umbrella before we go any further. It was not made for a lady, but I daresay you will manage it easily enough. I'd hold it myself if it weren't for the bags.'

Octavia said nothing. She stared, raising a hand absently to the gate. Under her gloved fingers, the iron was solid and cold.

'You would not think much of that sleet, it not being heavy, but it is the very kind that will give you a mortal dose before you have gone a hundred yards.'

'Georgie,' she said softly. He fell silent and followed her gaze. She felt a peculiar urge to stop him, to keep him from seeing.

But *did* he see? Could he?

'Lord above, sister.'

The girl was watching them from a little way beyond the gate. She was a frail creature, and profoundly pale. Though she wore only a thin and shabby nightgown, she seemed quite untroubled by the cold. But it was not that. That was not the strangest thing.

'Miss Tatton?' Octavia gripped the bars, thrusting her face between them so that nothing should obstruct her view. It must be her, surely. It could only be her. 'Angie? Is that you? I came for you, came to find you. Mrs Campion told me about you. And Neuilly, the man who cared for you? He asked me to come.'

If the girl had heard her, she gave no sign of it. She stood for a moment longer, solemn and unperturbed, and it was only as she turned away that Octavia was sure of what she had seen. She was no longer whole, this girl. Her right arm, from just below her shoulder. Her right leg, beneath the hem of her gown. They had faded, almost to nothing. Only a vitreous faintness remained, like isinglass in warm water.

'Lord above, sister,' said Georgie again.

Angie crossed the bleak gardens towards a ramshackle summerhouse that could be seen in the distance. She was silent and swift, seeming hardly to touch the ground. Octavia watched her for as long as she could, but the weather made her uncertain. She lost sight of her for a time, then glimpsed her again, or so she imagined. But perhaps it was only the wind among the dead leaves, or some illusory thing that she herself had conjured from the rain.

Lady Ada was out of temper. She had been quite at ease, the inspector said, when they had gone to view her brother's remains, and had afterwards announced her intention to bathe in seaweed, a practice she recommended. She had not expected to receive another visitor, however, and her mood had darkened considerably since she was given word of the new arrival. She was pacing about the drawing room when Gideon entered with his uncle, marking each turn with a brisk percussion of her cane. He had cleared his throat a number of times when Cutter did him the kindness of making the announcement.

'Yes, yes,' Lady Ada said, scarcely glancing at the visitor. 'Never mind that now. I have suffered quite enough in the way of disturbances. Let him take his seat until I am somewhat restored. Someone ring for Mrs Cornish. I must have whisky, before I perish. And some suet pudding.'

Gideon looked helplessly to his uncle, who dismissed the indignity with a benign look. He made his way unobtrusively to a chair.

'Where is Angela?' Lady Ada demanded, striking the floor with her cane. 'That is what I should like to know. Why haven't you found her yet, Sergeant? You have little else to occupy you, goodness knows.'

Gideon could not look her in the eye. 'I have been doing my utmost, madam, but it is no easy matter. I shall resume the search shortly, but I have in fact been otherwise occupied. My uncle has come, and he has much of importance to tell us.'

'Has he, indeed? What has any of it to do with me?'

Here Cutter intervened. 'Madam, I hoped I had made matters plain to you. We are now concerned with a serious crime. With a number of serious crimes. We have reason to believe that Miss Tatton was the victim of such a crime.'

'If I may, Inspector.' It was Neuilly who spoke. 'If it puts Her Ladyship's mind at rest, I believe Miss Tatton will soon return of her own accord.'

Lady Ada stared at him for a moment. 'And who are you to be venturing an opinion? You look like a clergyman of some poor sort. Is that what you are?'

'Forgive me, madam,' said Neuilly, rising. 'Allow me to—'

'No, never mind all that. I have no patience for pleasantries at the best of times. Keep your seat, and out with it.'

'I am Herbert Neuilly, madam. I was a clergyman, yes, and of a poor sort. You are right about that. But that life is behind me, I think. I knew Miss Tatton before she came to this. I cared for her, in my ministry, and for others like her. I did what I could to keep them from harm.'

'What kind of harm?'

'From harm of a common sort, in part. She was an orphan work girl, and faced all that such young women must face. But it was not only that. I knew her to be gifted in an uncommon way. To be marked out.'

Lady Ada greeted this with a strange silence. She turned after a moment to the window. 'The wreck will be disturbed,' she remarked, as if to herself. 'After a long spell of calm, it often appears that the sands will smother it entirely, then a storm comes and one wakes to find it exposed again almost to its keel. So, you see it too.'

Neuilly hesitated. He was not sure if it was him she addressed. 'The wreck, madam?'

'No, not the wreck.' She turned to him again. 'The brightness.'

'Ah,' said Neuilly. 'How remarkable. I so seldom encounter others like me. Yes, madam, I see it. And you? When did you first become aware of it?'

'As a child. At what age I don't recall. I suppose it was there from the first, but in early childhood one thinks nothing out of the ordinary. I used to see them in the streets. In people's houses, disappearing below stairs. It was more common in the lower orders, I found, which rather upsets one's way of thinking. And it seemed to be girls, always, though perhaps it was only that the girls came to my notice.'

'Such has been my experience,' Neuilly agreed. 'And I have seen a good many in my time.'

'But none quite like this one, I expect.'

'No, madam.' Neuilly lowered his head. 'None quite like this one.'

Gideon looked on, only faintly comprehending, but did not venture to speak. Cutter felt no such inhibition. 'What is this now?' he said. 'You might think of the ordinary mortals present.'

'Forgive me, Inspector,' Neuilly said. 'I have been so long in the habit of keeping these things hidden that I forget when I am among friends. Lady Ada is speaking of an interior brightness, a brightness of the soul, though perhaps we use the Christian word in ignorance. There is more I must tell you, but first, if I may – Lady Ada, did you feel compelled to keep it hidden, this perception? I have encountered others – in spiritualist circles, among a great many charlatans – and all told stories of a similar kind. They had learned not to speak of it, in their early lives. They had been subject to derision, and much worse. Some had been cut off from their families. Some had been locked up. I hope I do not touch on a painful subject.'

Lady Ada made a dismissive gesture. 'The whole of my existence is a painful subject,' she said. 'One acquires a certain fortitude. My experience was not quite as you describe, however; not to begin with, at any rate. I learned to be discreet, of course, when in company. I led rather a sheltered life, in my early years, though there were certain occasions that could not be shirked. My family had a certain standing, after all. But my father had no great liking for balls or field days. He preferred his study, his laboratory. I was like him, in that way, and it pleased him. And not only in that way.'

'Forgive me, madam,' Neuilly said. 'I do not follow.'

Lady Ada turned from the window at last. 'Isn't it obvious? My father saw what I saw. I don't recall when I discovered it first, but it became a secret we shared, at least for a time. I remember once, at Ascot – one was obliged to go, in those days – my father crouched next to me, when he was sure we weren't observed. He pointed out a little girl. She was scrubbing kettles in one of those tents where tea is served. An awning had been raised in the heat, and we could see the kitchen to the rear. "Look, Ada," he said. "Do you see how bright she is? Isn't it marvellous?" And that was all. He winked then, and led me away. I don't recall that we ever mentioned it again, but there was a look he used to give me, when we encountered them. A look, that was all. But it was enough.'

They were interrupted by Mrs Cornish, who entered the room with a rattling tea tray, setting it down with no particular delicacy. 'You might wish to take something, ma'am, having gone without your breakfast. I have put out some of your nuts and berries, along with the tea things. You might take a sup of something hot, ma'am, against the damp.'

'Take that rubbish away,' Lady Ada snapped. 'It is whisky I want. And some pudding. And what have you done with my cigars, woman?'

'You'll find them in their case, ma'am, nearly by your elbow. Which they ain't never moved, to my knowledge.'

'How dare you utter such a brazen lie?' Lady Ada replied with great vehemence. 'I scarcely know where to look for them from one hour to the next. Why do you persist in tormenting me, now that your paymaster lies dead?'

Cutter raised an eyebrow at this, but said nothing. He would have a good many questions, no doubt, but for now he seemed content to let this exchange run its course.

Neuilly seemed to acknowledge this when he spoke again. 'Well,' he said. 'There are other subjects we must turn to shortly, but if the inspector will permit it – and if you will indulge me a little longer, Lady Ada – might I ask if your brother came to know? About what you could see?'

'My brother.' Lady Ada had lit a cigar. She stroked the lid of the case as she closed it, then released a slow furl of smoke. This small ritual seemed to soothe her. 'My brother, yes. My brother always came to know of things. And somehow it never ended well.'

Octavia ran, clutching her sodden hat to her head. It was foolish of her, perhaps – she had no clear notion of which way Angie had gone – but she had acted on instinct. Poor Georgie had called out after her, laden with baggage and unable to follow, but there hadn't been time to explain. She caught another glimpse of Miss Tatton, or thought she did; a gauzy disturbance at the edge of her vision, crossing the shaded interval between two pines. She ran heedlessly then, letting her hat fly off in her wake. It didn't matter now how she might appear. Nothing else mattered.

She sighted her again and changed her course, realising she had gone astray. The grounds were wild and featureless in places, and a mist had risen from the shore. The sleet had ceded now to an insistent rain. She stumbled along choked footpaths and climbed overgrown terraces, searching the colourless vistas for something to orient herself by.

She turned back uphill, passing a blackened fountain, and came to a narrow walk of untended yews. At the far end – she was almost sure of it this time – she saw the girl again, and halted for a moment in confusion. The walk led to the summerhouse she had seen from the gate. She had doubled back without realising. The rain was heavier now, though it hadn't seemed to trouble Angie before. Perhaps she had sought shelter.

The summerhouse had been painted at one time in French grey, though it was now much disfigured. It was set out in an octagon, with doors that gave on to a mossy terrace. The wind caught them as she let herself in, so that she struggled for a moment to pull them closed behind her, fearful that a pane would be knocked out. She smelled the cigarette smoke before she turned to look. The scent of sandalwood. Then he spoke.

'Hello, Wavy.'

Lady Ada said no more until the housekeeper had cleared away the tea things and withdrawn, and even then she would not be rushed, choosing not to speak until she had smoked almost three quarters of her slender but noxious cigar.

'Tell me, Inspector,' she said at last, 'what do they say of me in London?'

Cutter looked up, slightly vexed at this digression. 'Begging your pardon, madam, but I do not take your meaning.'

Lady Ada strode to the centre of the room to face him. 'Do not try my patience further, Cutter. You are a policeman of some years' standing, I take it, and charged with looking into my brother's affairs. Am I to believe that you have discovered nothing of my family's history? That I have been shut away at my brother's whim for the better part of thirty years, and no explanation for it was ever put about in society?'

'As you say, madam, I hear a good deal in my profession about a great many things, and I heed very little of it. What I have heard of your circumstances, since you put it to me so directly, is that your brother obtained against you some finding of incapacity, and was given leave to confine you and to direct your affairs.'

'Incapacity.' Lady Ada repeated the word with a forceful contempt. 'Incapacity. Do I appear incapable to you, Inspector? Do I seem feeble in mind or body? No, it was not incapacity that concerned my brother. If I had been merely an imbecile or a lunatic, it would have suited him very well. The moment my father died, he would have consigned me to an asylum, and he would not have needed half a dozen medical men to make the case for him.

'It was not incapacity that made me intolerable to him, but the very opposite. Neuilly asks if my brother came to know of it – of this perception of mine, as he puts it. And he did, of course, though I never quite knew how. I imagined we were discreet, my father and I, but I was a child still. Who knows what he observed, what talk he might have overheard?

'Whatever he knew, he kept it to himself while my father was alive. He was a monster always, and filled with jealousy, but my father restrained him. Once he was gone, well . . .'

She broke off for a moment, and looked away.

'There was a serving girl, at the home of my father's cousin.

He saw me watching, I suppose, saw how fascinated I was. But he wasn't sure who it was. It was a large household, you see, and there were other serving girls. He couldn't pick her out. Not at first.

'He began to taunt me openly, to accuse me of hysteria, of madness, of witchcraft. But then he would alter course. He would claim that he perceived it too. He would try to describe how she appeared, this serving girl, as if from his own observations. He wanted me to confirm what he said, so that the details would seem convincing. And he wanted to be sure of who it was.

'When I wouldn't answer, he would torment me again. These were nothing but delusions. I was disordered, he said. My father had known it, but he had indulged me out of kindness. What he couldn't bear, you see, was the thought that he did not understand – that there might be secrets to which he was not admitted. He would show me, he said, that it was all in my mind. He would show me that the serving girl was perfectly ordinary.

'I didn't know what he meant, or what he intended. I couldn't tell if he had discovered who it was. But of course he had. I must have been careless. I must have paid attention to the girl when she was alone. He came to me with the newspaper, after it happened. She hadn't merited more than two or three lines. She had gone into the canal, near the Paddington Basin. The afternoon was dark, and the towpath was icy. Some bargemen from a brewery pulled her out. Alice Coakes, aged thirteen. In service at Gowden House in Mayfair.'

Cutter allowed a moment to pass before he spoke. 'Make a note of the particulars, Bliss. You will not object, Lady Ada?'

She ground out her cigar with a look of impatience. 'Let your sergeant get his notebook out and write down what I say, since he is diligent about such things. I am not speaking for the good of my health.'

'Did your brother confess to the act, madam? Openly or otherwise?'

'He was a brute, Inspector, and much less clever than he believed, but he wasn't an outright fool. How inconvenient for the Gowdens, he said. But I suppose it won't be terribly difficult to find another serving girl. One is much like another, after all.'

Neuilly gave a heavy sigh. 'Now we begin to see. "Thou look'st through spectacles", Donne said. Do you know his verse? When we look through spectacles, he said, "small things seem great". He was talking of the divine, of course, and how little we may know of it, with our pitiful faculties. "But up unto the watch tower get, and see all things despoiled of fallacies". I think we have begun to climb the watch tower at last, though it is a sad and wearying business. We begin to see.'

Octavia turned slowly at the sound of his voice. It was not shock that she felt, but a surge of revulsion. Elf had arranged himself on a bench seat at the rear of the summerhouse. His posture was languid, as if it were an afternoon in June and they had chanced to meet at a garden party, but he could not quite conceal his laboured breathing, his slight agitation when he tapped away his ash.

'It isn't possible,' she said. 'Ours was the first cab to be had. Master Alfred said you might be waiting an hour or more.'

'Poor Wavy.' He inclined his head. 'How confusing it must all seem.'

'My name is Octavia.' Her voice in her own ears was unfamiliar and brittle. 'You may address me as Miss Hillingdon.'

'Just as you wish, of course. And perhaps it will give you some comfort, Miss Hillingdon, to know that I might indeed be waiting still, if I had depended on your Master Alfred. But a man in my position would not keep it for long if he depended on the Master

Alfreds of this world.' He paused. 'Is it Master Alfreds, do you suppose, or Masters Alfred?'

'Why?' she said. 'All those poor girls. Why?'

'Ah, yes.' He sat upright, discarding his cigarette end and crushing it fastidiously beneath the toe of one shoe. 'I'd been wondering quite how much you knew. He removed certain items from Mr Brown's person, didn't he? Our friend on the train. Well, I suppose there's time to tell you just a little. Won't you sit down?'

He slid to one end of the bench, indicating the other with a courtly gesture. She backed away, pressing herself against the door and shaking her head. He sighed, as if in weariness, and reached into his coat. For a strange moment, Octavia did not recognise the object he had produced. The fear enclosed her then, like a skin of cold.

A gun, a pistol. How unobtrusive a thing it seemed.

'Forgive me,' he said. 'It's vulgar of me, I know. But do sit down, there's a darling. You aren't given to making a fuss, as a rule. I'm sure we can avoid any unseemliness.'

She glanced out over the gardens again as she edged towards him, keeping to the margins of the room. He held the gun with practised nonchalance. 'Who is it that you hope to see, my dear? Your poor, vanishing orphan? Not your brother, alas. He has found a use for himself as a porter, I gather, which seems about right.'

Octavia lowered herself carefully to the bench, gripping its edge and keeping her arms braced at her sides. She moved carefully, taking slow and even breaths.

'My brother is a naval officer,' she said. 'And a finer man than you have ever been.'

'A lieutenant, yes, how very splendid. He needed no more than three attempts, I am told, to pass his examination. Whereas you distinguished yourself at Girton College, and have charmed half of London into overlooking the matter of your birth. Who knows how well you might have married, if you had only given up that wretched bicycle of yours. How differently things might have turned out.'

'I want to know why,' she said quietly. 'Tell me why.'

'Well, as to the why of it, Strythe would have been the man to ask. He was the true zealot, the one with the grand notions. But I'm afraid he no longer has much to say. Hanged himself from the front gate in the night, I gather. I've been speaking to the servants here, who have made themselves useful in various ways, over the years.

'As for me, well, I came to the enterprise quite late. Much of what I've told you is true, you see, as far it goes. I do hold a position at the Home Office, in one of the more obscure Directorates. Secret, one might even say. We take an interest in cases of a particular sort, in certain phenomena. Strythe's little experiments were just the sort of thing that tends to attract our notice. I took a professional interest, nothing more. Or at least, that's how it began.'

'And then what? What *were* these experiments, as you call them? What did you want with those poor girls?'

'What does any of us want, my love? Life. To live. That's what they had, these bright ones. Life in abundance. Life to burn. But wasted on them, really. I mean, you've seen how these people live. Strythe's first was some little parlour maid, if you can imagine such a thing. I gather that he acted out of spite to begin with – the girl was a favourite of his sister's, if you take my meaning – and I suppose he meant only to take whatever coarse pleasure such a creature could offer. But he wrung rather more from her than that. Life, Wavy. A surfeit of it that infused his own being like some restorative tincture. The effects were modest at first, and persisted only for a few days, but he knew he had been given the merest taste. And the thought came to him that it might be distilled somehow, this vital essence – that it might be *purified*. And what use did they have for it, these girls? It would do nothing to better their prospects, this peculiarity of theirs. What harm was there, then, in taking what they didn't even know they possessed?'

'What peculiarity? What are you talking about?'

'Haven't you been listening, darling? They may be common, these wretches, but they aren't quite ordinary. They are gifted, if that's the word, with some rare superfluity of the soul, with a freakish excess. And we found a way to divert it, this excess, to *consume* it. Well, Strythe and his hirelings did, and naturally their method was documented for our files, but I never concerned myself much with the mechanics of the thing. The sickly ones were best, that much I gathered, the ones who'd been weakened in some way. It made them brighter, it seems. That's how it was manifest, you see, as a brightness of some sort, though I couldn't see it myself. Nor could Strythe, though he'd had certain instruments made. But we discovered that there were those who could. We learned to make use of them. Did you know that certain plants produce a great flush of flowers when they're dying? So that there will be seeds, I suppose. So that something will persist. At any rate, Strythe had employed all manner of people, even before he established his charitable institution. That was a delightful touch, don't you think? There was some disgraced medical man from Edinburgh, I remember – and a chemical agent had been perfected. A resin, I suppose you'd call it. It had to be kept in special vessels, made by a chap in Antwerp. You can't imagine the expense. It became a vapour, this resin, when the bottles were opened.'

'The black air,' Octavia said quietly. 'The smoke.'

'It was black, yes, and terribly noxious. Rather a nuisance to administer, too. It all had to be done very slowly, or they'd skitter over the edge before we'd got what we needed. But when it did work, my goodness. It just rose up from them afterwards, and we breathed it in. After the last one that worked – Felicity something, I think it was—'

'Hardwick. Felicity Hardwick.'

'Yes, that sounds right. After that one, well – my man Macken hardly recognised me the next morning. Said I looked ten years younger. Ten years. I mean, what wouldn't one do? And if there were someone brighter still, how much more might have been possible? Twenty years? Fifty? A hundred? But then there was all that fuss. That damned woman. That *cunt*. She destroyed the vessels, you know, when she jumped. And the resin that was left. A fucking *seamstress*, of all things. I told him it was a foolish risk. I warned him. But he had a weakness for theatrics, I'm afraid, and indulged all sorts of grand notions about higher knowledge. He couldn't just take a girl and get on with the job. He had to make a bloody ceremony of the thing. I knew it would be our undoing in the end. I knew what had happened that night, when word reached us at Ashenden House—'

'It was you, then. It was you I saw, climbing into his carriage.'

'Oh, you saw, did you? Ever the curious little cat, weren't we? Well, someone had to take charge of things, after all, if anything was to be salvaged from all of this. Someone had to conceal him, to begin with, since there was no question of his returning home. Besides, he'd rather exhausted my patience, and I wanted him within easy reach when the time came. But he grew suspicious, I think. He began to see, when he had had time to reflect, the predicament in which he had placed me. I could still maintain the appearance, just about, that I was doing no more than investigating this little case, but now there had been a grubby little incident. Questions would be asked, if there was anyone left to answer them. At any rate, my man Macken had been watching over him at Grosvenor-crescent, but he had fled when I returned from our little soirée at Mrs Digby's. I knew where he would go, of course. The carrier's cart was waiting still, and there were the remains of that ridiculous clergyman to think of – or so we believed. I knew he would come here – he always did – and it suited my purposes admirably. In the meantime, a story had to be put about that would allow me to conclude my business without any tiresome fuss, and in that regard you proved most obliging. Of course, I'd had to put the hours in first, telling you just enough to keep you keen. I'd had to cultivate you, as one always does with rare blooms, but my efforts were rewarded in the end. No one else was looking for Strythe, and I had a free hand. He robbed me of a certain satisfaction in the end, with that garish suicide of his, but at least he saved me some trouble.'

'What trouble?' Octavia said. 'What did you come here to do?'

He gave her a look of mocking sorrow. 'Oh, Wavy. You poor darling. Haven't you guessed?'

She glanced at the pistol, then scanned the windows again, searching the greyness for movement. 'There are others who know,' she said. 'They're probably here already.'

'Oh, they are. I wanted everyone here, where it's nice and quiet. One can kill people in London, of course, but it's always such a production. There's just so much to think of. Whereas in the country, well – there aren't so many distractions. One can get things done. Of course, it's tiresome all the same. You mustn't think it's what I wanted. I mean, I'm awfully fond of you still. I had other hopes for you, dear heart. I had other hopes for us. But you will insist on finding things out, won't you?'

'The policemen. There are two policemen here. If you – if there is shooting, it will bring them running.'

'Well, a policeman and a half, perhaps. But yes, they will make an appearance, I'm sure. Inspector Cutter, I'm afraid, has no great gift for looking the other way. It can be rather trying.'

'But they're *policemen*, for God's sake. And Scotland Yard knows they're here. You said so yourself, after the second death at Strythe House.'

'I say lots of things, darling. The second death at Strythe House was a bit of housekeeping, nothing more. Carew had been indiscreet, I rather suspect, or might have been later. No, our friends are a long way from home and haven't troubled to inform their superiors of their whereabouts. No one will be looking for them here.'

'He was right about you,' Octavia said softly.

'Who was?' Elf affected detachment still, but there was a sourness in his expression. 'Your secret correspondent? Your brother? You think they know me? That I have permitted *anyone* to know me?'

'I do. I know you. All your deceit, all your lies. Did you think you were so very brilliant? I may not have known what you were hiding, but I knew you were always hiding *something*. Always. And there were things you couldn't hide. The emptiness at the core of you. You couldn't hide it because you didn't recognise it. But I did. It's why I refused you.'

His sneer was undisguised. '*You*? Refused *me*? What can you be talking about?'

'Yes, you tried to hide that too, didn't you? To make a grand joke of it, as if the very notion were ridiculous. But you can't let it go, can you? That's why you taunt me still, about my birth. About how well I might have married. You thought you could become someone, didn't you, if I loved you. Someone real. But you never did. You never will.'

He looked away for a moment, and released a long sigh. 'Perhaps you are right, Wavy. Perhaps you are right, after all. I hardly know any longer. I admit I've never had your charming conviction in the matter of what is true and what is not. But it hardly seems to matter now.'

He stood up. His movements were unrushed, almost ceremonial. 'Perhaps you ought to close your eyes, old thing.'

'You loved me, Elf, but I never loved you. There was nothing to love.'

She closed her eyes. For a long time, there was only the sound of the rain.

When Lady Ada turned at last from the window, she held something before her, suspended on a fine chain. 'Do you know what this is?' she said. 'It is a key. It is a key that my brother wore about his neck, and which I removed from his body earlier this morning with the inspector's permission. It is the key to the gates of this cursed place, which he chained up almost thirty years since.'

'If I may, madam,' Cutter interjected. 'You have not forgotten, I hope, that you undertook to give me the key when our business here is finished. It may be submitted in evidence.'

'Yes, yes, Inspector. I have not forgotten. You need not remind me how little the world is changed. When one man dies, another is always at hand to take possession of the keys. A woman is never long without a keeper.'

Cutter frowned and cleared his throat. 'I have no authority to detain you, madam, nor any intention of doing so. You are suspected of no offence.'

'You mistake my meaning, Inspector. You spend your days

taking up thieves and murderers. It is natural that you have a simple view of such things. It is an easy matter, after all, to deprive a man of his liberty. He is put behind high walls, since he would otherwise climb over them. The window of his cell is barred, since he would smash a pane of glass without effort, and he is kept behind an iron door, so that he cannot batter it down. If you wish to understand the brutal force that men possess, you need only look at the measures that must be taken to imprison them.

'But when a man wishes to imprison a woman, Inspector, he need go to no such lengths. My brother put a chain on the gates because it amused him to do so. It is an additional inconvenience, certainly, since I cannot come and go by carriage, but there is nothing to keep me from leaving by the wicket gate. I am quite capable, I assure you, of walking all the way to Dover. But what good would it do me? I could not pay my passage abroad. I could scarcely afford to go into a tea-room. My brother's hirelings have long since tied up what is rightfully mine. Now that he is dead, perhaps, I may have some recourse at last, but until now I have relied upon the pittance he disburses for my upkeep, and even that is administered by Mrs Cornish.

'My brother reduced me to this state, Inspector, with no more than a few strokes of his pen. He accused me as only a woman may be accused, and he did so in the full knowledge that his charges would be laid before other men very like himself. You may wonder at this, perhaps. I am a gentlewoman, you may say, the daughter of an earl. But the truth is that I might just as well have been a village girl, brought up before the witchfinder.

'He had my journals admitted in evidence. I'd kept them for years. I documented things, you see. My father had encouraged it. I would go botanising, and so on. I was very meticulous. And I recorded them, all the bright ones I saw, whatever particulars of their lives I could come by. There were certain speculations, of course, as to the nature of their condition. And that wasn't all.

'The brightness, this phenomenon. It wasn't the only thing that drew me to certain young women. I hope I need not say more. I make no apology for my nature. In any case, I was meticulous, as I mentioned. I recorded my observations in considerable detail, and such small encounters as I could contrive. I recorded those too. You begin to see, I suppose, how all this might have appeared.

'He found a sympathetic ear upon the bench, of course. It was not even considered necessary to call me before the court, since by then my confinement had begun. My father being for some years dead, my brother was given unchecked power over my affairs, a power he did not stint to exercise.

'I tell you all this, Inspector, because I know that it was my brother's acts that brought you here, and that brought this man Neuilly here. I have told you all I know. I knew what he was capable of, I knew of his obsessions, but I knew no more than that. He would appear at odd intervals, always unannounced, and I would be confined to my rooms by those dreadful lackeys of his. The Cornish woman and her simpleton of a son. I wish I knew more, Inspector. Upon my life, I would gladly offer you any scrap that might damn his name, but I can think of nothing else.'

'Thank you, madam. It was no easy matter, I'm sure, to give us the account you did, and it may aid us more than you think.'

'As to the rest,' Neuilly said, rising from his chair, 'I believe I may now do my part. First, there are things I must show you. If I might have the use of this table, madam?'

Lady Ada raised her cane in assent.

He drew a packet from his coat, and from it he produced a number of documents and photographs. 'I obtained these yesterday,' he said. 'From a man on the train from London. There were other items of a similar kind, but it was necessary to show those to another person. That person is now on her way here, or so I hope, as is another less welcome visitor. Listen now, all of you, we may have only a little time.'

The noise. It was obliterating and complete. Afterwards, in the ruptured darkness, she felt nothing. There was a stillness, that was all, and a strange ease that kept her from pain or fear. Perhaps it was always so, at the end. Perhaps there was always this mercy.

'There now,' said the voice.

She stirred, sought his shape in the smeared light. She felt herself enclosed, made weightless. 'Georgie?'

'There now, sister.' He set her gently on her feet, keeping an arm about her. 'Mind how you go on the way out. There is a good deal of broken glass.'

'Georgie, is he—'

He guided her from the summerhouse, settling her coat about her shoulders. 'Gone, the bastard. I clipped his wing for him, but he got off before I could do more.'

'But the noise, the shot. I thought he had . . . that I was . . .'

'My boarding pistol, which between ourselves I have never fired in anger before now. It is an ancient thing – I bought it from a disrated master at Portsmouth – and none too accurate by the looks of it. Or I am a poor shot, one or the other.'

'But I left you behind, at the gates.'

'What do you take me for, Octavia Hillingdon, to think I would not follow you? It was only that I took a moment to stow the bags out of the weather. And I will own that I could not get my bearings for a time. It is a puzzle of a place, this garden, though it seems full of nothing, and the rough weather is no help. It has the makings of an honest squall. But hold up now, there is a fellow coming from the house at a fair clip. He is a stern-looking cove, by God.'

'You there,' the man called out, coming to a halt a little way off. 'State your business here, and be brisk about it. I am Inspector Cutter of the Metropolitan Police, and you are trespassing here at the very least. State your business now.'

'Good morning, Inspector.' She stood fully upright, though she felt a little unsteady, and offered him her hand. 'My name is Octavia Hillingdon, and this is my brother, George. I am here—'

'Your name has just come up, Miss Hillingdon. You are expected, it seems. But no brother was mentioned.'

'Lieutenant Hillingdon, sir, of the Royal Navy. I hope I see you well.'

Cutter gave a guarded nod. 'Another man was mentioned, who might be in your company. A Marquess, among other things.'

'He was here, sir.' Georgie's expression darkened. 'I came upon him just now in that summerhouse, menacing my sister with a gun. I had a go at him with my boarding pistol, but I was firing through a window. I did him some damage, but I'm sorry to say it was no more than that. He's made himself scarce for now.'

'You needn't be too sorry, Lieutenant. I have evidence before me of conspiracy in upwards of half a dozen murders. I have one suspect dead already, and I mean to put the other in the dock. Put your pistol away, like a good man. There is too much shooting and wandering the grounds for my liking. Come, you may tell me the rest while we walk. I will be easier in my mind when we are back indoors.'

When Cutter had returned with the new arrivals, there was a good deal of business to be attended to. There were introductions to be made, but he would not permit much in the way of ceremony. Lady Ada had other ideas, however. Although she scarcely acknowledged the lieutenant, she was most solicitous towards Miss Hillingdon.

'It is a shame you cannot see it, Inspector. She is not quite like Angela, of course, but her light is bewitching all the same. There is something almost autumnal about it. Forgive me, dear, if I embarrass you. I have been starved of such wonders for so very long. You must have some tea, of course. Or should you prefer whisky?'

'I am sorry for it, madam,' Cutter said, 'but our new guests must do without for now. Miss Hillingdon has been giving me the bones of what happened in the summerhouse. We need not go into every detail, but it seems you were right to have a low opinion of Mrs Cornish and her boy. I intend to lock them in your cellar for the duration. I have quite enough to occupy me without looking over my shoulder for those two. Bliss, is there any sign yet of the girl?'

'No, sir. I will go out now and look again. I was only waiting for you to return.'

'No, Bliss. It is best that you stay put for now. There is a man loose about the grounds, and I do not like the sound of him a bit. Make a circuit of the main rooms. Be sure the doors are locked and the windows fastened. When you have done that, you may keep watch at the French doors. They command the widest view of the grounds. Lieutenant, you might take up station there in the meantime, and keep a hand to your weapon.'

Cutter had already returned when Gideon completed his rounds. He was conferring now with Gideon's uncle, while Lady Ada kept Miss Hillingdon in animated conversation.

'I am trying to get the measure of them, Neuilly,' Cutter was saying. 'Or of the man who is still standing, at least. They dogged your steps for years, it seems, but never revealed themselves until the night Miss Tatton was taken. Do not take it amiss. I am only trying to account for it in my own mind.'

'No, Inspector, I do not blame you. The same questions have preoccupied me. In the end I believe it was a simple matter. I had failed in my vigilance, in the past. There were other girls I cared for, as I mentioned, before Miss Tatton. It grieves me to think of it now, but it seems to me in hindsight that there was more I could have done. They took the others while my attention was elsewhere, and I vowed that I would not fail Miss Tatton in the same way. But Strythe and Hartington had grown impatient, it seems. She was unique, you see. Brighter than the rest. They would not wait. They decided to take us both.'

'Forgive me, Reverend,' Miss Hillingdon interrupted. 'I spoke to Mrs Campion, who kept the boarding house. She said that Miss Tatton had been on an outing that evening. That she went out alone, to the best of her knowledge.'

Neuilly gave a sad smile. 'An outing, yes. To feed the ducks in St James's Park. She had a great fondness for them.'

Gideon had crossed to the window, but he turned at this and quietly lowered his head.

'I could have forbidden it, perhaps, but the poor girl had few enough pleasures in the world. Why shouldn't she have her outings? I asked Mrs Campion only to fix the times, and to keep to them strictly. In that way, I could be sure of keeping watch. I followed her, you see. Discreetly, or so I thought. But I was seen.

'They took me first, and brought me to the church – to St Anne's, nephew, where you later discovered her – and they bound me until they returned with her. They had begun dosing her already, those demons. It had made her faint, but she saw me there, just as she was meant to, so that each of us would know the worst at the end. Strythe left then, for his grand engagement, meaning to conclude the whole filthy ceremony at his leisure. Hartington too.'

Miss Hillingdon sat up at this. 'He must have known you, then. You must have known he would recognise you, when you came into our compartment on the train. Were you not at all fearful?'

Neuilly gave a rueful nod. 'Greatly so, miss, but the Lord granted me just enough courage, and directed the outcome as I had prayed he would. You see, I had staked all on the hope that he would attempt nothing in your presence, and so it proved.'

'If we might return to the events in the church,' Cutter said. 'They left someone in charge, I take it, having gone to so much trouble?'

'Indeed, Inspector. A sexton in their employ was left to watch over Miss Tatton; they had used that place before, I believe.'

'And you, uncle?' Gideon said. 'You were not there when I found her. What had they done with you?'

'They were agitated when they returned. Miss Tull, by then, had carried out her plan, though I did not come to know of it until much later. She had come to me, some time before, in torment and in fear of her life. I was grateful to her, God knows, and commended her courage, but I warned her against approaching me again, fearing that we would be observed. She told me that she saw a way – a way they would not discover until it was too late – to unmask those she feared and frustrate their plans. She would say no more than that, and I did not press her. I did not know the nature of her sacrifice, that night in the church, but it was plain to me that she had succeeded in her designs. They were at odds with one another, and uncertain of how to proceed. Poor Miss Tatton was unconscious, but she had received only a partial dose, and they could not predict what might happen if they waited longer. The sexton was to stand guard, and was to secure her somewhere out of sight if they did not return. I was dragged out to a carrier's cart that was waiting in the yard. The driver was not expecting to haul away anyone living, I believe, but he knew enough to stand apart and to look the other way. He was a regular hireling too, perhaps.'

'Devlin and Sons,' Miss Hillingdon said. 'I went to their yard, by London Bridge Station.'

'Yes, it was there that I managed to free myself, but it was only by the grace of God, for I was not meant ever to stir again. Outside the church they hauled me atop the cart and bundled me into a great chest. Strythe showed me a glass phial then, and said that he would unstop it before he nailed the box shut. It was coarser stuff than they had given to Miss Tatton – that would not be wasted on the likes of me – and it was meant for a cruder purpose. If I was going to pray, he said, I might do it then while I still had the breath in my body.'

'Devlin and Sons.' Lady Ada echoed the words. 'Forgive me, Neuilly, it has just returned to me. On those occasions when he came here, when they locked me away upstairs – I saw them, those carriers' carts, but they were driven somewhere out of sight. Valuables, the Cornish woman said. The master has valuables that want storing. And he did keep things here, objects that he'd acquired for his collections. The place is filled with them. But I ought to have known. May God forgive me.'

'You judge yourself harshly, madam. We guess at small acts of wickedness, since they are familiar to us. But crimes of this magnitude . . .' Neuilly bowed his head for a moment, and as he did so Gideon was struck by how aged he now appeared. 'The darkness, in that box. They nailed it shut, and the vapour began to rise around me. The taste of it, thick against my throat. I will not forget it soon. He'll give no trouble, I heard Strythe say. The dose was fit for a horse. Wait for an hour, then look for me at the house. If you do not find me, bring him back to the yard and await my instructions. The girl will be done soon enough, he said, and she can go in on top. That is how he spoke of her, of my bright one. It roused a rage in me even as I was passing from my senses, and as I scrabbled for purchase against the walls of the box I chanced upon a knothole. I pressed my face to it and tasted untainted air once more, then I kept as still as I might and did not stir for hours afterwards, when the cart had long since halted and all outside was silent. I was saved, though I was not worthy of it and could not fathom why. I retrieved the bottle they had used. It was empty now, but I wished to return it to them even so, as a token of my resolve. I took a room for the night, being very much weakened. I recovered what I could of my strength. And then I began the work for which the Lord had surely saved me.'

Cutter got up and went to the window, a growing restlessness in his movements. He had let himself be ruled by caution until now, but Gideon knew his dislike of confinement and inaction. 'Nothing stirring, Lieutenant?'

'Nothing, sir. The weather does not help our cause, mind, but I have stood watch in worse.'

'This man Hartington,' the inspector said, turning to the room. 'You know him best, Miss Hillingdon. You say he came here to snuff out a scandal that might bring him down, to put us all out of the way of talking. But what kind of man is he, beyond being bad to his core? How is he apt to go about it?'

Miss Hillingdon considered this. 'He will hide. It's what he does. He will stay hidden for as long as he possibly can. And when he shows himself, he will know that he has only one chance.'

Cutter gave a grim nod and worked at his neck. 'And still no sign of the girl.'

Gideon looked out over the grounds to the sea beyond. The

sky was burdened and gloomy, but a ribbon of radiance survived above the water, staining it with ochre and violet. This strange light touched the gardens in places, scoring them with long shadows. 'Inspector,' he said. 'We ought to consider, I think, that this may not unfold according to any plan of Hartington's.'

'What do you mean, Bliss?'

'You said yourself, sir, that Miss Tatton sees what we cannot. That she has a long reach now.'

'I felt her hand,' Neuilly said. He spoke distractedly, as if thinking aloud.

'Uncle?'

'On the train, with that man, the one calling himself Brown. When I did what I did, I felt her hand on mine. I *saw* her hand. You will think me mad, but look at me. I would not have had the strength.'

'And Strythe, sir,' Gideon continued. 'He did not come here, surely, with the intention of hanging himself from the gate. He believed he was carrying my uncle's remains – forgive me, sir – and he had come to dispose of them. What he did, he did at her bidding. You said as much yourself.'

'Yes,' Cutter said. 'That much I am persuaded of. I have seen the like before. But what is she waiting for, if that is the way of it? She wasted no time with Strythe.'

'She ain't waiting, Inspector.' It was the lieutenant. 'Not any more.'

They gathered at the windows.

'Angie,' Gideon said softly. She stood perhaps twenty feet from the house. She was waning still. He had been prepared for it, or so he thought, but at the sight of her he felt a helpless lurch of sorrow. The vanishing had spread to her left side, claiming her fingertips and the lower part of her leg. Beneath her nightgown, too, there were signs of fading, places where her silhouette did not seem whole.

But there were other changes now, of a kind he had not seen before. Her vanished parts had been imperceptible before in daylight, and by night only a faint and gaseous tracery had been visible. But they had brightened now, becoming distinct even in the strange dusk that the storm had brought, and she seemed formed in part of a gauzy tissue of radiance, sharpened at its edges so that it might have been etched into the air itself.

'Lord Jesus,' the lieutenant said.

Lightning flickered out at sea, and a moment after it there came a blunt surge of thunder. The French doors rattled in their frame, and out on the dunes, the marram grass was stirred and silvered under the wind. Angie raised her arm, holding the pale flame of it aloft in the darkness, then she turned away towards the sands.

'Well,' said Neuilly. 'There she is, come into her glory. Whatever she intends, I fancy she will give us no better sign that that.'

Cutter drew out his revolver and nodded to the lieutenant. 'Bliss, stay at my back and do not fall too far behind. Ladies, will you make these doors fast again when we are gone?'

Lady Ada strode towards him and met his eye. She was very nearly his equal in height, and no less commanding in aspect. 'Don't be absurd, Inspector. In the first place, Miss Hillingdon's is the gravest duty of all. She will be the one to put what happens here before the public, which she cannot very well do if she is cowering in a corner. For my own part, I have endured this withered life for long enough. I am quite prepared to die today if I must, but if I do, then by God, I will go down swinging this stick.'

The storm was gathering force again, and made for hard going as they crossed the grounds towards the shore. Cutter led the way, as was his habit, and since he too was armed, the lieutenant brought up the rear. They kept together in a ragged file, each straining to keep the next in view, but it was no easy matter. The way was downhill for the most part, but the terrain grew coarser and more uneven as they drew near the dunes.

From time to time they would glimpse Angie again, flitting back and forth – a quickness in her movements now that was beyond anything natural – as if to assure herself that they were following. When she passed out of sight she left brief traces in the air, like the arcs of brightness when a lamplighter swings his wick.

They could see no sign of her when they came to the open shore, and at first they struggled even to orient themselves. On the sands there was no shelter from the weather, and the rain came now in obliterating shoals. The tide was out, and the waterline so distant that Gideon could not make it out. There was nothing that might be called a horizon, only a wash of tainted pallor in the lower reaches of the sky.

'There!' Neuilly called out. 'Do you see, Lady Ada?'

'I see her. Cutter, look. It is this way.'

Gideon trudged after them, coming level with Neuilly. 'Uncle, a moment. I saw nothing. Are you sure?'

'The brightness is growing, nephew, and soon it will be fully manifest to all. But Lady Ada and I have an advantage still. I see her plainly, over that way where the sky is brightening. You will see for yourself soon enough.'

Gideon accepted this grudgingly. He put his collar up against the cold, and for a time he kept pace in silence. 'Uncle,' he said at length. 'If I may speak frankly, sir. I have not always shown the gratitude that was your due. You provided for my education, setting prospects before me that many young men might have envied, and I regarded them with indifference. I have neglected my studies, I regret to say, and allowed myself to grow resentful at those few limits you were obliged to set. I am sorry for it, sir. I regret it exceedingly.'

Neuilly slowed at his side, coming nearer to be heard above the wind. 'Do not reproach yourself, nephew.' He gripped Gideon's shoulder, though perhaps it was only to steady himself. 'I did no more than my duty, and stintingly at that. You had no great cause for gratitude.'

'On the contrary, sir. You were generous beyond all—'

'What were you to think, finding yourself all but banished? There were reasons, as you now know, but how were you to guess at those? I did wrong, I think, in keeping them from you. I had other duties, yes, but to those I devoted myself heedlessly. It is I who have been derelict, my boy. It is I who ought to be contrite.'

'But consider all you have done, uncle.' Gesturing vaguely, Gideon raised his face against the rain. 'All those you have aided.'

Neuilly halted, surveying the scoured sand at his feet. 'And what did it all come to, in the end? Where are they now?'

Gideon was about to answer, but his eye was caught by a change in the light. A curious silence descended then, and even the weather was brought to an unnatural stillness. What followed seemed remote from him, as if witnessed from some vantage apart from his own body. He knew dimly that he had been struck. That he struggled, but was held.

'Hold still, there's a good chap.' The voice smooth and hard, and a cold pressure beneath his jaw. 'If you'll just come this way.'

And there, as he twisted. The white of her, in the thinning mist. The bright miracle.

Angela mea.

He was hauled now, up into the dunes. He bucked, heels dragging. 'Can't breathe,' he said. 'Can't.'

'That's all right, old thing. You won't need to. Not for very much longer.'

The others below, gathering around her. She was paler now, and brighter. Untouchably calm. Cutter was approaching, slow and grave. His gun was raised.

'Hartington,' he called out. 'I would sooner have you in the dock, but if I am put to it I will gladly have you in a box.'

'I think not, Inspector.' Gideon tried to turn, but the blunt cold was pressed now against his throat. 'No, I rather think not. You will throw aside your gun, and the lieutenant will do the same. Otherwise, I shall be forced to put down your little pup. You have learned a little about me, I fancy. You know not to doubt me.'

'Easy, Bliss.' The inspector was wary and intent, a fierceness coiled in him. 'Easy now. You hold still, and I will see about this specimen. You did yourself credit in the end, Bliss. You have the makings of a sergeant, after all, and we will live to put away another chop or two at Leggett's.'

'Yes, sir. I hope so, sir.' A gull passed, sliding in silence through the leavening mist.

'Hartington,' the inspector called again. 'I do not like your odds. That shoulder wound is showing, you know. You can hardly keep your gun arm straight. Do you see what I am pointing at you? It is a Bulldog, the most reliable thing a man can carry. Put down your pistol, there's a good fellow, or as God is my witness, I will take off a quarter of your head at the first twitch of your finger. You will not harm that boy.'

Angie was raising her arms. He sought her face, tried to fix upon it, but the brightness made it indistinct. A tremor then, somewhere beneath his feet. Miss Hillingdon came to Angie's side.

'Miss Tatton?' she said gently. 'Why did you wait for us here? What is this place?'

Angie had joined her hands, but spread them now as if parting a veil. Gideon felt the dune slump beneath him, fissured now and spilling upon itself. Hartington's grip tightened as he struggled to keep his balance. 'Whatever she's doing,' he said, 'I suggest you dissuade her. There could be a nasty accident.'

'How little you have learned,' Neuilly said. 'How little you have learned if you believe she can be dissuaded now.'

Angie's arms were fully outstretched, a radiance growing at her core.

'We might take a few paces back,' the lieutenant said. 'Another minute and the whole lot will give way. You have gone for the wrong high ground, Hartington.'

'Bones,' Miss Hillingdon said. 'My God, Georgie. All those bones. Inspector, do you see?'

'I will look soon enough. I am occupied just now.'

Gideon twisted, fighting Hartington's grip. He glimpsed the wreck, stark and solitary in the distance, and beneath him in the lapsed flank of the dune – it puzzled him, this strange nest of cages, or he kept himself for a moment from seeing. But he knew the shapes, the pale knurled hafts and fractured orbs. He knew, he knew.

Behind him Hartington lurched, and Cutter was roaring, pounding towards him. The noise came, vast and brutal, and somewhere in him a fierce influx of hurt. He was flung away, as if by a wave, and knew only faintly when he came to rest. Above him, for a moment longer, Hartington stood suspended, then a maw widened in the sand and he was gone.

The sense of things failed then. The order. There was a heat, an upswaying of the sky. A light from somewhere, and the arc of a gull. Slow, considering.

'Bliss!' Cutter was near him, but his voice was not. Nothing solid was left, nothing whole. He clutched himself, and near his skin he found the sixpence. The bright thing from long ago. 'Oh, Christ. Bliss.'

And she now, kneeling. Seeing him. *Seeing*.

'There you are.' To him, at last. To him. 'You came back. I knew you would.'

'Angie. I promised. I have it, look. Angie Tatton.' Her hand found his, enclosing the token. 'In ribbons. I found it. In ribbons of. It hurts, Angie.'

'Hush.' She lowered herself, came near to him. Dreaming, it was like, or the stillness just before. The falling away. 'Hush now. I know. It won't be long. Hush.'

She lay by him, held him and made him still. He let himself be quiet. The other voices had faded now, and the greyness was very gentle. The gull returned, just once, then passed away on a soundless bend of wind, intent on something far away and out of sight.

VI

LUX PERPETUA

June, 1893

At New Scotland Yard, since she could fix upon no suitable place to conceal it, Octavia conducted her bicycle directly into the public office. A good many people were coming and going, since the evening was fine, and the mere proximity of a large body of policemen would be no deterrent to thieves.

'Miss.' A duty sergeant stretched from behind the counter, thrusting apart a pair of agitated callers to address her. 'Excuse me, miss.'

'My name is Octavia Hillingdon, Sergeant. I am here to see one of your inspectors.'

'I'm sure you are, miss, but what do you call this?' He jabbed a thick finger in the direction of her bicycle.

'I call it a bicycle, Sergeant, but the term is not of my own invention. You are welcome to come and look, if you haven't encountered one before.'

The duty sergeant wiped his mouth with his knuckles. 'You're a right scream, miss. Which, my point was, you can't bring it in here. This is the public office at Scotland Yard, not Wimbledon Common. You're causing an obstruction.'

'Very well, then, I shall bring it with me.' She crossed to the low gate at the far end of the counter. 'Would you mind letting me through? I know the way.'

The sergeant lumbered wearily to the gate, folding his arms as he confronted her. 'Miss,' he said. 'I'm going to say it nice one more time, but after that I ain't going to be answerable. You see that lot up there? I've got two drunks, three witnesses to arson and some nutter says he's the Bishop of Wapping. Just 'cause you say your aitches right don't mean I can't haul you in for breaching the peace.'

He laid his palm with emphasis on the counter flap, but no sooner had he done so than a larger hand enfolded his and removed it without ceremony.

'That will do, Foyle.' Inspector Cutter clamped the sergeant's arms to his torso and shunted him aside. 'It is a long while since you hauled anything into this place beyond your own apparatus or the odd pound of sausages. Good evening to you, Miss Hillingdon. I have an appointment, I'm afraid, but you are welcome to keep me company on the way. It is pleasant out, I believe.'

The inspector held the doors as she manoeuvred her bicycle from the building, but made no other concessions to her presence. When they had crossed the forecourt, he strode away without a backward glance, setting off at an energetic pace along Victoria Embankment. Octavia had grown accustomed to his peculiarities, and if she found them tiresome at times, she knew that no personal slight was intended. She might simply have caught him up, as she had done on other occasions, if not for the encumbrance of keeping the bicycle at her side. After a moment's deliberation, she simply took to the saddle and followed by way of the road. When she drew alongside him – or nearly so, since the avenue was lined with plane trees – his fearsome expression was softened for a moment by something approaching amusement.

'Well, Miss Hillingdon,' he said. 'Will it hold fine, would you say? You are at a considerable elevation, I see. You must have sight of the storms out at sea.'

'I daresay it will,' Octavia answered. 'I do hope so, at least. I shouldn't like your evening out to be spoiled.'

Cutter passed behind another tree and did not reply at once, but his aspect had darkened again when he reappeared. Octavia had come to know him only a little – there seemed to be no one at all who knew him well – but from those of longer acquaintance she had formed certain impressions. He had tended always towards a certain bleakness of disposition, it seemed, and if recent events had left their mark on him, the changes might be less apparent than in a man of easier temperament.

Inspector Cutter was, in the opinion of one plain-spoken sergeant she had consulted, the same hard old dog he always had been. The same dog, only more so.

'I am not having an evening out,' said Cutter at length. 'I am no great man about town, as you are well aware. I am abroad on police business.'

'I see,' said Octavia. 'And where will this police business take you, if you don't mind my asking? I don't mean to pry. It's just that I'm wondering how long will it take us to get there.'

Cutter looked about him briefly, raising a hand to halt the traffic as he crossed Northumberland-avenue towards Hungerford Bridge. 'How long?' he said. 'Are you in a great hurry, Miss Hillingdon?'

'Not at all, Inspector, I'm just wondering if there'll be time. I'm afraid I've come to go over your recollections again. It's my new publisher, you see. He's been perfectly agreeable, for the most part, but there are aspects of the case that make him rather nervous. There are particulars I must verify with the officer who was present.'

'Officers, Miss Hillingdon.'

'I'm sorry, what?'

'Officers. During the events we are speaking of, there was more than one officer present.'

'Yes, of course. I'm sorry, it's just that—'

A train had come in at Charing Cross Station, and the inspector was obscured for a time amid the tumult of emerging passengers. The cabmen were arriving to contend for fares, and their disorderly rank swelled halfway across the road. By the time she had made her way around the obstruction, Cutter was some distance ahead, turning from the footway so as to continue by way of the gardens. He was nearing the bandstand when she came abreast of him again.

'London Bridge,' he called out.

'I'm sorry?' Octavia was out of breath, and momentarily at a loss.

'I am going as far as London Bridge, to answer your earlier question, at which point I must bid you good evening. It is a distance of two miles, or near enough, so you may question me at your leisure. I am glad, by the way, that the arrangement is turning out to your satisfaction.'

'What arrangement?' Octavia veered around a darting youngster, whose mother regarded her with the sternest disapproval.

'With this publisher of yours,' Cutter said. 'Are you not sorry, though, that you kept it from the papers? It would have made your name, I am told.'

'Hardly,' Octavia said. 'It is not the practice to put names to articles, for one thing. I had nothing to gain but the promise of advancement. That no longer interested me, though the editor of the *Gazette* found it hard to believe.'

'So he told me. A Mr Healy, if I am not mistaken. He came to see me, you know. I believe he hoped I would intervene.'

'Yes, that sounds just like him.' Octavia looked away in

amusement. They were rounding a bed of young roses, and the still air held a faint sweetness. 'What did you tell him?'

'I showed him the door,' said Cutter.

'Did you, really?' she said. 'I should have liked to see that.'

'It was no great spectacle, I'm afraid. He came to see me at Leggett's, which is an establishment I am fond of, and seated himself without my leave. You will not be familiar with Leggett's, I expect, but in the back parlour there is a pair of armchairs. They are not much to look at, but they are reserved, in a manner of speaking. It is a thing that has always gone without saying. And all the more so, since what happened.'

'Of course,' Octavia said quietly. 'Of course, I do understand.'

'I told him to pry his arse from where it was, and to take his leave. He did not trouble you afterwards, I take it?'

'Oh, he pestered me for a time, but he knew when he was beaten. He has his position, still, but he has been a little less sure of his ground since my grandfather's passing.'

'Is that so?'

'The arrangements that had been made were not quite as he had hoped. They grant me considerable freedom, I gather, though I have not looked into it fully. It no longer interests me greatly, as I said, and I have other matters now to occupy my time. Georgie has begun to take a hand in things, which I am glad to see. He had not thought of it before, having a poor opinion of his own abilities, but he has an aptitude for it, I believe, and a doggedness in getting at the truth of things. I rather think he is better suited to it than I ever was.'

'Is he not minded to print the story himself, then? He had a good deal to do with it.'

'He doesn't think it his place. In any case, his hands are tied for now. Proceedings are still under way, for one thing, so a good deal would have to be omitted. Strythe and Hartington may be dead, but their underlings will be tried, since you were so diligent in making cases against them. And then there is the committee of inquiry, which will drag its feet for months, even if it comes to no conclusion. The dead cannot be defamed, of course, but Hartington was attached to the Home Office, and it seems there is such a thing as seditious libel. Did you know that, Inspector?'

'I did not, Miss Hillingdon. I have put a good many fellows in the dock in my time, but none of them rose to the likes of that.'

'Well, my publisher has retained a QC, so I am learning a good deal. No, the *Gazette* would be confined to tattle and speculation, and Georgie has no fondness for either, especially in this case. It's my story to tell, he says. He wants to see me do it justice.' She paused to choose her words. 'And to honour those who were lost.'

Cutter grunted mildly at this.

'I suppose it sounds terribly tedious, and perhaps it will be. But I want to try, all the same. I shall have to touch on the scandal, of course, but no more than that. I want to show people the lives that those poor girls lived, the conditions that made such easy prey of them. I want to document the inequities of our society, much as Mrs Harkness did. Perhaps you know her work, Inspector? She is the author of *In Darkest London*.'

Cutter seemed dimly entertained by this notion. 'I am no great man of letters, miss, but I believe I have seen my share of London, dark and otherwise.'

They carried on in silence for a time, leaving the gardens and crossing towards the river at Waterloo Bridge. This put Octavia at the further disadvantage of bicycling against the oncoming traffic, but she carried on as if it were the easiest thing in the world. As Cutter kept up his resolute pace, she began calling out her questions, regulating her own speed so as to come abreast of him in the intervals between the plane trees. His demeanour was hardly welcoming, but he gave his answers readily enough, hesitating only when his professional discretion required it, or – once or twice – when she came near to matters that touched him personally. These he would not discuss even now, and it was Octavia's belief that he would never speak of them again.

She was as methodical in all of this as the circumstances permitted, but was obliged to conduct her questioning with a certain briskness. At Blackfriars Bridge, when an omnibus passed in front of them, she made a brief study of her notes and found that she had satisfied herself on nearly every point. She had even managed, in those moments when the press of traffic had halted her progress, to jot down some particulars that she feared would slip her mind. London Bridge was some way off still, and she did not wish to appear rude by leaving as soon as her business with the inspector was concluded. She cast about for some suitable subject, but it seemed impossible to imagine conversing with him about anything other than his work.

'Well, Inspector,' she said, when the obstruction had been cleared and they continued on their way. 'Perhaps you will tell me a little about whatever business you are on. It must be rather important, since you are setting out so late in the evening.'

Cutter gave her a keen look, then halted abruptly and appeared again to her right. They had turned in at Thames-street, where the going was mucky and there was no footway to speak of. 'You might keep in by the wall, miss,' he said. 'They are hard at it still in the wharf yards, and the carts are loaded at a ferocious rate. There is no telling what you might be splashed with.'

'You are very gallant, Inspector,' she said with amusement. 'And I hope you will forgive my curiosity. It is no more than that, I assure you, since I no longer take a professional interest.'

He let out a snort of amusement, leaping smartly over a puddle as Octavia swerved to avoid it. 'You are mistaken in that, I believe.'

'Forgive me, Inspector,' she said, coming alongside him once more. 'In what am I mistaken, exactly?'

A wharf-hand veered into his path, jostling him as he swung up a sack. Cutter took hold of him, and with a fierce oath hurled him bodily onto the laden cart. 'Mind where you put yourself!' he bellowed. 'I will put you under it the next time, you witless monkey.'

Octavia let the incident pass without comment. If the inspector was more easily provoked than he had formerly been – *the same dog, only more so* – his outbursts could be depended upon none-theless to subside as quickly as they arose.

'I meant, Miss Hillingdon,' he said, continuing after a time as if nothing had happened, 'that you are mistaken in what you say about your professional interests. You have set them aside for now, being so much occupied by this book of yours, but you can no more cast them off than I can set myself up as a governess. You may no longer care for high society – and you can hardly be blamed for that – but you will be back to your old ways once you have finished your little act of penance. I may not see this bright-ness of yours, but I know all about bringing things to light. We are both in that game, whatever else we may be, and we will never want for business. There will always be a surfeit, in this world, of fellows who wish to keep their doings from coming to light, and there will always be the likes of you and me to plant boils in their arses.'

Octavia laughed, and for a moment a levity came to her that she had not felt for some time. 'Perhaps you are right, Inspector.' She hesitated for a moment. 'Do you think us alike, then?'

He glanced up at her again, and there was a wryness now in

the set of his face. 'I cannot quite match your elevation,' he said. 'A fellow must be born to that, and if he is not he must go about things in a plainer fashion. But in the ways that matter, I fancy, we are more alike than not.'

'Goodness me,' she said. 'I had assumed you thought me a nuisance.'

'And so you are,' Cutter replied. 'You have hardly given me a moment's peace in three months, but I can hardly fault you for it. It is in your nature to make a nuisance of yourself, just as it is in mine. It is the rightful order of things.'

They passed into the dank shadows beneath Cannon Street Station, where their conversation faltered amid the clamour of an incoming train. Cutter strode ahead again, and was presently engulfed by a lowering drift of steam. They were drawing near now to London Bridge, and for all his professions of regard, it would not have surprised Octavia to find that he had gone on his way without another word. He was on police business, after all, and all else was secondary to that.

She pedalled on, emerging once more into the light, and it was a moment before she realised that she had overtaken him. He had moderated his pace – had slowed, in fact, to a contemplative stroll. Octavia dismounted in mild astonishment and fell in alongside him. It was a more comfortable arrangement, if nothing else, and she saw no pressing need to question it. They carried on in more or less easeful silence until he returned abruptly to her question.

'I am pursuing a gang of slavers, since you ask.'

Incredulous, Octavia halted to confront him. 'Slavers? Here, in London? You are making fun of me, surely? The practice has been outlawed for decades.'

'A good deal has been outlawed that goes on all the same. It is an unpleasant bit of business, but there is nothing new in that. I would pass my days in idleness otherwise.'

'But where are they bringing these poor creatures from? And how?'

'There is no shortage of shipping, miss. England must have its cotton still, and its sugar and silk. Such things are brought in by the ton, as you have seen for yourself, and where there is trade there is apt to be contraband.'

'But living men, Inspector? Living men, packed into the holds of ships, in this day and age?'

Cutter had turned in at Fishmongers' Hall and was mounting the steps towards Adelaide-place. He paused for a moment, as if in weariness. 'It is not men they are bringing in, miss.'

She stared after him mutely, and presently he turned and descended again, taking hold of her bicycle and hoisting it to his shoulder. 'Allow me,' he said.

He set it down, reaching the top, and produced his pocketwatch, rattling it vigorously before consulting it again. He looked out over the square towards London Bridge, shielding his eyes with a flexed hand against the declining sun. 'Do not alarm yourself unduly,' he said, catching sight of her expression. 'It goes on in a small enough way, and the fellows we are watching have no great heads for their trade. We will clip their wings for them, you may be sure. The next thing will be worse, no doubt, but that is the way of it. We can only keep house, in this life. We cannot tear up the foundations.'

'Perhaps you are right,' she said again, lagging a little way behind him as she fell into thought. 'About me, I mean.'

Cutter gave no sign that he had heard. Reaching the bridge, he planted his feet apart and looked about him. He settled his coat about his shoulders with an agitated air, as if he had been waiting for an hour or more.

'The book will be finished soon enough,' Octavia said. 'And a woman ought to have something to do.'

The inspector scanned all approaches, leaning out over both sides of the bridge before returning with a dissatisfied air to resume his station.

Octavia brought her bicycle to rest against the parapet, glad to be relieved of its weight. 'All of this.' She surveyed the grand facades, the spires massed against the mild sky. 'It is built on suffering, isn't it? All of it.'

'It is cheaper than Portland stone, miss.' Cutter was looking distractedly about him still. 'And never in short supply.'

'Perhaps you won't object, then, if I continue to call on you from time to time?'

'It would do me little good, I suspect. Besides, you will not depend on me entirely. You have more than one officer at your disposal.'

'Ah.' Octavia hesitated. 'Has he mentioned my visits, then?'

'He talks of little else, lately. He is very nearly restored to himself, in the talking line, though I fear his spirits are far from recovered. He does a good deal of pining still.'

'It is to be expected, I suppose. He has his own portion of the story to tell, after all. But I have been mindful of the doctors. I have tried not to tax him.'

'You may tax him to your heart's content, miss, if it will stifle his yapping in some small way. He has hardly been back on duty a fortnight, and I have forgotten what it was to know peace and quiet. Ah, here we are now. He has decided to put in an appearance after all.'

Octavia turned at this to see Sergeant Bliss, hurrying towards them from the opposite side of the square. It had been nearly a month since she had seen him last, and he seemed remarkably improved. There was a sickliness to his complexion still, and he could be seen to favour one leg, but there was little sign otherwise of how near to death he had come.

'How astonishing,' she said. 'I thought it would be months yet.'

'I put him under our own Dr Carmody,' Cutter said. 'But he gives much of the credit to Lady Ada, for the job she did in plucking out the bullet and sewing him up. It was as handsomely done as he has ever seen, he says, though she has no training beyond her books. As clean as you like, which was the main thing. There is nearly always infection, when the shot is to the gut, but it seems she knew what she was about. Matters might otherwise have taken a different course.'

Octavia raised a hand in greeting as the sergeant approached. He touched his hat, catching sight of her, and made an effort to straighten his gait.

'And he had more than that in his favour, if his uncle is to be believed. He had help from another quarter.'

'Another quarter? Who?'

'His little match girl, or so Neuilly maintains. When she passed, he says, there was an excess of some kind to be taken up. Not in the way that our friends tried to engineer, but in the natural course. I do not pretend to understand all the particulars, but it seems it did him no harm.'

'She is with him still.' She spoke without reflection, and was at once persuaded that he would think her foolish. 'I mean, there is always that comfort, when someone passes. She will be with him always, in some small way.'

He turned away with a dour look, but it seemed to Octavia sometimes that his sentiments were gentler than he pretended. 'Yes, that is a great comfort, I am sure,' he said. 'I suppose it was too much to hope for that he might have grown brighter in the common way. His timekeeping shows no great improvement either. Show a leg there, Bliss! You are not in procession behind a hearse, blast you.'

'Good evening to you, Miss Hillingdon.' Sergeant Bliss was out of breath, and as ever, somewhat dishevelled in his appearance. 'A pleasure to see you, as always. I do beg your pardon, Inspector. I left with time to spare, but I came upon a pair of youths who were attempting to drown a litter of kittens. I was forced to intervene, sir, in an official capacity.'

'You were forced to intervene?' Cutter looked upwards, working a thumb into the hollow of his cheek. 'In the drowning of a sackful of kittens?'

'Yes, sir. It was a most distressing scene.'

'We have more pressing matters to look into, Bliss, as you might recall. I will thank you to make no further interventions this evening, unless you are called upon to do so. Did you pay a visit to the wharf-master, as I asked?'

'I did, sir.'

'And did you copy out the bills of lading for the days in question?'

'In their entirety, sir.' Bliss clapped a hand to his coat.

'What about your study of Portuguese? Have you made headway in that?'

'Well, sir, it has certain peculiarities, I find. Did you know, for instance, that it has twenty-one distinct vowel sounds, though these are represented by the same five letters as our own?'

'You are not giving a lecture to the Royal Society, Bliss. Can you converse passably with the captain of a merchantman, is all I want to know?'

'I believe so, sir.'

'Well, I expect we'll see. Come, we have lost enough time. The man we want may be gone with the next tide. Miss Hillingdon, we must part ways for now.'

'Good evening to you, Inspector. And to you, Sergeant. I hope you will spare me an hour or two of your time some evening soon. We have a great deal to talk about still.'

'I shall look forward to it, miss,' said Bliss, turning to follow the inspector. 'I shall look forward to it with the utmost eagerness.'

He raised his hat again as he scurried after Cutter, a neglected bowler that he replaced at a slightly comical angle. The inspector had reached the steps already, and was descending at a clattering pace to the wharf below. Octavia went to the parapet to retrieve her bicycle. She had meant to return home at once, so as to begin transcribing what she had learned, but found herself lingering. When he reached the wharfside, the inspector paused. He made a show of working a stone from his boot heel, but it was plain that he meant to allow Bliss to catch him up. Cutter swung his arm to chivvy him along, but must have noted his halting gait, for when he set off again it was at an easier pace. He was obliged to sidestep a bollard, allowing Bliss to pass him for a moment. As he came abreast of him he raised one great hand, thinking himself unobserved, and held it a little way from the sergeant's back, as if to keep him from harm.

They passed out of sight at last somewhere beyond the Old Swan Pier. These were the longest days of June, and the sun had only now begun to set, seaming the river with rose and bronze. It infused the lightly shrouded air, setting a blush on the great calyx of St Paul's and, far below, gilding the trusses of piers and the buckled ridges of tin sheds. Octavia had spoken in haste about Miss Tatton and what might remain of her. She could not say where the words had come from, or what she herself believed, but some nameless conviction had formed in her all the same. There was this light, if nothing else, and a sense that it was sufficient. There was the plenitude of this midsummer dusk, exalting all that was ordinary. It seemed impossible, even as it faded, to imagine that it was anything other than eternal.

Afterword and Acknowledgements

Passenger carriages with side corridors had been in use since the 1880s, and in March of 1892, the Great Western Railway introduced the first complete 'corridor train' (as *The Times* described it) on its Paddington to Birkenhead service. However, trains of this design were not yet in service between London and Kent by February of 1893. This minor historical liberty is the only one I have knowingly taken, and by confessing to it openly I hope to escape censure.

Among the locations in London that figure prominently in this novel, some were chosen for their personal significance, and wherever possible I have walked – but not, admittedly, bicycled – the same ground as Gideon, Octavia and Inspector Cutter. In other instances, especially where streets or structures no longer exist, I have relied on contemporaneous records, and in particular on the Ordnance Survey's 1894 map of London. The National Library of Scotland has not only digitised this resource but made it available – in a gift beyond price to the shiftless novelist – as a fully navigable overlay for Google Maps. My debt to the archivists involved is incalculable.

A full bibliography, when appended to a work of fiction, serves only to assure true scholars of the author's delusions, but such has been my reliance on certain sources that I cannot in good conscience fail to acknowledge them. Jerry White's *London in the*

Nineteenth Century (Vintage, 2008) is indispensable to understanding the transformation of London's built environment during this period, while *Victorian London* (Weidenfeld & Nicolson, 2006), by Liza Picard, is likewise essential if you want to know what people did all day (and all night, for that matter) and exactly how much it cost them.

Of the many works of scholarship on Victorian spiritualism, only Alex Owen's *The Darkened Room: Women, Power and Spiritualism in Late Victorian England* (University of Chicago Press, 1989) has – at least to my knowledge – examined its singular cultural importance to women, both as a source of social capital and a means of expressing subversive or even illicit ideas.

Joan Lock's *Scotland Yard Casebook: The Making of the CID, 1865–1935* (Robert Hale, 1993) serves, albeit incidentally, as an invaluable guide to the procedural and administrative intricacies of the Scotland Yard that Inspector Cutter would have known, while *The Invention of Murder* (Harper Press, 2011), by Judith Flanders, illuminates not only the journalistic practices of Octavia's predecessors and contemporaries, but their engineering of conventions and expectations that have shaped our depictions of crime and punishment ever since.

I am deeply grateful to Melissa Harrison, who laboured through an early draft of this novel in manuscript, and who has offered wise counsel and candour throughout its difficult history.

I would like, finally, to make a small act of reparation. Writers tend, by convention, to acknowledge those we love only for what they enable us to do. We dedicate our books to them, as if such dedications were gestures of tribute, truly, and not further increments of vanity.

Sinéad O'Donnell has heard quite enough about this book, and so have Sophia and Jacob. What matters is not that their brightness sustains me, but that it surpasses me, exceeding these meagre inventions. Never mind the book, then. To them I dedicate only my love, and – as poor a gift as it may be – whatever else remains of me.

Leabharlanna Poiblí Chathair Baile Átha Cliath
Dublin City Public Libraries